THE IN-BETWEEN

MOLLY O'DOWD

The In-Between
By Molly O'Dowd

ISBN: 978-1-911740-14-8

First published in 2025

Managing editor: Bridget Reaume
Copyeditor: A.R. Thompson
Design: Tasmin Briers
Artwork: Nicole Stone

Published by Palavro, an imprint of
the Arkbound Foundation (Publishers)

Arkbound is a social enterprise that aims to promote social inclusion, community development and artistic talent. It sponsors publications by disadvantaged authors and covers issues that engage wider social concerns. Arkbound fully embraces sustainability and environmental protection. It endeavours to use material that is renewable, recyclable or sourced from sustainable forest.

Arkbound
1-3 Gloucester Rd
Bishopston, Bristol BS7 8AA

www.arkbound.com

THE IN-BETWEEN

MOLLY O'DOWD

CHAPTERS

CONTENT WARNING

Dear Reader, if you don't wish to have spoilers of content within this book- please promptly skip this page (don't read on here-seriously, it's about to specify what could (and will) happen within this book... these are potentially major spoilers... continue reading at your own discretion).

This book contains some content themes that may not be suitable for all readers, and some passages that could be triggering. The possible triggers include- domestic abuse, sexual assault, suicide and various depictions of grief.

That being said, if you still choose to keep reading The In Between, I hope you enjoy the ebbs and flows of the story. All acknowledged content warnings are crucial to the storyline, and none of it is taken lightly or glorified.

To anyone who's ever felt unworthy of love,

this is for you.

CHAPTER 1
THE SHALLOWS

The waves crest the edges of the beach, tentatively pulling away in preparation to push forwards again; little by little towards my toes.

The sand doesn't itch and the waves aren't cold. The sky is whatever I want it to be.

This isn't real.

I've had lucid dreams since I was 14.

6 years of consciously navigating my subconscious.

I always follow through the mental checks. Can you feel your clothes against your skin- or do you just know what they feel like? Are you blinking? Can you rewind?

Count your fingers.

Most nights I bring myself here.

I conjure up the night sky above the beach, encasing my inner-vision in a layer of blue-black darkness; the silvery luminescence of the moon is the only light source by which I can watch the waves. I've read that if you dream of bright, light spaces that it can disrupt your sleep. It doesn't let the brain relax. Since I am, for some reason, in control of my brain even at night, I should at least do right by it.

I lie myself down in the sand, taking comfort in the fact that I won't have to scrub myself raw later- trying and failing to remove every last grain from my body. I let my long dark hair ease into the beach, the strands falling one by one between the granules.

Eyes closed, with nothing but the soft brush of the tide on the shore, I wait to hear it.

Her name.

The name that I don't conjure, but persists without hindrance. The name that summons me from my peace, awakens the deepest parts of .

The sand flies up around me and suddenly I'm spun off the ground and I'm falling-

No, *flying-*

Fighting the wind as it buffers me in a storm cloud of glass shards and icy winds.

I shouldn't feel the wind's chill here. The glass shouldn't cut me. Yet the small pieces dig into my arms as I make to shield my eyes, giving in to the power of the storm and balling myself as tightly as I can; as it keeps screaming-

-Her name.

Aletheia

Aletheia Aletheia

The wind howls it, the stars shine for it and the world opens up to cry it-

Aletheia Aletheia

CHAPTER 2
ALETHEIA

She heard me again. I know she did.

I've been trapped here, suspended in the void of light and dark for an inconceivable amount of time.

Immeasurable- not just because it's been a devastatingly long time, but because time passes differently here. Or perhaps doesn't pass at all.

I'm not entirely sure.

My silver hair trails down my naked frame, long enough now to curl past my toes and descend into the nothingness.

Stoic still in the breezeless air.

My right arm is bound by the ropes of darkness, my left by those of the light, my body suspended in the grey.

I am weightless, yet firmly held.

I raise my head until the back of my neck clicks. I kick out my legs. Roll my shoulders. Stretch out one leathery wing, then the feather one.

My diamond eyes could see for miles in my realm, could observe the goings-on of neighbouring planets without so much as straining.

Here they are wasted on the wasteland.

I whistle lightly once, preparing my ears again for what I must do.

What I must repeatedly do- lest I give up. The tips of my ears cringe, capable of hearing a baby's cry from several streets over- now painfully aware of what must be done.

I sigh, shaking out my hair so it falls around me in the void, fanning out like a spiders' web, with me trapped at its centre.

"Come on my darling," I say in barely a whisper, "Say my name."

And I scream it.

CHAPTER 3
CARRY ON

I bolt up in bed, breaths coming out in spurts as my body returns to the room. My brain is still hurtling through the air as I blink away the remnants of the dream, as my *'family'* bedroom slowly comes back into focus.

My bookcase, a standard white flatpack desk-space with obligatory houseplant in the corner. My dressing gown on the back of my chair that haunts me in the dark. A typical university-student room.

The coldness still lingers on my skin, the harshness of the nightmare still marring my subconscious. It happens every other night nowadays. I fall asleep, go to my beach, and wait to be swept from it. The nightmares started shortly after mum passed away, the better part of a decade ago now, and they've only got worse over time.

Once they were a blessing, to distract my restless mind from painful memories- when the police had me identify her body, when I had to be the one to speak at her funeral because dad was too lost in grief- I didn't mind getting taken from those.

They were my saving grace.

Now all they accomplish is sleep deprivation.

But the feel of them, the determination and almost desperate quality to the disruption...

It's only a problem if I allow it to be one.

I wipe the sweat from my brow and clap quietly once, the dawn-lighting flickering to life, breaking across my room. I swing my legs off the bed, grabbing the small slip of e-paper from the bedsheet and chucking it on the floor. The device blinks black and white momentarily before becoming one shade lighter than the floor; engaging heating-mode.

My feet touchdown on tepid floorboards and I drag my body up and over to my desk, where the small pink notification-light attached to my computer is flashing at me.

I barely notice the scratch marks on my arms leftover from the non-dream, , as I reach to open the screen. The projector spins illuminations around me in different colours, the small cubes of light like the night's sky in my room. The cubes are colour coded of course: yellow for work, green for extra work, red for family, purple for friends, and white...

The white block blinks at me expectantly, daringly- I hesitate.

Irene had said they would source my details; I just didn't think they'd be able to find me so soon...

Potions class is always my favourite, never failing to make for an exciting afternoon. The professor, Mr Spelinski, was as charismatic as ever. It wasn't enough for him to just teach the basics. He wanted us to practice skills outside of the curriculum- to exceed his and our own expectations. He's the kind of professor that likes to place a myriad of ingredients at your feet, and have you deduce what to make of them. To take a heating lotion and work out how to erupt a volcano, to produce a sleeping draft and work out the maths for both a flea's dosage- and a hellhound's.

Needless to say, no task was left unmet- at least not by me.

Potions gave me a sense of purpose. That, and investigating the most curious off-limits knowledge in pursuit of my future career- a Researcher. A path without limits, where nothing is restricted. University has changed since the days of single-subject studies. Now students take three to five different subjects, focusing on the areas that will help them succeed in very specific careers. Far fewer go to university, but 99% of those that do walk away do so with a job already lined up that suits their specialised qualifications.

I'm lucky to have gotten to my final year here. Southlakes University isn't just the most prestigious in the country. It's the hometown for those who got magic banned in the first place- hence my curiosity in the out-of-bounds.

Magic.

We were world builders, once. Star-travellers. Beings with the powers of the universe at our fingertips. Until a few too many found dark-magic, their morbid curiosity instigating the downfall of all magic-users.

They travelled through dimensions not even the Gods were supposed to pass through. Making their destructive pathways across the cosmos, to the far corners of existence.

The Gods fought valiantly, battling a great many wars against earth-dwellers from across the galaxies. But in the end, for once, mortals actually held the upper hand.

Only when the Fates reared their ancient heads at the commotion did the chaos cease. They swooped in, mercilessly stripping the magic of earth-dwellers. Without which, we didn't even know how to cross our own galaxy, let alone jump through dimensions or hop into different realms.

So once again, we were cut off. With only the basics in herbology and potions to suggest we ever touched what people might class as 'magic'. That was over 500 years ago now. People forget. And others become fearful, anxious that we will once again anger the Fates. The most anxious of all being our leaders, who have, for centuries, prohibited any mention of magic, let alone the acquisition of it.

"Tenaya!"

I hear Amaya's determined footfalls racing up behind me and prepare myself for impact.

One Mississippi-

Two Mississippi-

Three-

"Gotcha!" She squeals, swinging her arms around me as we pass the room for Creatures Class.

Amaya is a force to be reckoned with, 5"2' and fierce as a fire nymph, with hair to match. She hasn't left my side since the start of university- and I wouldn't have it any other way.

Besides her, Rylan is the only other soul in university who makes me feel like I have a home.

"Mind my hair you ninny." I scold, snaking the strands from under her arms and giving her a squeeze.

She's a wild spirit, tamed only by her incredibly upper-class home life. Her mum and dad made a point of educating her in manners of every culture and cuisine. I don't think I've ever even seen the girl slouch.

Her parents tried to shield her from life's horrors, including- Gods forbid- diversity. They enrolled her at the least inclusive of all universities: Southlakes. From what I understand, her parents are devotees of a similar faith to my father, but taken to a new extreme.

However, they failed to shield her from one particular tragedy. At fourteen, she'd been the first to come upon a dead body- a corpse washed up by the tide. She rarely mentioned it, but when she does, her eyes glaze over and she loses some of her usual spark; so I know she's still shaken from it.

I couldn't dare tell her how much I empathise. It's her tragedy- not mine. She trauma-dumped it on me on practically our first encounter- sipping tea whilst spilling me the details- and I couldn't summon the guts to open up in the same way; it would only serve to overshadow.

"Oi! Weirdos!"

Our heads snap around at the assertion, both of us peering over the side of the stairway to where the Outliars crouch.

'Outliars', aka Outright liars.

That's what the rest of the university liked to call them.

The band of alternative nobodies that fancied themselves truth-seekers, 'Magic Fanatics'.

Unfortunately, I also fall into that bracket. It's only our dedication to our studies that keeps Amaya and I from joining them. That, and Amaya's complete distrust of anyone even mildly nonconformist.

The group huddles in a mist of multi-coloured clothes and marijuana haze, their stares following us as we descend low enough on the stairs to talk to them. The leader, a cocky brunette with purple highlights and eyeliner that extends beneath her hairline, places a hand on the ledge opposite us.

"Yes?" I ask, taking the lead- Amaya had taken a step back.

The girl cracks a smile, her mauve lipstick drawing wider as she holds out a hand.

"Irene." she announces, as I take her hand.

Her tongue piercing pokes through her teeth as she grins, rattling noisily from one side to the other.

Ticketty-ticketty-tack and back again.

She's certainly beautiful, no doubt; in the alternative way that kind of takes you by surprise. Startling at first glance, until the harsh exterior and dark glimmer behind her eyes come together to create something kind of spectacular.

Realising that I should probably respond at some point, I hurriedly reply, "Tenaya," I clear my throat, "And this is Amay-"

She pulls my hand towards her and I lurch into the ledge that separates us with a thud, my face now close enough to hers that I can smell the sage.

"We know who you are," She says, her voice silky in contrast to the vice-like grip she has on my hand, "Word gets around Tenaya, that you know how to unlock a Veturcaela."

The word haunts my breath, stilling and stunning me- I'm assessing each and every detail of her being.

She's strong but slight. Hidden muscle along lean arms- concealed beneath layers of mesh clothing and baggy jeans. A façade? Her friends are much the same. A lanky boy with mousey hair and a long nose stands arms folded in the corner. A pink-haired sprite of a girl in bubble-gum clothing. A heavy-set girl in all-black with as many piercings as there are colours in their combined palettes.

These people were jokes to magic Researchers- amateurs. Mimics of authentic magic-finders who dedicate their lives to uncovering the hidden truths of the universe; respecting the set government boundaries.

Of course, I know what a Veturcaela is, everything about them, from their creation to their usage.

In essence, they're a door. A portal to another realm. They hinge on the utilisation of deep-set innate-magic- or rather, they allow for the unlocking of it. Only those chosen by the Veturcaela itself can wield the magic required to travel through it. I've been searching for one since I first read about them, just to see one- to understand it.

To unlock it.

I gulp back my anxiety and try to remain calm.

"So what if I do?"

Amaya grips my arm.

"You know how to unlock a Veturcaela?!" She hisses Under her breath, "Why didn't you tell me?!"

I shrug.

"Hypothetically I know how, I figured it wasn't much use since you don't exactly have one lying about." I raise an eyebrow at her, and she frowns, her mouth pouty.

Amaya wants magic just as much as I do, only difference is- she lacks the drive to do the research. Or the lucid dreams and weird voices in her head that push me to find reasons for the randomness; other than madness. A logical explanation for to the voices.

The ones that chant her name.

"We do."

My heart falters for a few absent beats, only to begin racing as I look back to Irene. Her smile has turned devious as she pulls me in even closer.

"We have one, not lying around per se. But it's safe- and with your help..." Irene trails off, looking between us for confirmation.

Amaya tugs on my sleeve, her jitters uncontainable as she practically vibrates where she stands.

Giving them the benefit of the doubt didn't really have a downside, besides possibly getting drugged and mugged- but the downsides of that could even be limited by just not bringing anything valuable. Note to self- leave my purse at home.

No, those downsides weren't the issue.

It was getting out of the house.

It was getting out of the house undetected by the tyrannical force that bludgeons me for the smallest infractions, including getting home past curfew.- let alone going out at night.

Bargaining for extra time after school was out of the question- she would know I was lying. I learned this the hard way once- I told her I'd signed up to help clean the hall after a portions class, just to spend some time with Rylan and Amaya at the park. She went to Spelinski himself, and even though he tried to cover for me, the downside-incarnate could smell the lie.

The punishment was brutal. I couldn't sleep for a week, the bruising from where she'd struck me repeatedly with her rolling pin rousing me every time I turned.

"When?" I ask, steeling myself.

Irene finally releases my hand, my palm now clammy under stress.

"We'll be in touch," She says, with an air of mystery their group so obviously craved, "Keep an eye on your notifs, we'll find your info. All you have to do is turn up."

I place a hand over Amaya's, feeling her pulse going just as crazy as mine as they slink off towards the local bar; like they hadn't just been plotting to open a portal between worlds and conduct the most illegal activity of the modern age.

"Tenaya...!" Amaya squeals, and I can't help the nervous grin that spans my face.

I'm finally going to do it.

I'm going to have magic, real magic, in the palm of my hand.

I'm going to unlock a Veturcaela.

I can find her, if I do it correctly, I can find out if she is real or a repercussion of the damage inflicted on me by my stepmother and if I am, in fact, insane.

I might finally find Aletheia.

...that was only two days ago, and yet there it is.

Hovering obnoxiously in the centre of my room.

I cast my eyes around the room anxiously, gripping my upper arms for a sense of stability. The glow from the notification block casts just enough light to illuminate the two foot-shaped shadows lingering behind the door.

My heart drops through the floor, and I wish I could drop with it. That I could fall through the centre of the earth and burn away.

Outside my room, she's stood still, which can only mean she's had another bad night.

I often catch myself thinking- what if I'd picked the room at the end of the corridor? What if, before mum died and Hydra moved in and Tabi took it- what if I'd chosen differently?

Instead of placing myself right in her path, right where she passes by every night to get to her bedroom and every morning to leave for work. Like a pit stop where she can pause and relieve tension if she sees fit.

The longer the shadows stay there, the more I know she's not going away.

I close my laptop screen and the lights evaporate into nothingness, just as she opens the door. Her shadow stabs its way across the floorboards and into the room, clawing towards me until I cower.

Until she sees me.

"Why're you causing this *racket*?"

Her voice is like a whip through the room, cracking down upon me like her wrath surely will.

Floorboards creaking at 5am, I should've known.

It's as good of an excuse as she needs.

CHAPTER 4
CHEMICAL REACTIONS

I massage the egg-shaped bulge on my head as the bell chimes for start of first lecture. In all fairness, I was the one who left my hockey stick right by the door.

I practically handed her the weapon.

A tube of pale-yellow liquid comes falling from my left and lands on my desk.

"A tonic for the headshot." Amaya grumbles, coming to sit in her usual spot next to me.

Always the left and only the left.

She eyes up my latest injury with the same disgust as the last hundred or so times I've had to excuse minor or major wounds; those that are visible anyway. Amaya is under the impression that my stepmother takes an interest in my extracurriculars and enrolled me in jiu-jitsu classes on the north side of town.

It's safer this way.

I take the balm in hand and begin smoothing the cold lotion against the bump in slow circles, wincing at the sharp pain.

I just have to survive university, get Tabi sent off to boarding school and make a swift exit.

Keep him safe.

I won't let her shift her violent outbursts to him just because I can't take it. Tabi got the room at the end of the hall, just past her path. Not that Tabi knows what happens behind my closed bedroom door, but he's seen me hobble to the bathroom once she's gone to bed enough times now to have suspicions. Even at seven years old, he's seen too much to be completely ignorant.

It started small. Insignificant.

She'd make a snide remark, knock something off my desk, crumple an assignment. I'm not sure when it turned from a head tap to a hockey stick. But at this point what was I going to say- *"Oh, hey dad, yeah, you know the one true love you found after mums tragic death left you desolate and depressed? Yeah, she's been beating the crap out of me since she moved in six years ago, funny right?"*

It would kill him.

"I still don't understand the point of learning martial arts if all you do is get your ass whooped," Amaya snarks, "Not as if you're gunna get attacked in Siveyra."

I snort- she had a point. Siverya could barely be considered a town, with little more than a supermarket, church and maybe three bars across the surrounding areas. The only real concern was the ziplong in and out of the city, and even then the security for that mode of transportation is insane; cameras line just about every inch of the place, and guards standing at every exit and entrance point.

"You should see the other guy." I mumble into my jumper as I lounge forwards onto my desk.

Without missing a beat- she sticks a pen in my side and I jump, massaging my ribs.

"Sit up straight." She reprimands, and I'm reminded for the billionth time what an uptight excuse for a best friend I have.

But she *is* my best friend.

"This isn't even your class, why the hell are you-" I begin, but my eyes are dragged to the entranceway- which currently hosts the most beautiful person in all of Siveyra.

Madeline Costello.

The only girl to have transferred to this small university from the local school, besides me. The only person other than Amaya, Rylan and Tabi that makes staying here worth it at all.

She sways into the room in a cloud of lavender perfume and hip-length brown curls. Her deep blue cardigan hugs her figure, matched with a pair of shapely black leggings and a snowy white scarf that she holds up close against her cheeks.

A porcelain doll escaped from the cabinet.

Guided by her boyfriend, Max Harletain.

The second most popular person in university- after Madeline. He stands nearly a head and a half over her- tall enough to reach around and snake her waist against his as they ascend the stairs to the row in front of mine.

"She'll slap you for looking at him like that one day." Amaya hisses in my ear and I bat her into silence as they come within earshot.

It was better she thought it was him.

Definitely better.

Safer.

Not only did I not know how she would react, I don't know how the rest of the university would.

How my dad would...

I can guess, and I sure as hellfire know what Hydra would say. Tabi isn't ready to be the object of her attentions, I hope he never will be- but if dad finds out about who I like, I could be out of house and home before I can even decide on the right label.

Dad's a follower of the Hieramans, as is most of this backwards town. Hieramans are an ancient faith, highly into their "Natural ways". They take influence from old religious texts that overlap-

and combine them. Unfortunately, that also extends to having a direct opinion and ruling over other people's personal lives.

Funny that having a romantic preference towards a person can be unholy, but capital punishment is the *'Gods' way'*.

"I don't do any harm in looking." I mutter to my left and she gasps, holding a hand to her chest dramatically.

"I'm such a bad influence." She pantomimes theatrically.

"The worst." I grin, and we both return our attention to the backs of their heads.

I met Madeline in fifth grade. Initially an exchange student, with eyes so large and green- so curious- that seemed to unsettled everyone around her. Being from the north, her features stood out in ways that others didn't quite understand; larger eyes and shinier skin. This town was not known for tolerance. They avoided her in the playground, pulled their eyelids open wider to mock her, tripped her in hallways.

Until I made them stop.

I've always excelled in school, potions being my speciality. Even at ten years old I knew what elements to combine to turn the whole class green. It took an entire month for their skin to stop glowing in the dark, and even then- they never picked on her again. They knew it was me of course, the silent girl with the coy small smile. Oh, and the only other student in school not to be turned green other than Madeline herself. But what were they going to do? Pick on the girl who knew how to wield the elements like a knight weilds a sword?

They knew better.

Madeline gives me a small wave, Max twisting slightly to do the same, before blocking her from my view with his hulking frame.

I should turn him green too.

Still, I can't stop the small blush that bleeds into my cheeks at the brief hello.

"You are *shameless*." Amaya laughs, and I give her leg a kick.

"Hush your face."

A gangly body comes sailing in from my right, I swerve just in time to avoid an elbow to my temple. I curse at Rylan as he grins at me like a Cheshire cat, his eyebrow cocked as he places one leg over the other on the chair in front.

"I was informed I've been missed?" He muses, waggling those infuriating eyebrows up and down at me so that they practically disappear beneath his gold-brown hair.

Giving him an evil glare, I shove his legs until they fall to the floor with dull thuds.

"Do you pride yourself in drawing the most attention humanly possible whenever you enter a room?"

Rylan was notorious for making a spectacle, and for irritating me, usually one habit complementing the other. He is, unfortunately, also one of the three reasons I stayed at this university in this cursed town, in my Gods-forsaken '*family*' house. He's the only one of my friends who knows the full extent of what goes on at home, he's my only safe place.

My small sanctuary.

His eyes do the usual up and down of my exterior, assessing for damage and lingering longer than necessary on the third eye poking from my cranium.

His smile turns into a grimace, before righting itself begrudgingly as he grabs his laptop.

"One more year." He groans, extending his fist to me.

"Three-hundred and forty-two days." I smile, bumping his outstretched fist with my own before reaching down for my own book-bag, busying myself with setting up.

He would never say anything.

I made him promise.

A promise which will only stay in place so long as I can walk into university. Apparently, my stepmother literally crippling me is the hill he's willing to die on.

He only agreed because his dad makes him suffer the same.

I'm not sure if it was the Fates wanting to play out some twisted game, or maybe just dumb luck that two people in the same circumstance found themselves not only in the same university- but the same classes.

But I'm so grateful.

I twist my mouth at him in mutual understanding as he presses his fingers into his eye-sockets, massaging away the evidence of a sleepless night as best he can, covering it well with false bravado and extravagant gestures.

We all have our coping mechanisms- and our camouflages.

"Will both of you quit your rustling and hush up!" Amaya hisses at us as Mr Spelinski scurries into the room, his wiry grey tufts of hair the only things that peek out over the mountain of sheets.

"Settle down every-" He tries to shout, bumping into the desk on stage as he does so.

Dumping the papers, he moves to his pockets, half the class still lost in a muffled frenzy of newly-returned student gossip.

Little did they know what was about to happen.

"Duck." I say, grabbing Amaya and Rylan by the knees and gesturing for them both join me behind the chairs. I manage to reach a hand through the gap in the chairs and shove Madeline's head down just before Mr Spelinski throws the contents over the class.

The spray of potion lands on every oblivious student. The crimson specks that fall on clothing instantly grow into roots and shoot toward the ceiling like big red banners of shame, sprouting mercilessly from whatever section of clothing they are embedded in.

Half the class, including Max- but excluding Madeline- immediately have red vines circling their heads like demonic halos.

"Righteo!" Spelinski claps then throws a hand to the right side of the hall, "Troublemakers to the right. That means all of you with the red roots of Cryosayde attached to your gossiping bodies- up you get."

Spelinski is a nerd, but a powerful one. Which makes him a bit of a legend in my eyes.

Half the class slowly gathers their stuff. Huffing and puffing their way to the other side of the room, they gather as a small forest of red branches and mortified faces.

Max shoots me a glare as he gathers his stuff and storms past Madeline to the opposite end of the hall, his aura as aggravated as the plant on his chest. Madeline on the other hand gives me a small smile, mouthing a *thank you* once Max's back is fully turned.

I can't help the warmth that comes over me, and I thanking the Gods for Spelinski's mayhem.

"Now then-" Spelinski says, hopping up to sit on the desk so his legs swing. The projector turns on and an ingredients list for a potion pops up on the screen, "-Half the class has been infected with Cryosayde, which will spread like wildfire if untreated." He smirks as some of my classmates on the right of the room hang their heads.

"The ingredients for the remedy are as shown above- and knowing what you learnt from *last* year-" He says pointedly, "You should all know the logical sequence to prepare an antidote."

He locks eyes with me and grins as I begin scribbling down the order as easily as I would write my own name.

"Class," He yells, spreading his arms wide before clapping his hands together excitedly, "Begin."

"You're such nerds, you know that, right?" Rylan, his hands still sore from incorrectly handling the Baynersnyde grass, bristles as we head out of class.

That stuff is itch-inducing if you don't coat it in olive oil first - which he'd know if he ever paid attention.

Amaya and I raise our hands without looking at one another

and high-five our pain-free palms, smirking at him.

"Don't we know it." Amaya grins vindictively, elbowing him in the side, "Better luck next time, rookie."

Rylan grimaces. He's lucky she's too short to see the slightest of blushes that creeps up his cheeks at her touch.

"Did you guys get the, uhh, notif?" I ask, my heart pounding as I recall the message that got me caught this morning.

Tonight, midnight, TF3a GAAD, bring your big girl undies -
this is about to become real
See you for a magical night
xox

Rylan and Amaya nod emphatically. Not quite the reaction I had, but not unexpected. Unless the Outliars want to kidnap, murder or torture us, the other two have a lot less to lose. Amaya's parents give her free rein for the most part, and Rylan's parents barely notice if he's in the house regardless. So long as the authorities don't catch us, they'll be fine.

Unlike me.

"Do you think we need to bring snacks or something?" Amaya asks, and I can't help massaging my temples. Sometimes she's too innocently sweet for her own good.

"It's a-" I pause, walking in closer as people pass so that Rylan is in the middle, and lower my voice, "-*Séance*, in an abandoned basement, on a Wednesday night- I'm pretty sure snacks are at the bottom of their to-do list."

Amaya pouts, waving me off theatrically.

"Imma bring some anyway, midnight snacks if nothing else."

We both stare at her, before cracking smiles and rolling our eyes at her. We wouldn't have her any other way.

For such a little sprite of a thing, the girl can eat.

"Whatever, firecracker," He says, playfully shoving her to

the side and leaning an elbow on my shoulder, "I thought our little miss over here would be more interested in the latest bit of goss'." He smirks, clearly knowing something I don't, "Unless Her Esteemed Nerdiness considers herself above such childish nonsense... when it concerns Maddy and Max."

I stumble, Rylan creasing as I try desperately to regain composure.

"Spit it out if it pleases you." I say, holding my head as high as my fall from grace will allow.

Rylan hooks me and Amaya round the neck so that our heads clash together as we walk. The experience is more painful than it's comedically worth.

"Well, word around is- Miss Popular dumped his sorry butt over the summer." He says in a mock-whisper, and my heart stutters, trying not to get caught up in the plausibility of such a turn of events.

Madeline and Max have been together since the start of university - a sorry sight for many of the university's students, myself included. They'd been inseparable, and I'd done my best to be happy for them. But he always seemed to dictate her every move, shoving her in seats or steering her in directions. They seemed more like Max and his accessory than Max and Madeline.

"But today-" I say in confusion.

"Ah, yes- well." He coughs, drawing us in closer, "I said she dumped him - I did *not* say they stopped partaking in certain... shenanigans."

"Ew." I say at the same time as Amaya says "Gross." And we both push away from him.

Rylan holds his hands up in bafflement.

"What?!" He exclaims, "It's better than controlly-mc-controllerson being with Mrs up-her-own-ass, isn't it?"

"You wouldn't happen to be talking about me," Madeline's voice from behind me is like a harpoon shooting into my back and straight through my heart. "Would you?"

I turn towards a face made up of cherry lipstick and green eyes. her green eyes blinking back at me expectantly.

"Uhhh..." Rylan utters, and Amaya slaps him harshly on the arm.

I'll have to thank her later.

"Umm, we- Rylan was just-" I stumble over my words, my face flaming in embarrassment.

"Hey, it's okay." She says, and her words only fan the flames of humiliation, "Word was going to get about anyways. Not that I care." She grumbles, clearly caring.

She's had this habit since middle school of pinching her sides when she gets anxious.

She's pinching now.

"It must've been hard." I find myself saying, and I'm glad it comes out sincere, "I'm sorry."

Her eyes meet mine and I try to remember to not look at her mouth and just breathe.

In and out.

At a normal rate. Gods dammit, why is a normal rate so hard to find?

She smiles, "Thanks Tenny, it's sweet of you to say." She shrugs, "But he is kind of an asshole. Just, you know, good at certain things I guess."

I try to keep the vomit down.

Just the thought of Max touching her in that way is enough to make me want to run to the nearest bathroom.

"Girls gotta do what a girls gotta do, am I right?" Amaya butts in, waggling her eyebrows and ironically pointing finger-guns.

I laugh, but stop when I see Madeline cringing.

I wish she liked Amaya. They could've been friends. Madeline climbed the social ladder pretty quickly once we hit middle school, and her popularity had skyrocketed by the time we reached university. Amaya, however, had never quite got the hang of social climbing. After finding Rylan and I in her first week of university, she never felt the need to branch out - especially if doing so meant changing who she was to fit the trend.

Madeline's trend.

We could've been friends too, if I'd just been... different.

Better.

More like *her*.

"Yeah, *sure*." Madeline says, and I can tell her tone hits Amaya, as she recoils.

I really *really* wish they could've been friends.

"Come on flame-o," Rylan dives in to rescue us, "Come to the canteen with me, I'm lonely- and there's a vending machine sending me mixed signals that I'd like your professional opinion on."

He takes her by the shoulders. Amaya's face is still set in a grumpy line- but slightly appeased by the mention of snacks.

"I'll catch up with you guys in a sec." I call back to them. Rylan chucks a thumbs up in my direction, with Amaya only sticking her tongue out and folding her arms.

I can't blame her too much.

I turn back to Madeline and she's smiling, but my own smile falters when I see who's stalking up the corridor behind her, dying Cryosayde-roots still sticking out of his jumper.

Max.

"Actually, I'll have to c-catch you later." I stammer, backing away in the direction Rylan and Amaya went.

She looks hurt, but I can't go back now.

His hand lands on her shoulder and she jumps, before realisation sets in on her features. Her lips twist into a light frown that he will mistake for her resting face.

She would rest far more easily away from him.

But I can't save her- Gods know I can't even save myself.

I turn my back on them as his arm goes around her shoulders. I walk at a quick pace until I stop thinking about them and

I'm reunited with my friends. Rylan's face morphs into silent sympathy whilst Amaya gives me nothing but raised eyebrows and grumbled mutterings, only letting it be when I place a vending machine goodie in her hand.

CHAPTER 5
A SECOND SERVING

I scrape the empty ketchup sachets and napkins from one plate onto the other. The table is coated in an array of sauces and sugar granules. How anyone managed to make this much mess- let alone think it was acceptable- is beyond me.

I chuck the small-change into my apron pouch, swiping a rag across the table before heading back to the counter.

I've been working at the Silver Server Diner for over half a year now, and it's got its charms- the red and white tiled walls, long curving countertop and beige booths. Sure, the chairs are peeling in places, there's damp in the right-hand corner of the diningroom, and so help us if it gets cold.

But it serves its purpose, both in earning me money for when I make my great escape, and the comfy-casual appeal for the regulars.

There is just one thing that makes me want to up and leave-

Him.

Casimir, his body arched over the counter in a lazy slouch, makes no move to allow squeezing into the kitchen any easier for me. As the manager, dress code is apparently optional; his rotund belly extends out from underneath his shirt and his belt is slung low. He's a slob of a man at the best of times, and at the worst...

"Nice job." He snarls as I suck in to get past him. His beady eyes scream something worse. I feel his eyes stalking me until the swinging doors obscure his line of sight.

I breathe out.

One more year- barely. That's all I have to get through, then the savings from this place will take me as far away as physically possible. Away from Hydra and Casimir and this whole town.

Away from Madeline.

She's here today, in her usual booth with several other hideously pretty girls. All sipping their decaf no-sugar no-milk no-nothing coffees and nibbling at their 'skinny' fries. That's the luxury of growing up and being able to buy your own food- you get to limit yourself more than your parents ever thought to. Madeline never used to, but I guess needs must when you're the most adored student in the whole of Southlakes University; of all Siveyra for that matter.

I busy myself scrubbing at the mountain of plates in the sink. The mound Casimir so blatantly ignored.

The door swings open-

If one could summon the devil by thinking his name

-and Casimir steps in, one hand on his hip, the other down by his side closest to me.

His very presence exudes grime, the sneer he wears only ramping up the disgust he instils in me.

To anyone else, he's a manager, a husband, an upstanding member of society. But to me?

"Intrusive thought alert! Nearly tried to slap your ass out of my way!" He grins, like it's the funniest thing in the world.

What does he want from me? Permission?

When it's abundantly clear I'm not going to share in his amusement he shrugs, winking as he moves past me.

"It's alright- then I remembered you aren't my wife."

The urge to puke runs through me as he collects the napkins he presumably came in for, slapping the work surface hard for emphasis and making me stiffen, before leaving.

One more year one more year *one more year*.

If I ignore it- it will go away.

If I don't rise to it- I can keep my job, make my money.

If I just...

I shove the tap off with more force than I meant to, making the head of the pressure-washer swing like a snake possessed.

From outside I hear the familiar notes of Carla-XI, her sweet melody harshly accompanied by Casimir's off-key singing.

And just like that, he's ruined one of my favourite songs.

I exit the kitchen as quietly as possible, hoping he just stays at his desk. Praying he doesn't come over to ask me about my sex life or tell me about his, talk to me about his '*trauma*' or about how he married his wife for convenience.

If I were stronger, I would tell him he was being inappropriate. If I thought it would do me any good and I could keep my job, I'd report him. Even better, I would quit.

But I can't.

Call it weak, call it foolish. But I can't find another job that pays as well in this Gods-forsaken town, and it's only a year.

I have to stay, for my future- and for Tabi's.

The door jingles and I raise my head. Irene and her posse stroll in. Two with their hoods low over their faces, and the pink haired girl- her girlfriend?- with an arm looped around Irene's as they search around for a booth.

I come around to the front desk, before seeing my mistake-

I hadn't realised he would still be lurking.

"Want to hear a new word I learnt the other day?" Casimir's voice sounds way too close and I do my best not to yelp.

His grin is repulsive and I try not to let it show as I shrug, looking down and busying myself with counting up the cash in the register. He moves closer, and I can feel his breath on the side of my neck.

"Go oooooon," He drawls, his mouth left open like a dog's as he pants at me, "You know you want to."

From his tone I can tell it's going to be gross. Probably something off the alter-dictionary. Something he looked up just so he could make me *squirm*.

"Sure," I concede quietly, hoping to appease him in the briefest way possible, "What is it?"

His face scrunches up, and I can tell I haven't done a good enough job of pandering to him.

"If you don't wanna know, just say so," He grumbles childishly, folding his arms, "Just thought it was interesting."

I know he won't give up until I ask again. It'll be the same remark for the rest of shift, and then finally he will tell me anyway.

Best to rip the band-aid off early.

"No- no I want to know, what is it?" I say.

His demeanour immediately shifts back to slimy. He grins and places a hand in front of me by the till, so half his body is practically over mine. Too much enthusiasm- my mistake. My heart kickstarts sickeningly, but I know he won't do anything.

I pray he won't.

Not out here in the open.

But the till hides us from the customers and his body blocks the camera-view.

He wouldn't...

"The word-"

"Can I order?" Irene's irate voice snaps us both to attention. He releases his grip on the countertop immediately.

There's a beat where no one says a word, Irene simply looking between us both. He gives her a thin smile before curtly nodding and skulking off to the office area.

My cheeks flame with humiliation, and I'm not sure how much Irene understands until I look up.

Her eyes shoot daggers in the direction of the office, her arms folded. Her pink-haired girl/friend stands to her full height of 4-foot-nothing beside her, her head barely poking over the counter. I recognise the girl/friend- I don't know her, but she comes in every evening to order the same strawberry and banana milkshake, and her bright hair is hard to miss. Today, She's dwarfed in a giant muted-green hoodie that looks to have long rabbit ears attached, and a bright pink skirt that matches her hair trails down to her knees.

I always wear skirts. Hydra said it made me look like a man when I tried to leave the house in trousers, insisting I go back up and change.

When I came home that day, she'd disposed of all of my trousers - all save a pair of joggers I wouldn't be caught dead in.

Irene's expression shifts immediately when she turns to me, sweeping me from my reminiscing, Her arms come loose and one hand extends over the counter to touch the surface closer to me, her eyes full of pity.

Gods I hate being pitied.

I'm not weak- I'm not. But with this...

"Is he-" Irene begins.

"You wanted to order?" I say at practically the same time, mainly to avoid the conversation.

I've kept this place as drama-free as I can for the past six months. I'm not risking it all for the sake of comfort.

Irene gives me a small smile- a knowing one? Her girl/ friend steps around her and hoists herself up and over the counter before I can stop her, rushing to hug me around the waist- the only place she can reach.

I can't think of a way to react. I can't even breathe. All I can think is that I don't know the last time I was properly hugged.

Irene smirks from the other side of the counter, "Meet Sayra. Sayra- Tenaya."

I look briefly to see if the coast is still clear before hesitantly reaching my arms around her in return.

She mumbles something into my side.

"Hmm?" I ask, and she lifts her head so her chin leans into my ribs and all I can see are her bright pink eyes.

"I saaaaid," She smiles, "We've got your back *nerd*."

She's the most ferocious tiny thing I've ever seen. Her hair isn't even her true statement piece. Her eyes are so vibrant, her face heart-shaped, and her lips spread wide in a pristine toothy-grin. She's almost feral in her actions, but I can see the years in her, the understanding behind the quirkiness and doe-eyes.

These guys are so unique, so themselves... And I'm just Tenaya. Tall, dark-haired, brown-eyed Tenaya. I'm not skinny, I'm not fat, I'm not heavy-or-small chested. I have nothing that separates me from the next smart girl.

But these guys- they're different.

They speak different, smile different. Even *feel* different- as soon as they enter a room, the mood is an amalgamation of chaos and anticipation.

I snap myself back into the room as her smile begins to falter and she loosens her grip, and I catch Irene's eyes narrowing in my periphery.

"Th-thank you," I stammer, giving her another squeeze, before taking her by the shoulders and steering her back around the counter, "But I assure you I'm fine. Nothing to worry about."

I know I'm not convincing, but I hadn't exactly predicted them showing up- let alone showing interest.

"Honest," I say, straightening up to a point Amaya would deem acceptable, "It's nothing, he's like that with everyone."

No he's not.

Not even close.

"Sayra doesn't seem to think so," Irene muses, leaning one arm on the top of Sayra's head for emphasis, "And she comes in most days."

"He's gross." Sayra harrumphs, her arms crossing her chest, "And you're too nice."

Nice- a good word.

Nice is another word for shy-

Boring

Invisible.

Forgettable.

These are the characteristics I need to be in order to survive the year- to Hydra, Casimir, Madeline, even myself.

I shrug, scribbling on the order pad and letting some of my hair fall forward to hide my face.

"It's not so bad," I lie, "Can I count on another strawberry and banana milkshake? Or is this the day you take a new suggestion? Banana, peanut butter and chocolate is a pretty legendary mix."

Irene twirls a few strands of her lavender-streaked hair between finger and thumb, scrutinising me. Sayra on the other hand has latched on to what I hoped she would.

"You- you can have- THREE flavours?!" She squeals.

I catch Irene rolling her eyes endearingly at Sayra's unquenchable excitement at such a novel thing. It's not dissimilar to how I react to Amaya- the two seemingly indistinguishable in their passions for confectionary.

"That'll be a '*yes please*', then." Irene says, leaning over and giving Sayra's head a kiss.

Girlfriend then.

Images of Madeline run through my head unfettered and I try not to let the jealous part of me rise. We would never work. Madeline is sunshine and enthusiasm and all things that scream '*hey world! Look at perfect little me*'. Whilst I'm busy hiding under the nearest rock.

I don't think I let anything register on my face, but something in the way Irene smiles at me makes me wonder. The knowing look, the camaraderie.

It would be nice, I suppose, to have someone who understands.

"Coming right up." I say, practically bowing before rushing into the kitchen.

I busy myself with the order, my mind a million miles away.

They saw how Casimir is. It's not just me being paranoid.

I had always wondered if it was. He started out with general questions, like why I thought he was the way he was or if I was interested in hearing about his day. But then hearing about his day led to hearing about his stresses, which led to the deeper stresses, which led to his whole family background- his parents, his childhood, his friends or lack thereof. It led to his deepest secrets. To him confiding, and me abiding because Gods know it's beyond me to leave someone to struggle on their own.

But that led to familiarity, over-familiarity, breaching of boundaries, the comments the closeness the staying late the unwanted intimacy the lack of personal space the-

The bag of frozen bananas bursts open in my hands.

"Crap." I hiss, hastily picking the runaways off the counter and righting the bag and myself in the process.

I slam the rest of the ingredients into the blender and press start, hoping the noise will drown out the racing thoughts in my head.

This is why it's best not to think about it, to pay it no attention until I can leave. Because what am I going to do? Tell on him?

See where that gets me. Fired at best.

I steady my hands before stepping back out, stopping short only when I see Casimir and Irene exchanging a begrudging handshake, before he slips away back to the office without looking at me. I watch as Irene wipes her hand- the one he shook- not-so-subtly on her trousers.

She notes my confused look and smirks.

"I begin repainting the walls on Monday." She says, "I'll be here every evening you are for the next couple weeks."

I'm not going to cry.

I'm *not*.

Sayra leaps up onto the counter like the wildcat she is and slips the milkshake from my hands. She winks at me before taking a ginormous gulp of the stuff. Her eyes bugging.

"*Oh* yeah," She grins, pointing at me for emphasis, "We gotta keep her- she's smart."

I smile before I can think not to, and Irene's grows wider as she hands me a couple of coins and a piece of paper.

"I'll see you on shift, *work buddy*."

I open the paper as Sayra slips from the counter into her girlfriend's extended arm, making their way to the other two by the door. "It's for whatever," Irene says, and I see that she's scrawled her number accompanied by a smiley-face, "See you tonight."

My head snaps up and I have just enough time to see the excited and devilish grins that span all their faces as they leave, Sayra waving manically with her mouth still glued to her milkshake.

I gulp.

The séance is tonight.

CHAPTER 6
GAME OF SURVIVAL

The house is void.

Void of noise, void of feeling.

Except tension.

The house is tension incarnate.

I purposefully left my door ajar tonight, not enough to grab her attention, but enough that it wouldn't make the jarring squeak that threatens to condemn me every time I need the toilet.

She'd been too tired to bother with me when I got home, for that at least I was grateful. It's harder to creep out of somewhere with aching limbs.

The hallway has never seemed so menacing.

It's six paces maximum- I can do six paces. The 'pillow-me' has been arranged, the lights off, the usual signs I have been present are all distributed. I even heated up a hot water bottle to make the room smell and feel slept in- should she pry.

It's just six steps.

Then ten downstairs.

Then five to the front door, a swig of shrinking potion, through the cat flap, a gulp of the antidote, a sprint and home free.

Quite literally.

I clench the small jagged potion bottle in my hand until it brings me back into the room, the tremors in my body subsiding slightly.

I can do this.

I slowly press two fingers around the side of my door, gripping it and bringing it tentatively towards me and silently into the room; having oiled it earlier. It glides without complaint until I have the space I need to slip outside and into the darkness of the hallway.

I grasp the door again and place it back where it was initially resting, making sure to get it precise to the millimetre of floorboard that was visible before.

The grey walls give only blank nothingness as I feel for their edges, stepping toe-heel the six paces as quickly and quietly as possible. If sweating made noise then I'd be long dead, my t-shirt clinging to my spine like a wet blanket; weighing me down as I descend.

Two beady yellow eyes glare up at me from the base of the stairs.

I'm surprised I don't pass out from shock, my brain kicking-in last minute to tell me it's Hyacinth- Hydra's cat.

She stands like a demon doorman at the bottom of the stairs, a feline gargoyle of grey fluff, flicking her tail back and forth.

I have two options.

Two feasible ones anyway.

Shoo her away and risk her causing a scene, or slowly step around her.

I take a deep breath, gripping the bannister and selecting the latter option as I creep down even slower than before.

Hyacinth's eyes track me, not even blinking as I get within two steps of her. Three and we'd be on level ground.

I take the first.

Nothing.

My heart is ricocheting inside my chest and I can't pause to breathe or I'll turn back and forget the whole thing. Magic be damned, this exertion would cripple me- and then Rylan would tell on me.

I take the second.

She blinks once, a quiet understanding- or a threat. I can't be sure. Hyacinth is only really seen on the couch or by Tabi's feet. From this I've always gathered she preferred his company or none at all. Perhaps me leaving the house is what she wants?

I take the third.

I'm on her level.

She pauses for only a moment, her tail no longer flicking and the hairs on my arms standing erect in fearful anticipation.

She turns and bolts for the living-room, her pampered paws making no more noise than that of cotton-balls on bathroom tiling.

I don't even breathe, doing so may turn into a sob, and that would definitely be the end of me.

I rush the last steps to the door and take a swig of the potion I'd made earlier in class, thanking the Gods once again for Mr Spelinski.

I take just enough to make my shoulders and hips fit through the cat-flap, snaking out into the fresh air of the front lawn.

I don't even bother using the antidote yet.

Not yet.

Let me get free- really free.

I sprint, the wind in my hair and my footfalls barely registering on the ground as I race down the drive and out onto the road, my skirt flying up behind me as I pace it down two streets before slamming on the breaks and letting out a breath that sounds more like a cry. My voice breaks on it and the sweat on my temple rolls down onto the pavement, mimicking rain in its abundance.

My breaths quickly turn from near-sobs to laughs as I brace

my hands on my back and lean into the crisp night air, closing my eyes and feeling the rush of oxygen swoop in on my lungs, turning my silent prayers into songs of praise.

I made it.

After taking the antidote it was less than twenty minutes-walk before I arrive outside the hovel they called a meeting-place.

There are cracks in the paintwork of the for-sale sign and the bricks host more vegetation than cement. That clearly didn't stop Amaya from thinking it was the perfect place to lean against and pop a ciggie.

Rylan crinkles his nose at her, and I can't say I blame him. She'd been trying to quit since start of first year, now entering our third- the quest's completion doesn't seem likely.

"I can *feel* the judgement." She groans in way of greeting, stamping out the end on the floor and digging her heel in for extra measure, "It wouldn't kill you to be more subtle." She grumbles.

Rylan snorts.

"Wouldn't kill you to quit either," He remarks, mock-pondering and tapping his chin, "Come to think of it, it's actually the opposite of quitting that'll kill you. Huh."

"*Har-di-har*." She says, elbowing him in the side before turning and knocking on the door with a loud rap.

Rylan looks me up and down in the way he always does.

I do the same to him.

"No Jiu-jitsu this evening?" He asks, and I cringe, already trying to suppress the memory of fleeing the house; even unscathed it felt like an ordeal.

"Not tonight." I reply curtly, not asking him the same in case Amaya twigged something.

I wouldn't drag her into this mess, if she knew- she'd run straight to the officials; she's not one to stand by and let her friends get hurt.

She wouldn't understand.

Rylan nods and his mouth thins into a smile, flicking his hair from his eyes as the door to the building creaks open; the excessive sound still sending tension through me even this far from the house.

Irene stands on the other side of it, her phone light in one hand and her body cloaked in what looks to be ancient monk-robes. Brown sandbag-like material drapes over her body and head. The hood hides her face from full view, but her lipstick and devilish grin are enough of an identifier.

"Welcome, fellow mages." She says eerily, ushering us in and down the stairs towards the basement.

She gives me a once over and a wink before closing the door behind me. I've never made friends quickly, but I already feel like Irene has stuck her neck out for me as much as any friend would. It could be nice to join her ragtag group once in a while.

It's not every day you get to sneak out of your abusive home in the middle of the night, hangout with a rebel group in a deserted basement- with the hopes of unlocking an ancient artefact in the pursuit of illegal magic...

So I'll try to enjoy myself.

"You failed to mention they were part of an occult." Rylan grumbles from behind me as we descend the stairs, his eyes darting back to the door nervously.

"It's for aesthetics, dumbass." Irene hisses, her mouth twisting into a frown; only visible by the light coming from under the door at the bottom of the stairs.

Upon entering the room, I can see that she wasn't kidding- and that Rylan may have a panic attack.

The others sit around in a circle on the floor, a coterie of weirdos all wearing similar monk-esq cloaks and staring us down from under their hoods. The room itself is little more than a storage room. Square in dimensions, maybe 8foot on all sides.

The walls are old and peeling, dust at the base suggesting the weight of the house is getting to them. I choose not to point this out to Rylan, who already looks ready to bolt. Amaya barely does a take, her eyes zoning in on the same thing that mine do.

Sat in the centre of the room, smaller than a human head.

The Veturcaela.

I have to stop myself from grabbing for it. I'm pretty sure that if I do, they'll kick us out, and then I'll never get my chance to find her-

Magic.

Just the Magic...

Irene steps forward into the middle of them, taking the Veturcaela in hand- and throwing it at me.

Amaya yells and Rylan lurches backwards, my hands flying forwards to catch it as it lands in my palms. It's dense- but squishy, like some sort of exotic fruit.

"What do you think, nerds?" Irene asks, her arms folding across her chest and the others standing, watching us intently.

Sayra skips over to Irene's side, giving my ribs a jab as she moves past me; I barely register it.

My heart is beating a million miles a minute and I can't think. Amaya and Rylan come to my sides to take a closer look.

In my hands lies the closest thing to magic I have ever encountered. I have made potions to morph sizes, change temperature / colour / species.

But *this*?

This could change the world as we know it.

I had expected it to feel more alive, or present at least. But the Veturcaela only sits. It fills my hands, dusty and ancient and looking for all intents and purposes like it's been ripped from a tree. In fact- exactly that. It looks like the heart of a tree, all vines and ivy and dirt, with an unknown and potentially unknowable epicentre.

All my research has taught me what to look for, the signs and symbols that I now see engraved into the things very being. The lines and markings that single it out as a Veturcaela.

"Well?" Amaya asks from my side, her fingers clammy on my arm, "Is it the real thing?"

I look between them, both searching me eagerly for confirmation.

There's no doubt in my mind.

I nod.

They all gather round in a circle, their eyes transfixed on me and the thing in my palms.

A Veturcaela is essentially a magicians' broomstick through space. It allows the holder to take away one dimension and replace it with the next. It's driven by thought and desire and will follow the mentality of the host. Essentially, it's a living thing- fully capable of deciding whether you go or don't, based on your conviction- it won't send you halfway across the known universe if you're not sure you want to go. The person who wields it has to be certain, strong, versed on the ins and outs of it.

And they have to be compatible with magic.

Open.

Their mind has to be able to take in and let out magical components, becoming a vessel for the inter-dimensional elements.

Since no one else steps forward, I'm guessing the first bet is me.

"Are you guys sure about this?" I ask Irene, looking from her to Sayra, who's currently hopping up and down in the spirit of the rabbit ears she's haphazardly stapled to her monk's hood.

"We may only get one chance at this." I push, knowing that failing the Veturcaela can result in its disintegration.

Irene nods, taking Sayra's hand in hers to halt her bouncing. Amaya's gaze darts between their clasped hands but she doesn't say anything.

I'd give anything to see Amaya's thoughts- and for Irene to never notice the look that passes across her face at their intimacy; too quickly for anyone else to notice.

But I do.

"We trust you, Tenaya." Irene says, shrugging, "We've done our research- into it, and into you." She smirks, flicking hair from her face, "It's you or no one at this point. And we are far too impatient to go around hunting and persuading another nerd."

Sayra nods emphatically.

"Nerds are a tricky business, you're the first who's even bothered to hear us out!" Sayra pipes up.

I hold the Veturcaela closer to my chest, tight enough that I can feel my heartbeat echoing in its core.

"I'm so grateful you chose me," I say, looking to Rylan and Amaya, "-*Us*. Thankyou for bringing us here, showing this to us- whatever the outcome."

The group grins, even though I can't see it, I can feel the other two smile from behind me, their hoods low enough that they hide their eyes from view.

I step into the centre, not looking at anyone else and taking a breath.

Closing my eyes.

I press into the flesh of the Veturcaela-

Simultaneously delving into the deepest parts of my mind until all around me is darkness and blankness. Until the solipsistic existence I've manifested in my head is all that is and all that ever will be and I can feel it.

The Veturcaela.

It calls- pools into the void from my hands and it feels cold. A cool breeze after climbing a mountain, a river rushing over me after days in the sun. Blue light runs into my cavern and I'm surrounded with lines of iridescent beauty that swarm me, observing me, scrutinising my worth, my aptitude.

And only then do I allow myself to think it-

Shout it.

Beg for it

-to the spirits of the magic realms that circle me like aquatic vultures.

Aletheia.

They pause.

They literally stop, and nothing exists but me and the blue lines in the void in my head.

They suddenly blink an angry red, so quick I could have imagined it.

Pink vertical lines dart and slash through the blue, interlocking with them and spiralling until I can't distinguish where one colour begins and the other ends.

From the outside world I feel it then, hear them yelling, my body vibrating and lifting. Hands grab at my clothes, sides, anything they can get at.

My eyes fly open and I'm suspended above them, my hair fanning out around me like I'm attached to a current.

Maybe I am.

The floor and walls begin to ripple, to shift and sway and everyone else is holding onto parts of me for dear life; the Veturcaela scattering any free-standing objects to the outskirts of the room. And I know it then, before I even see it.

The Veturcaela has opened.

A cornucopia of colours and light stream from within it as the heart shaped mound of dirt opens up like a flower in my hand.

There's a crinkle in the fabric of the realm.

A two-dimensional crease in front of my face, like crumpled paper. One that wasn't there and shouldn't exist and completely tears apart my perception of the known universe.

Before I can question it- I take the crease in hand, the feel of it thinner than tracing paper, and tear it away; taking the room with it and spinning me and everyone else away.

Their bodies touch down in a hellscape, and I cling to the

Veturcaela like a lifeline as it suspends me in the air several feet above the others. The ground is blood red and oozing, the sky a heliotropic dystopia. Bats as big as jet planes and dark as obsidian fly past us, their jaws unhinging like that of a snake's as they dive us. Caves larger than mountains loom in every direction and crimson rivers flow between them, our group sprawled on the small embankment.

Distantly I hear Amaya and Rylan screaming my name, but I don't know how to help them. Other than finding another way out, looking for the crinkle in the realm.

But there's nothing, and I know the Veturcaela can sense my panic, my indecision; it's floral petals quivering and threatening to close again.

From below me I hear a howl, looking down to see Irene's leg between the jaws of a demonic creature as big as a mountain lion but with the exterior of a porcupine, sharp daggers from all directions preventing the others from helping her as it tries to drag her away. Sparks of purple spit in and around her and the creature - *magic*. We have entered a realm where magic is wielded.

But I can't focus on that- she needs medical help - she needs *saving*.

I push these feelings through me and into the Veturcaela until I see it, the crinkle, the scar-tissue in the skin of the universe.

"HOLD ONTO EACH OTHER!" I yell, throwing a mental image of them up in my mind, condensing the current into two-dimensions and ripping the physical-field from view.

Stepping into the new again.

My feet collide with ground this time and I fall back, my body encased in soft grass and the most brilliantly lilac sky. The strands are so long I can't see over them to check for the others. I can only watch as the grass bends and weaves, curling around my head- the part that yields the bump and hair loss. They press tenderly to my temple and hum, lulling a melody so sweet that I can't help the tears that spring to my eyes, the indescribable joy that flows into my body as I am healed.

The Veturcaela works on thoughts, I knew that much. But I hadn't realised how much of a mental strain it was- that with the push or pull of any emotion you could send yourself halfway across the physical plain.

The two-dimensional aspect is a new one though. The idea that by connecting to the Veturcaela, you can pull out of your world, tear it away and step into a new one. Condensing the current plane to a two-dimensional field in order to step into the next three-dimensional one.

Curious.

I hear sobs from beyond the grass-level, and the strands fall away seamlessly as I lift myself up to sit. I can't help the smile that splits my face as I see the rest of them- four fake-monks and two weirdos, all encased in healing foliage.

The demon-pine is gone, Irene's leg firmly strapped down by the greenery that has begun to heal her. Everyone else's eyes are as wide as saucers as they take in the magnitude of what's just happened, what could *still* happen.

What I'm doing.

"You actually did it." Rylan whispers in awe, and I turn to see him running his hands through the grass, their tips glowing faintly at his touch.

I did it.

I used a magic portal.

Transported us through the universe, across galaxies, in *space*.

What if...

I stand, and the others join me as if on queue, likely terrified of getting left behind. As nice as a world of healing grassland is- I should think given a lifetime of it you may go slightly insane. Not that the grass would let you kill yourself to escape it either, or die of old age...

I don't let myself think on it too hard. Don't let myself think about wandering the plain in search of lost souls who couldn't escape and therefore never left; kept alive and captive by the very things they sought out to save them.

...I thought about it.

But other than the good-but-bad-grass-

-I can find her.

The thought comes unhindered and I'm suddenly more anxious than I was when entering the hell-scape. I can find the thing that invades my dreams, that disturbs my peace; or what little of it I can scrounge together at least.

So long as she exists- I can find her.

"I'm going to try one more thing." I say to them, and they all nod their heads; only too excited to see what the universe can show them. Rylan bends down to Amaya, scooping her up by her arm and brushing her down before checking around to make sure that the others are okay.

Closing my eyes, I bring my attention inwards and let the Veturcaela raise me again, the signalling blue swirls swimming around in my head as I collect myself in the darkness.

Bring me to her.

If she's real, in this dimension or the next.

If she can be found- find her.

Aletheia.

Find me Aletheia.

Take me to Aletheia.

Aletheia Aletheia Aletheia Aletheia Aletheia Aletheia Aletheia Aletheia Aletheia Aletheia Aletheia ***Aletheia.***

I chant her name until it's written in the blue and pink and then the red

Red

RED-

it feels angry

It feels inevitable

I summon and demand it until it's *understood*, and I feel the tug on the other end- a small but growing presence.

I open my eyes to see the crinkle, right in front of me, begging to be seized.

And I do.

I rip it open with a force so eager I fear it will leave a permanent crack in the fabric of the universe, stepping us from one field of existence to the next with an urgency unparalleled.

She has to be real.

Has to be.

Aletheia...

Our bodies are suspended in a void of black, grey and white, with blinding light to the left and an abyss of darkness on our right; holding us in the grey.

And right in front of me is a girl.

The most ethereally perfect person I've ever seen.

A girl with diamond eyes and hair so long it cascades beneath us all, her body buoyant but restrained.

Staring wide-eyed back at me.

Her lips fall open, as if this Goddess of a creature was capable of shock. Her eyes are full of wonder, hope and something else-

Fear?

"You..."

She breathes, her voice softer than silk.

She... she's real.

Suddenly and without warning- giant clawed hands of amaranthine and ink-black power rip through the white, shattering the moment and reaching for us.

The girl's face first plastered in fear now shifts to that of defiant rage. Her hair spreads wide at the same time as wings of leather and feather fly out from behind her, blocking the hands from us momentarily; the claws ripping harshly through her porcelain flesh.

"LEAVE!"

The command flies at me, shoving me and the others backwards, the words a physical push in the void. One of her hands snaps loose from the restraints, the claws having severed it, and something orange and white slams from her hands into my chest.

"Aleth-" I try to say as I'm sucked out of the void.

"GO!"

She screams, and even as she tries to lurch towards us the hands come around her middle, big enough to envelope her, stealing her from my sight.

They take her just as the world takes us, the Veturcaela stripping us from her dimension and slamming us back into the basement with a thud, our bodies colliding harshly with the concrete floor; a dark circle of soot all that's left to say anything ever happened.

The Veturcaela dims and shuts, a sign it won't open again for some time, and I shove the thing in my pocket before anyone can see.

"NO!" I scream, throwing myself onto the floor and pounding at the ashy concrete like it will do any good. "Bring me *back*, bring me back there bring her back let me go back to her!"

I can't think straight, and as blood from my palms dirties the soot, I feel arms lock around me from both sides, hauling me back and against them; but I keep screaming.

She was real- she- I *saw* her. I found her and now she's gone again.

The tears freefall from my eyes as I sob into Rylan's chest, Amaya's fingers running calmingly through my hair.

"Nonono I need to go *back*! I need to go back *please* let me go back, they'll hurt her they'll *kill* her..."

Amaya strokes some strands from my face, her wildly concerned face blurring its way into my periphery. I know they've never seen me like this, I know distantly I must look as insane as I truly know myself to be- but I don't care.

They took her

"Who's *she*?" Amaya asks cautiously.

"Who's *they*?" Rylan presses, his expression equally baffled.

I feel the blood drain from my face.

It can't be-

"Wh- what did you see- in the last realm. What did you *see*?" I ask, my lips trembling as I grip onto Rylan's arm for an anchor- a sense of stability that he so often provides-

-but doesn't now.

Irene steps forward from the corner, massaging her left arm from the impact. I can still see the scars from where the beast had its jaws on her leg; faint white lines visible through the rips in her cloak.

"It was a void, an empty void of light and dark." She says and my breath hitches, "Nothing. It felt like the closest thing to a place of nothing. It was thick with it, and it rejected us being there."

Irene steps closer, "What did you see, was sh-" But she stops herself.

My vision blurs and I can barely think for the feeling coming over me.

I am going insane, that much is clear.

She doesn't exist, she never did.

I'm seeing things, and this latest event confirms it.

I try to speak but no words come out, my lips barely moving

as darkness threatens my periphery.

"Woah, hey- Ten. *Ten*? Tenaya stay with us now."

"Is she alright?"

"What's happening?"

"That was more than I ever thought possible."

"Where's the Veturcaela?"

"Is she passing out?"

"*Tenaya*."

The voices blend together and I can't discern who's talking. All I can think and feel is that I am doomed. I tasted magic and it has dosed me with the truth- I am going insane, and it's only a matter of time before they all see it too.

"I need to go home." I hear myself say, like watching a film play out from behind a pane of glass.

I watch my body rise from the ground and prop itself up on Rylan, Amaya's arm going under my other side hesitantly.

"Rylan." I say, and he looks more worried than ever- which says a lot, considering he sees the aftermath of beatings on a semi-regular basis.

"Take me home?"

CHAPTER 7
SOMETHING IN THE ORANGE

The trip back to the house at near-dawn is barely a memory. All I know is I had myself shrunk and thrown up to my bedroom window by Rylan, instead of going through the whole sneaking through the house ordeal. I hid the Veturcaela under the floorboards in the bathroom- I know I should tell the others it didn't die. I know it's betraying their trust. But I'm the only one there who can wield it, I know I am- and I won't be using it without them, I just... I can't shake the feeling that I need to keep it close.

I'm the only one who's ever made to clean the bathroom, so I know it'll be safe there. My room certainly isn't. Half the time I come home to a room that smells like *her*; like cheap perfume and disdain.

Now I lie awake, staring up at the ceiling as it grows from black to blue-black to grey to yellow through the passing hours.

She hasn't snooped, so I'm safe for now.

I barely feel the relief through the pounding in my skull.

I'm going insane, and there's nothing I can do to stop it. Is it her fault? Did she break me?

Did I break myself?

My body shivers and I try to shake off the feeling of something crawling on me. The goosebumps that travel up my spine and around my neck, continuing down my chest and pooling on my stomach...

Goosebumps don't pool on your stomach.

My hands scramble for the base of my shirt, gingerly lifting it until my belly is exposed.

...*Impossible*

An image of a Kitsune stares up at me from my navel, its beady fox eyes staring into my soul as I roam over its details.

I never got a tattoo.

That means this isn't real.

It spans as big as my open hand and points towards my chest with its snout, its nine tails bunching just above my pant-line.

Run through the facts Tenaya. Don't. Panic.

I have a tattoo, I never *got* a tattoo, but I have a tattoo.

The tattoos blinks.

Everything in me freezes and I think for a moment time stops. I don't scream, I don't throw anything- the thing in question I would throw being somewhat attached to me.

"*Breathe* Tenaya," I wheeze through claustrophobic lungs, "Talking to yourself is the first sign of madness, seeing fox tattoos that aren't there is probably the second... seeing them *move*..."

I try to take my eyes off of him but I can't. I don't even know why I know it's a *him*- but I do.

For certain I do.

"Okay," I breathe, the image of the fox juddering with my every breath, "Let's try something."

I swing my legs off the bed and stand, removing my shirt so

I can keep the kitsune in full view. His claws extend and retract like he's making biscuits, and there's no doubt in my mind now that this thing can move. Either he's not real, or he's magic.

Please let him be magic.

"What's your name?" I ask, trying not to second guess myself for talking to a possibly-not-there kitsune tattoo on my stomach.

He blinks at me slowly, before nodding- the feeling stirring up goosebumps as he fully extends. His body stretches and contorts itself until he's positioned his body and nine tails into a shape.

A pose that looks like a letter.

"K?"

He shifts again, flowing into the next one, a mischievous gleam in his eye.

"U?"

Again but faster, the feeling overcoming me one of excited joy- one that I can't tell if it's his or mine.

"R?"

He backflips into the last one.

"O?" I say, placing fingers along his spine and watching as he moves into them, nuzzling against them through the flesh barrier.

"Your name is *Kuro*?"

If a fox could smile- he just did.

The image shimmers and bursts into orange glowing beads that fizzle and tear from my body in a shower of golden light. The atoms bend and reknit in the air in front of me, swirling and stitching until they reform in the middle of my room.

Stood on my rug, barely taller than knee-level, all nine tails flowing in the air- is a kitsune.

Kuro.

I have summoned a being from another realm, that Aletheia threw to me- or I am really losing it.

Either way, he's real enough to rush towards me, darting in

between my legs in a figure-of-eight; coming to rest between them with his tongue lolling like a dog's.

His fur glows an ethereal golden-orange, burning like the last embers of a fire. His feet herald dagger-sharp claws of onyx, contrasting with the snowy white of his paws, snout and underbelly.

"Hello, Kuro." I murmur, squatting gingerly down beside him and running my hands through his coat.

The softness is unexpected, and I marvel at the way my fingers glide through it, seamlessly and leaving it as if untouched.

He *feels* real.

"You're going to have to stay here," I say, already stressing about what the hell I'm meant to do, "No *way* are you coming to classes with me."

Kuro whines, his head dropping and paws padding lightly at my stomach, like a baby-joey begging to re-enter the pouch.

"I don't-"

"Naya?" Tabi's voice comes from the other side of my door and my heart plummets.

"Just a second!" I yell, turning back to Kuro and stroking him behind the ear, "Kuro- *on*." I whisper, placing a hand to my chest, summoning him in the only way I can think of.

He lets out what can only be described as a low chuckle before bursting into a billion tiny lights and slinking back onto my stomach in a flurry of sparkles; re-morphing into the kitsune on my flesh and darting back to rest by my navel.

I grab on a shirt and rush to the door, breathing normally for all of two seconds before swinging it open.

Tabi stands on the other side, sleep still sagging his eyelids and a blanket clutched to his chest. He's barely 7, and it's moments like this that remind me why I have to stay. He needs me, not just to be his big sister. He needs me to take the hits. Because if I don't, then he will learn too young what it is to become a human punching-bag.

Not on my watch.

"Hey Tabi-cat," I sooth, hunching down and scooping him up into my arms so that he rests on my hipbone, one of his tired fists scrunched in his face, "Why're you up, huh?"

He grumbles, gripping the blanket tighter and leaning his head on my shoulder.

I sigh, hoisting him up a little higher and heading towards his room.

"If Hydra sees you up at this time, she'll have my head." I whisper as I rush past her bedroom, pushing through the door to his room. It's all blues and greens and sketchbooks, colourful pages littering the ground.

I feel him tense against me at the mention of Hydra and I almost regret saying it- but it's true.

I don't want him to feel he can't come see me or can't be around me, but the more he does the more danger he puts himself in. And the more I'll suffer for it.

I feel Kuro bristle against me.

I wonder how much of an insight into what I go through, what this body is put through, he gets from just existing on its surface. Does he get the mental feed to accompany it? Or does he have to piece together the mess from the connect-the-dots work of scars on my body?

"I wanted to see you, Hyacinth told me." He mumbles against my shoulder, and not for the first time I let myself believe he has a hidden gift.

Tabi and Hyacinth have been inseparable since Hydra first moved in. Where Tabi went, Hyacinth could be found slinking close behind, fluffy tail swaying behind them. Tabi knew when she was hungry, when she wanted to go out, when she needed attention- even when Hyacinth was sick, Tabi was the first to say she needed a Vet. Dad and Hydra managed to convince themselves it was because he loved her so much, but I see the way he is with animals.

I know magic when I see it.

Either that, or he's just as insane as I am- and I'm not ready to condemn him just yet.

"Did she now," I say, setting him down on the bottom bunk of his bed, "And what exactly did Hyacinth say about me?"

Sometimes I come in here, only on the nights she doesn't come searching for me. I creep in and stay the night on the top bunk, never waking him, just to be here; to remind myself why I stay. Tabi has so much joy to give. He loves football and play-fighting and jigsaws, he draws and builds new worlds with his toys. He's smart and funny and *so* brave, more than anyone realises.

Because he's not naïve.

He may not see everything, if anything, but he knows enough to understand; and he stays quiet. He doesn't say anything because I don't say anything.

And it breaks my heart.

He was barely a year old when mum passed, a new-born never to properly know his mother.

She'd be so proud of him.

"She says not to sneak out again." He mumbles tiredly.

I stop tucking him back in, my fingers tense on the quilt.

He couldn't know that I snuck out. My door was shut in the way I'd last placed it and he was asleep when I left. The only person who saw me leave was Hyacinth.

Tabi's dark brown eyes meet mine, and whilst I can see the sadness in them, I can also see how mad he is. He doesn't get it completely, but he knows that what I did was risky. He's mad because he knows that if I had been caught then I would have been in trouble.

He just doesn't know the extent.

And he knows this because *somehow*- he can talk to the cat.

I press the quilt down on top of him and stroke the hair back from his forehead.

"Listen Tabi, you can't be saying these things. To me it's fine, but if anyone else knew that you can communicate with Hyacinth-"

He pushes against the covers.

"It's not just- that wasn't my point, my point is-"

"I know your point, Tabi-cat," I interrupt, and he sticks his bottom lip out at me in frustration, "Your point is you want me safe." I let my breath out slowly, and I feel the tension slip from him a little. "You want me to look after myself. I know, and I promise you from now on- I will. No more risks, no more sneaking out. Just going to look out for you and me."

It takes him a moment of debate, thoughts going through his head that a seven-year-old shouldn't have to think. But after a moment, he smiles, a small one- but it's there. He squeezes one hand from under the blanket and extends it to me.

"Pinky-swear?" He asks.

I give him my biggest smile, snaking his pinky with my own, linking forefingers and touching thumbs to lock it in place.

"Pinky-swear."

I stand, letting his hand fall away and waving him off as I make to leave, gently shutting his door behind me. He is still so young, another year and I can get him to safety- and then me. I can save us both, and now I have promised to save us without risks.

Kuro skims along my skin and appears on my inner arm, belly out and eyes on me, a reminder of my new complications.

Gods, please don't make me break it.

CHAPTER 8

PULLED FROM THE TRAINWRECK

Amaya and Rylan are absent.

Neither turned up for Nature-Nurture, and now Potions class they're still a no-show.

I've notif'd them but it hasn't even registered as read yet, which could mean a number of things. But considering what went down yesterday and the mess I was afterwards- I can't really blame them if they need to take a minute.

Madeline sits in the row in front of me, Max nowhere to be seen.

I wish I could concentrate, but with no friends to ground me, and a tattoo kitsune doing backflips on my body, I can barely hone in on what Mr Spelinski is saying enough to take in the basics.

I just have to ignore this for now. Get through the day, week, *year*- get home, sleep- hope this all turns into nothing.

But... do I *want* to ignore it?

Or do I just want to get back to my beach so I can try and contact her again?

Spelinski throws a hand in the air dramatically, sparks flying from his fingers in a gimmicky gesture in aims of maintaining our attention; for once, failing.

What do I even mean- contact *her*? She's a figment of my insanity, a conjuring of my own making to get through the year. She's not a saving grace or someone I can depend on.

She's not real.

She's not.

But... I wish she was.

My hand comes into contact with crumbs of dirt in my pocket, lacing the stitching in the aftermath of magic; the remnants of the Veturcaela still dusting the inside. I turn the dirt between thumb and finger, grinding the granules until my fingertips are coated in a fine powder.

Aletheia...

And the world implodes.

The hall feels like it's being sucked into a vacuum.

The walls bend inwards and ripple, time stops and bodies fluctuate in and out of focus as the realm tries to fold in on itself.

No one blinks, no one seems to register the shift in reality.

Everything drains into the background as a body bleeds its way into the hall. Like she's on the other side of the projector-sheet, being drawn forwards by invisible strings, forcing her way through.

I know it's her.

I don't know how and I don't know why.

But it's her.

There's a shimmer, an outline, a mask of a face and body in the film of the projector screen and it's screaming.

She's *screaming*.

It's on the tip of my tongue. Teasing it. Everything in me clenches as the vacuum threatens to suffocate me and I feel like I'm drowning in it.

The silence, the empty but ever-so *ever-so full* feeling.

If I give in to this it's giving into the insanity, admitting that what is happening is real for me and me alone. It's letting her in, and all the mayhem that may come with it. My world, the one I've been meticulously crafting for myself- for Tabi. I promised no more risks and I meant it, but *this*?

...*her*?

I say it-

whisper it-

breathe it-

"***Aletheia...***" The word escapes almost soundlessly from my barely parted lips.

The air returns to the room in a tidal wave and I feel crushed against my seat as the sound surges back in and the universe removes itself from my chest. The outline against the screen warps-

morphs-

grows.

The shadow becomes a phantom becomes a person.

Her body is held horizontal, like a person crucified, the dark leaching from the right and bonds of light clawing her left.

Her hair covers her from end to end and most in between, and my eyes travel the length of her. No one turns, no one so much as blinks as Mr Spelinski continues to explain the multipurpose benefits of Lymarian seeds.

No one sees the crack in the universe or the angel trapped there.

She lifts her head slowly, carefully, until she's staring me down.

She smirks.

"Hello Darling."

The bonds shatter and her body drops like a stone, her hair fanning out above her on the descent before falling like a cape over and around her, landing cat-like on the desk.

I look at the students along every row, none of them batting an eye at the completely naked girl on stage.

No one can see her except... me.

Before I can so much as question it- she's leaping from row to row, languidly stretching over classmates and chairs alike, her body moving like flowing water-

Until she stills in front of me.

There's a chair between us, but that doesn't stop her leaning forwards until her face is millimetres from my own, her hair no longer quite so concealing as her diamond eyes blink up at mine.

"You called?"

CHAPTER 9
BOUNDARIES OF THE MORTAL WORLD

This world tastes different.

It's the first thing I notice, other than her, as I rip myself from the clutches of the Fates and fall face-first into the mortal realm. My world smelt like a tavern, but also like sea and sky and dirt and home home home

She smells like jasmine.

She hasn't moved since she summoned me. Hasn't blinked. To their credit- neither have her associates. But their lack of attentiveness seems less purposeful.

I take her chin in my hand, feeling her tense at the movement, her hazel eyes widening.

...I can't feel her.

I peer closer to where my fingers meet her face. A millimetre- if that- but there's a barrier. Clear and barely there, but enough to keep my body suspended from hers.

"Bear with me, my darling," I say soothingly, "Just need to test out logistics."

I await her response, her eyes so big and dark they could hold entire voids in their depths.

I found her, this girl, again-

Amica mea, I've found you.

After what feels like an eternity she nods, slowly, and I feel her swallow back what smells like fear as I take a step away. My wings don't want to appear in this realm, although they were beyond-damaged last I checked anyway; so that's disappointing. Other than that, I appear to have taken most of myself with me in the escape.

Sneaking a glance back at her, I see the edges of Kuro's tails slinking under her skirts.

Dirty fox.

I'm glad he's stayed put though, hunting him down in Selheim is hard enough, but in this vast expanse of unknown territory?

My fingers run along the velvety texture of the chairs. I can feel the bristles itching to graze my skin, but they don't. My hand leaves no mark along the chair jackets, my voice carries no power and my presence makes no impact on the rows of mortal students; their slightly glazed eyes still trained distantly on the manic man dancing his way across the stage.

I skip over their heads until I'm back at the front, the balding leader of the group seemingly unaware of my existence. What if I just...

"*Don't touch him.*" I hiss at Aletheia, a couple of annoyed faces swivelling in my direction.

I cringe into my seat, wishing and praying that the world will open up and swallow me whole. Let me sink into the depths strand by strand, *grain by grain*, until I just disappear.

This can't be happening.

Aletheia smirks at me, but doesn't move towards him again. Instead, she busies herself with trying and failing to take hold of the remote for the display. Her hands glazing over the surface as if repelled by it, and I watch as her face goes from a breeze to a storm cloud; the frustration spilling from her skin in great waves.

I close my eyes.

Breathe, in and out.

Slowly in, easy out.

Now again.

I know these things:

I am the only one in the room who can see Aletheia. Aletheia is real to me. Aletheia followed me from the séance- if not before. The Kitsune belongs to Aletheia. Aletheia isn't human. Aletheia is naked. Aletheia is beautiful.

No

Try again.

Aletheia was trapped- now she's here. Aletheia can't interact with the rest of the world. Aletheia was summoned by me. Aletheia Aletheia Aletheia ***Aletheia***-

"If you keep saying my name like a prayer my darling, you may as well get on your knees."

Her voice in my ear snaps my eyes open.

My face immediately burns scarlet.

She's sat on my lap.

Aletheia is curled around me like a braid, her hair falling over me and her limbs covering the rest. Her eyes parallel with mine and both her arms wrap around my neck; without the sensation of it.

I can't feel her, only the faintest sense of her weight.

"I am kind of a 'deity', after all,"

She continues, as if this is normal for her- maybe it is-

"Or at the very least- the offspring of one."

My heart threatens to beat right out of my chest. Everything in me feels like it's glass. Glass that's slowly being heated to a point, a breaking point, one that will come out of nowhere without word or warning.

Her leg slips between mine and I splinter.

"I-"

"Tenaya?"

Madeline's eyes meet mine from the row in front, dousing me in ice, her expression concerned. She reaches a hand back to me, coming to rest on my knee, a hand I can feel- a weight that is real in this dimension.

"Is everything alright?"

I don't know. I'm here but I'm also in whatever purgatory dimension Aletheia is snared in. I'm in between two planes but also in both, expected to interact with both, *be* with both.

Aletheia rises, maintaining her seat but leaning forwards so that her hand covers Madeline's and her face comes within inches of hers; obscuring Madeline from my line of sight. All I can see is the length of Aletheia on my leg.

"Oh? And who's this pretty creature?"

Aletheia says with something akin to menace.

She's too close.

"No!" I try to say- but shout, and all heads turn to me, Madeline's eyes bugging.

I shatter.

"S-s-sorry- sorry, I have to-"

I avoid Madeline's gaze as I stand, grabbing my bag as Aletheia slides off of me, like a silk dress from a tired body. I always try to take an aisle seat and today is the day I know I make smart choices- as I race efficiently from the room without another word; much to the confused faces of both Mr Spelinski and students alike.

I'm in the hallway, the linoleum floors glinting up at me, my feet slapping down on them and the red red blood-red lockers begin closing in on either side of me.

This can't be happening

This cannot be happening

This can't

I can't breathe

I can't-

I feel my body begin to fall and I lean into it, crashing between where one row of lockers stops and another begins, a crevice in the columns.

The wall is cool on my skin and I feel consciousness try to slip from me as I slide down the length of it and into a ball, my legs splaying at jarring angles.

I'm not in either dimension now.

The fog rolls in on all sides, the only feeling one of slow numbing as my heart beats too fast for my body and my brain succumbs to it.

The last thing I see before the red turns to black, are silvery whisps floating in from behind the lockers.

She followed me...

Can't blink, can't breathe, can't feel the sand.

I'm dreaming again.

I let the waves rock in slowly, but I can tell I'm fighting them this time. They want to crash and storm and smash the sand further into pieces. I fight the tension and I slow it to a dull cresting against the shores, my feet sliding in to nearly meet it.

Not quite though.

How did it get to this?

She can't touch Madeline, that much I'm sure of. That didn't stop the alarm bells sounding when the two were inches apart, separated only by the veil between worlds.

I rest my head back, letting the rhythm of the tide wash over me without touching me, letting the sky above breathe calm into me.

Gods I wish you were here, mum. You'd know what to do...

As it stands- I have no idea.

Hydra will kill me if I start acting off, that much I know. And fainting at university?

I fist my hands together, cursing myself for my weakness. If she's called in to take me home it'll be the end of me, it'd take more than just concealer to hide the ordeal I'd be going through should I disrupt her day.

And now with Aletheia...

"Well, this is curious."

I sit up and the waves have stopped, the breeze is gone and the lump in my throat that can't be here- returns. Aletheia sits beside me on the sand, an arms-length away, her hair slinking around and over her like a silvery shawl; elfin ears peaking-through. She takes up a fistful of sand in her palm, dropping it from one hand into the other repeatedly.

Her body is practically the same colour as her hair, shining iridescent in the moonlight.

"Who are you?" I ask, in what I hope is a strong voice- but I've never had to use it here.

No one's ever invaded my dreams before.

No one except her.

She pauses, her outstretched hand still encasing granules.

She shrugs.

"A fair question."

Without another word, she flings the sand into the breezeless air.

The grains stay fixed there, like someone hit pause on a video. Then they change, but I don't change them.

And that's not possible.

The granules grow to galaxies, shifting up and outwards. My body no longer rests on sand but floats buoyantly in the middle of a universe foreign to me. The planets aren't circular but spiky, their shapes straggly and covered in tendrils that snake out amidst the crimson sky. The universe is deep red in one direction and a brilliant purple in the other as far as the eye can see, broken up only by the curiously shaped homelands.

Aletheia floats ahead of me, her hair up and around her and I try not to stare.

She wheels backwards so that her spine arches and her hair creates an ouroboros with her body.

...I stare.

She's like a goddess, suspended in the nothingness. The brightest star in the known galaxy and the next, sacrosanct in her beauty. Each sculpted and toned limb flowing into the next with effortless ease...

"My darling, you make me blush."

I can feel the heat in my own cheeks as I realise my staring mustn't be as inconspicuous as I'd thought; but there's nowhere else to look.

well, nowhere I'd rather look...

She smiles wider, I beg she can't read my mind.

Soundlessly she pulls the smaller stars nearest her around her body, plucking the dots from the sky like they aren't lightyears away.

They swirl and mist until a thin veil of silvery-white covers her from chest to thigh, held up by strings of starlight.

She gestures at herself.

"Better?"

I swallow back the panic enough to nod.

She takes two fingers then, placing them together and drawing them apart again. We're sucked in, or teleported, or the universe condenses. Either way- the galaxy focuses in on the lilac side, highlighting the single-most beautiful colour I've ever seen. It's a million colours in one, glowing in its magnitude, enough that my dream-eyes water at the sight of it.

"This," I say, delighted at her awe, "Is my birthplace. Empyrailla, or as your people call it- The Land of the Elder Gods."

She twists in the sky and suddenly we're stood in a forest of galaxy-trees and rivers of starlight. Nymph-like-beings glide through lengths of water, careening alongside prehistoric creatures with auras so pure they emanate it. The sky is like crying tears of joy, the forest floor the thought of coming home; the breeze alone is ecstasy.

The beings around us are so much more than beautiful, their shapes so carefully crafted they could never be captured by pen or paintbrush.

Everything feels too much, there's too much too much too much too much-

"Hey-"

Her arms come around me and her shoulder obstructs my view.

Before I can blink, we're in the foreign galaxy again. Her arms, arms that I can't feel, hold me together as my brain finishes reeling from the utopia of sensations that it was just subjected to.

"I didn't know, I'm sorry, come back to me. My darling, come back."

She soothes, taking my face in her hands in a way that doesn't help with feeling overwhelmed.

"Where... what..." I can only manage the basics as I begin piecing myself back together.

"That was the place of my birth, and the home of my childhood."

She murmurs, and I focus in on her diamond eyes to try to right myself, but instead I lose myself in them.

"My father was Fides, God and ruler of the Diamond Isles- this galaxy. He hid me from the rest of the Isles for as long as he could. But when the Fates found out that he had been seduced by my mother, they tried to take me."

She brushes my hair behind my ear, and in the same moment we are transported to what can only be described as a Hell dimension; the second I've seen in as many days.

The cracked ground bleeds ink into the streets and skyscrapers scar the sky. This place seems drained, like Empryrailla took up all the colours in the palette and these muted greys and dulled pastels were all that could be salvaged. Bodies quiver in corners and silver parasitic-like shapes crawl up the buildings; spindly metal limbs stabbing into the exterior to drag themselves higher.

"Don't move"

Aletheia says, just before a jet-black tsunami rounds the street corner and slams into us.

It's not real it's not real it's not real-

I watch, unmoved, as the wave passes into and over us, not touching us, Aletheia's eyes the only thing that pierce through the blackness of it.

That is, until beings of otherworldly grace follow along the current, emerging like shoots from the earth through the darkness. Lithe bodies, illuminated by the highlighter colouring visible only in the darkness the water provides, slip by us in the murk. Creatures of every shape and size, all with bioluminescent dots lighting up their exoskeletal features. Human turned fish, dragons with humanoid features- demons. That's the only thing that could come close to their description; however ethereal they may be...

The wave passes before I can fully comprehend what's happened, Aletheia and I as dry as if it had never been. I watch as the fifty-foot wall of water continues to traipse through the city, winding around a corner as if sentient, but without purpose or direction.

"This is Selheim, homeland of my mother."

She says, her voice seemingly more strained as she gestures to the living graveyard of a city.

And yet, I can feel that there's more to this place than its exterior. Even just dipping beneath the waves- there was more life than I'd ever expect to see in a place like this.

"My mother, the Demon Queen Relinque, heralds the ability to traipse between realms. The single most-greatest threat to the Fates- reproduced with the God of the stars, to create me. I am what is known as a Realm-Hopper."

She explains, and from behind her back bursts one leathery and one feathery wing, twice her height and width even whilst closed. Her eyes shut briefly, and her smile is one of relief. I remember then- the claws that ripped through them last I saw her. She probably didn't know if she'd ever see them again.

They are breathtaking...

"From the age of 16, I worked out how to leave- and I left," I continue,

"After being banished from father, and held hostage by my mother, I escaped with Kuro."

She points to the kitsune that has since sprung from my skin to slink between my legs, his snout bashing against me persistently.

"I travelled between realms, stars and dimensions like I was crossing streets. That is- until I fell through time, straight into the exact place I was never supposed to step foot into. The realm of the Fates."

Without warning Selheim crumbles into nothing and I'm floating aimless in a void. My left arm has ropes of light lashed around it, my right held captive by ink-like restraints and my body is suspended in the air, pulled taught from either direction. To my right is blackness and to my left is blankness, and I'm stuck in the grey. Back in the place she was when we found her, right where they almost...

I try to pull free but the ropes are like vices, and I feel the panic that came with seeing her being taken sweep over me again.

Aletheia hovers buoyantly in front of me.

"The Fates are not people, they are existence personified, they are control incarnate, but they cannot kill. They are ruthless and unstoppable. You can never beat them."

She says, and I can feel the fear and tension in her words, the challenge.

The smirk.

"But I thought I could outrun them."

She hooks a finger into my shirt and pulls her body against mine so that she's flush against me.

"I am Aletheia, Demi-God of the Diamond Isles and offspring of the Demon Queen Relinque. I was taken by the Fates at 19. From the feel of your world, I have deduced I am now 23." I look left, right, up and down, back to her; fear spiking at the memory.

"I was here, alone, for four years." I press closer and poke a singular finger into her collarbone, "Other than for you, my darling."

She brushes the ropes of light off first, then the dark, sweeps the Fates' room away like the unveiling of a canvas. My mental body lands on my beach, and she's sat straddling me, her smile slowly creeping back into her features as she lowers herself.

"I'm here to find out why."

CHAPTER 10
AS THE FATES WOULD HAVE IT

My body returns to me in a haze of pins and needles, the light above me appearing to swing and dance- before righting itself. The long strip-bulb tells me that I've been moved to the nurses' office; that, plus the plastic mattress.

I won't cry.

I know that they will have notified Hydra though. The thought alone has me receding into myself more than any of the other events ever could.

I move my head to my right and come face to face with a sleeping Aletheia. My movement hasn't woken her, but from where her face had been pressed against my head she has been moved away. I can't touch her, and she can't interact with the physical world either; held apart by the faintest of forcefields.

Her breaths come out shallowly and I can't help but marvel at the long white lashes that fan over her cheeks, the fairest of freckles splashing across her cheeks like paint spray.

Like stardust.

She said she was born of the Diamond Isles and what appeared to be Hell. What kind of person can come from two such extremes? Not to mention being imprisoned for four years with nothing but my dreams for solace.

"Your brain is whirring, my darling."

She murmurs, jolting me back to the room as she places two fingers to my temples, fingers I can't feel but can sense the barrier between all the same,

"Make it shush whilst we rest."

Darling?

Why is this person- no- my hallucination, calling me their '*darling*'? It makes no sense.

None of this does.

I can feel a concussion coming.

"Ssshhh."

She hisses, scrunching her eyes and replacing her two fingers with her palm above my face, blocking the light from view.

Hallucinations really shouldn't be able to block light, but then again- what did anyone insane actually know of the logistics of insanity?

From her open hand spreads light, warm and yellow, vibrant but not blinding. It heats my skull, emanating from her skin like a radiator. The warmth pools at my temple and I watch as slithers of light spiral down to touch me, circling like the grass had on the field-scape; spreading over my head until the wave of pain subsides.

She smiles, her eyes still closed, taking her hand away and moving closer until her head rests on my collarbone.

My body tenses like I've been stunned.

Hallucinations shouldn't maintain weight, should they?

They certainly shouldn't be able to *heal* people.

But I can't feel her, not really.

And that's what helps me logic this out. I can beat this insanity through understanding its mechanics.

The logic doesn't help the feeling of my heart in my chest though, or the awkward blush that seeps into my cheeks as the nurse appears by my bedside; completely oblivious to the secondary figure slung along my body like a human-handbag.

Nurse Sillen's hair looks so taught atop her head that I wonder if Aletheia would mind also saving her the headache.

"What have we here then?" Nurse Sillen mocks, flicking me on the arm.

We've had run-ins before, so there's a degree of familiarity.

"Overdose?" She jokes, not unkindly, prodding me with the end of her thermometer.

Nurse Sillen is barely touching her forties, not that you'd know it. The general touch ups to her exterior making her look nearing thirties at most, with curly hair and dark skin, she was what one might call '*popular*' with the boys here.

"Don't you know it." I grumble sardonically, lifting into a seated position so that Aletheia's head rests in my lap, my cheeks on fire.

"Something the matter love?" She asks, her eyes darting to my cheeks.

Can't fool a nurse, I guess.

"Everything's fine, in fact-" I say, swinging my legs off the side and causing Aletheia to faceplant the bed with a squawk of indignation, "I think I should be going- I'm already late." I say hurriedly.

Quarter past seven.

Fifteen minutes later than I should be.

An hour later by the time I get home.

“Oh no you don’t-” She says, “Last I checked your concussion was pretty severe.” She places the thermometer in my ear and peels my eyelid open with a carefully manicured finger; blinding me with a handheld light.

“You’re not going any-” She stops halfway through her sentence, and I make an effort to breathe normally- obediently staring into the tiny torch.

She releases me and takes the thermometer from my ear to inspect it, blotches of colour blurring my vision as she clicks it off.

“Huh.” She muses, tongue between teeth as she blinks between me and the instrument.

Aletheia can’t really have healed me.

She can’t.

She’s not *real-*

“Looks like you’re magically healed.” She says, “Guess you’re free to go.”

Oh, if she only knew.

She can’t be real.

Aletheia’s hand now gripping my leg feels *almost* real though.

“She said we are free to leave, yes?”

Aletheia checks, before promptly launching herself- using my leg and the bed- across the room.

She halts by the door, her hair spiralling around her as if sentient; unwilling to dirty itself on mortal floors.

“Coming?” I ask with a wink.

“Tenaya?”

-Aletheia and Nurse Sillen ask at the same time.

Nurse Sillen places a hand on my shoulder and I blink blankly back at her, "You sure you don't need me to call someone?"

That's enough to snap me back.

"Yes- No! Sorry, I'm okay. I just need to head home. Thanks, Miss Sillen." I say, grabbing my bag from the floor and scurrying out of the room after my hallucination.

The hallways are abandoned, and I thank the Gods Rylan and Amaya are absent. Else I'd have them to answer to right now- and I'm not sure I can think straight, let alone work out what to tell *them*.

"Well, that was interesting."

Aletheia muses, delicately tiptoeing through the hall ahead of me, her feet making no sound or impact on the floor. The dress of stars she stole from my dreams still sweeps her body down to her knees, the material hanging low on her back.

A hallucination- a making of my own malicious brain. That's all she can be- all I can *allow* her to be.

"I need you to leave me alone." I say abruptly, and she stops dead. Even her hair pauses in it's semi-sentient curling.

I don't know why I said it.

I do- but I don't.

She shouldn't be here- but she is also what I've been searching for since she first started turning my lucid dreams into topsy-turvy nightmares.

But now she's here...

Her shoulders sag as she turns slowly, shrugging.

"You need time to process, I understand."

Well... at least my imagination is understanding, that's always nice to know. I sigh, releasing a breath I hadn't realised I'd been holding.

"Besides,"

She says, bouncing over to me,

"Gives me time to explore your world- I do so love world-wandering!"

Before I can so much as reply- she leans in and presses a kiss, that I can't feel, to my cheek; grinning and dancing away down the hall.

I feel hot and cold and everything in-between.

"Call me!"

She yells as she turns the corner and disappears, her silvery locks the last thing I see before she's gone.

And I'm alone, dumbstruck, the day having gone from absurd to insane.

It's about to get a hell of a lot worse.

Before I even make it to the kitchen, I know she knows. I know they called her, and I know unequivocally that each step I take into the house damns me further.

"Tenaya? Is that you sweetie?" Her sugary sweet façade drawls as I halt at the base of the stairs.

I twist my body around the bannister in order to be seen from the kitchen.

Dad sits at the table, unaware of the tension that will now continue to grow and mutate until she can get me alone. One leg crossed over the other, he spoons soup absentmindedly into his mouth as he scrolls through the daily column.

Tabi sits quietly next to him, his mouth drawn into a line of concentration as he rakes his homework for answers. A line that breaks into an excited grin at the mention of my name.

My heart aches and I can't help but smile back at him, his dark-brown hair a mop that he occasionally whisks from his eyes in little jerks. He's all gangly legs and uncoordinated miss-steps. But Gods if he isn't the single most perfect person in my life.

"Yes, home late t-today- I was in th-the n-n-nurses office." I stutter in what I hope is an appeasing voice.

"Oh?" She asks faux-innocently.

As if she doesn't know.

As if she isn't already planning exactly how she will make her exit and ruin this day and the next with her brutality.

"How're you feeling now, poppet?" Dad says around a mouthful of soup, his dull grey eyes meeting mine over the lip of his paper.

He's more here than he used to be, I guess I can thank Hydra for that if nothing else.

When mum passed away, Hydra had been around anyway. A family friend, who then got more than friendly. At first she was just caring for him, making sure he was safe home from bars and texting him awake for work in the morning. A few dates and drinks later though and she was planted. Moved in, cat and all. Not that he ever remarried, but she was his; and he was *definitely* hers.

She's always been around, at gatherings, to babysit, to be in and around this household since before I can remember.

And she'll never leave.

"Tired." I reply, making an emphasis of yawning, "I think I'll skip dinner if that's okay? Just going to finish some assignments then head to bed."

He smiles, and although it's tinged with sadness- I can see

he doesn't think any more of it. If Tabi was concentrating, he would sense my dread. But with dad it's still a state of blissful ignorance. He was just a loving widowed-father, providing for a harmonious family and reading his papers in peace.

He wasn't the father to a clinically insane daughter, wasn't sharing a bed with a monster who beat his eldest child.

And he could stay this way.

He needn't suffer the burden of knowledge on my behalf- he's been through enough.

"If that's what suits you, just mind you don't push yourself too hard." He says, nodding me away before turning back to Hydra.

She's not even looking at me, flicking on some music and humming along whilst stirring the leftover soup on the hob.

"Thanks dad." I say, and head up the stairs, choosing the less creaky ones without even trying.

I guess learning the easy route-out doesn't suddenly go away, my body predisposed to be quieter; less existent in her presence.

I don't even make it into my room.

I should've known from the turning up of the radio, or listened for her footsteps- or even stayed downstairs.

Her fingernails drag across my scalp and yank my head back against my doorframe. I feel hairs rip from their follicles, stars dancing across my vision as she holds me there, her teeth bared.

"You *conniving* little *minx*." She hisses, spittle flecking from her lips across my face.

I haven't broken yet

The wave lurching forwards, higher-

-But I recede.

I watch from a mental-distance as she rips me from the wall and back against it by my hair. I feel a cry surge up and die in my throat, a guttural sound as I bury the pain.

"Don't think I don't know what you're doing," She spits, her blonde hair flying manically in jerky movements, "You're trying

to turn them against me, both of them. But it won't work."

Sometimes she doesn't even need reasons. Sometimes it's just all in her head.

She pushes me off the wall by my hair and I stumble into the room, my feet barely finding their place.

"Hydra, I swear, I'm not-" I begin to plead as I turn back to face her.

The slap sends my body crashing into my desk and onto the floor, the edge digging into my ribs hard enough to break them and this time I can't separate. Tears leak from the corners of my eyes as I swallow the agony through clenched teeth.

"What have you done you stupid *bitch*!" She scowls, eyes darting around the broken pieces, "Clean up this mess, before your father sees you've had another one of your *pathetic* tantrums."

She slams the door behind her before I can fully register the near-panic in her eyes at the thought of trying to worm her way out of this. She was made for hasty acts and sugar-sweet façades.

She isn't built for on-the-spot lies.

But this is one she's had on the backburner from the first year after mum died. I was inconsolable, and she leached off that.

I was the troubled child with undealt-with anger-management issues- when she needed me to be.

My papers and pens litter the ground around me as I cry soundlessly into the rug, my tears turning the muted red of the fabric crimson.

I reach tentatively towards my head, not yet steady enough to test moving anything else.

My fingers come into contact with matted hair and pull away damp, tangled strands curling and sticking to them as I bring my fingers to my face to find them stained.

My laptop lies opposite me, open but unbroken.

From here though I can make out my reflection, drawn from

the lamplight outside; displaying my tearstained face back at me.

She's so tired

My body lies at a disturbing angle, one I can't bring myself to move but know I must.

I won't have the strength to clean up *and* move tonight. One will have to do, and my bed will make the efforts I have to go through tomorrow easier to bear.

I unbend my arm from beneath me and bite back a cry as I push off the ground to a seated position.

I touch a hand lightly to my ribs, searching out the bruising that lines the ones closer to my chest, cringing as the lightest of touches sparks up the deepest of aches.

It wouldn't be so bad if this wasn't regular. The slap and the fall likely wouldn't hurt so bad. But the repeat injury, where my ribs almost expect to be marred purple at this point, heralds a pain so deep I can't begin to express.

Taking a deep breath, I push off the floor, biting into the arm that hurts less to muffle the noises that I can't keep down, my head rocking as I fall onto my single-bed and curl myself into a ball.

I let the last of the tears fall onto my pillowcase.

I want to leave here, recede into the depths of my brain, dream myself a desolate island and stay there until this world doesn't want to hurt me so badly.

And I will.

But...

"*Aletheia...*" I whimper.

A prayer into the darkness.

These streets aren't dissimilar to Selheim.

A little more rustic, reds and browns and living things. Grass lawns on the verge of over-watering, porch swings used by this generation and the one before it; and likely after it and the one after that.

This town is small and samey.

Some may see my actions as fatuous, irresponsible-

Life-endangering.

But they know not what I know, and I need to know what neither of us knows-

Will this car hit me- kill me- brutally maim, or mortally wound me?

I am an inveterate risk taker. You kind of have to be, as a realm hopping Demi-God with the most powerful beings of all creation hunting you down.

Logistics - They will help me orientate myself in this new plain of existence.

I am lying in the middle of the road, so I'm gambling even now- will the automobile come first for my legs- or my skull.

Darling didn't respond badly to my family history, good to know I can depend on the one person who can see and hear me to refrain from judgement.

She's scared though, I can smell that.

Something else though, not just fear- anticipation.

My darling desires the adventure I bring. She wants to leap between realms, dance amidst the galaxies, dip her feet into the oceans of the universe and sing my name with the waves.

Craves it-

Me-

Escape.

And I will give it all to her.

Remove her from this insipid town, with its despondent inhabitants and vacuous exterior. She is so much more than this.

I knew it from the moment I met her. The same moment they took me.

I look to my right and the car headlights blind me momentarily-

Skull it is then.

I daren't close my eyes as I brace for impact

We've gone through worse

One Empyrailla

Two Empyrailla-

The car falters and stops, its headlights still insisting on burning through my corneas before the day is out.

I roll my head away from it.

Curious-

-I don't even have a shadow here.

Rolling back, I flip myself upright, my body lighter in this realm; allowing me to reach higher, run faster, swim deeper than any mortal.

I can see better too-

So I can see that there's no one in the car.

There never was.

And now I can feel them.

My blood runs cold, my feet already backing away from the ghost vehicle, its yellow beams glaring at me- daring me to run.

Black and purple tendrils snake from the top of it, winding together, snaking upwards and growing

growing

growing

Until the ink morphs together into a clawed hand, as high and wide as the telephone poles, tangling in the wiring and only hesitating for a moment.

The moment in which I choose to run.

My momentum pushes me fast enough to not get crushed by the giant limb, but not far enough to escape the rubble that breaks and shifts under the weight of its closed fist. Tarmac and cat-eyes crack and splinter, propelling me through the air in the direction I'd been running.

They've found me.

And it appears I can be harmed. Blue blood oozes from my chest as I extricate myself from the shard of road now poking up from the street.

The Fates are here

They've come for me

To take me back back back to the grey.

I won't be taken again.

"I. Will. Not. Bend. To. YOU." I grind out, sprinting away from the arm that now has a body, three bodies morphing into one with three heads that howl and wail and tear up the night sky with a fiery vengeance.

And I scream for her.

My name my name my name my name
She will hear me and summon me
My darling will save me
My darling will
Please...

She's in the middle of my room

I'm in the centre of her room

As if I conjured her just by wishing

She heard me- again she heard me

I don't know what to say, she doesn't move. Just breathes like she's been running a marathon and stares at me.

I can't take my eyes off of her, she might disappear

"Aletheia..." I say quietly, but my throat is hoarse and my head won't let me pry myself from my pillow.

I just want to not exist for a little while.

"You called." I reply breathlessly, and I can smell that something's wrong.

Someone has hurt my darling.

I will eviscerate them.

But first- she needs me.

Aletheia slinks her way over to me. Placing both hands on

the edge of the bed, she handstands into the air and slowly walks her feet down the wall that my bed leans on until she bridges over me.

Bridges the gap between us.

One arm then the other, she rights herself and slides into the small unoccupied space nearest the wall, facing me.

It's too dark to see her face.

With the moonlight unable to reach us, I hope she can't see the tears that fall from my eyes.

From relief? From fear? I don't know.

I don't care if she's not real. She's here and she came when I needed her. Right now, at least, that's enough.

My sanity can wait.

It's too dark for her to be able to see the tears that leak from my eyes, from relief- for her.

I cry for my sanctuary.

I cry for the tears that I can see winding down her cheeks.

I cry for home, my darling is my home now.

I move slowly so as not to spook her, placing one hand on her shoulder and the other under her head, I push lightly against the barrier between us that withholds my hand from her skin.

She moves without resistance, turning until her back is to me. I loop my arm around her waist and tuck an arm under her head and hold her as close as the Fates will let me.

I can't feel her, but I know she's there. Holding me as tightly as I hold her. I know she needs me just as much as I need her right now, from the exigent way her being clings to mine and vice versa. We are life rings bobbing just above the surface, tied together to stay afloat.

I close my eyes and imagine it, drag myself towards it, beg my subconscious to let me submerge in the safety of my own waves.

My beach.
Mum's beach.
Let me bring her with me?

I can feel a tug, a pull at my subconscious.
Did she do this? Is she calling me without even realising?
I smile.
Against her hair and wrapped around her I smile.
I'll follow you, my darling, through this realm and the next.

CHAPTER 11
LOVED YOU BEFORE

We aren't at my beach

We are far far away, further than the stars and past the point of what is known.

And I'm not anywhere.

This time it's my turn to not interact with the world around me.

My surroundings blur in a sea of white sheets and technicoloured lights. Yellows and pinks drift around me like the ones from the Veturcaela, like I'm at the centre of the hurricane and these colours are navigating the winds.

Aletheia stands at the epicentre, her eyes closed and arms spread wide, her hair cascading and skin glowing- humming- thrumming with energy.

She doesn't see me.

It's oddly comforting to feel non-existent for a change. Like there's nothing to fear, nothing can hurt or touch me.

Kuro stands resolute at her feet, his height reaching her hips this time and his nine tails moving in synchronicity with her hair, his eyes similarly shut and his fur alive like the flames of a fire.

All the lights in the sky and all the colours they emit, yet all I can look at is her.

As if sensing my thoughts- the sheets fall, the tornado cast out and everything slips away except for those two.

Aletheia sweeps the paper-thin veil aside, and steps out into the new-

New everything.

Around and above me are mountains and clouds- clouds made of mountains. Tunnels of luminous turquoise zip through their centres and vivid amber hues decorate the sky; courtesy of the red and yellow suns that appear to circle each-other in a dangerously powerful dance in the sky.

Vast lakes of amethyst and vermillion swirl in and around the sky-mountains, dotted with emerald circles; Lilypad-looking stepping-stones that Aletheia takes two-at-a-time.

Before I follow her, I crouch by the edge of the water, lowering my face until it's just below the surface.

And open my eyes.

A world of deep greens and golds shifts beneath me, vibrant and alive. Plants that curl and creep towards the surface, creatures larger than the biggest manta-rays surge deeper and out of sight. Pixie-esq beings of lime-green and yellow ride on the backs of what look to be dragonflies; their wings ten times their body size- and layered. Flowers open and close with the movement of the suns. Houses sit carved into the sides of the underground cave systems, barely bigger than my palm- but in their millions.

There's more to the universe than I ever dreamt possible.

And she's seen it.

I flip my head out of the water, my face and hair remaining dry and untouched, and I scamper over the pads in the direction she hops. My steps aren't nearly as precise and delicate as hers; yet I make no sound or suggestion that I stepped at all.

She flows with the grace of the Gods, every footfall purposeful and effortlessly calculated. Even Kuro seems to take his time in the air before deftly leaping from one place to the next in pursuit of his master.

From the depths rises a creature so large it moves the mountains, the clouds parting and pushing backwards so the beast can enter the sky.

It's flesh is covered in foliage from the deep, encasing its silvery body. From what I can tell- it's more fish than bird, but that doesn't stop it from floating up and out of the water; gravity non-existent.

If I don't exist, then consequences be damned.

I see a fin emerge from the water and I don't think twice. I leap, running along the appendage until my hands grasp the vines that strangle its torso, the beast unaware of its uninvited passenger.

The vine isn't hot or cold and my grip makes no dent on the plants- I am a ghost voyager on a living ship.

The tails flow from the water, paper-thin but powerful, reflecting the sunbeams like stained glass over the water; refracting the colours around the lake. It doesn't move higher, drifting weightlessly just above the water alongside Aletheia; a floating ecosystem from the deep.

I lean back, my feet next to its body and my hands gripping tightly, I let my head fall back and hair fly free and stare up into the face of a universe I've never met before.

And it stares right back.

A dark abyss of suns and stars and planets I've never charted, a dimension I've never reached.

Aletheia's playground.

From behind me I hear a light splash, turning just in time to watch Aletheia jumping from the pads onto the fin- just as I had. She runs with a grin plastering her face right to where I stand and grips the vine I hold- just as tightly. Kuro follows suit but stands closer to the beast, whilst Aletheia laughs, leaning back as I do and letting her hair fall as mine did and...

She can't see me.

She's not mimicking or playing along. She's showing me a memory. This is a memory I'm bearing witness to...

"This is the day it all went wrong, my darling."

The voice comes from all sides, her voice, but not from the version that breathes and grins beside me. This voice comes from inside my head but on a different level.

It's all inside my head.

Suddenly, a crack emerges.

A tear in the fabric of the universe- a Veturcaela calling- and it's right in front of her face.

A temptation and a dare.

The smile she wears tells me she's never backed away from either.

"Come along, Kuro," She smirks, her hand glowing as she reaches for it, "A pit stop on the way to father-dearest."

Kuro yips from her side, and with that, she peels away the world.

The sheets swim around her, but this time it's different. There are words and symbols and the sheet is darker but the lights are brighter and for the first time- Aletheia looks confused.

It calls to her, repeats and demands

Esta Tua

Custodire eam

Et servabit te

Amica tua

Amica tua amica tua amica tua

Repeats and demands it in a voice that I can feel but not hear, words I know but are not said. They echo in my mind in a voice with no sound, louder than life.

From Aletheia's side, straight from her ribs, she pulls a scythe. As long as the tallest man and sharp enough to cut clean through marble; it glows purple in reflection of the chaos around her.

Aletheia howls and rips the words away, the scythe tearing a gaping hole in the fabric of the universe, the darkness falling with it and-

-we're in my bedroom.

In two plains of existence we're here-

In... three?

Aletheia stares down at our sleeping bodies wrapped around each other, battered and bruised.

I know I am still asleep- I know that I am both here and there and that this is a memory all happening in my own head. I have to remember these things, orientate myself, or I will get lost- possibly in my own head.

This is Aletheia's memory, being gifted a glimpse into the future, the 'now' that was the 'to-be'.

Aletheia... she travelled through time.

No one is allowed to do that. That's how we got our magic taken away- what cost humanity everything.

"How-" She begins, but Kuro places a paw on her leg, his eyes boring into hers and shaking his head..

He knows better than to meddle with the future.

Aletheia nods, and I watch as past-Aletheia crouches by present me, my body both stood at my desk here as an observer, and lying on the bed there. Both being watched by her past self and held by her present.

Her face is so close to mine. On the back of my neck and now also in front of me, and somewhere in the back of my mind- her breath registers on my real face.

But something crosses over Aletheia's, joyous and pure, as she reaches out a hand to stroke a lock of hair from my eyes, her hand lingering on my cheek as she sees me for what must be the first time.

"So, how do I get here then?" she whispers, and I fight consciousness as somewhere in the back of my brain my real-world body draws on my mind. To the point I watch my body stir on the bed, and my phantom body flickers in and out of existence.

*"No- let me stay- I need to **see**." I command, stomping my foot into the ground as if it will help plant me here.*

The memory-Aletheia looks up at me.

This shouldn't be possible.

She can't be seeing me.

This is a memory- and it's happening inside my head; I am but an apparition.

But she walks over to me even so, her eyes fixed on mine, memory-Kuro growling at my seemingly sudden appearance. Her face is inches from mine and she looks me up and down in what can only be described as curious wonder.

And she smiles, the kind of smirk that sends my blood racing through my veins and my heart pounding; feats that shouldn't be possible in a dream or memory.

"Well, this is new." She murmurs in a curious and yet somehow sultry voice.

And all hell breaks loose.

One moment I'm in my mind-bedroom-memory, watching my body in real time with a past version of Aletheia- the next we have fallen through the centre of the earth.

The ground gives way and the room disappears and we're falling

falling

falling

Through time and space and darkness, purple hues slashing across my periphery and I catch the briefest of blues.

Blue is transport and magic and power and I grab it just as she grabs my hand.

She shouldn't be able to do this. Her hand shouldn't be holdable, mine shouldn't be tangible and I shouldn't have a presence here. The list of things that shouldn't be feasible is getting far too long for me to keep track, I only know one thing for certain-

I won't let her go.

My hand is coiled in light blue swirls that suspend me in the air above a fiery pit; a pit that emanates purple and black ink and smoke that swims and intertwines into hands.

Three hands.

Three Fates and they're coming for her.

"HOLD ON!" I scream as I try to summon the crease- get her out of here- get her away from them and save her from that fate.

Their fate.

The Fates that have come for Aletheia.

Kuro whimpers and howls as he falls, bursting into a million lights that swarm and suspend themselves on Aletheia's skin as she grips onto me for dear life, her wings useless in holding-off the flames that draw her down.

"I- can't- hold-" She grinds out, her grip already slipping.

The cavernous hole roars with the fury of the old Gods, and I can only look at her then, her terrified face. The face of Aletheia from four years ago when she was just a teenager escaping her mother's reach. When she was just starting to explore the universe and its secrets.

I can't save her from her past fate... but I can try and understand the present one.

Even if this is a dream devised from insanity, even if this is a hallucination born of trauma.

I'll save her- I have to.

I know that now.

"Find me." I say to her, as she slips from my fingers.

She gasps but doesn't scream, her eyes never leaving mine even as her body falls into the palms of the Fates, their claws wrapping around her body, just like they did at the séance, until her face is once again stolen from me.

The cavern falls in on itself and I am taken by the darkness.

CHAPTER 12
RULE 1, HYDRA

We didn't move.

From the moment I closed my eyes to that of waking up- my physical body at least- lay curled in the untouchable arms of a girl who may not even be real.

It's the first time I've woken up in anyone's arms, let alone a girl's.

The brain is a powerful thing, a monstrous thing- but a strong one. I have no doubt in my mind- in my monstrous brain- that if I was struggling enough, it would send me a hallucination to ease the burden.

Did it have to make the hallucination so chaotic though?

My body feels like it's made of pins and needles, like it really did travel through space and time to meet a memory. But I can't have- not even magic allows for that.

No magic that I know of anyway- and I've done my research.

Dream travel is the work of the Gods, namely the more ancient deities. Those found to be real when humans struck up a time war that got us banished.

But if she did time travel, that would explain why she was

taken by the Fates in the first place...

Seemingly as soon as I wake- she's up, cartwheeling over me and into the centre of the room to stretch. As if what she and I dreamt wasn't traumatic. As if last nights' memory was just that for her. Not something she had to relive and re-work through. Not to mention the actual physical pains we both endured.

Gods I wish she wouldn't stretch like that.

All graceful limbs and smooth skin...

She's not real.

Monstrous brain.

I slip from the sheets, cringing but trying to hide it as I bypass her and out to the bathroom before she can see or say otherwise. The mirror taunts me as soon as I shut the bathroom door, my puffy eyes and blood-threaded hair glaring angrily back at me.

I raise my shirt on my right side, the dark bruising reaching from just below my breast down to the end of my ribs, the blue-purple haze striking against my pale skin.

At least this one is easier to hide than the headshot.

The door flicks open as if on springs and Aletheia pushes through, her devilish smile stopping short only when her eyes flick to where I threw down my shirt. Her gaze travels up to my bloodied head in the mirror, only then meeting my eyes.

"In this realm- we knock." I snap, moving to shove the door- and her- out of here.

So, she *can* move objects- some at least. The rules of this barrier between realities really aren't very distinct.

Her foot remains lodged in the doorway, her arm an immovable force on the other side. Barrier or not, she still has strength. Whether she can interact with people or not is another matter.

"In my realm,"

She says slowly,

"We eliminate those that threaten our people."

She won't look at me, her eyes trained on something behind me but not there. A memory?

Hallucinations don't have memories.

"Well, we are not in *your* realm," I say, giving the door a softer shove, "And I am not *your* people."

She smirks, leaning on the door so that her face is so so close to mine.

"My person, then."

She slides into the room as I push the door again and it crashes shut. Fear spears through me and I hold my breath, praying she's already left for work. She should've- but Tabi's still downstairs so she likely will be too.

Please don't come upstairs

She's terrified.

I can see it, as easily as I can see her- she is irrefutably paralysed with fear. And that narrows it down.

"It's someone in here,"

Aletheia says quietly, placing a hand next to mine on the door,

"The person who did this- is here."

I squeeze my eyes closed tighter and lean on the door. She isn't real, she can't tell anyone, she can't do anything.

But even the *idea-*

I pry open the door again, confident enough that Hydra would've appeared by now if she was going to. I stand to the side.

"Please just- let me shower." I say, and I hate how broken I sound.

Just from slamming a door.

From the idea of Aletheia- a person who isn't even real in this dimension- telling dad, doing something on my behalf.

She folds her arms, holding her ground for a moment too long.

"Please." I beg, pathetically.

Her shoulders sag and she sighs, stomping out of the room and grumbling something about disembowelling people.

I lock the door this time, hopeful for limits to her interactions with things, tentatively removing the clothes around the painful areas. I turn on the faucet and slip into the spray.

Kuro whisks up my spine, slinking along my collarbone to rest with his head across one of my breasts; his tails fanning out contentedly.

Someone really needs to give me the handbook for hallucinations.

Towelling my hair dry with as much care as possible, I make my way downstairs, my heart already thumping as I hear Hydra's shrill laugh.

It kicks into overdrive when I turn the corner to the kitchen, my eyes locking in on Aletheia. Her feet slung on the table as she reads the paper over dad's shoulder.

It would be comical if it wasn't giving me a heart attack.

She gives me a wave that contains way too much energy for this early in the morning, making it *that* much harder to pretend like I don't see her.

Tabi sends me a beaming smile through his mouthful of cornflakes as I pass him. I ruffle his hair and he leans into it like the cat-whisperer he is.

"*Mind*, dear," her voice rings like a gunshot through a cavern as I turn to where she's stirring some oats on the stove, "I just brushed his hair for school."

To my dad and Tabi and anyone else it would've sounded innocent, a precautionary measure.

"S-sorry, Hydra."

I don't mistake the death sentence for caution tape.

Innocent to *almost* anyone, I realise, as Aletheia tip-toes onto the counter in her perspicacity and squats by Hydra's head, staring daggers into the back of her perfect blonde-bob.

"This one."

Alethcia seethes, her nails desperately itching to stab holes in the countertop.

Hydra smiles sweetly before turning to dad, unaware of Aletheia's fury simmering hotter than the breakfast she stirs; a quiet menace.

"Your muesli's ready, dearest." She panders, flicking off the stove and carrying the steaming pot over to him.

Dad looks up, shocked that there're people around him- let alone breakfast in front of him.

Once he's in his paper, he's like me with my research- in another world. People could talk and music could play, and the world could carry on spinning- but he was content in his little pool of knowledge.

"Ah-oh right, right- beautiful, Hiddy- thankyou," He says in a rush, taking the ladle in hand and noticing me, "Tenaya! good morning, poppet- w-would you like some-"

"Oh no, dearest," Hydra admonishes quickly before he can so much as proffer me the ladle, "Tenny's on her little *diet* at the moment, remember?"

I don't bother arguing, even though I am on no such thing. To argue would be to cause a scene.

Dad looks to me, confused, his spectacles having slipped down the length of his nose. They age him. For a man barely touching his 50's, the glasses add ten years at least.

"Yes- dieting. But thank you, dad." I say, saving him from the awkwardness as much as I can.

This is another reason why I prefer to leave early or late. It saves me from trying to navigate the toxic social environment that is my family breakfast.

"There should be some fruit in the pantry." Hydra says tiredly as she spoons some more food into dad's bowl and the excess into hers.

"You can have some of mine!" Tabi pipes up.

Gods I wish he hadn't.

Hydra's eyes fixate on me almost imperceptibly in the moments it takes me to respond, and I know I'm in trouble now- regardless of the outcome.

"Ah, no thank you Tabi-cat," I reply, giving his shoulder a rub instead of his hair, "I'm not even hungry, you enjoy."

And I mean it, the 'enjoy' part at least.

I clench my abdomen to try and stop the grumbles that threaten to expose the lie.

He shrugs, diving back into his cereal like a lion might an antelope, Hydra's temper placated for now.

Aletheia's- less so.

"I will incarcerate this demon,"

Aletheia announces, as she slides off the counter and comes to stand at my side without looking away from Hydra,

"I shall scourge the flesh from her bones until her pitiful existence expires... Then you can have all the 'cornflakes' in the world."

I snort without thinking.

I slap my hand over my mouth and freeze as they all turn to look at me, even dad glances up from his paper.

Aletheia smirks at my side, clearly serious in her threats, but glad to make me laugh.

I, for one, am less enthused by my outburst.

"S-s-sorry," I stammer, wiping the smile from my face as I make my escape to the pantry, "S-something S-Spelinski s-said."

I dart into the cubby-hole of a room and close over the door as Aletheia slips in after me. I hold onto a shelf for support as I try my best to breathe.

"That was intense." I grumble, gripping the top of the doorframe by my fingertips so that I dangle.

My darling looks more stressed than ever, and I can't help but want to relax her. My methods are clearly off the mark though, her doubled-over-body not the most well-hidden indicator of discomfort.

"Rule one,"

She breathes, lifting upright and pointing a finger at me,

"No making me laugh in front of Hydra."

Her statement sounds funny, but I can see the sincerity there, the earnest desperation fuelled by fear. So, 'Hydra' is the yellow-haired demon responsible for her pain.

My darling, what has she done to you?

"Difficult, because I am naturally hysterical." I say, taking a glance at the only fruit in the pantry. The blackest banana and bluest orange I've ever seen.

"Aletheia."

She says as quietly and sternly as possible.

Her use of my name sends beautiful tension through my body- a calling, and a demand.

I sigh, swinging forwards so her still-pointed-finger collides with my collarbone. I watch as the blush creeps undeterred up her cheeks and I smile.

"Rule one accepted." I say, returning my attention towards the desiccated remains of what used to be fruit.

I follow her eyes to the pitiful portion of fruit on the side. Hydra probably left it there purposefully, but I guess I shouldn't always assume the worst.

I pick it up, knowing that if I don't then she will come for me later. Maybe for wasting perfectly good food, maybe for not throwing out food I wasn't going to eat, letting it go mouldy, leaving mouldy food lying about-

There is always a reason.

"Hey,"

Aletheia murmurs, placing a hand over the fruit in my hand,

"Let me try something." I say, praying to the new gods and the old that they allow this.

"I don't think-"

"Then don't."

She interrupts, encasing my hands and the fruit with her own.

I try not to think about how close she is. Ridiculous, not

only because I'd spent the night in her arms- she isn't real. A conjuring of my own devices for the sake of my sanity.

Talented monstrous brain.

I have to go to university with this... 'this' going on. The diner, home and everywhere in-between. If I'm going to make it through the next year- there are going to have to be more ground rules.

...I want to know her though.

If she's real, then she's putting everything on pause to be here- her freedom, the universe- just to be near me.

But *why*? I'm not special, certainly not enough to take pause on the universe for.

Aletheia closes her eyes, and for a moment nothing happens. Then her hair begins to lift higher, like tentacles from the deep, around and above her. Her skin shimmers with iridescent light, like that of those from Selheim but brighter- lighter and technicoloured.

Even the freckles on her cheeks burn silver.

All the light that dances along her skin moves and pools until it circles down to her palms and dims, falling from her flesh to mine in a shower of light and silent sparks.

Slowly, as if scared of the result, she peels away her fingers.

I gasp.

The freshest orange and ripest banana lie in the palms of my hands.

I did it.

I helped her. I knew I could heal her, but now I know I can interact with the world on this level- if not the directly physical one.

I can tell by her eyes and her heart I did good. I can use healing magic- I can help her, even if I can't touch her.

She smells like jasmine and hope.

"You- you used magic?" I ask, not even sure what I'm asking

but knowing I need answers.

Aletheia jumps up and down excitedly and my bewilderment threatens to be swayed to something else, as the flimsy stardust dress stretches furiously.

"Aletheia!" I say, holding her down by her shoulders, "How...?"

"Does it matter?!"

She asks, smilingly devilishly, as if fully aware of why I'm really gripping her shoulders. She runs her hands along my arms until she reaches my shoulders, pausing only momentarily before catapulting herself over me so she stands behind me.

Her face is next to mine as we both look towards the pantry door, the fruit still in my hands.

"Now," I quip, my lips barely grazing upon her jaw, "You are going to peel that fruit, pocket the other, and walk out of here with your head held high."

The ice bucket of a prospect that dunks over me is an unwelcome awakening to reality. So what if a hallucination in my pantry just reincarnated fruit using magic- real life consequences still exist outside that door.

"I can feel you thinking,"

She says quietly, and I stiffen, her arms looping over my shoulders and her chin taking rest there.

"Don't. Just peel-"

She flicks open the banana using my hand,

"Eat-"

Brings the fruit towards me by gently bending my arm,

"And move."

She shoves me hard enough that the door opens on impact and I have no choice but to step out.

The kitchen is exactly as I left it. Tabi's bowl a bit less full, but dads face still in his paper. The only people to look up are Hydra- and Hyacinth from under the table at Tabi's feet.

I've never seen her shocked.

I've seen her angry, fake, doting, hateful...

The sight of Hydra with her mouth hanging open though, is a new one.

I don't stop to take it in, I keep walking.

I can make it to the front door.

I grab my bag from the seat by Tabi, smiling at dad and giving Tabi a squeeze on the arm as I go.

"See you later!" I say hurriedly, watching as Aletheia stands to the side of the pantry, arms folded and a wicked smile on her face.

It gives me the strength or stupidity to do what I do next.

I pause at the door, taking the peel from the banana and dropping it in the food waste. I slip the orange from my pocket, lifting it to the light so that Hydra can see it in all its glory; I smile.

"Thanks for the fruit." I say.

And I leave.

The sound of Aletheia tittering follows behind me, and the image of Hydra's pale face ingrains in my brain- making friends with my pounding heart; the cat under the table the last thing I see.

I swear, if it's possible, Hyacinth grinned.

CHAPTER 13
MY OH AMAYA

"Well hello stranger!" Amaya plonks herself down on the seat to my left, Aletheia tucking and rolling onto the floor by my feet to avoid getting crushed.

"Long time no manic meltdown, how've you been?" She goads and I cringe, not just from the reminder.

Aletheia has taken up a more permanent seat, cross legged on the floor, the back of her head resting between my legs.

After begging and cobra-clinging around me for the entirety of the walk to university, my choices were next to none; I conceded to her joining for class...

"No touching Mr Spelinski." I say sternly, as we approach the university gates.

"The mad dancing man on stage?" I smirk, skipping along beside her.

"Yes, him- or anyone else for that matter." I grimace, massaging my temples.

She smirks evilly.

"Okay my darling, I'll restrict myself just to you."

...It'd taken me a whole 20 minutes for the blush to creep down from my cheeks.

"Still not what I meant." I grumble under my breath.

Aletheia tilts her head back towards me until I can see her upside-down face between my thighs, smiling devilishly.

"You say something?" I chide sweetly.

I grit my teeth, placing a hand atop her head and pushing on the barrier until she faces forwards again.

Amaya gives me a curious look, and I quickly remember she can't see her.

Of course she can't.

I busy myself with reaching down to my bag, as if that was always the intention, to get my books and laptop out.

"I've uhh, had some complications." I mutter.

"That's a pretty sobriquet darling, so sweet of you."

Aletheia sneers, pinching my leg and making me swallow a yelp.

I cinch my legs together, hoping it'll get her to quit. I need to get through this year, having her here is fine so long as I can concentrate enough to pass Finals.

"You really believe this to be a deterrent?" My pulse dances along the

tension her legs place upon my neck.

She smirks, snaking her arms through my legs in a figure of eight behind her head with a wanton demeanour,

"By all means, deter away." It takes everything in my power not to nip her.

There is no winning.

"Jiu-jitzu again?" Amaya sneers, and for a moment it seems there's more she's not saying, her mouth twisting as she looks me up and down.

"Not this time, just... thinking through what happened the other night." I reply, busying myself with my files.

"That really was mad," Amaya agrees, shaking her head, "I don't even know what to say. I mean, it's a shame we lost the Vet-" She catches herself, looking around before continuing, "The uhh, the thingymewhatsit. But what we saw was freaking *wild*."

I smile. It was- and I am going to see it again if it kills me.

I'm not ready to tell her that I managed to salvage the Veturcaela, nor that it's currently hidden beneath a floorboard in my bathroom.

"We'll find a way back." I say, and I mean it.

I'll take her with me if I can, when I work out how to reopen and use it. Amaya and I can travel to wherever- whenever.

"Incoming!" Rylan yells as he tumbles over us and trips straight into Aletheia, clearly having miscalculated the jump.

I'd bring him too of course.

Aletheia lies perfectly still, Rylan's body squishing her into the floor.

To everyone else- Rylan is floating.

Floating Rylan isn't normal.

I shove him quickly to the side, past me and off of Aletheia. Rylan grunts, clambering up onto the seat next to mine, staring back at the place he'd been with bafflement.

"Did I just-"

"Where have *you* been then?" I cut him off, pretending to reach for my bag and grabbing a book- at the same time I hoist Aletheia up, stroking her shoulder consolingly.

"Another friend of yours, I presume?"

Aletheia grumbles, massaging her shoulder where my hand rests and righting her dress.

I nod subtly without looking in her direction.

Existing in two planes is Gods-damn difficult.

Rylan shakes his head, clearly not coming to the conclusion that he just floated from the ground due to an invisible barrier coating a figure from another dimension.

Best he doesn't question it, I don't even know what I'd say. How do I tell my two best friends- who are already shaken from my meltdown the other day- that I'm insane?

"Been busy, doing stuff, this and that. What's it to you, crazy-pants?" He mocks, nudging me lightly with his elbow.

So, we weren't going to just bi-pass my meltdown, fair enough I suppose.

"I'm sorry for how I was," I say awkwardly, "I know I went a bit mental. I think it was more than I thought I would see, I just-" I pause, not sure how to finish what I'm saying with Aletheia staring up at me.

"What happened?"

I close my eyes and take a breath, working out how to answer her and explain to Rylan at the same time. The feeling akin to that of doing mental-maths when the whole class is watching you.

"When we... went where we went, the black and white," Realisation sparks in Aletheia's eyes, "I didn't know what I was going to see, I didn't know it was possible. So, I kind of just broke down. I wanted to stay there and understand, but then when we were cast out-"

"I'm here now,"

She says, curling into my leg and stroking me reassuringly,

"I found you again."

My cheeks warm, luckily Rylan seems to take this as embarrassment over how I was the other night. Not because there's a whole-damn-person draped over my leg.

"It's all good dude." Rylan says consolingly, bumping my leg with his and jolting Aletheia. She casts a glare his way, "We were all a bit star struck, just a shame we can't redo it. I'd show that *demon-pine* what-for." He says, comically cracking his knuckles.

Amaya and I scrutinise him, neither of us believing him capable of fighting his way out of a paper bag, let alone a monstrous spiky creature from a hellscape.

"I'm sure you would." Amaya says sarcastically.

"Totally." I concur, scrunching my nose at him.

He doesn't flinch, taking it in stride.

"What can I say, some of us are born to be absolute legends." He says, fanning his hand out in front of him.

I see the bruised knuckles before he can snatch them away. His eyes widen for a second, before he shrugs and places his hands behind his head.

His father is a prick.

A drunken bastard in the mornings and a drugged-up wife-beater at night. I guess the brutality alternated between wife and son though, as I note the mild discolouration of skin under his floppy hair.

A bad concealer-job.

Trust him to try and hide it. Not for my sake of course, and certainly not for his.

I turn back to Amaya, who has luckily already zoned in on class material too much to have noticed either of the flesh wounds.

He can't hide it from her forever though, the bruising- or the feelings.

Madeline turns from the row in front, serving as a physical reminder of my hypocrisy. Max still a no-show.

"Did you get the notes from last class?" She asks, prodding my leg with the rubber end of her pencil, "I missed it for uhh, well..."

She trails off, gesturing to the empty seat next to her, which, logically, could mean a whole host of things. One of which I really don't want to entertain the idea of. The other being much more of a daydream than a reality. That she cut him off, had the talk and was done with him forever, letting her be open to the attentions of others...

"Yeah- yes, I did!" I say hurriedly, as Mr Spelinski enters the room, I lean forwards so as not to talk loudly in his class- I know better.

She leans in and I can smell her sugary perfume.

"I can give them to you after school-Thursday? I have diner-work, but I should be finished around 7?"

I don't know where the ease of talking to her came from. Maybe it was that every other situation in my life seems to be more stressful at the moment. Maybe it's a small step in taking back a modicum of control in my life.

Maybe I'm just sick of sitting about and doing nothing.

About Hydra, Casimir- I'm even avoiding confronting Aletheia, for fear of what she means. Besides, I have a whole two days to prepare for a conversation alone with Madeline.

She smiles, bringing me back to focus.

"Yeah, that'd be nice," She says quietly, "It's a date."

She turns back to the front of class before she can note the shock on my face.

"A what now please?"

Aletheia seethes from between my legs, crawling forwards till she's climbed up on top of the chair, all four limbs clawed into the seat to keep her suspended above Madeline like a lion over prey.

Her hands come down to rest on Madeline's shoulders, and I have to grip the edges of my seat to stop myself from vaulting forwards.

She can't hurt her- she can't touch her.

"Everything okay, hun?" Amaya asks, her eyebrows drawn low over her eyes, and I look away from Aletheia, trying my hardest not to think about it.

She's. Not. Real.

What she does- doesn't matter.

"Yeah, don't worry about it." I say, trying to chant my own advice into my head, even as Aletheia lowers her face to Madeline's.

"Listen here you insipid harpy," I hiss in her ear, corresponding with her subconscious as hard as I can- though I know from the feel of the barrier that I can't penetrate it, "I can see what lies in your heart- and it is darkness. It is selfish loneliness and manipulative notions of grandeur-bred from insecurities of the lowest nature. Mark my words, you take them out on my darling, and I will find my way through this incommodious trammel- and you shall be exenterated."

The demon Madeline shudders, making me smile. Perhaps in some way, my mental field imprinted on hers. I lean forwards even closer.

"And I shall do it oh so slowly, so that my darling might be able to see

just how ugly your insides truly are."

Aletheia

Her summoning comes loud and angry through the link and I swivel so I can see her.

I attempt to send daggers through my eyes at Aletheia, her body propped up like a meerkat above Madeline. I saw Madeline shudder- I know I did. Which means something, somehow, got through from Aletheia to her.

Or she shuddered because it's cold, or any number of this-dimension reasons for shuddering.

Get. Down. Now.

I mouth at Aletheia as subtly but strongly as I can manage- which isn't much with Rylan and Amaya either side of me.

She harrumphs, blowing strands of hair out of her face in despondent resignation as she leaps down to the floor again arms-first; taking up her curled position once again by my legs.

"She started it."

Aletheia grumbles, whatever that means.

"Can you tell sir jumpsalot over there to quit his knee jiggling." Amaya whispers, indicating at Rylan with an irked grimace, "I don't particularly enjoy being vibrated whilst I work."

She pauses, her hand above her keyboard and her face pensive.

"On second thoughts- scratch the vibrating part. Just tell him to quit it."

I can't help but giggle, Rylan's curiosity peaking and half his body leaning into mine as he quite literally scrambles for our attention.

"Explain the hysteria, por favor?"

Amaya scrunches her nose at him, leaning across me to swat

him away.

"You're a pain in the ass." She snarks.

"You're a human vibrator." I say, and we both share a look, turning back to him.

"Same difference." We say at the same time, and quickly dissolve into giggles that don't go unnoticed by Mr Spelinski.

If we weren't his favourite students, we'd have a lot worse than redroot inflicted on us by now.

Rylan sends us both the finger, but I can see the hint of a smile there. He's used to it, what did he expect having two girls as his best friends?

"You know they're-"

Aletheia tries to say but I place a hand over her mouth as if I'm fixing my skirt, an indignant squawk slipping from between my fingers; her teeth bared against them.

I don't want her opinions on Rylan and Amaya, not right now. Not with them literally being the one solid thing in my life right now. They always have been.

I shake my head at Aletheia and her eyes narrow. She swipes my hand from her face, standing.

"I shall not be so casually silenced and dismissed, especially as I'm causing no disturbance to any other being in creation but you."

She says, her fists clenched by her sides.

I freeze, not knowing what to say. What am I meant to do? Tend to both her in one place and everyone else in another, whilst not making her existence known? She's asking for more than she knows.

She takes my silence as answer.

"Figure it out yourself, I guess. I'll be back."

She strops, and without further word, leaves.

Her hair trails behind her down the middle isle of the hall and out of the room, facing away from me and not looking back once.

How the hell did I manage to insult-away my own hallucination?

What did she mean, *figure it out*?

When is she coming back?

These questions almost have me up and chasing her down, calling her back to me.

Almost.

"No rest for the wicked." Rylan sings-songs as we parade him to his next class.

Whilst Rylan is perfectly capable of using his intellect to work alongside Amaya and I at the top of the class, he is also a renowned skiver. Meaning, he skips more classes than he attends, and only through sheer willpower and natural intellect does he manage to scrounge his way back to a decent grade.

Not that I can really blame him. I'd be the same now and again if I didn't think I'd be crippled for it- both by Hydra, and my father. Neither would stand by such acts of disobedience. His parents aren't quite the same breed of strict, and he needs the extra downtime more than anyone.

But classes skipped meant class-catch-up, and that sometimes meant he had no time for lunch- or us, by extension. Today's catch-up includes chem-ed and ancient-creature studies.

"The wicked bring on their own undoing's." Amaya pokes, and although I see the playful nature of it as she hugs onto his arm, I also note the pained look in Rylan's features.

In some ways, he genuinely believes he is responsible for what goes on behind closed doors. Whether it was for not always being home in time to stop his father, letting it go on for so long that it's too late to say anything, or not being strong enough to stop him.

Mirroring the reasons I blame myself for my own ruinations.

I shake off the feeling and loop my arm in hers.

"Honey, we just don't know how to have *fun*." I say, giving Rylan a half-smile over her head.

His eyes go wide and excited.

"Does this mean you guys will-"

"Not on your life." Amaya says, unlinking with him and gripping tight to me. "We are nerds for life, get away from us- foul smelling creature!"

Rylan smirks, knocking on the door to creature-studies as she does so.

"How apt an expression to part on, I bid you both- *adieu*." He says with a flourish, blowing us both kisses as he goes.

"Absolute ninny." Amaya mutters, hauling me away and towards the exit, "You know, I think we lose brain cells just being in his presence. Let alone the mayhem that would ensue if he actually got us to skip class. I just know he'd try to get us to try '*it*'."

I smirk, giving her a squeeze.

She must smell the stuff on his clothes, the green has a way of sticking to you. It wasn't for her to know that it was his dad, and that Rylan was as clean as the day he was born.

"You're so uptight you can't even say the word." I say jokingly, and she goes red, her mouth pouting.

"I can too." She harrumphs, "I just choose not to."

"Go on then," I push, as we arrive at the exit to the university, unlinking us and turning to her with arms folded, "Say it."

Amaya looks around, her eyes darting left and right anxiously.

"...*Here*?"

I can't help but laugh at her, turning and stepping out into the fresh air.

"Nerd my ass, you're a flipping saint. Can't even say *'weed'* without feeling the heavens' eyes upon you." I mock.

Amaya mimics me in a high pitched voice, hands coming up to gesture crudely at me and I gasp in mock-astonishment.

"She blasphemes! What shalt thou mother say?!" I cry dramatically as we descend the stairs, which earns me a shove.

"Meanie." She whines, half-heartedly.

My attention is suddenly grabbed by the smell of incense and a flurry of colours.

Irene and the others sit by the steps, chowing down on what look to be diner-fries. I give them a wave and Sayra hops up and down excitedly, having just been chasing a pink butterfly. The other two look up and give me a nod, their demeanours loud but voices silent as ever. Irene grabs Sayra round the middle and scoops her into her lap, squeezing her until she squeals.

I glance over at Amaya then.

And really wish I hadn't.

I really *really* wish I hadn't.

Her eyes are on them and her nose is crinkled in what can only be disdain.

It doesn't un-crinkle in time for me not to notice, or for me to play it off as something unrelated.

I look back to Irene, who has her eyes resolutely locked on mine.

In a *planned* way.

Like she needed me to see what I'm seeing. Sayra is none the wiser, kicking her legs frantically in her trapped state and risking everyone's food in the process.

"Amaya?" I say, my voice monotone and so detached from the care-free familiar tone we'd been rallying back and forth all day.

Amaya's face plateau's back to curiosity, concerned as she notices my shift.

"Yeah-huh?" She asks innocently.

I pause, steeling myself.

"What do you think of gay relationships?"

Her back straightens to a line, and if there's a picture in the dictionary next to the word bristled- it's this.

"Why would you ask me *that*?" She asks, avoiding the question and not meeting my eyes.

"No, I mean it." I say, stepping closer to her so she looks up, my height for once coming in handy and bearing down on her.

Her eyes are wide and almost nervous, I guess she's never really seen me mad before. Or strong. Or standing up for anything other than studies.

Is this new attitude Aletheia's doing?

Amaya's face is turning a shade of red that's too close to her hair, her palms melding together and her eyes still struggling to meet mine.

"What do you think of a relationship like *theirs*?" I say, inclining my head towards Irene and Sayra, who have seemingly stopped their shenanigans. Their whole group, even though they're out of earshot, appear to have paused; none of them looking our way.

Amaya twists her hands in her skirt to the point I think it may rip.

"You know my parents don't condone that sort of thing-"

"No," I interrupt, cutting her off harshly and making her jump, "Not your parents, not *their* beliefs. Yours. What do *you* believe?"

I hold my breath.

I beg to the old Gods and the new. To the Fates.

Please...

She shakes her head, not looking at me.

"It doesn't matter, why should it matter to..."

Until she does look at me. And I know you can't see sexuality like a hair colour but it's like she sees it- me, for the first time.

I can't even summon a friendly smile.

"Amaya, I'm bisexual." I say, for the first time in my life.

It feels like the release of a weight, a dam breaking. It floods out and I feel like crying but don't, I hold it in. Amaya's mouth parts but she says nothing.

She moves to say *nothing*.

And the nothing is too much for me to stand idly by.

"Right." I say stoically, hoisting my bag higher onto my shoulder, "See you around then."

And I leave her standing there.

She doesn't call out to me, doesn't try to get me to stop, or to hear her out, or even plead her case.

She just stands there dumbfounded as I make my way down to Irene and her friends- *my* friends. Sayra bounds over to me, grabbing my hand in hers and dragging me the last of the way.

"I- sorry, umm, I just-" I stumble, the last of my confidence ebbing away as I take my seat next to Irene on the steps.

"We know." She says, having the decency to look bashful as she shakes a small vile of Ecutayder solution at me.

Eavesdropping potion.

I look around their group, all giving me equally ashamed looks.

But I don't care.

They heard everything, they heard what I said and they didn't flounder. They didn't pause.

They aren't the ones who have known me for nearly three years and still don't know how to accept all of me. No, *they* welcomed me. Took me by the hand and let me in.

"How's the leg?" I ask Irene with what sounds like a laugh, but comes out broken.

Irene's leg in question is still in bandages, but probably more of a precautionary measure from how it looked after the séance- can't have people asking about a monster-sized scar spanning her entire calf.

"Healed and beautifully scarred- I'm going to tattoo around

it n' everything." She grins, clearly not wanting to go into what happened just yet either.

I wouldn't know where to start right now either, not with having just lost...

"Welcome to the club?" Irene says with a lilt, cutting of the thought, her eyes assessing me.

I smile as much as I can manage. I allow my shoulders to sag in a way that would have Amaya chastising me, trying to dull the tension forming in my heart; I don't stop Irene from pulling me in, or my head from resting on her shoulder.

Sayra rushes me, jumping up and giving me a chaste kiss on my cheek.

"You're gunna fit *right* in." She says sweetly, offering me her milkshake- or at least what's left of it.

It's a strange contrast.

To feel so welcomed, yet so hollow at the same time.

CHAPTER 14
FATHER DEAREST

I have a little time before I should get back to her, I can make this work.

The crease ripples and bends in front of me, shining in the iridescent blues and pinks that I've craved and missed so badly. I sigh, partially in relief that they even appeared.

A resplendent semaphore of hope in this abysmal excuse for a realm.

What with this imbecilic bubble-barrier between me and the rest of the universe, I worried I wouldn't be able to summon it at all.

It'll do her good to miss me for a bit. Clearly the information that her comrades are- and have been- intimate behind her back for so long, is nothing of consequence to her. Should've let me speak.

Not to say this is not a pernicious risk, a destructive one potentially. But I haven't had the chance to visit father in nearly half a decade.

He'll be in dire need of some tormenting by now.

A quick trip to daddy dearest, that should slake my urge to flit between the dimensions. At least quench it until she's ready to come with me.

I'm sat with my legs curled on a weird human contraption that I overheard a smaller human call a 'swing'. The curious creation only serves to move you between two spaces in the same dimension. The small human next to me seems ecstatic though, as it uses all of its might to send itself higher and faster from one spot to the next.

Ah, if only it knew.

You people used to be star travellers, world benders, galaxy-explorers and realm hoppers. You people with your magic and your infinite desire for what's new.

Ruined by the warpath of your ancestors.

"If you jump at the end, you'll go further." I find myself saying, the little human male not even blinking in way of response.

But he jumps.

Right at the pinnacle of his efforts where his body turns parallel with the earth, he leaps. Soaring through the air for all of two seconds before plummeting back down.

Right on his ankle.

I hear the crunch before the scream, an older female human rushing over to his aid- his Mother? Mine isn't quite so attentive, unless my life is at risk; her lineage being of somewhat importance to her. She never wanted kids, that was made abundantly clear from a young age. However, since I pissed off the fates, it's unlikely they'll ever permit her another child again, so she's stuck with me.

The boy wails hysterically and his mother hoists him into her arms, carrying him away.

"Unfortunately, the risk of pain does come with the territory of leaping, tiny human," I say, and for a second his big brown tear-infested eyes seem to meet my own, "But don't let that deter you. There're jumps to take that'll break more than just your bones- but what you serve to find makes it all the more worth it."

Like my darling.

The boy child blinks away the last of his tears as he moves out of earshot, holding my gaze a moment longer before burying his face in the safety of his mother's shoulders.

The mini-assault course is now deserted. Time to leave.

I allow the power to surge up inside me, closing my eyes, the feeling akin to that of being lifted into the air by your heart; the strings pulling taught.

Oh, how I've missed the tension.

The brief but blissful feeling of the universe stretching to capacity for a moment, just so that you might step through it.

So that I can step through it.

I picture him then, sat on his throne, presumably with several ungodly-level-beautiful beings caressing every appendage. My hand comes up without instruction and I open my eyes to see the crease in front of me. Glowing blues, pinks and golds.

The purple was bad. The darkness was bad. But they aren't here today.

I flick through the layers with my fingernails, making sure not to peel any away- I have to be precise with this. Realm hopping is a delicate work. Darling managed it so fluidly, but with the same ease that a new-born might accidentally say its first word. The act itself purposeful, but it has no idea what it's saying or even why. Same with her, she had known she wanted to wield magic, to jump between realms, but she didn't take the time to sort through the layers or visualise what she wanted to find.

I will teach her. Soon.

I find the layer that feels like he feels, gripping it between finger and thumb. It seems odd not to talk to Kuro as I make to leave, but he will keep her safe in my absence, and serve as a beacon back.

The world flattens, the visual field that of a painting, and I move to step out of it; pulling away the canvas and stepping out into the three-dimensional realm of Empryrailla. When you've been to a specific realm as many times as I have, you needn't learn the long route- you simply tear and step.

It's not the forests this time, or the throne room that I envisioned him in. Instead, I find him sat with his lower half submerged in bubbles. The golden bath house hosts him and a number of the beautiful beings I had thought to imagine him with, three in particular are draped over him like silks; over each shoulder and between his legs.

One out of two assumptions- I'll take it.

"Oh, father dear!" I yell theatrically, throwing my arms wide and

strutting forwards, sing-songing so that my voice bounces against the gold-lined ceramic and back to him, "Your baby bird hath returned to the nest once more."

I saunter along the side of the baths, not daring to submerge myself in water that is touching so many of his people and... things.

His eyes track me the whole way.

His antlers reach high above him, draped in vines and floral foliage, connected to his head beneath a mane of platinum blonde hair. His diamond eyes are strikingly white and mimic the shape of my own, although I guess mine do the mimicking per se.

For a God, he is to be what is expected. Larger than life and chiselled, even for a male entering his thousands. His skin is the only thing that makes us at all different- other than his horns. His skin is a seamless stretch of golden-tan, basking in the reflections of his bathhouse. In contrast to mine, which chose to replicate the complexion of our hair.

I've always been jealous of the antlers.

"You dare intrude on the land of your birthplace again, daughter." He rumbles, his voice giving me pause where I stand not twelve feet from him, although he doesn't seem surprised. "After last time, after everything, why do you still pursue me?"

His tone is saccharine, but the words juxtapose them. He may or may not have a point.

I try to visit him once every year, never on the same day and never at a particular time. If he knew I was coming, I'd never get in.

I never meant to let what happened- happen. He must know that. Yet I've never been able to win back his affections. Not since mother stole me away.

We were both so young, Liedha and I. I had no idea what I was doing, realm hopping as an eight-year-old.

I never meant to kill her.

"You don't have to say it so much father, I know you missed me." I goad, squatting by the water and flicking some droplets in his direction.

His eyes roam over me in confusion, lingering on the draped stardust I wear fashioned across my body.

"And what exactly is that?" he asks sardonically, sidestepping my joking nature to gesture at the thin veil.

Must he always be so dull and ruler-like?

"Oh, this?" I say, picking at the wafer-thin material as if I'd just noticed it myself, "I made this for my darling. You see father, they're rather modest. You'd like them though. A rule and ruler follower for sure."

It's true, he'd like her. If he didn't know she was mortal. Or female. Whilst father would rather have me killed than conceiving, he still demands the utmost say in whether I do so or not- and who with; he is a God after all.

"Your darling?" he queries, like I knew he would.

If I am to obtain his attentions, it would have to be subjects on his terms. And for the first time, I actually have something to spark his interests.

Just... not in quite the way he wants.

"Yes, my darling. They're quite shy. But secretly a tenacious spirit with an untapped destiny." I say, her face bringing a smile to mine and his eyebrows raise in mild curiosity, "Effortlessly whimsical and existentially curious, and her eyes-"

"'Her' eyes?" he bellows.

I slipped up.

That was fast, even for me.

Well, that's my queue.

Father sits straighter but doesn't make to move, only shaking his head in obvious disappointment.

"I thought they were tricking me," He says sombrely, resting his hands on the women around him, "Whispering harsh falsehoods in order to get me to hand you over."

Suddenly purple and black swirls pool into the water, slinking from the bodies of the women, their smiles stretching.

I stumble backwards, already summoning a way out as I watch their beings shift.

"Now I see, I was foolish to think better of you." He says.

Their mouths open, ripping at the corners, tearing apart and *unravelling over their heads and down their bodies. Undoing their flesh coats and revealing my worst nightmares curled around my father.*

The Fates.

The crease seems to shrink as my fear grows and I lose the concentration I need to snatch it, the room fluctuating in and out of two and three dimensions.

"Father no- please- let me go-" I plead, my hands shaking and failing to find possession on the tiles as I scramble backwards, away from the hands of black and purple mist that claw for me.

"This is for your own good." His voice is stone, no way I'm getting through to him now.

"Please..." my voice is barely a whisper as I tremble, helpless as the hands reach for my ankles.

"Not today, my darling Fides." Mother's voice comes from behind me, followed by a crimson lava-encrusted fist that slams down on the hands of the Fates with a fiery vengeance. "Not my daughter, you crusty old hags."

Her other hand wraps around my waist, fingers coiling over my body possessively; big enough to snake around my entire middle.

"Stick with her, my child," She cajoles, as her face peers at mine with obsidian teeth bared, "Your darling is the only thing in this universe and the next that they can't touch."

She thrusts me backwards with the force of ten men, my torso moving faster than my limbs as I freefall, my hair a silver banner flying out behind me.

I don't even realise she's thrown me through a crease until I'm staring at a two-dimensional image of the bathhouse before it closes. The last thing I see is my mother's looming demonic silhouette, one hand on her hip, staring down at my father with an aura of complete and utter power.

"I had it under control." I bristle, shuddering off the feeling of my mother's hand on me.

The mortal realm feels dull without the excess of feelings and sensations that Empraillya so naturally exudes. The coppery outer-building of the university campus glares at me from behind. I can hear her laugh, smell her jasmine, and I turn to see her huddled up with a technicoloured conglomeration of individuals.

Father betrayed me, Mother saved me.

Funny, if they had taken up each other's roles, my mood would be the opposite as well. As it stands, all I feel is an aching pit of despair and indignation.

I can't realm hop alone, that much is now known. What had she even meant that the Fates can't touch her? The Fates have control of everything and everyone- bar a select few Gods.

But as I stare at the back of her head now, watching as she senses me- as I sensed her- and turns to me with a smile that falters, I can't help but wonder-

Maybe my darling is even more spectacular than I already thought.

CHAPTER 15
IT HAD TO BE MADDENING

Aletheia hasn't been trouble in the build-up to Thursday, spending more time talking my ear off about different realms than anything else. I hate to admit it, but I was relieved when she came back; smile shy, hands behind her as she took her seat next to me in Irene's group.

Since then, she's not left my side.

It's a solace of sorts, a quiet ease of the mind to just hear about all the dimensions and worlds I have yet to visit. Like the spiral spiderweb-planet that hosts beings with multiple limbs and the power to see the future. Or the six moons of Sirena, that orbit each other in such a way that once a year, they all collide together for a day, allowing the inhabitants to switch moon-ports- before pulling apart again the following morning for another year-long rotation. The year presumably works on a different time-frame than earth- but I don't need to know the logistics.

Not yet.

The feeling of ease in her company only serves to solidify the knowledge that this must be from my own head. How else could

I feel so comfortable in her presence after only a couple of days?

Even with Amaya, it had taken over a year before I was comfortable getting the surprise hug from her. Not that we've spoken since I made my big announcement.

Yet, with Aletheia I can lie beside her and listen to her talk. Sleep in her arms and never question it. Sure, my heart beats a thousand times a minute when she gets too close; but no part of me wants to run. She calls me her darling- and I'm not sure what to make of it, but I know I don't want a different name.

Today though is work-day, diner day- Madeline day.

A consequence of such being that my hands are shaking, and refusing to do even the simplest of tasks properly. I've nearly dropped orders eight times now, minor spillages on nearly every tray. Casimir noticed of course, telling me off in a way where he stands to his full height and looks down at me through his nose, occasionally making a point of slamming his fist down on work surfaces after a slip-up. Not that he got closer than that though- not with Irene in the corner, painting away and always keeping one eye set on him.

Her friendship is officially invaluable to me.

I've spent the last two days with their group. It felt almost too easy to blend in with such a flamboyant crowd, when I feel so bland in comparison. The dull daisy in a garden of tropical flowers.

But they make me feel seen. Irene introduced the other two, Corbin and Emmy. Corbin is pansexual and loves the study of taxidermy, Creature Classes being the highlight of his days. Whilst Emmy is studying to become a physiotherapist, specialising in acupuncture and herbal remedies on the side; making potions class and the concept of magic ever more intriguing for her. She's transgender, as I later found out, and has been out as such for over five years. Turns out, Corbin and her are dating. Which made it a little odd that I am the only single person in their little group.

But it never feels wrong- never making me feel outwardly rejected or like I'm missing anything.

Sayra is obsessed with my knowledge of magic, picking my brains with notebook in hand whenever she can get a word in edgewise. Corbin and Emmy are more-so the video-game geeks, hyper-focused on the new holographic VR you can tap into even during REM sleep.

I chose not to mention that my lucid dreams have led me into full-blown hallucination territory; best not to scare them off just yet.

And then there's Irene, who feels so easy to be around that it's like she's known me for years. She's quirky in a more subtle sort. Defiant in a righteous sense and strong in the most obvious way; no one messed with Irene.

Aletheia sits next to me, lounging on the counter facing the booths, one leg bent and the other bouncing off the side.

"I told you you'd get bored here." I whisper in her direction, prodding her in her side with the end of my pen.

She hisses, grabbing the pen before I can fully pull away and dragging me closer with it. Gods knows how that looked to everyone else, and I make an effort to bring the pen and her hand down onto the countertop as subtly as I can.

"And I told you,"

She says, leaning down so her hair dangles next to mine,

"That I don't care."

I don't add that I have no choice. That as of two days ago, my newfound perceived-freedom turned into the kilometre surrounding one mortal female.

My mortal female, but a kilometre radius nonetheless.

She goes quiet, her mind drifting elsewhere and her eyes to

that of beyond the diner windows. How epic it must be to have the imagination she has, after seeing everything she's seen. She's lived a thousand lives and hasn't even scratched her mid-twenties.

Gods knows why she sticks around here- provided she isn't just a figment of my own misguided subconscious.

I have to admit though, I like that she does.

It would be humbling if I believed her to be real.

"Yo-" Irene says as she lounges against the counter, with Aletheia's legs dangling by her shoulder unbeknownst to her.

Aletheia seems to pick up that this is a conversation I'd prefer to have unattended by an uninvited third, blowing me a kiss and slinking off towards an empty booth.

"-have you seen Sayra today? She hasn't come in to bother me yet. And as we both know by now- she *always* wants to bother me." Irene smiles affectionately, but I can tell there is some concern attached to the humour.

I lean in so as my voice doesn't carry as far as the office, "She uhhh..."

I don't know quite how to tell her that I'd seen her leave here earlier today, skipping along beside a rugby lad from the year below us.

Irene's eyes narrow before they seem to register understanding.

"Ahh I see- was she with Tyre?" She asks.

I don't know his name, so I lift one arm above my head to indicate his height, the other tensing to make as much bicep visible as possible; measly as mine are.

Irene grins and nods, pointing her paintbrush at me, "That's Sayra's other partner, *slash*, partner-to-be," She says, a slightly gleeful look coming over her face at my shock, "We're polyamorous honey, chill."

I hadn't even considered that an option for them, they seemed so close all the time and so weirdly perfect, why would they need another?

"Polyamorous?" I ask, trying to appear unperturbed.

She nods, leaning her head against her arms on the countertop and looking up at me.

"Lemme explain so you get it- because you're clearly confused- and that's okay-" she says hurriedly as I feel the colour drain from my face at the thought I'd offended her, "But maybe some clarity will help."

I twist my hands together nervously.

"Whatever you guys choose to do is up to you." I mumble.

She bats her hand at me, waving me off, "Shush your face, I don't mind. Look," She says, placing her hands in front of her like two walls, "First off, and not to get all political or up-myself about it- but the only people in history not allowed multiple partners were women." She rolls her eyes theatrically before continuing, "Throughout history, men have taken mistresses-multiple of them, without repercussions. The ancient Greeks held orgies for both the rich and the poor. The Egyptians could take as many wives as they liked- even in the bible, in Genesis, Lamech married two women. In the Quran, men are allowed multiple wives if they are all treated equally... I'm getting off-topic-" She says, blushing slightly and waving herself away; clearly passionate about the topic.

I lean forward.

It may not be *my* thing, I don't think, but it's hers- and she's important to me.

"-Any-who, monogamy is good and all, I get the amazing notion of one true pairing and singular devotion. But people used to live a *lot* shorter lives when they agreed to the whole 'till death do us part' thing. I think being bisexual, Sayra included, we understand that people have the capacity to love more than one person- without it taking away from their other loves." She shrugs, "Love is love, we just feel we have more to give."

I guess I'd never thought of it like that.

To be honest, I've never given the topic much thought at all. I'm still working out how to love *one* person, let alone split that love between people equally.

I clear my throat, "So what you're saying is- monogamy is just a concept made up by men to restrict women's pleasure and maintain their power?"

"Bingo." She says, shooting me finger guns and grinning.

Maybe she does have more love to give, maybe that's why it was so simple to get to know her. Because she was more open to people and their quirks.

"Don't worry though," She says, patting my arm over the counter, "You're stunning honey, just not my type."

My mouth falls open as she sticks her tongue out at me, the metal ball glinting, and proceeds to strut away.

It's only when she passes the office door that I notice his shadow move against the blinds and know I have to make myself scarce-

Busy-

Out of sight.

Giving Irene a nod I quickly pass through the kitchen doors, turning my attention to the mountain of glasses and plates haphazardly thrown in the sink; the pile so high that he's taken to placing the dirty dishes on the clean work surfaces as well.

How thoughtful.

Apron on, head down, get to work- then Madeline's coming.

My hands freeze right above the power washer.

Madeline is coming here- to talk to me- one on one.

They begin to shake, and I grip the nozzle for stability, busying myself with the workload.

Madeline, who hasn't talked to me properly since middle school. The most sought-after girl in the whole of Southlakes and the object of my affections for the past eleven years... and I'm going to help her with classwork.

I'd be excited, if I wasn't still wishing I could talk to Amaya and Rylan about it. Amaya is still a no-show, having skipped the last two days of university. She can't hide her face from me forever, but the more she tries to- the more it hurts. We are best friends- *were*, best friends, and she's willing to give it up over my sexuality. I-

I can't blame her.

Perhaps it feels to her like I've lied to her, made her become friends with someone who inherently goes against the beliefs of her parents; and by extension, her. I never meant to start lying to her, but when it came to Madeline, I always kept my feelings secret. So, when Amaya naturally assumed I was into the person that was a human limpet to Madeline... I don't know.

It felt safer.

Rylan is a no-show as well, presumably with Amaya- he'd notif'd me that he was okay, so I'd know it wasn't his family. But that leaves me here, without my best friends, to talk to my crush for the first time alone- whilst also trying to work out why I'm seeing a demi-demon-goddess when others can't.

I wish I'd told them when it started.

But that would've meant the dreams, and the beach, and mum...

A glass slips from my fingers, crashing back into the sink with clangs that bring me harshly back into the room. Enough that I hear the loud and aggravating footfalls that can only belong to Casimir, as he enters the kitchen.

He wears a pout today, as he takes his time lowering each individual glass into the sink; hovering over me close enough that I can smell what he had for dinner.

Something fishy.

"You going to be my friend again soon?" He says in a cooing tone, leaning his head down so he can look up at me past my hair.

I try not to react on impulse, refraining from pulling away.

"I- I d-don't know w-what you mean." I stutter, Gods I hate

when I stutter.

From behind me I see the door lightly blow open, silver whisps curling into the room.

"Darling?" I call, stopping short when I see how pale she's gone.

Casimir's fist hits the side of the washer and I can't help but flinch, the remaining glasses clinking noisily against the side of the sink.

"Maybe next shift?" He says in a calculated tone, just as I hear Irene's voice summoning him from the other room.

This man is a bad man. Another clear enemy in pursuit of my darling. He shall be disembowelled alongside the blond-haired demon.

Aletheia stands to the side, but at full height, as Casimir moves to leave the room. Her eyes bore daggers in his head until the door swings shut again.

I wish she wouldn't look at me like that.

"I don't need your pity." I say harshly, flicking on the jet-spray again and not meeting her eyes.

I know all I'll see is a reflection of how bad I've let things get, staring back at me.

I feel the weight of her arms, without the heat or her presence attached, wrap around my middle; her head resting on the barrier against my own head.

"I have been aware of your existence for four years,"

She says, her mouth moving against my hair without being able to touch it,

"I have felt who, and how you are, every fleeting emotion, through your

dreams and through what you have consciously or unconsciously sent me over the years."

I feel my heart pounding in my chest. *Every emotion?* How much of me does she know? How can I know so little of *her* in return?

"I have known you, and only you- for the years I was trapped by the hands of the Fates. I have lived through you. Felt compassion, hope, anguish, heartache and ineffable joy for you, my darling," She breathes, *"But never once, have I ever felt pity."*

I turn to face her, my hand slipping down to hold hers as much as I can. She smiles, looking at me through her bright-white eyelashes and placing one hand on the back of my neck; pulling herself forwards until our foreheads meet.

"Pity is for the weak, my darling, and you are the strongest person I know." She smiles, her mouth so close, *"And I've known a lot of people."*

I can't look away. I ache to know her like she knows me. To feel as understood and to understand in the way that she claims to. Is it even possible to feel so known...

"Aletheia..." I whisper, her diamond eyes huge and focused on mine.

I... I don't...

The door crashes open, or feels like it does, my head banging against Aletheia's and separating us as Irene makes her entrance. One hand holds the door ajar, her eyes roaming my face, presumably to check how bad the situation had been.

Gods knows what she must think, my cheeks are on fire and Aletheia's hand is still in my own.

She frowns, shaking her head but not saying anything.

"Your *'friend'* is here." She says, adding quotation marks with one hand and pushing the door open by her fingertips so I can see around her.

Madeline comes into view, sat in a booth and wearing a face that's drawn and closed.

My fingers slip from Aletheia's and I distantly feel her bristle.

"I'll be right there." I say, untying my apron and checking the time.

7:02- time to clock off anyway.

Irene nods, her eyes lingering a little too long on where Aletheia stands, before letting the door swing closed.

I breathe out a sigh, running my hands through my hair to try and make it look somewhat presentable.

"She is a falsehood," I say, folding my arms and leaning against the silver bench as she adjusts herself for the sake of a hellhound, "She is a charlatan, a fabulist, a romanticist for her own machinations."

She shakes her head at me, not looking in my direction as she places the clothing-covering on the countertop. Gone is the girl who looked back at me with an ageless wonder, gone is the woman who yearned for me as I did her.

In place is the child who chases bad choices.

"She's not what you think."

She says, moving to leave.

I can't let her engage in acts of such miscalculated naivety. I know she wants to feel known, craves it even- but from this girl?

This rancid excuse for a mortal will drag her down to the pits of hell right alongside her for the sake of ministrations.

I grab her arm, halting her from her doomed endeavour.

"Aletheia, let me go."

She hisses under her breath, her eyes darting between the door and me.

I wonder when she will feel comfortable enough to announce me to the rest of her realm. Likely not in this lifetime. But I understand, just as I understand what she's doing now and why.

That doesn't mean I'm not going to at least try to save her from her pitfalls.

"She doesn't care to know you," I say quietly, saying it but not being able to meet her eyes as I wound her, "She doesn't even know what she wants-'"

"Enough." I say, stopping Aletheia from spewing any more of the hate she so clearly possesses.

I know what she thinks of her, but I have known Madeline for eleven years of my life. I've only known Aletheia properly for a number of days; the four years having only been rude awakenings from my dreams.

She has no right.

I rip my hand away from hers and move to leave.

"Stay *away* from her." I point at Aletheia, before stepping out into the bar area.

The anxiety slams into me like a tidal wave upon seeing Madeline, pushing harder and higher as I approach the booth. This is going to be fine- normal, even. Just two friends helping each other with an assignment.

Nothing more.

Madeline spots me in her periphery as I come around the side of the bar, her eyes lighting up.

"Tenny!" She squeals, jumping up from the booth and slinging her arms firmly around my neck.

This is fine.

This is normal.

So can my heart *please* give it a rest and act normal too?

"Madeline- hey- hi, how're you doing?" I finally manage to get out once she extricates herself from me.

She beams, as if that was somehow the best question she's

ever been asked.

"I'm good! Yeah, sit! Sit-sit-sit." She insists, patting the space opposite her in the booth.

She is definitely anxious. I know that palm-sweating, eye-darting stress like the back of my hand. Something's happened- and she wants to talk about it.

Aletheia climbs up on the booth behind me, her legs dangling down so that her feet rest either side of my head. I can't do anything about her now- but we will be having words later.

Suddenly, Irene appears at the side of the booth, making me feel rather crowded- and I'm the only one who's aware of it.

"Howdy Miss Maddy!" Irene serenades, leaning on my chair-side.

Madeline scrunches her nose a little but doesn't pick on the weird term of endearment; if that's what you could call it. She was happy enough to cringe at Amaya, but no one messes with Irene.

"Hello *Irene*." Madeline replies, dragging out the middle of her name and giving her a small wave.

"Fancy seeing *you* here," Irene says sarcastically, "Not like this one has been going on about it for the past three hours or anything." She says, with a thumb towards me.

If my face could produce flames, the building would be ablaze. I shrink into my chair, hoping the worn leather fabric will swallow me whole.

"It's been a boring shift." I mumble awkwardly, internally cursing Irene.

Madeline only laughs, covering her mouth with her hand at my obvious embarrassment. I can't help but smile nervously back.

"Well, I'm glad I could come along then." She says sweetly, "Tenny's actually helping me with some classes I missed."

Irene's eyebrows raise and her smile grows maniacal.

"Is she now!" Irene exclaims, like I hadn't told her as much at least ten times already, "Is that what *Tenny* is doing?"

The nickname feels forced on Irene's lips and I cringe.

"Well, I should leave you two nerds be, then." She announces theatrically, mock-saluting me before turning to leave, "Happy nerding!"

Irene struts back over to her corner, waving her paintbrush in the air as she hums a tune loudly and off-key. I shake my head endearingly.

"She's quite a character!" Madeline remarks.

I try not to read too much into how her voice tilts towards insulting, hoping I imagined it. I'm just negative, looking for the bad because of the literal demi-demon hovering on my shoulders.

I can *feel* her seething.

"She's a good friend," I say, "Her and her girlfriend Sayra come in all the time for milkshakes and fries."

I don't know why I bring Sayra into it, maybe to test the waters? Maybe to see if she was being insulting? Maybe I'm scared that she will react the same as Amaya.

Madeline's eyebrows raise and she nods.

"Those two are *so* cute together." She says, and I feel lighter.

This isn't going to be a repeat of Amaya.

Not with her.

She grins at me, taking out her bookbag and extending a pen to me.

"Shall we?" She asks.

I grin, taking the pen from her, my heart doing flips as our fingers brush for the briefest of seconds.

Aletheia's feet swing forward, before kicking back into my shoulders, effectively shoving me backwards against the seat and away from Madeline.

I grimace, but don't react, Madeline being none the wiser.

"We shall." I say, determinedly.

We spent the next hour and a half slogging over the classwork, chatting about Mr Spelinski and time missed since middle school. Aletheia clocked out soon after Madeline began talking, claiming she *'wasn't interested in petty tales of glorified mortal memories'*- from Madeline anyway.

Aletheia now sits in the booth behind, occasionally kicking the back of my seat if things we say irk her.

One of the key notes Madeline had missed was actually the redroot that ensnared Max on the first day back.

"Bet you wish you'd known this stuff last week, would've helped..." I begin, stopping as I note her discomfort.

I watch as her shoulders sag, a marionette cut from its strings.

"Hey," I say, leaning forward, "Has something happened?"

She looks away shyly, tucking her curls behind her ear and lowering her head.

"It's nothing, really." She says, clearly meaning it's something.

I move closer, placing my hands on the table in front of me to steal her attention.

"You can talk to me, you know," I say, "I'm not going to tell anyone. I'm rather a professional at secret keeping."

Her eyes light up at the mention of secrets, a devilish gleam passing over them that Aletheia would've called demonic, leaning in.

"Oh? What secrets?"

Too close.

She is very very close.

I can smell her perfume and see where she's slightly over-drawn her lipstick. Even the eyelash stuck to her cheek.

I'm going to leave it.

I'm not going to-

"You have an eyelash-" I say before I can stop myself, my hand moving of its own accord to take it from her cheek, "-there."

Even Madeline looks shocked, a soft blush creeping into the

edges of her face.

Her cheek is smooth and warm and her eyes never leave mine.

I rub my fingers together from where they brushed her, surprised to find them dusty. Upon looking I can now see she's painted. Beautifully done, expertly in fact, but the perfect face that I'd assumed was a natural part of her growing up, is merely a façade.

I can hear Aletheia's cruel remarks in my head.

No.

Her face is still beautiful, just more so in the way she chooses to present. It's just me thinking the wrong thing, not her telling me a lie- makeup isn't a lie. I really need to get Aletheia's opinions out of my head.

"I need to tell you something."

Madeline interrupts my thought spiral before it's even begun, twisting her hands nervously. I watch as one of them goes to her side.

Pinching.

"Sure, shoot, I guess." I say, internally cringing at the forced-casualness.

She twirls one of her curls in her hand, slipping it between her fingers as she speaks, unwinding it.

"Well it's just... me and max, we're kind of- over?"

I practically feel Aletheia's ears prick up at the announcement, her head peering not-so-subtly over the edge of the booth behind me.

"Oh?"

"Yeah." She breathes, biting her lip and looking over at me, gauging my reaction.

"I-I see..." I begin.

Her hand reaches across the table, taking hold of mine between both of hers.

My breath catches and I dare not take another, my eyes locked on my hands in hers. She bridged the gap.

In public.

Here.

"I've missed you, Tenny." Maddy smooths her thumb over my knuckles with the utmost delicacy, "It was always him saying I couldn't go near you, couldn't even speak to you. The first chance I got away from him I tried, but... well, you know how well *that* went."

My brow furrows, my mind reeling back to the hallway over a week ago. The way she had approached out of nowhere, how surprised and hurt she'd been when I walked away. How resigned she'd seemed when she realised why.

"He followed you."

"Yeah, he did. But now..." She trails off.

Her hands squeeze almost imperceptibly tighter around mine.

"I'd really like the chance to get to know you better again?"

I think my world stops.

I feel catapulted through my body, the rest of me left reeling, as the sentence I never thought would come from her mouth reaches my ears.

I should probably answer at some point.

"I-I- I would like that too, Madeline." I stammer, clenching my other fist under the table at my inarticulate nature.

She titters, one hand coming up to hide her pristine smile.

"You can call me Maddy you know, seeing as I call you Tenny."

It's moments like this that I have to convince myself I haven't lucid dreamt myself a perfect reality.

Blink, breathe, count fingers-

Fingers still held in Maddy's hand. Maddy who said I can call her Maddy- because we're going to be closer now, and she's not with him.

"Maddy then," I reply- albeit unsteadily, "I'd like to know you better again, too."

She claps her hands together, cold air rushing into the space she left in the wake of her excitement.

"Great! I was wondering if you'd like to come for a sleepover, end of this month?"

"Basilisk said what?!" I shriek, unable to contain myself any longer.

Aletheia leans over the top of the booth, her eyes daggers and her lips curled to reveal sharp canines.

If I don't get Maddy away from here- and fast- I don't know whether the barrier will be enough to deter Aletheia from ripping into her.

"You- what- oh, umm-" I stutter, my words failing me in my time of need.

Maddy lets me squirm.

I see it in her eyes as the smallest of smirks bleeds into her features, looking up at me through dark lashes.

Aletheia's nails dig into the back of the seat.

"It'll be so much fun- trust me, there'll be loads of us coming... why? Wait, what were *you* thinking?" She asks, her eyes widening.

But I can see her smile.

She knew what she was doing and she liked it. *I* liked it, even if she was trying to scare me into admitting I liked her.

At least, I think I like it? I like *her*...

The blush creeps up my face like a forest fire.

"Oh- nothing, no that's... yes. Who's coming?" I flounder, pulling my hair forward and not meeting her gaze.

Maddy sighs, "Well, a couple of the girls, I've sent an invitation to your two as well don't you worry! And oh- yes- I should invite Irene! Bear with."

Before I can so much as say the word Amaya, she's up and out of the booth, her hand reaching down to give my shoulder a quick squeeze before sashaying down the isle in Irene's direction.

...*What the hell just happened?*

Maddy, Madeline, my crush for the past decade, is now broken up with her boyfriend and... what? Wanting to get to know me better? What does that even *mean*? Why did she let Max dictate her friends up until now? Unless he saw me as a threat...

Aletheia does a handstand over the booths, her hair falling over and around me and disrupting my attempts to make any sort of sense of things.

"Brace for barrier-withheld-impact!"

She announces, moments before she lets herself fall half-on half-off me, her legs draped languidly across my lap.

I flick her on the forehead, causing her diamond eyes to go cross-eyed at the assault.

"Whilst I can't feel that, it's still rude."

She smirks, flicking me back with the same pain not registering.

"She's coming back, you know." I swat at her, weirdly thankful for her intermission.

Somehow, with the demi-demon-goddess from another dimension, that I can't touch and only I know exists- who may be a figment of my imagination- I feel more at ease with than I do sitting across a table from a mortal girl.

"But darling, am I not a rather exigent distraction."

She purrs, kicking her leg up to turn my head towards her.

I sigh, fighting off the butterflies with a flamethrower.

"Wicked demi-demon." I hiss sarcastically, gripping her

ankle and flinging it down into my lap.

"*Tenaya*?"

Amaya's voice comes from behind me, my neck snapping towards her so fast it gives me whiplash.

She stands flustered and windswept, having likely ran from wherever she came from. Both hands are clenched at her sides and Rylan stands a couple paces back from her, eyes wary.

She's breathing deep through her nose and her ginger hair is a ball of static around her head. In all the years I've known her, I've never seen her look anything less than pristine; with posture to match.

Dishevelled would now be putting it lightly.

My chest tightens and I avert my gaze.

"I don't want to talk to you." I say, my voice attempting harsh, but falling more on pitiful.

Aletheia's hand comes up to cup my face, her thumb stroking my cheek and gently pushing my face back towards Amaya.

"If you hear her out, at least you will be done with it." I say, hoping she will listen.

She'd mentioned what happened of course, how could she not? The exchange was written all over her face from the moment I stepped back into her realm.

I hadn't had time to assess how my darling was realm-defyingly different or magically competent. Not when she was off speaking-terms with one of her only human companions.

My darling is lonely enough as it is.

I allow Aletheia to turn me around to Amaya's puzzlement.

She shakes it off though, not willing to dwell on off-looking actions when she has something to say.

"Look, let me just get this out, because I know you don't want to hear from me, but suck it up- no-"

Rylan holds up his hands in surrender from where they had gingerly landed on her shoulders.

"-I need to say this, Rylan, and you can't stop me-" She huffs, slapping him in the side affectionately before turning her attention back to me.

"Tenaya. You are my best friend. You have been for years. I care about you more than you will ever understand, I love you- even, so much. And that isn't weird for me to say, because I do- love you, that is. And I love Rylan." She pauses, the crimson curse creeping into her cheeks, "But I love you and Rylan in two different ways, you see- I love Rylan because... I want to be with him, have been with him. We're kind of together..."

"Wait- *what*?!" I exclaim, but she holds up a hand.

"-let me finish." She says, sighing.

This was not going in the way I'd anticipated. I had expected her to resign from our friendship, begrudgingly want it back, desperately want it back or just explain her viewpoints on LGBTQ+ relations.

I hadn't expected her to announce her secret relationship with my other best friend.

"Tried to tell you." I grumble, earning me a sharp swat to the stomach.

"Yes," Amaya continues, ignoring the fact I just swatted at mid-air, "We've been together for a while, but only casually. But now we want to be open with you because you were open with me. Rylan and I are dating, and you're bisexual- and *neither* of those things matter to me enough to stop me being your best friend. So, I don't care who you want to date, love or screw, really- I will support you with whatever. Just... let me be your best friend whilst you do it?"

She looks at me like I'm holding up her world by a string, scissors at hand.

She... they...

"I- But..."

I am completely lost for words.

Amaya and Rylan are dating, Amaya doesn't care if I'm bisexual, Rylan now also knows...

"You're *bisexual*?" Maddy asks from behind my booth.

Cold ice rushes into my chest and I watch as the colour drains from both Rylan and Amaya's faces.

"Uh oh." I hear Irene murmur from further down the hall, at the same time Amaya says- "Fu-"

CHAPTER 16

ANYWHERE AWAY FROM HERE

It's been an entire week and I still can't process what's happened.

Aletheia steps up onto the ledge beside the path like a tightrope walker, hands outstretched either side of her and face skyward; taking in the sun on our way to university. She had a few choice words to say about the whole situation, mostly laughing at my expense.

Irene had come over as soon as she'd heard, poised and ready to steer away whoever required steering.

Amaya's face had paled to the point we all thought she might pass out, Rylan's arm going around her protectively.

But Maddy just smiled.

"You're bi? So am I! Who'd have guessed!"

It was the most unprecedented, wonderful sentence I'd ever heard come out of her mouth.

My world, which was already complicated enough, suddenly heralded new opportunities I hadn't even begun to fathom. Or rather, fathom into a realistic prospect.

My childhood crush is suddenly becoming a potentially real thing... So, why am I not more excited? Amaya and I had spent that evening getting to know each-other's beliefs. It wasn't necessarily that she disagreed that people should be allowed to love whoever they wanted- it was more that she didn't understand it. I have since promised to be more open with who I find attractive and when. Which made her scrunch up her nose a little, but I think she will come around to it, given more time.

It's a lot to suddenly rearrange in her head, I guess. But I'm patient, and I love her enough to bear with her whilst she comes to terms with it.

Rylan had been only too eager to discuss the potential for shared crushes, pushing me to name my most favoured celebrities; followed by ranking them using their first names as categories. It felt nice, warm, to be accepted with more of me on the table. It's not that my sexuality needs to bleed its way into every corner of my life, or be the pinacol of who I am; but it's good to be able to just be myself with the people I feel closest with.

And now? Now I am free to look at Maddy in class without worrying about judgement from Amaya's end. I can talk to Amaya and Rylan about her, about how I've felt since school.

I can tell them how it started, how she warmed to me back then- how she's inviting me to hers and seeking out my company and-

"Are you quite done?" I snap, the pressure having built to an intolerable level.

She has no idea, she mustn't. If she knew I could feel her emotions, surely she would do a better job at hiding them.

Especially when she so clearly has mixed emotions around the pretty prevaricator.

She looks at me like I've slapped her. The way her mouth moves around words she hasn't chosen yet, her deep brown eyes trying to decipher the meaning in mine.

The feeling she pours into me when she looks at me without even realising it.

It's ecstasy.

Contrast to what she sends my way when she thinks of her. I wish I could save her from this, but it may just have to play out.

Thank the Gods I'm a patient demon.

Her face morphs from irked to indifferent in a matter of moments, and I can't understand what I've done. We've been walking in a comfortable silence for the past ten minutes. Perhaps I misjudged the comfortability?

"I- umm, is everything okay?" I ask cautiously.

I don't quite know where I stand with Aletheia. Then again, I don't know where I stand with most people at this point. Amaya and Rylan have returned to a semi-normal state of being, Irene and her lot are as manic as they've always been, and Madeline...

She said I could call her Maddy.

In the moments she couldn't even wait for me to respond, her emotions have drifted back to her. To the seductress, the succubis, the siren of Southlakes.

I've had enough.

"Field trip time." I say in a deadpan voice, begging the Gods to let me do this.

I can feel them pushing, tugging, just under my skin- at my shoulder-blades and waist and I smile.

Praise be.

Aletheia crouches, her spine arching before leaping onto my back like a leopard.

"Aletheia- *woah*!" I yelp, trying to find my balance.

She only chuckles.

"Hold on darling." I say, interlocking my limbs around her so tight that I can't help but blush even through my frustration.

She grins, before wings of onyx and iridescent white burst free from her back.

They span three times my height on either side, a demon and an angel, attaching at her shoulder-blades and torso. Four segments. Each of them rising skyward as far as they can point, before thrusting down with a force unparalleled in this dimension; skyrocketing us up into the open air.

The air-

Is *so-*

Thin.

We're travelling so fast my vision blurs, a comet through the sky that could block the sun for half the town; if only she could be seen.

As it stands, all people will see is a terrified girl freefalling through the sky with an unknown trajectory. The clouds part for us and she sweeps us up above them, the mist grazing my cheeks and coating my clothes and skin in a layer of cold dew.

"Aletheia! *What-Where-*" I can't even find the words, my lungs too focused on driving air into me.

Air that's quickly thinning out to a point I can't even draw breath.

She only grips me tighter, smiling.

"I'm done with other people for the moment,"

She says, the wind seemingly bending her words so they reaches me,

"I want out."

Out?

What does she mean, *out*?

The clouds rise up beneath us and I realise we are descending. My brain thankful for this at least, as oxygen begins streaming into my parched lungs; clearing the mental fog that was enclosing in on all sides.

I have university to go to- I have to go or Hydra will know and I'll be doomed, *and* behind on classwork. Aletheia knows at least the second half of this, so why is she taking me away?

I close my eyes against the water this time, bracing myself for the cold.

And open them to my nightmare.

The beach spreads as wide as the eye can see, the waves crashing in harshly against the sand. Pummelling, tearing it apart, breaking it down-

Drown-

Drowning it

Drowning drowning *drowning*

"ALETHEIA ***NO***!" I scream, my hands ripping at her and my legs careening in every direction, like I can steer us away or transport us elsewhere by panic alone.

Pure panic

I can't breathe

Think

Feel anything

"NO- no *please*- Aletheia *nonono* take me *AWAY*! Get me *AWAY* from here!" I scream, and Aletheia drops like a stone from the sky.

Her wings tuck and we torpedo downwards, spiralling until all I can see is blue and gold, sand and sea.

That beach

This beach

Mums beach...

"Hold on!"

She says through gritted teeth, and I have enough sense to tighten my grip before she veers harshly right, and everything is bathed in darkness. My body slams into the cavern so hard that we burst apart, rolling over and over until I stop near its base; my body convulsing.

She's steered us into a cave just off the beach, up and into the cliff-face, deep enough that I can almost imagine we aren't here.

But we are.

And I can hear the waves and the gulls and the wind and the water and the *sea*-

The water that took her from me, Tabi, dad.

My eyes see thousands of lines on the cave walls, thousands where there should be tens. My arms and legs won't stop shaking and I can't draw in air even though we've come down from the sky.

I'm having a panic attack

And I can't stop it

Worse worse worse than the ones in my bedroom

Worse than the ones I got in the weeks after I saw her lying on that metal bed, a white sheet draped over her bluish bloated body; fouled by the tide.

This is *her* beach, this is *her* sea.

Darkness perforates my vision, or what's left of it, and I succumb to the nothing in my state of inordinate being.

This is the sea that drowned my Mum.

CHAPTER 17
ARMED WITH SHELLS

"I didn't realise, please, you have to know I couldn't have predicted this would happen- please talk to me, my darling I wish to understand-"

Aletheia sits crouched in front of me on my dreamland beach, both hands on my knees as I tuck myself as small as possible; not meeting her eyes.

She was never supposed to know, no one was.

She won't look at me. It's like I'm truly not here. The one person in her realm that can see me and she's refusing to.

Please see me

I just want to understand-

This is my safe place. My version of events where there is no danger. I control the tide, the sand, even the airless breeze. In my dreams there is no danger, so it's fine. It's a therapy of my own devices, I conjure the place but I take away the fear, the painful part, out of it.

And I don't touch the water.

I scoot my feet a little closer towards me, burying them in the sand and throwing the water back further from me.

"How is this beach good and the other not?"

She asks, and I can feel how earnestly she wants to make things okay.

But she can't.

Because shortly I will wake up. And when I do, it will be in a cave above the place that my Mum's corpse washed up. The beach where she was found a day post-mortem by a family of 3. By their daughter no less.

Amaya had told me the story perhaps a handful of times, always when she was around that sort of topic; death or trauma. How she had been on the beach one day with her parents, collecting fossils, shells and skimming stones, when she went to investigate what she thought was a log. It was the first dead body she had ever seen. It was veiny and white and bloated to a point where she couldn't even tell if it was a man or a woman.

She was only fourteen.

It had been very traumatic.

There was even an article in the local news about it: 'Teenage girl uncovers corpse at Southlakes Cove'.

I've never told her she was the one who found my Mum.

I don't think I ever will.

How could I? When she was so traumatised by the event, taking on the pitying eyes she got every time she told the story.

I don't want that. I've never wanted that.

I just want to forget.

To move out, move on and forget the image of my mum with her skin oozing and translucent, her eyes unseeing.

Aletheia's hand brushes my chin, and I allow her to drag my eyes to hers.

"Why do you feel so hollow?"

She murmurs, barely above a whisper but registering like a punch to the gut.

The ache returns to my chest as the memory burns with fresh pain.

"My Mum," I begin, without thinking, "She... she was the single most perfect person in the universe."

Aletheia moves without disturbing a single grain, flowing around to my side and curling around me like a comfort blanket as I speak.

"She was funny without trying, with a laugh so amazing you'd wish they'd play it on the radio. She was adventurous, she would find the magic in everything- take me and Tabi to the woods, to the beach, to anywhere she could that was new- breathing life into it with her stories. It's why I fantasise about magic and new dimensions now. Perhaps in one of them..."

I drift off, not wanting to voice the idealistic wish that my Mum in some realm still exists. Somehow preserved by the magic that she was in life.

Aletheia squeezes me, bringing me back, and I continue.

"She left on a Sunday morning, she wanted shells for a project- spirally and pink, they had to be that way she'd said. Demanded them in the way that she would. Dad put up no objection, but I-" I pause, swallowing the lump in my throat that shouldn't be a hindrance in my dreams but still manages to be.

"I was ill, and Tabi was still only a baby. So, dad stayed behind to watch us whilst mum went to the beach alone. I still remember the last thing she ever said to me," I say in an almost-laugh, "'If you don't get your butt out of bed by the time I'm back, I'm sending a demon after you- and they'll be armed with shells!'"

Aletheia smiles, but it doesn't quite reach her eyes, her arms still locked around me, holding me together.

I shrug.

"She was weird like that."

Aletheia places a hand over mine, and I unclench my fist to allow for her fingers to interlock; my heart breaking a little more with every truth I tell her.

"She drowned, on that beach?"

Aletheia asks.

I scrunch my eyes shut, but I still see her lifeless body.

I nod.

"This one." I say, opening my eyes and gesturing around us. "This is the only version I let myself near. A harmless version. One that I know can't hurt me or anyone else and never has. It's my almost-exposure therapy- one that I haven't ever really progressed in. I haven't even made it to the water here, let alone out there."

I twist so we look backwards up at the cliff-face.

"We're up there." I say, locking onto the small incision in the rocks, picturing our real-world bodies curled up in the furthest-most corner.

They'll have to wake up eventually.

"They asked me to identify her." I say, and she tenses, anger seeping into her features; barely concealed under the surface.

Her father is a coward, and she still chooses to save him every day.

My darling is worth so much more than the people she saves from harm.

That's something I don't talk about, not once- not ever.

Dad had been too emotional, grieving before he even knew for sure that it was the case. He knew in his heart. We all did. But the hospital and the police needed assurance. So, they took fourteen-year-old me into the hospital, down a lift that felt rickety and a snap away from plummeting. Past swinging doors on either side of a hallway that looked too much like the one in college. To the room that held her- to the metal bed and the white sheet and her too-pale body that was definitely hers.

No question.

She still had my hair, but that was about all that remained the same. The rest was marred by water damage and death.

I look at her then, at Aletheia. Her diamond eyes blinking back at me expectantly. I have no words to offer her, no way of explaining how deep the pain goes or how far down I've shoved it in order to carry on.

Without a word, she presses up into a crouch, slipping both hands up until they're cupping my face. She places a kiss to my forehead.

"It wasn't your fault," another kiss, "She loved you more than life itself," another, "You were too young to go through what you did," and a final one before she leans her forehead against mine, "You are so much more than the tragedies that befall you. My darling- you glow."

I shouldn't be able to cry here.

It shouldn't be possible and neither should she.

But the tears freefall down my cheeks, silently and onto the sand where we sit, Aletheia's tears mixing with my own and shimmering in a way that feels ethereal.

She strokes my cheek, stretching up to stand and taking me by the hand so I move with her. Only she lets go, and takes a step towards the sea, waves, danger-

I nearly make it disappear.

And she feels it. I know somehow she can feel my immediate panic because she smiles at me. Smiles the whole time as she slowly, through the magic that she is, calls the water to where her feet are. The rivulets travel over and between her toes and wind up her legs like the vines of a tree. They run over her whole body, making rivers and waterfalls across her entire being until she is a world of water and I take a step back.

"One step at a time." She says softly, walking backwards until the waves rock against her heels, "You are braver than you know."

I can feel the waking world pulling at my mind, distantly the wind sends shivers down my aching body. But I don't want to wake up, I don't want to be there.

But with her...

"I'm scared." I say, and I feel the cracks in me appear as I admit how weak I really am.

I am helpless and paralysed by the fear stored in the memories, powerless to it, as I stand before a being of inordinate strength and potential.

Aletheia.

She splashes me.

Before I can lift my hands to stop the spray or even react to what she's done. The water hits my skin and sticks, dark spots forming on the clothing I've conjured here.

She- she just did that.

"Did you just- after what I just told you-"

She does it again, and this time I bring my hands up, covering my face but failing to stop the dozens of individual pellets of water from grazing my face. My heart beats faster than I can count and I want to be angry. I want to throw things and cry and bring a tornado down on the sand and flip the world on its axis.

But what I really want is to splash her back.

What I really feel like doing is crying, not with sadness, but with a deep feeling of painful relief.

I didn't have to take the first step.

For once, I didn't have to make the first move towards what I knew I needed to do. What I always know I need to do.

Because she was okay doing it for me.

She was perfectly fine in being that helping hand, that starting shove- the villain even, for a time. So that I can do- be- have- what I know I can.

What she has always believed I can.

"Like I said," *She smirks, as if reading my thoughts; swishing her skirts nonchalantly in the salty foam,* "One step- at a time."

The world blinks back at me as my eyes slowly adjust to the pseudo-darkness of the cave. The dark-red walls blur into focus, my heart kickstarting again at the sounds coming from just beyond the lip of the cave.

Aletheia is nowhere to be seen.

I scramble to my feet, my bones and muscles aching from lying in such an awkward position.

"Aletheia?" I call, not wanting to go closer to the edge but knowing I need to if I'm to leave, let alone search for her.

I creep closer to the precipice, only when I start to see blue and then yellow as I reach the very edge, do I notice what she's done.

Steps have been carved into the face of the cliff, jagged and rushed, but purposeful, leading in a winding route down to the edge of the sand.

She did this. She can't interact with people other than me, but I guess she can manipulate non-living things.

That's when I spot her.

I take the steps before I even register what I'm doing, some of them two at a time, until my feet hit the grass before the granules and I pause.

The tide is in, the waves not more than fifty or so metres from where I stand, and I'm immobile; the beach deserted other than for us.

She stands in the waves, an ornate statue in a literal sea of blue. Her hair spills amidst the white horses and her dress skims the surface as the waves roll around her. She doesn't move towards me, but she does lift her arm back behind her. For a moment I cower backwards- afraid she will send the waves at me. I can't control them here- but she can. It should scare me, and it does, but the other part of me knows she won't hurt me- she knows me. Possibly better than anyone else in the universe in this moment.

She throws her arm forwards, flinging something small and glinting directly at me. I follow it, tracking it's course and leaping forwards in order to catch it with both hands.

I don't notice the sand beneath my feet until they begin to sink slightly in its softness.

I'm on the beach.

It's the first time I've been this close to the water since before mum passed. First time I've seen the waves again in real life, let alone touch real sand.

My fingers uncurl from around the object and all the air rushes from my lungs, tears immediately springing to my eyes. I stare at its glossy surface, the water droplets reflecting the dying sun back at me.

A spirally pink shell.

I close my eyes, bringing the shell to my chest and allowing myself to feel it. The pain, raw and unfiltered, that comes with my Mum's last living memory.

Mum did what she said she would in the end, and I laugh, unable to contain the ridiculousness of it all.

I open my eyes, placing the shell in my pocket and letting the feeling wash over me like the tide- as I take myself one step at a time- towards the water.

She's there waiting for me, arms spread and circling herself in the spray, her fingertips delicately breaking the surface and sending the water spitting around her like a halo.

The waves reach out to me, but I pay them no attention. I focus only on her. At her hands in the water, at her body twisting beneath the stardust dress, at her hair that spills over and around her in a silvery cape, at her face. Her eyes her mouth her smile-

I'm in the water and the waves are around me, and still all I do is stare at her, taking her hands in mine and stopping her movements for a moment.

"Good steps, my darling." She says, sliding her damp hands out of mine and wrapping them around me. Holding me close and together in the place I never thought I'd ever go again; the sea enveloping us and pushing us closer.

Mum did what she said she'd do.
She sent a demon after me- and she was armed with shells.

CHAPTER 18
HIGH TIDE CAME CRASHING IN

Salt clings to my skin like saran wrap, the feeling inextricable without a deep soak in the shower.

I don't mind though, because she's walking beside me, holding my hand as tightly as the interdimensional barrier will allow.

I don't know how or when she became the closest person to me. Not just physically speaking, but altogether the person who just understands me. But then again, maybe it makes sense. This person from the realms of which I yearn to explore suddenly appears and takes up an interest in me, claiming to have known me through my dreams for the past four years.

It isn't hard to imagine that I'd develop a connection with her.

I don't know what that connection is, and I'm not ready to try to work that out. There's too much already on my mind, what with Hydra, Dad, Tabi, work, university, Amaya, Rylan and now Madeline- Maddy.

The realm-hopping demi-demon-goddess connection will

just have to wait.

If I can help it.

But as she bumps her hip against mine, I lose both my balance and my focus, my heart skipping for just a second.

I can push down a second.

But it's the smell that comes with it, and suddenly I have to stop.

"Aletheia-" I shake my head, trying to think of how to word it nicely as she looks at me, "I think... I think I can... *smell* you?"

Her eyes glow and her grin spans her entire face.

"Yeah? And what exactly is it that you think I smell like?" I ask, ecstatic at how quickly the bond must be developing.

She swings my arm theatrically, urging us to keep moving as the sun travels past the lip of the earth; the soft pink afterglow the only thing lighting our way.

I don't quite know what comes over me.

One minute I'm swinging her arm in mine. The next, I'm holding her still by the hip and my face is by her neck, breathing her in.

She doesn't move a muscle, one arm hovering above my shoulder and the other still linked in my hand.

"You smell like..." I say, breathing in again before smiling and pulling back, the embarrassment creeping into my cheeks, "Earth, pine and green." I say, "But also salt and sea and blue- but I don't know whether that's from you or the beach."

Aletheia doesn't say a word, her eyes wide and tracked on me and my foreign movements. For once, speechless.

Dark blue stains across her cheeks.

"Aletheia your face- it's turning-" I panic, cupping her cheek in my palm as she tries to hide her face.

The dark blue stain spreads quicker.

"That's me blushing, darling."

She mumbles under her breath without meeting my eyes,

"My blood is blue."

My fingers slide from hers as she starts moving forwards without me.

One step forwards, two steps back.

Aletheia is a being from another realm. A demon. A demi-god. A realm hopper and possibly something that's not even real.

What am I doing?

I can't be getting caught up in everything she is. She's so much, so complex and intricate and beautiful-

Beautifully put together... and I'm messy.

She's better off figuring that out sooner rather than later.

"Oh." I say softly, falling into step beside her and choosing to ignore her fingers that still stretch towards me.

Her fingers that then clench tightly before swinging by her hips again.

We make it the rest of the way home in silence.

"Can you meet me in my room?" I ask Aletheia as we arrive at my front door, "I need to talk to Tabi."

I pray she doesn't see through my crap, that she doesn't realise that I just don't want her seeing what Hydra will do to me. I've been absent from university all day. Now, standing in front of my house, all I can feel is the sickening pit in my stomach that's telling my brain to switch itself off for a bit. To vacate the premises because the body needs to take this one.

She gives me a perplexed look before shrugging.

"Sure."

I unlock the door and swing it open far enough that she can slip through, her body gliding silently up the stairs and out of view. I wait until I hear my bedroom door shut behind her, before closing the front door behind me.

I slip my shoes off one by one and hang my jacket over the bannister, my heart thumping as I hear her approach.

I don't want to get blood on my jacket again.

"He's in his study." Hydra's voice echoes harshly from the kitchen archway.

I turn, my hand still on the bannister, hovering like the option of escape still exists.

"S-s-sorry?" I stammer, clenching my other fist behind my back to ground myself.

She tilts her blonde head at me, her eyes gleaming in a way that scares me far more than if she were mad.

I'm used to mad- I'm used to manic.

I'm not accustomed to smug Hydra.

"I *said*, he's in his study." She repeats, gesturing to my left like I haven't lived here for the solid twenty years of my life.

Like I don't know where my father's study is in my own home.

But I guess I did ask twice. And at this point, it's probably more her home than mine. It sure doesn't feel like my home anymore.

"Oh, thanks." I mumble, before knocking softly on the study door.

"Dad?" I call gently, easing the door ajar and squinting into the near-darkness.

His study is little more than a cubby hole with all the papers and filing cabinets stored in there. A small window-chair beside a wonky bookcase- hosting several framed photos of him and Hydra; gifts from her over the years. A tiny desk and a giant computer screen, with just enough space to fit a keyboard underneath. A squeaky office chair that spins only once before it falls apart, behind which is the fold-out camp-bed that usually stands upright against the bookcase.

But today- now- it's unfolded.

The mysterious yellowing-stains and coffee-marks displayed for the world to see.

Dad sits in the centre of it. His feet on the floor seeming to be the only thing that's grounding him as he carries his head in his hands; his elbows on his knees and his body buckled forwards. His hair is dishevelled, and his reading glasses have fallen onto the floor at his feet.

"Dad..." I whisper, my shadow falling upon his broken frame.

His head snaps up at my voice and I see that his eyes are red and puffy, his mouth hanging open like he can't believe I'm standing here.

"Tenaya? What- where have you..." His voice trails off as he takes in my sea-encrusted clothes and sand-strewn skin, the salt still palpable around me.

His face shifts so quickly, I forget what he normally looks like.

He stands to his full height, a storm cloud incoming as he moves the three steps it takes him to breach the distance between us; towering over me. His eyes roam my body, breathing in the sea-stench and my stricken face.

He knows.

He knows where I've been, not like I tried to hide it.

He looks so angry.

"Dad- I know you're mad. But I'm okay- I'm *safe*-"

"No text." He interrupts, like a slap across my face, silencing me. "No call. No word from school. No sign of you anywhere in town. No police sightings, no travel documentation, no *note*."

As he lists off the ways in which I've failed him today all I can do is listen. I don't know what to say. But now he's left those things in the air, they feel thick; heavy. In need of acceptance or dismissal and I can do neither.

"I was safe- I promise I was only trying to-"

"DO YOU EVEN REALISE WHAT COULD HAVE

HAPPENED?!" He yells, grabbing me by the shoulders and shaking me like a rag doll.

"You could have *drowned*. You could have *died* today- out there. I wouldn't have even known where to look for you." He says, and I see the fear in his eyes; kept at bay only by the anger forcing its way to the forefront.

He never speaks like this.

I did this to him.

"You went to the one place that I wouldn't follow you. I could've lost you, Tenaya. I could've lost you like I lost *her*, your *mo-*" He swallows harshly, squeezing his eyes shut and releasing me.

His arms fall limply to his sides and his head droops, his jaw set.

My chest feels like he's stood on it, stomped on it, and I'm crushed by my own guilt.

"I can't lose you too." He says solemnly.

I've broken him.

This is all my fault.

If I had just sent a text. Didn't go down to the beach. Didn't follow her into the water-

"I'm- I'm so s-sorry, Dad." I whimper, not meeting his eyes.

I stare holes into the floor until the silence becomes too much and I watch as his feet retreat into his study, slamming the door behind him.

The wood misses my nose by millimetres.

"You're such a disappointment to him." Her curse comes hard and fast, hitting its mark as I place a couple fingers on the study door to steady myself.

I cast a glance through my hair at her, watching as she stirs baking mixture in a bowl; the movements slow and purposeful as she looks at me with eyes that *could* hold pity.

But I know what pity looks like.

Hers hold nothing but spite as she smiles smugly at me.

"At least he's starting to see the real you," She says, licking the spoon before indicating the stairs, "I think it'd be best if you went to bed without supper tonight, don't you?"

My brain has officially clocked out, and I find my head nodding automatically, my legs taking me towards the stairs without another word.

A sharp and brutal pain stabs into my foot, bringing my focus back to reality and causing me to trip. I hit the floor with a crash, cradling my right foot in my hand.

I'm so trained to be silent when hurt that it's second nature, and I double my efforts to bite my tongue with the reminder of Aletheia upstairs.

With shaking hands, I take the rusted nail between thumb and finger, grunting from the white hot pain as I gently extricate it from my flesh; holding the two-inch bloody metal aloft in front of my face.

"Oops! Silly me!" She says, marching over and plucking it from my fingers.

I catch her eyes though, the wickedness in their depths that she won't let loose when he's in such close proximity.

"Must've dropped that earlier. Be more careful next time, won't you?" she smiles, before striding away to the kitchen without another word.

Loosely translating to- *stay out of sight and out of mind- or else.*

I use the skirting board to lift myself up, cringing as my sea-water-infested sock adds literal salt to the wound.

I push through the pain, placing my clean hand on the wall and taking up my jacket in the other to place over the bannister.

I sigh, watching as my bloody fingers press stains into the material of my jacket.

So much for what I want.

I make it to my room but keep going, heading straight to the bathroom and bolting the door to clean up before Aletheia can see.

She doesn't need to know.

It’s safer this way.

CHAPTER 19
WHAT DID THE FOX SAY

"Is the silent treatment indefinite? Or should I schedule in a termination date?"

Aletheia grumbles from her upside-down position on my bed.

It's only been a couple of hours, but she's been incorrigible. It's like she can sense that something happened. Even though I cleaned up the wound as best as possible and scrubbed my face and body free of sand, salt and heartache. I swear she can smell it on me.

The stench of secrecy.

"It's not silent treatment," I say stoically, continuing to type at my desk, "I have work to catch up on- no thanks to you."

She flinches, and I wish I could take it back- but I don't. It's safer to keep her at a distance, and I'm not entirely lying- I really do have work to catch up on. Luckily, Spelinski loves me enough to send over what I missed; not that I don't already know the stuff, but revision never hurt.

"Naya?" Tabi's curious voice filters in from under the door and my heart splinters a little more.

Seeing dad worried probably had him fretting all day too. Seriously, is there any way in which I haven't messed up today?

Before I can answer him, I hear Hydra's footsteps approaching from the stairwell.

"Not today Tabi-wabby," She coos in a voice too young for him, "Naya has been awful naughty today, so she's taking some time to think about what she's done. Why don't you come downstairs with me, *hmm*?"

There's a pause, where I can envision him glaring at her- rejecting her. I don't want him to make it harder for himself, but I'm glad he can see through her pretence.

"*I'm* the only one who gets to call her Naya." I hear him grumble, but then follows her down anyway; away from me.

Probably for the best.

Aletheia's eyes track from the door to me and back again before realisation comes dawning in on her face. I can only hope she doesn't fully understand.

"Break time me-thinks."

She announces suddenly, swinging her legs over her head till she's backwards-rolled off the bed and into an upright position; stretching skyward. It's only then that I notice the feinter line in the material and the dark line that mars the flesh underneath.

I'm up and out of my chair in an instant.

"Wow, didn't actually think you would- Woah!"

She says in surprise as my hand comes into contact with the wound, covered loosely by her dress.

"When did this happen?" I ask, my voice tight.

I hadn't noticed.

This isn't fresh- this is days old if not longer, and I've been so wrapped up in myself that I haven't even seen it. She bats my hand away lightly.

"I fell on a piece of your mortal pathways." I say, not wanting to divulge that I'm still being hunted by the Fates just yet.

"Tis nothing to concern yourself with- anyway!"

She gestures to my stomach.

"Gimme."

It's a demand, not a request.

"Uhh..." I say uncertainly, just as my skin ripples and I feel the tiny being on my body shift- having completely forgotten about him up until this point.

How did I forget about a *kitsune*?! My life is getting way too full if I can just casually forget about a magical kitsune-tattoo on my own body.

"Kuro."

Aletheia commands more harshly, flicking me in the stomach where he hides.

"Hey!"

"He must do as he's told."

She sniffs, crossing her arms and tapping her foot.

I feel him scurry down my leg, winding around them and sending chills from head to toe. He pauses on my wound at the base of my foot, and for a second it burns- white hot and electric to the point where I have to hiss through my teeth to stop from stomping him.

"What's he doing?! Is he...?"

She asks suddenly, grabbing me by the shoulders and trying to get my attention.

I shake my head vigorously as the pain subsides, ignoring what she could possibly mean, watching as glowing yellow and amber flecks flow from my skin and reform into the knee-high kitsune at Aletheia's feet.

He yips excitedly, running to me and shifting quickly in his little figure of eight between my legs; bumping into me harsh enough that I nearly buckle.

"Good boy."

Aletheia purrs, crouching and holding out her hand so he runs into it; nuzzling his snout into her palm affectionately.

His fur seems to flow on an imaginary breeze, flecks of orange and yellow still occasionally dancing from his fur into the open air; before returning to him.

"I suppose I don't need to introduce you two then."

She says, more to him than to me.

I decide to take a seat on the floor, moving the heat-square from my chair to the wooden slats and watching as it blinks a couple times before settling. Kuro leaps over to it, enthusiastically pawing at where he last saw it blink.

"That's a heat-square," I say to him, stroking his soft fur behind his ears as he continues to scratch at it, "Makes five feet of surrounding space a warmer temperature- so please stop killing it!"

I say the last bit a tad harsher, gripping his scruff and pulling him back a little.

His amber eyes meet mine then, darkening, and his whole body stills- even the flecks in the air pause as I take hold of him.

The tension is gripping, and I feel like I can't move or even look away as he stares into my soul.

"Kuro- calm."

Aletheia says sternly, breaking the spell and turning him back into the playful boy I'd become accustomed to.

But for a moment there...

For just a second, we felt connected. Like he'd been exploring more than just my skin over the past few days. I take a quick glance at my foot to check the blood hasn't seeped through the sock.

Odd, it seems clean.

Too clean.

I peel it back and have to stop myself from gasping, else Aletheia ask questions.

He's healed me. The gaping hole in my foot that had been crusting over, is now no more than a tiny white scar along the pad of my foot.

I try to see him out the corner of my eye, and he seems to almost smirk.

I shiver, maybe I should have kept a closer eye on the non-tattoo kitsune roaming free on my skin.

"How did you meet him?" I ask, as Kuro takes to lying down between us, Aletheia taking a seat opposite me and raking her fingers across his fur.

She pauses, Kuro doing the same as he looks up at her. For a fox, he's so expressive- anthropomorphic even, in his movements and level of understanding.

Kuro's eyes are trained on mine, and I can feel him urging me to tell her- to explain fully.

But it feels too soon.

Maybe one day. Maybe when I'm no longer condemned to a bubble dimension, and I can take her with me through the galaxies. Maybe then she can bear witness to the weird and wonderful depths of what he is.

Who he is.

But for now, the initial meeting couldn't hurt... if phrased a certain way.

She deliberates, biting her lip, before shrugging.

"There's not a whole lot to say."

She says, lying down so that she's eye-level with Kuro.

I follow suit, both of us taking it in turns to smooth down his coat.

"I'd been in Selheim a while, barely touching teenage years. The borders seemed to shrink with every passing day. The outcasts and the damned- that's who I shared my first drinks with."

I raise my eyes from the specks of gold I'd been brushing from Kuro's back.

"You were drinking as a *teenager*?" I ask, astonished. The idea of going out for drinks even nowadays only serves to scare me. I'm not as free as others my age- and have more to lose if I'm not back within curfew.

Hydra would never allow it.

Aletheia smirks, flicking away my disdain.

"When you've learnt all that you need to at the age of eight, from

mental transference from the Gods, there's little point in abstinence."

She rolls onto her back, tucking one arm under her head and closing her eyes. I can't help but take the opportunity to look at her. Her skin is flawless, without blemish or tarnish, save the stardust on her cheeks. Her ears point out of her silvery locks, and I catch myself wondering what they'd feel like.

I have to stop myself from reaching out to try.

I wouldn't be able to find out either way. The barrier that separates us won't even allow for heat transfer, let alone texture.

My eyes roam to her face and linger longer on her lips than they should.

I wonder what they feel like...

"Anyways,"

She says, snapping me from my self-destructive imagination,

"I had been served enough that my daily dose of daydreaming had been quenched. Alas, me being the gregarious fool that I am, I followed the other delinquents downtown."

I say, remembering how mother had always banned that; that side of town and the folk in general.

She hated the groups that she so often found lurking around the gates of Cisdle Bay; the only place worth drinking at. Said they were raucous halflings with nothing better to live for.

Funny, for some reason she thought I was different.

Couldn't see I was sewn from the same cloth, born from the same miscalculations, and raised with the same level of love those unlucky 'halflings' were dealt.

"They were headed to Ail Gyfle, like what you mortals know as a 'tattooist'. But this one was more of an... adoption clinic." I continue, "See, most of them were after weapons- allies and demons. Caught or bought

by the host to be transferred onto the individual's flesh for their own tormented devices. Me?"

She glances at me from the corner of her eyes, her lashes swooping up to touch her brows.

"I just wanted a friend."

For a second I can visualise her childhood. Grasp the level of loneliness from her eyes and feel it as deep as mine goes. Aletheia had all the freedom of her planet with no one looking over her shoulder- she had a world to explore, but no one to do it with.

Me? I had the freedom of my own mind. My home is no sanctuary and I'm watched everywhere I go. But I have friends. I have people. I have a little brother who I've adored for seven blessed years.

She had no one.

"Ail Gyfle had many to choose from." I continue, as she watches me, unblinking, "A collection in cages, with enchantments powerful enough to capture the most vicious of villains. I stumbled my way down cage after cage, isle after isle, of demonic figures and bloodthirsty familiars. Until I came to the very- last- one." I smile at the memory, and Kuro raises his snout, sensing it.

He leans into my palm, and I have to fight the emotions coming over me from the memory.

"He was so tiny," I murmur, her eyes fixated on my every word, "Curled in the corner with his head buried in his tails. I had no interest really in bonding myself to another for eternity. But when I leant my sorrowful head against the bars of his cage, and he crawled over and met mine in the same movement- I just knew. He was a pariah no different to myself, a solitary resistance against the rest of the universe. In a way, I think he was always mine."

Kuro yips, his tongue lolling out and his mouth spread wide in a grin. I see her smile in awe, like I had that day, his tails flicking sparks of brilliant fire into the air in his excitement.

I chuckle, shoving him over so he falls into her side. He blanches for a moment before smirking at me and nuzzling into her, her arms coming around to pull him closer.

Dirty fox, that's my darling you're canoodling.

"The procedure hurt enough that I was sober walking home, but I've never felt a connection quite like it. That is..." I trail off, searching out her thoughts in the space I've left between us.

My heart ricochets in my chest, enough that Kuro looks up at me, his head tilted in concern.

What am I doing?

Lying in the middle of my room with a demi-demon-goddess and her pet Kitsune as she explains their meet-cute. Am I really going *that* insane?

But as I try to breathe through the tension that's been cast between us, I realise something-

I... don't care?

I don't care if she's real or not, a hallucination or a fever dream. In this moment, she has gifted me the closest thing to a reprieve- a sanctuary, and a home outside of my own dreams, that I've had the honour of having in the past six years.

"I-" I begin but can't seem to form the rest of the sentence.

It would change everything.

And I... I don't even know what I'd be changing it into. What it's changing *from*.

I shake my head, closing my eyes and breathing a calming sigh through my nose.

"Anyway, that's how I met Kuro." I say softly.

She needs more time.

I've let her down.

Another person I've let down.

I close my eyes and press my face into Kuro's fur, pushing as deep into his neck as possible in an attempt to distract myself from the guilt.

It's odd that I can interact with him but not her. Like the universe itself knows I'm not ready, or worthy.

Both?

"I best get ready for bed." I say, collecting Kuro into my arms, with every intention of bringing him with me.

"I wouldn't bring him with you to shower, darling,"

Aletheia says suddenly, her arms outstretched to take him from me,

"He's quite pervy at the best of times. And if I don't get to watch- he most certainly doesn't."

She says wickedly, and I can tell she's relishing my reaction.

She's adorable

I glance down at Kuro, his limbs hanging limp in my arms. He gives me a not-so-innocent head-tilt, and that's enough to have me placing him back down. I don't put him in her arms, I can't even look her in the eyes.

If I do I think I might just implode, my heart a ticking time bomb.

"I- yes, okay. I'll- I'll be back in a bit." I say hurriedly, grabbing my towel off of the radiator and rushing from the room to the sound of her giggling; for my second shower of the evening.

It's okay, my darling. We have time.

CHAPTER 20
FLY FOR RYLAN

Time flies differently with Aletheia in the house. For the most part, I can get on with my day as normal. So normal that it's easy to forget she's just upstairs or around the corner. She's either lounging, investigating rooms, or leaning over Tabi to assess the intricacies of human studies.

It's a Wednesday, and for the first time in a while- I have nothing to do. I try not to make a sound as I pass by dad's study.

"Poppet?" Dad calls, just as I think I'm clear.

I scurry back to the doorway, leaning into the room with my hair falling forwards. He's been back to normal after a week's rest, forgetting of my near-death escapade. But I can tell it rocked him, aged him. But then again, I always think he's looking older than he is. Time wears away at people when you're not watching, and I get to see him less and less as the days go by.

"Yeah, Dad?"

He's busy at his desk, piles of pages stacked high with to-do's and to-don't's. Dad is a businessman, whatever that means- I'd never deemed it interesting enough to ask about to any length of detail. But there were the occasional interesting projects. Investments that sought to look into magical arts, or the invention of new materials to make the mortal race an easier existence; the ones that went above and beyond the general hubbub of meaningless jobs for bills and pay-checks.

"Would you be an angel and pour me a cup of tea?" He asks, looking up over his spectacles at me with squinted eyes.

I nod, but something gives me pause. He senses it too, as he removes his glasses and leans back in his chair.

"What is it, poppet?"

I scuff my feet, twisting my hands together and steeling myself. I never ask questions, never take his time- but today? After what happened?

"How did you and mum meet?" I ask timidly, my heart in my mouth.

His eyebrows raise higher, a film of sadness clouding his dull greying-eyes. I know he must try not to think of her, as I do- but the other day surely left some stuff at the surface.

"We... well, we met in a café." He stammers, leaning further back precariously on the half-broken chair as he recalls.

I step more into the room, resting against the door and not looking at him directly so that he carries on.

"She was a regular at my favourite spot in the city." He says with a nostalgic nod, "I had barely time to sit during the day, busy man that I was. But since spotting her, I couldn't help but keep carving out the time to try and see her." He smiles, and I don't think I've seen that smile in the better part of a decade.

"She had just started at the school a couple blocks away; a primary school teacher. Always there on her break for a mid-afternoon cuppa." He looks at me then, catching my eye. "It wasn't till five years later that she admitted she had to run there and back for it. Just to see me."

I smile fondly, rubbing my arm and nodding.

It's something mum would do. I can almost picture her, calmly getting up from her seat and quietly exiting the café, before sprinting like a woman-possessed back to her job; papers flying and hair askew. She loved dad to the moon and back- of course she'd run a couple blocks a day for him.

"So, you asked her out?"

"Not on your life." He laughs, shaking his head, "No, your mother got what she wanted when *she* wanted it- and in her own time. It was maybe a month after I first saw her that she bumped her hip against mine- spilling my coffee in the process- and demanded my number." Dad folds his arms, shaking his head, "Best cup of coffee I ever bought."

"She knew what she wanted and got it." I smile, nudging my hand against the door.

"She always did," He mutters, looking me up and down, "You do too you know."

I stop my hand from swinging.

"You look more and more like her every day, poppet." He says, his eyes glassy.

I don't know what to say, choosing to look away, hiding my face. Maybe it's because I look so much like her that he doesn't pay me any attention. Maybe it's too hard for him.

If he did, he'd notice the bruising, the swelling- maybe even hear the horrors occurring.

All he sees is his little girl, not so little anymore.

"I should be so lucky," I say, shrugging off the feeling, "I'll grab you that tea... thanks, Dad."

I slip from the door without looking back, his eyes sad as I abruptly leave the room towards the empty kitchen.

I'm so glad it's empty.

"You could also help me take a look at this new investment- think it'll be right up your alley." He yells after me.

I wish he wouldn't yell.

She's taking a midday nap, but yelling can- and will- rouse her and ruin my day if she wakes up before she's ready. Because it will be my fault.

It always is.

But I want to spend time with dad, however brief.

I grab the kettle off the side and start filling it up with water, the sound serving to drown out the paranoia rising in me.

"What's that?" Aletheia asks, startling me as she leaps up onto the counter to watch me.

She leans in, her hair pulling back of its own accord so she can stare down the spout of the kettle with one eye. I gently push her head out of dangers way.

"You'd think, what with mental transference from the Gods and all, that you'd know what a kettle is." I say, smirking at her as she folds her arms indignantly.

"Mortal objects didn't really feature in the handbook." She mutters, casting her eyes back to it curiously, *"Although I'm certainly wishing it had done. Your world is bizarre."*

She's so different. Refreshingly so, from everyone else I've ever met.

I grab two mugs from the cupboard, pausing for a moment before reaching for a third, and placing them down on the counter in front of her. She stares at them, somewhat unsettled as I throw in the teabags and reach for the sugar.

"How many sugars?" I ask, Aletheia's hand already in and out of a mug, examining the teabag.

"You're suggesting I consume leaf-juice held within precarious packaging...for pleasure?" She recoils, waggling the packet.

I snatch it from her, whacking her with it before shoving it back in the mug.

"Yes, now do you want your '*leaf-juice*' sweet, or not?"

She pauses, scrutinising me and the bags until the kettle clicks to a boil and steam rises into her hair.

"*Sweet.*" She says, still skeptical.

Dad always takes his without sugar, but I can't resist a spoonful in mine as I lather the stuff over Aletheia's. She strikes me as a sweet-tooth.

Pouring the water in, I grab the milk from the fridge, not waiting for her remark as I finish making them. I want to get back to dad, he never has time for me nowadays and I don't want to miss the opportunity.

"Enjoy the *'leaf juice'*." I say hurriedly, grabbing up the other two and heading back to the office.

I stare down at the strange liquid, the depths of which continue to spout vapour up into my face from where it sits between my legs. I understand it's her father, she should dote on him when asked of course.

But the jealousy- not from lacking her attention, but from never having the same affection from my own father- it cuts deep. Not once in the past fifteen years after the incident has he ever called upon me.

Not once.

I know I should also spend time with her, or even invite her along- but... it's dad.

I don't even get the chance to knock.

"Oh sweetie, is that for me? You shouldn't have!" Hydra drolls, stepping in the way of the door and taking the mugs from me before I can even decide to protest.

She's still wrapped up in a dressing gown, and from the looks of things- a little out of breath. Surely she didn't run down from their bedroom just to intercept me?

"Your father and I are a bit busy right now- why don't you go help your brother with some homework, hmm?" She says, closing the door on me without waiting for a reply.

I'm too stunned to move.

He could say something, he could say he wants to show me the investment or that I can stay and talk too...

The door remains closed.

I take a deep breath, clenching and unclenching my fists before turning back to the kitchen. It's not as if it's unexpected. Maybe it's Aletheia being here, making me believe I can hope for better.

What a cruel thing it is, to wish for what you know has never been, and never will be.

Aletheia hasn't moved from the counter, the tea still sat between her legs that dangle over the side. She looks up at me slowly as I enter, and I don't doubt she heard what happened. I'm sure she's sussed out the dynamic of the household by now.

There's a beat of silence, and then-

"You can share my leaf-juice, if you like?" she offers quietly.

I go for a smile, but it doesn't quite reach my eyes as I walk over to her. I take up the mug in hand, placing it to the side; not hesitating before wrapping my arms around her middle and pulling her in. Her arms go around my shoulders and I feel the weight of her chin on top of my head. It's not exactly a hug, I can't feel what one usually can.

But it's enough for now.

"Thanks." I say into her shoulder, trying not to hold on to the feeling of rejection left behind by the closed office door.

I don't know how to offer her words of kindness. I know her father's type, I know the blond demon's type too. Neither of them are redeemable in their actions, at least not in my eyes.

But I must tread lightly with her- she still believes he can be saved.

"My father has never acquired a new wife," Aletheia says, her jaw bumping up and down atop my head, *"He's had many lady-callers since my mother though. Hasn't made him any more attentive to me. So, I can empathise with having an apathetic and somewhat discourteous father-figure."*

"Mine's not that." I snap, the words barely having left her lips, "My dad's kind, caring, devoted and..." I trail off, not even knowing if I mean what I'm saying.

He's...

A shell of a man since your mother passed, I think but don't say.

I know that she understands what kind of man he has become. He is blind to the abuse of his children and crippled by the depressive nature that so often accompanies great loss.

He stopped being her father a long time ago.

She's been bringing herself up since the age of fourteen, cohabiting with a man she barely knows.

I'd be comparatively vexed under the surface too.

"He's only human." I say instead, a mundane critique for a mundane man.

I can tell she's biting her tongue, and for that I'm grateful. I don't even know where I'd begin in trying to defend him.

"Naya?" Tabi's voice trails in from behind me.

I quickly slam my hands down on the counter, hoping he didn't see what must've looked like me hugging onto thin air. I forgot his school called a strike this week, unused to having him around the house so much.

"Yeah, Tabi-cat?" I reply, turning around and Aletheia's hands now coming to rest on my shoulders, her legs circling my hips, stealing half my focus.

I've come to know quite a bit about the boy Tabi. He is pure of heart, with certain tapped-into magical abilities. An artist, with a curious tenacity.

He's not good at maths though.

Tabi holds out the phone to me, "It's for you."

People never call the house line, but I've gotten into the unfortunate habit of leaving my phone in my room. I know this isn't going to be a casual call though. No one calls me, unless it's an emergency.

Unless it's Rylan.

I take it from him, "Thanks, all okay in there?" I ask Tabi, the phone to my chest as I indicate the living room where he's supposed to be working.

He shrugs.

"Maths is hard." He says defeatedly, before scuffing his feet and shuffling back out the kitchen.

I shake my head at his receding form.

I shall teach him the fundamentals of the universe, transfer my all-calculating knowledge of mathematics into his tiny human head- then he won't be burdened by this 'homework' anymore.

I nod to myself as he slips from view, and my darling brings the portable communicator to her ear.

"Hello?" I say into the phone once Tabi is out of range.

"Ten- heyyy Ten, ol' buddy ol' pal." Rylan's strained voice crackles over the line.

Something's happened.

"Where are you?" I ask, shrugging off Aletheia and grabbing my coat off the bannister, knowing he'll need me to be there.

"That's- no Ten, well... ugh." He groans, arguing with his moral compass.

"Coordinates- now." I say, flicking open the cupboard under the sink and grabbing out the first-aid kit.

I'll have to replace whatever I take whilst I'm out, but better to arrive there prepared.

There's silence, a sigh, and then a submission.

"The park, up the hill- bench nearest the swings." He says, and as an afterthought, "Thanks."

"On my way." I reply, clicking off the phone and turning to Aletheia, her eyes narrowing.

She wants something, but she's unwilling to ask for it.

Oh, my darling, why must you make me flounder over such trivialities.

"Whatever you want- yes." I say, leaping off the counter.

Her eyes track me to the door, before following me out and grabbing her shoes along with the green box under her arm.

It's only when we've made it out the front door that she turns to me, her head lowered as she cringes.

"Can uhh, look- I wouldn't ask unless I really needed to hurry- but..." I say, hoping she'll take the bait.

Please just let her understand that I want her to fly us there.

She's going to have to ask, she's able to and she shall.

"Yes?" I poke, folding my arms and waiting.

Her face screws up adorably, and I'm almost tempted to let her off the hook, until she sighs theatrically.

"Fine. Aletheia, can you please fly us to the park swings? I can direct *y*-" I begin, but she already has her arms under mine and her legs jump up to wrap my waist like a demon-backpack.

"I actually know where that is." She says, before shooting up into the air.

I clasp the first aid kit firmly against me as we spiral upwards above the clouds and out of view of the neighbourhood.

It feels like moments, seconds even, before she dives us back down. Spinning us in a corkscrew fashion until her wings fan out, hovering us a metre above the ground of the playground and dropping me there.

There're a couple of children in the playground, only one that noticed us though. His eyes are as big as saucers, looking between me and his mum, who's thankfully preoccupied with her phone.

It's the leaping boy-child from the other week. A couple scrapes fewer, and his confidence thankfully restored.

See- the jump was worth it.

I place a finger to my lips before hurrying away, not looking back as I hear the boy calling anxiously for his mother.

"A little more subtlety would've been nice." I mutter as I spot Rylan bent forwards on his knees, like a drunk on the bench.

"And a 'thankyou' would suffice." Aletheia retorts, smirking at me as we pace it to where he slumps.

His head lifts groggily upwards at the sound of my approach, reflective sunglasses obscuring his eyes from view.

But they can't hide the swollen lip, the cut from which is still stained with dried blood. Nor can they distract from his mangled right hand, the knuckles crusted over and the bruising already flaring up. His other hand lifts momentarily from cradling his ribs, saluting me hello with as much of a smile as his battered mouth will allow for.

"I know what you're thinking," He says sarcastically as we approach, "Sight for sore eyes doesn't seem to cut it. No rush, take it all in, I'm in no hurry." He laughs but then wheezes, his face scrunching up.

"On second thought though- maybe a little rush. I'm hoping you have the bloody powerful stuff in that sexy green box."

I try not to let it phase me. Really it shouldn't. We've both been in this situation enough times now that I should be used to it.

But knowing he goes through this almost as much as I do, and that Amaya doesn't know-

Aletheia's face says it all. The concern bleeds into anger across her features as she takes in the devastation that is Rylan's broken form.

She can't possibly condone this. How can she bi-stand to such brutality-

I look at her then, her eyes full of understanding and an empathy I can't touch on as she takes in the state of her broken friend.

She allows it because she lives it.

"Three hundred and-" I begin to say.

"Don't." He snaps, wincing at the harshness of his voice. "Sorry, just- not today. I can't count down today." He says, wringing the back of his neck and closing his eyes.

It's too long.

The unspoken words hang like dead-weight between us.

I nod, opening the first aid kit and squatting by his side, Aletheia moving to the other.

"You know," I say instead, "When one is mortally injured and looking like the neighbourhood drunkard on a Wednesday afternoon, the children's play-park probably isn't the go-to."

Rylan smirks, morphing into another grimace from the splitting of his lip.

"That's where you're wrong- you see, kids aren't going to judge you too harshly, and the parents generally stay away out of fear- so actually it's probably the safest place in town."

I give him a look that speaks the volumes of idiocy he's spouting.

"Tell that to the authorities." I grumble as I open the box.

Rylan gestures around before slinging his good arm behind his head as nonchalantly as possible whilst in extreme pain.

"So long as they feed and fix me in the cell, I'm happy to serve my time."

His hand appears broken, the knuckle-bone severed at the junction. If I can heal my darling, and inanimate objects, it serves to reason that I should have the capacity to heal others in this realm too.

Before she can stop me, I reach out, placing my hand over his and pressing on the barrier.

Her eyes go wide, but she doesn't stop me, only tracking my hair as it flies up around me, my magic flowing through me and glowing furiously across his broken hand without his knowledge.

"What was it this time?" I ask, trying my best not to focus on Aletheia and set myself to work putting Danderayan healing cream on the bruising around his ribs.

All the remedies in the box come from Mum's old creations and potions books. All of them, in my opinion, far better than any local pharmacy or corporate product.

Rylan hisses a breath in through his teeth as the mixture winds its way below the surface of his skin, bubbling slightly. I know from experience- the process isn't easy, but worth it in the end.

"It was bad as soon as I got up," He grimaces, closing his eyes and removing his glasses, the extensive purpling surrounding his right eye and bridge of his nose now in full-view, "Mum'd gone to the shops, don't know where and don't care. But Lily was left on her own. She's only five, funnily enough- no one thought to teach her the difference between glitter and cocaine when engaging in arts and crafts."

I close my eyes against the imagery. Lily was younger and far more naïve to the ways of her parents than Tabi is. Meaning she's that much more important to protect from it. At least Tabi can sometimes pick up on tone, Lily doesn't even know there are reasons to fear her parents yet.

"He didn't-"

"He tried to." He snaps harshly, massaging his temples, "He was drunk of course. Saw her shoving his stash all over some glue-and-glitter masterpiece she was working on and lost it. Bastard couldn't think of a better place to hide the crap than under the kitchen sink with the pipe-cleaners. He-" Rylan presses his lips together and takes a steadying breath.

I place a hand on his knee, still watching Aletheia out of the corner of my eye as the glow around his hand intensifies.

"If I hadn't been there," He grits out, "She would've been hospitalised. Man saw red and went for it. If I hadn't heard the yell- if I hadn't been in the other room- Ten, he would've-"

"But you *were*," I say consolingly as Rylan fights against the mist clouding over his eyes, "You protected her. She is safe because of *you*."

He barks out a sharp, humourless laugh, his eyes meeting mine in a moment of resignation.

He gestures to the playground with the hand Aletheia had been holding; the luminescence dimmed and her hair returned to its usual state of semi-sentience. I turn, following the direction to see Lily, one of the children scurrying round on the jungle-gym.

"She is in danger every *Gods*-damned day- because of *me*." He grinds out, looking away in shame.

She's so little. Barely entering pre-school and blissfully ignorant to the hardships of the world. Golden ringlets to match her halo.

I can't tell him he's wrong. It's the same reason Tabi's in danger. But we both know that for now, this is the lesser of two evils.

For now.

"So, she didn't see...?" I ask, Rylan already shaking his head.

"I shoved him over to buy me the time to run her to the stairs. Somehow she knew that meant it was time to make herself scarce." He mutters, "Mum found me a couple hours ago. To her credit, she bought frozen peas." He laughs bitterly, "Almost as if she *knew* what she was leaving me to deal with."

He looks at his hand then, his- still-bruised, but definitely not broken anymore- hand.

"See," He says slowly, turning over his palm and flexing his fingers, "I thought it was the concussion that had me seeing you fall in from out the sky- but *this*?" He says, looking at me then, serious and unwavering. "I've got to at least ask. We don't do secrets- not us. So, I'll ask you this once, Ten- what's going on?"

The question is so loaded.

Where do I begin?

Do I begin?

I look to Aletheia, her eyes not meeting mine as she crouches by his leg, unmoving. Does she want me to tell him about her?

Rylan follows my gaze to his other side, confused.

I guess... if I'm going to tell anyone...

"I- well..."

I think I'm going crazy

I've been living with a demi-demon-goddess

The girl from the realm followed me home

I interact with a girl no one else can see- a girl who healed your hand

"I'm not going to tell anyone," He says, leaning forward even as the healing lotion froths viciously against his skin, fighting for a smile, "Come on, Ten. Gimme some good news. Or at the very least- a distraction."

I take a deep breath. This was not how this meet-up was supposed to go. I was meant to help him, catch up briefly and leave.

This may be getting too close, even for him. But still...

"I can see someone that no one else can." I say before I can stop myself.

Rylan doesn't react, not at all. And from that, I know he's holding back.

I can't blame him.

"Since the séance," I continue, my heart hammering, "I have been able to see a girl, Aletheia. She is a goddess and a demon and I brought her back from the Fate's realm- the white and black void. She can't interact with people, not on any level- other than healing I guess." I point to his knuckles, "She healed your hand."

I don't move.

Rylan leans slowly back, hands reaching behind his head as he gazes skyward.

"You... told him?" I say in utter bewilderment.

I crawl over to her, wrapping my arms around her neck, clinging to her.

She's accepting me, showing me to her friends.

Her arms hesitate before coming around me as well.

"Woahhh-" Rylan exclaims, lifting off his sunglasses again and pointing at me, "Is that her there? Is she hugging... Oh My *Gods* is that why I *floated*?!"

He starts babbling and I feel as though I can breathe again.

He didn't call me crazy- I'm not crazy.

She's *real*.

"Yeah, we're still working out the technicalities." I say, giving her a squeeze before taking her arms from my shoulders, "Seems as though people can feel the barrier around her- but she can't enforce that on others?" We both shrug, "It's a glitch in the system."

Rylan scoffs, rising up on the bench.

"Trust you to keep your first girlfriend to yourself, selfish witch." He remarks, and I try my best not to let it show; the level of panic that just went through me at the label.

I felt it.

"Can she do something?" He asks, "Like- I believe you, clearly- but it'd be cool if I could communicate with her. She's gotta be getting pretty bored with just your nerdy ass for company."

"Never."

Aletheia says defiantly, gripping me tighter to her before I even have the chance to worry over it.

She is always so sure, of herself and of her feelings.

And me? I don't even know how to look after myself, let alone be there for a whole other person- much less an interdimensional being with powers even the Fates are fearful of.

"I'm not sure," I say, touching Aletheia's shoulder, "You don't have to do anything if you don't want to."

I smirk at her, my always ever-so-careful darling, worried about my wants and needs.

"I suppose I could briefly entertain the half-wit." I sigh, earning me a chuckle.

"What did she say- what did she sayyy!" Rylan whines, pushing on my shoulder as he bounces up and down like a child.

"She called you a half-wit," I groan, pushing him off, "And that she'll give communication a go."

He rubs his hands together excitedly before remembering the still-fresh pain, switching to bouncing his leg up and down gleefully.

"Not even mean names can spoil my fun." He grins, looking around in anticipation for whatever Aletheia chooses to do.

She rises, stretching and cracking her back and knuckles theatrically.

"Show time." I muse, revelling in the attention she's giving me.

But what to do, what to do...

Whatever it is I'm sure to achieve his esteemed adulation- I am an invisible girl after all, presumed to be his accomplice's girlfriend.

Mortals are so easily entertained.

The girl he named his kin scuffs her feet in the dirt, clearly growing tired of running around the same twenty-metres horizontally or vertically as the plastic play-thing allows.

This show will also be for my darling.

I summon Scythe from my ribs, gripping the hilt and hoisting it from my side with a flourish.

"Aletheia... what are you-" *She begins, but I thrust the end of scythe in her direction, the tip coming within inches of her face.*

"Trust me, my darling." I say, grinning at her before rushing off towards the gated-off area, Scythe a-swinging.

"Where is she- where is *sheee*!" Rylan shoves my shoulder repeatedly, his eyes dancing every-which-way.

I'm going to regret telling him.

"Umm, she..."

How do I tell him she's currently stalking towards his baby-sister with a scythe?

She stabs it into the ground by the blade a metre or so in front of Lily and I do my best not to flinch.

"There." I point, and he follows my finger to the indent in the dirt.

The child Lily stares at the point my blade made, curiosity getting the better of her as she crouches to inspect it further.

You're lucky you're in a realm where such idle curiosities won't get you killed- I wouldn't advise realm-hopping to this one. The creatures of the deep universe would feast upon her innocence in a heartbeat.

She reaches out to touch what must be just a small hole in the dirt to her, tiny fingers splayed. I pull back on scythe, dragging the dirt with me so there's now a fine line in place of a dot.

She hesitates, her eyes widening as she tracks the movement.

Come on child, think about it.

Her tiny features break into a grin and she launches for it, just as I'd hoped. Time for a quick game of 'catch me if you can'.

I leap backwards, keeping my scythe firmly in the dirt as I run, pacing it in intricate swirls and zig-zags as she pelts after me on stubby legs; giggling hindering her breathing.

One must learn, in battle, breathe first- laugh later.

She keeps coming though.

"She... she really..." Rylan fumbles.

"Yeppers peppers." I say with a smile, as he stumbles over what to say.

I move up onto the bench, folding one leg over the other and breathing a sigh of relief.

It feels good, to be assuredly not insane.

But that also means accepting her as real, fully real. A part of my life and a real person, with emotions and feelings and however those interact with me.

I can't help but smile though, as I see Aletheia's play turn into something effortful, her movements becoming purposeful as she tries harder to evade Lily. She's quick for a five-year-old, but still young enough to run after a suddenly-appearing-line without much thought as to why she's doing it, or how it appeared.

Aletheia ducks and weaves, her body arching gracefully, slicing through the playground and dodging other children who haven't even noticed that a makeshift track is being formed before them.

She will never cease to amaze me.

I swing under ropes and catapult over tunnels, keeping my scythe in the ground and creating a route for the child to meander through. She squeals as she closes in, her determination admirable.

If I could let her catch me, I would.

Instead, I make it back to my starting mark, connecting them end to end before shooting up into the air and bringing scythe back into my ribs with a flourish.

My darling waits patiently on the bench, her friend stunned speechless at my performance; his mouth practically unhinged as he gawps.

Like I'd previously ascertained- easily impressed.

The girl-Lily stomps on the spot where I started, clearly not yet tired of spiralling through the tiny arena with her air of wild abandonment. For a girl of the circumstance I've come to hear of, she still manages to hold onto her childhood.

Perhaps the brother - Rylan - is to thank for that, more than he realises.

Lily starts up the hill at the same time Aletheia makes a dive-bomb for me, her wings halting her just before she gets to me; having them recede before plopping down into my lap.

She looks up at me with eyes that seek approval.

"Yes, that was very good- if slightly unnerving to watch." I say, still trying to shake off the weirdness of watching a girl whizz round a playground with a bladed weapon.

Feels like something I shouldn't be praising.

Aletheia's eyes light up and she smiles, wrapping her arms around me tighter. My cheeks burn as her dress droops lower and her chest presses firmly into my neck.

"Twas nothing," She says, bringing me back to the present, *"The child has a zealous soul, she will grow up to be strong, regardless of circumstance."*

"This- this is- I don't even know." Rylan stammers, shaking his head and watching my movements that work around Aletheia, unprepared for Lily coming-up and colliding with his legs; his knees buckling on impact.

"*Ry*- Rylie did you *see*?! Did you see me?" Lily bounds up at him, grabbing at his shirt and sides.

His face creases briefly in pain, held back with a not-so-convincing smile.

"I did, I did- you were so *fast*! How'd you get so fast Lilypad?" He enthuses, mussing at her hair so that she bats him off.

"It was the fairies- Rylie they were *here*!" she says defiantly, pointing back to where the lines still mar the dirt.

Aletheia chuckles, squeezing me.

"Never been called a fairy before," She murmurs quietly, almost seductively, as if they could hear her, *"Suppose I do have the wings for it."*

"Not to mention the magic." I mutter back under my breath, Rylan being the only one to catch it.

He crouches down by Lily, holding her head and pretending to inspect her mouth.

"Well, I don't see any missing teeth." He muses, "So that rules out one option. Do you know any others?"

Her eyes light up in excitement.

"I have a 'fairies of the forest' book back home! Maybe she's in that? Please please *please*?" Lily begs, yanking on his trouser-leg.

Rylan's face flinches for a second, and I know what he's thinking. Right now, home isn't a safe place- that it rarely ever is.

"How about we go into town and find a *new* fairy book for you to have a look through? I'll even get it for you to keep?"

I didn't think her eyes could get any bigger.

"For *keeps*?!" She squeals eagerly.

Rylan smiles, "For keeps," He points to the playground, "Go grab your stuff and I'll meet you by the gate."

Lily giggles ecstatically as she races from his side and back down to the jungle-gym, arms flailing.

He watches her, his eyes tracking her path until she's on more solid ground.

"I don't even know where to begin." He says, shaking his head and grabbing up his bag from the side of the bench.

"You and me both." I grumble, shuffling Aletheia off my lap and onto the bench.

He picks up the healing potion, hesitating and raising it to me.

"Are you trying to make her visible?" He asks, shaking the bottle at me and I wave him off to suggest he can take it.

I hadn't really thought to...

"There's nothing you can do," I say before she can think too much on it, "I'm working out a way in my own time, you needn't concern yourself with it."

I can't have her questioning why I'm trapped or how to un-trap me. Then I'd have to explain about the Fates, about Liedha, about mother and father and how I'm bound to my darling due to her untapped prophetic potential.

A prophecy my mother refuses to divulge to me, a knowledge of a power apparently great enough to combat the will of the Fates.

She already has so much to worry about, let alone delving into her untapped powers.

I consider her for a second before responding.

"She says she's onto it." I say, not quite sure of it even as I say it.

Is she... *hiding* something?

I know the panicked look of someone holding back. Every time I see Rylan, every time I glance in the mirror. The look that is as plain as day across her face.

Rylan sighs, stealing me from my paranoia.

"Well, what's one more secret I guess." He sighs, waving to Lily to signal he's on his way. "We do need to talk more about this though, when I'm not childminder-or-hospital-bound. Notif me, yeah?"

I nod, closing up the first-aid kit as he salutes me off. "Thanks for the lifesaving, Ten," He says as he meanders down the hill, "I knew you weren't crazy."

I smile, closing my eyes and trying to calm myself enough to head back to the house. I can only pray she hasn't realised I've left.

At least one of us has faith in my sanity.

CHAPTER 21
MUM AND MOTHER DEAREST

Aletheia is becoming more agitated by the day.

When we got back to the house the other night, dad and Hydra were still in his office; probably her tactic of trying to keep me away from him for as long as possible. This one time though, it worked in my favour; incurring no further injury on account of me leaving the house unannounced.

Aletheia's taken to pacing my room in the evenings, I've even caught her doing it when I come back in after showering in the mornings before university.

I know she's ruffled but she won't tell me by what. And what with Maddy's sleep-over being only a couple days away, I really want to find out before then.

She's kicking her feet, swinging them over the side of my bed- the precursor of pacing.

I'm going insane.

She does the same things every day. Never divulging from the path, never even walking a new way home. It's morning then it's university then it's the diner then it's home again.

Repeat.

And I have to follow for every same-day steps, all to avoid capture.

Of course, I want to be with my darling- but I want to show her worlds. I want her to taste new delicacies and experience new textures and dip our fingertips into the waters of the universe without knowing how they'll come out again.

If only I could...

"Do you want to get out of here?" I ask, anything to stop her itinerant footfalls.

My neck nearly snaps at the speed I face her. Did she... did she just read me?

I can tell that's what it is. She's fidgety at the best of times, but this is getting ridiculous.

Maybe... maybe she could show me new places.

"I... want to realm-hop with you." I say, standing up from my desk and walking over to where she gapes at me from my bed.

For a second, I don't think she'll even respond.

For just a moment, I let myself believe I've read this wrong. That she has no interest in taking me anywhere and that I've been wildly presumptuous and demanding by requesting such a thing.

But then she smiles- the greatest thing I think I've ever seen. A smile that feels like I've just made her day- month- year, just by asking.

Aletheia bounds off the bed into the air, my arms flailing wide as the weight of her lands on me. Her legs wrap my middle and her arms slink over and around my neck; slotting into place like they were always meant to land there.

My face is alight.

"Oh, my darling," She purrs, brushing her nose against mine in a way that makes me feel like I'm falling, *"I thought you'd never ask."*

If this is how flustered I get when she's blocked from me by a dimensional force-field, I'm terrified of what I'd be like without it.

She's too much, and I'm... I'm not worthy.

I shake my head, blinking back into focus as she slides from me and takes one of my hands in hers.

"Hold on tight." I say, squeezing her hand in mine, "As tight as the Fates will allow us."

"The *Fates*??" I begin to ask, but she's already raking her hand through the surface of our dimension.

Her nails track the length of a crease that seemingly appeared from nowhere, bleeding down the blue line until she folds her fingernails under it. She looks at me, her grin spanning wide.

"Here we go."

She whips it round us and suddenly we're in the centre of a hurricane, the eye of the storm. The white sheets like the ones from her memory swirl around us; the blue and pink lines dancing across the membrane.

So, *this* is how she travelled all the time. Not the chaotic dimension-condensing version I'd experienced with the Veturcaela. It feels like shifting between the layers of the universe, coasting through the semipermeable sheets of the dimensions and then choosing one to slip into.

And she's at the heart of it.

Her hand glows in mine.

Kuro leaps from my skin in a flurry of fiery fragments, yelping excitedly and bounding around us. He's clearly missed this as much as she has.

They both waited for me.

Aletheia grins and only then opens her eyes.

I gasp, not knowing whether to be in awe or fearful. Her diamond eyes are completely made up of white light; even the iris is indecipherable amidst the glow. She smirks at me, and I let myself breathe out a little as she winks, reaching out to the sheet and ripping it away.

The film folds in on itself like fresh linen, crumpling and falling into nothingness around us and revealing a whole new world.

She pulls on my hand before I can ever register where we've landed, thrusting it onto a vine as the rest of my body tries to float away.

"What the-" I begin but falter, wrapping my legs around the vine I cling to.

We are held weightless in a world of wires.

Green vines of different shades burst skyward in every direction, so plentiful that it's all I can see; a forest of inch-thick plants that sway in the air. Above me, where the world seems to be pulling me, burns a vibrant blue that gives the feeling of being underwater.

It's like we are at the bottom of the ocean, clinging to seaweed to evade the surface; whatever that may herald.

Kuro has the plants between teeth and tails, low growls emanating from between clenched teeth; clearly not so enthused with the choice of realm.

"This is Marineise." I say, watching as she takes it all in, ignoring kuros protests.

This is what I wish to do for the rest of my days, watch her bask in the abstruse nature of the universe.

Tiny metal bodies skim past me, dodging around our bodies.

They appear to be fish-like in their structure, but with their skeletons on the outside. Exoskeletal structures comprised of silvery flesh not unlike metal- glinting in the blue from above. They swarm in groups of tens at least, gliding between vines and swirling up through Kuro's tails. I can practically feel his overwhelming urge to snap at them.

"Let's explore." She says, beckoning me to follow her as she releases one hand to grab another vine and then another; dragging her body along behind her.

I follow, the weightlessness a baffling concept, but nowhere near as weird and wonderful as what I hoped we would see; what I know must be out there.

We don't speak as we pull ourselves through the foreign realm. Occasionally dodging right or left to avoid new creatures. This place seems to have the metal-like-exterior theme, all the creatures being vaguely aquatic-esq in their features; all of them with their insides on the out. They have no fur, no softness. Just harsh, bee-line bodies to dart through the reed-like environment with ease.

What mum would've given to see this.

The thought comes unhindered and I take pause, as do Aletheia and Kuro to wait for me.

I never think of what she would have wanted. I never dwell on the past like that, never so casually. But since the beach and since I told Aletheia so much, mum's snuck to the forefront of my mind more and more.

I wonder...

"Take hold." Aletheia says, snapping me from my thoughts, her hand outstretched.

I push forwards to grip her hand in mine as she rips this world from view, dropping us in the new one with such ease that it doesn't feel real.

This new one though, it feels... different.

"Where... where are we?" I ask softly, afraid to make more than a whisper in such a place.

The world itself is hidden. My feet, which feel as though they're on some squishy marshland, are indistinguishable; my legs disappearing shortly after the edge of my skirt. The world is completely covered in a thick-but-misty layer of fog. Tendrils of the stuff rising around me, even the sky is obscured by it. In and amidst it though are balls of colourful lights.

I know they're alive. I can't quite explain it, but the small floating orbs are *thrumming* with life. Some so full of it they feel fit to burst; others dwindling. All of them suspended in the fog.

"This is Enaidorffwys." Aletheia says, sifting her fingers through the mist and cupping one of the glowing balls into her hands.

It bobs up and down in her palm, burning brighter under her gaze, before lifting up and out again.

I turn to one myself, one that emits a dull blue haze of light. I cup my hands in the way she did, mimicking the scooping action and gently raising the thing to eye level. On inspection it seems to be only made of light, but I can feel there's more to it. The weight that it holds is heavy, even if no one can actually hold it; the barrier between myself and the orb feeling much like that which exists between myself and Aletheia. I'm aware it holds weight, but I can't properly touch it.

I'm getting really bored of barriers.

"Why are we here?" I ask, my hands raising it up so that it floats away and up into the fog; obscuring itself from sight.

"We've come to find your mother."

I think my world and all others fall out from under me.

My heart stops.

It genuinely stops.

"What... what do you mean?" I manage to ask, a lump quickly rising in my throat.

Aletheia smiles softly, brushing her fingertips across another orb and making her way over to me; Kuro close at her feet, only his tails and snout visible through the haze.

"This is the land of Souls, should they choose it." She says, ducking behind me and snaking her arms under mine to cup another orb in front of my chest. *"These floating beings are what's left of people once they leave their realms. Not just mortals of course, and this isn't the only place souls can travel to."* I fight the glassy film that's coming over my eyes.

"But between here and every realm available to those moved on, we will search for her. If she's able to be found- rest assured, we'll find her.

We shall peregrinate to every corner of the cosmos, if that's what it takes."

I feel the pressure of her lips as they graze my cheek. Never have I wanted to break a barrier more.

Does she realise what she's doing?

"But...H-How do I find her?" I ask, my voice choked as I gaze around the large expanse of fog and floating lights.

This can't be real.

It's not like I believed there to be a Heaven or Hell, Underworld or Olympus just lying around the universe. But a place for souls?

But my mum- would she have travelled however far souls are required to, to spend the better half of an eternity in purgatory in the hopes her child would find a way to visit her?

To be fair, that sounds like her.

"You take your hands," Aletheia says, sliding her own along my arms till hers mimic my own movements like a shadow, *"And hold them out, open."*

Her words are soft against me, and I lean back into where I know she is. Holding me. Coaxing me in the right direction.

Her fingers bend and lace between mine for a second, the pressure of them enough to ground me, before she slips them out and back to snake my waist.

A part of this, but not.

"Now think of her."

"What?" I ask, my hands faltering in the air.

I turn to try to look at her, but her hands travel lightening-fast up to my head, keeping me facing forwards as she moves to cover my eyes.

I have tried my best to push down every memory of mum. Keep her precious and safe but away from the rest of my life. She was so pure. An angel amongst mortals. And I can't bear to hold such a person in memory knowing I can never touch, see, hear her again.

The pain is ineffable.

"Tell me about her again." She prompts gently, and part of me breaks.

Like a dam I feel myself aching to pour outwards. The pressure like a physical weight on my chest, begging for release.

She already knows so much.

Maybe... maybe I can do this.

"My Mum," I begin, "Tara Gaialla Syn. She was a teacher. She loved to show children the magic that still lived in the earth. Gods, she loved anything that breathed." I say, taking my time and allowing myself to tell her, *only* her, "She was a dancer- a terrible one. Dad used to twirl her around the kitchen till she was too dizzy to stand, and then carry her till the song finished."

I feel Aletheia's hands come away from my eyes but I dare not open them.

When they're shut it's just me and her and the void in my head.

"She was beautiful, in an obvious but not in-your-face kind of way. I have her hair and her height, but her *face*- her smile could light the universe. She smelt like springtime and walked with the confidence of the Gods. She had a laugh that would grab the attention of just about anyone," I smile, "So loud and present that you couldn't help but join her. She..." I feel a warmth in my hand but still I don't open my eyes.

I can't.

I'm too scared.

"Sh-she was... she..."

I try to keep the thought pushed down. I can't say it.

It's not fair.

It was never fair.

"Darling." Aletheia murmurs against my skin.

I open my eyes.

In my open palms floats an orb, with pinks and blues and greens swirling and dissipating at its edges.

And I can feel it.

Her.

As clear as I know I am myself I know it's her.

Mum.

The orb opens.

The light morphs up and stretches into a colourful sheet, bigger and wider than both me and Aletheia combined. I feel the weight of Aletheia's body leave my own and I panic, nearly tripping.

"Aletheia- *wait*!" I yell as the sheet folds down and over me and I'm swallowed by it.

My feet fall out from under me and the floor is gone. I'm floating in a wide expanse of white, not unlike the land of the Fates.

"Ale... *Aletheia*!" I shout into the abyss, my hair moving about me like hers does, in a state of zero gravity.

I hear it but I don't believe it.

The sound that causes an ache so deep I feel I may die from it.

Her laugh. *Mum's...*

It echoes in and around me and I flip around like a fish out of water, desperate for the source.

Images.

All around me like they're sent from invisible projectors. Holographic memories. Mum pushing me on the swing she'd insisted dad wouldn't build. Tabi on dad's shoulders flying round the living-room. Mum and dad at a restaurant on their anniversary, smiling over their wines at each other; perfectly and happily in love...

These aren't my memories.

"They're mine."

The voice, *her* voice, comes from everywhere. All around me and it's like I'm losing her all over again. I can't see her, I can't feel her, I can't smell her. It's like I'm trapped in the camera-roll of the phone I threw away when it happened. Like the photo albums that lie in a box under my bed.

Untouched.

Safe.

"Mum? Mum I'm here!" I yell, whipping around in all directions as best as I can in the frictionless abyss.

"What was the last thought?"

...

No.

Because I don't believe it. It's a childish thought. A hateful one that I have no room for anymore.

It isn't real.

I don't even believe it. Not really. Not when it all comes down to it, when I logic it out...

"You must say it, to let it go- you must set it free."

Mum's voice grows more demanding, louder. The memories seem to speed up and I can barely think straight. Mum holding me in her arms the day of my birth, my tiny pink fingers wrapped around hers. Dad spilling flour on the kitchen floor as mum mops and the towel-whipping frenzy that ensued. Tabi in the bath with mum, bubbles on her head as she wiggles ridiculously for his entertainment. Mum holding me as I cry over the bullies at school, rocking me on our chair.

The chair that Hydra threw out, that dad *let* her throw out. Because...

"*You left us.*" I whisper, tears slipping like rivers from my eyes as the image of me and mum in the chair pauses and focuses in, as I say it.

"You left us. You left me to do *this*- all of it. All by myself." The tears come strong now and I crumple in on myself, unwilling to look at her holding me then- when she can't now.

"You left me in *hell*. You abandoned Tabi. Dad has never gone back to how he was. I had to be a mum, and a life support, and a human punching bag at *fourteen*. You left me alone. *Mum...*"

Arms go around me and I inhale spring.

My heart fractures into a million pieces as I open my eyes to her… mum…

"…*Mum*?" I whisper, barely audible but it feels like a shout.

Her hazel eyes blink down at me. Her strong arms, *real* arms, pull me closer to her, like she would in our chair, and holds me.

"I'm here baby," She says, "I never left."

I am broken.

I wail.

I am a child.

A baby.

No more emotionally competent than an inconsolable infant as she rocks me in her arms and I cling to her.

"You- you're here- you're *real*. I- I don't know what I'm doing mum, I *never* know what I'm doing- and I wish you were here. I miss you. I miss you so much and it *hurts*…"

"I miss you too, my beautiful baby girl, you're so grown up." She says in a voice like heaven into my hair.

I raise my face, unwilling to stop looking at her else she disappears.

Her face hasn't changed, her smile still the best thing in the universe and her eyes like mine.

She brushes the tears from my face and I hold onto her arms as she does so.

I can't let her go again.

"You've been through so much, *too* much. I didn't want to leave you honey; I never would have if I'd had a choice." She consoles me, washing away as much of the pain with her words as she can manage.

"I know, I just- I can't, not without you. I've tried so hard without you…"

"I know you have honey." She murmurs and I see the pain in her eyes as she looks at a daughter she probably barely recognises.

Nearly seven years.

She looks the same, wholly and brilliantly the same as she always was. But me? I've changed more than she could ever have imagined.

"Do... do you still..." I can't wrap my mouth around the words, but she understands.

She always did.

"I would recognise you whether you were old and grey or five seconds old Tenaya. You are mine, always have been- and always will be. No matter what you go through or how many years pass between us. Even when you outlive me-" She smiles, pausing as tears from her own eyes spill over her cheeks, "-I will always recognise you, my beautiful baby girl."

There's a rumble that sends the image, and us, juddering; her arms falling away from mine and our bodies suspended in the air.

Hers is fading.

Too fast.

Too soon.

"Mum- mum no- *wait*! I'm not *ready*!" I scream, reaching fruitlessly in her direction as she floats mere metres in front of me.

She's already out of reach again.

"I can't lose you again! *Please*! I just got here- there must be a *way*-" I wail as the abyss shudders again, this time jarring cracks appearing in the walls of the room.

She only smiles, blowing me a kiss with a hand over her heart.

"I will always be with you, Tenaya. *Always*."

I cry as she fades, her body now almost completely blended into the nothingness.

My world is ending all over again, and once more I am helpless to stop it.

"You are stronger than you believe. I am so proud of you, please- look after yourself. Care for yourself in the way I wish I could." She says, her smile never faltering even as my world does.

"*Mum…*" my voice is so small.

"I'll see you again, my beautiful girl," She says, and I feel her warmth wrap around me one last time as the void unravels, "In another life."

Her body disappears along with the walls, and I plummet back into the foggy realm.

Strong arms catch me and I look up into Aletheia's face. Hers is concerned but stony, her eyes darting between mine and something in front of her.

I turn, my feet faltering but finding their place on the floor as I right myself.

I shove the feelings down down down

Back into place

Back into their box

For now.

The fog has parted in a circle that hosts me, Aletheia, and a woman-like creature seemingly made of molten lava.

The lady stands twenty-feet tall at least, covered by a black silk wrap that accentuates her curved-but-bone-slim figure. She holds a staff in one of her massive clawed hands, which heralds horns at the top that mimic her own; spiralled and pointed.

She scowls down at us, one taloned foot in front of the other, her golden eyes blazing.

"I told you not t- *oh*," She growls, before her eyes fall upon me, shifting to curiosity, "Well, what do we have here, daughter?"

She moves in powerful strides, closing the distance before Aletheia can so much as protest.

Daughter?

The pain from losing my own mum a second time bubbles up, but I cork it.

It has to wait.

At least until there's not a giant demon-lady threatening my very existence.

The heat she radiates warms my skin, but I don't flinch. The tears from before drying on my cheeks and the salt falling freely from my face.

The woman up close is beautiful, not just in her physique. Behind her previous scowl, she has a kinder demeanour. With high cheekbones and strong structure, the cracks of gold in her face only serving to highlight her more prominent facial features. Like her eyes- they bore into my soul.

"You must be my daughter's *darling*." She deduces, reaching a hand forward.

Aletheia flinches but doesn't move, and it's only her inaction that keeps me in place. If I know one thing, it's that Aletheia wouldn't purposefully put me in harm's way.

Her mother's long fingers scratch the surface of the barrier, coming up without having contacted my body; her eyes dancing in wonder.

"Curious creature." She murmurs.

She moves lightening-fast, hand clasping fully around my waist and arms, trapping me, lifting me in the air to her eye-level.

I squirm and kick, grunting indignantly as Aletheia rushes forwards.

"Mother- Put. Her. Down." She commands, but I can already tell she has little control over her mother's choices.

Her mother merely smirks, shushing her before turning her attentions back to me. Her hand doesn't burn, but the heat is still there, and I know if it wasn't for the barrier, I'd be charred to a crisp by now.

Gods knows how Aletheia's father managed.

"We haven't been formally introduced," She says, inclining her head at me, "I am the Demon Queen Relinque, ruler of Selheim, and Mother of Aletheia." She says the last bit with a grimace as Aletheia half-heartedly kicks at her legs.

I can't help but scowl back, my manners deceased.

"I'd call it a pleasure, but you just interrupted a once-in-a-lifetime reunion with my *Mum*." I snap, trying not to get emotional, but angry all the same. "Forgive me if I'm not ecstatic at the introduction."

Relinque only grins, demonic sharp-black teeth in full view.

"She has a fiery spirit after all. Well chosen, daughter."

From below me I hear Aletheia grumble something about not needing her approval.

Relinque shakes her head, her smile dropping.

"Regardless, my dear, it was imperative that I did. I'm certain my impetuous offspring has failed to apprise you of the imminent danger you both are in by being here?"

I twist to try and see Aletheia, but she won't meet my eyes, her hair falling forwards to obscure her face.

Kuro, who'd been hiding behind her for some time, leaps forwards and bursts into flecks and into my skin; scampering up my leg and resting on my shoulder-blade, facing off with Relinque.

Protecting me?

"What... what do you-"

"The Fates are-" Relinque grunts, looking down I see the end of a bladed object retracting from her leg.

She can't know, not yet.

My scythe sticks out of my mother's leg, only just edging beneath the surface of her molten flesh but still. Enough of a warning.

If my darling thinks the Fates are after me then she won't accept me. I can't guarantee she won't forsake me to protect her friends. I am no danger to her, neither are the Fates- they don't mess with mortals much anymore, least of all the innocents. But still. Why would she believe me?

I burst my scythe, watching as it disintegrates back into my ribs. My second of three familiars, and likely my last.

Relinque's gaze hardens but she draws no attention to it.

"The Fates are angry, I told you daughter, as I'll tell you again- stay... in *her* realm." I watch her face screw up, like her words pain her to say.

Why did Aletheia stab her?

"Why are they angry?" I ask instead.

Relinque curls me towards her like I weigh no more than a paperweight. A pebble in the palm of a giant.

"I have warned you enough dear child, I should not be taking to meddling with mortal affairs." She says, not unkindly, her smile returning a little.

"Place her down and be gone, I did not venture here to be castigated in this way. You are not my authority." Aletheia snarls, stomping her foot for emphasis; but only showing how much of a child her mother makes her feel like.

I can only imagine what power she must hold to make even Aletheia obedient.

Slowly, so as not to startle me, Relinque brings her other hand up; her joints glowing, crackling and reknitting with every movement.

"What're you doing- mother desist!" Aletheia demands but Relinque heeds nothing of it.

Instead, she moves two extended fingers to the top of my head, her long nails scratching, itching, tapping at the barrier.

And then pierces it.

I feel the tips of them touch and burn my skull, subtly and barely there but definitely through that which separates me from her daughter.

I don't break eye contact. I don't move an inch as she rests there for a second longer, her eyes locked on mine but unseeing.

She inhales deeply before relinquishing my head, drawing her finger to her lips in a way that suggests I say nothing; embellished with a wink. She lowers me to the ground, her fingers falling away and Aletheia's hands immediately replacing them, standing in front of me.

Protecting me.

"We're leaving." She says, her body tense and her hair already swirling around her in a flurry of white.

The last thing we see before she rips the world from my sight is her mother, smiling down at us.

"Always a pleasure, daughter dearest."

The sheets wrap and surge, angrier and harsher than before. It feels like mere seconds this time before the world returns, and I'm stood in my room, stumbling for balance as Aletheia moves to sit stubbornly at the edge of my bed; her head in her hands.

And that's when I hear what her mother said.

Really hear it.

"She said *again*." I state more than ask.

I watch as Aletheia's form stiffens, slowly raising her head.

I knew my mother would be my ultimate downfall. She didn't proffer the information about the protection my darling grants me without her awareness.

But she tattled on me just the same.

"Yes, she did." I reply tentatively, my hands slipping to the edge of the bed to cling to something for support.

Gods knows I'm going to need it.

I'm not going to lie though, not more than I have to. Deception for the sake of ease is one thing, but lying openly to my darling? I could never.

She stands resolute, and for a moment she appears larger than mother did, towering over me and making me feel barely inches tall.

"I left, on my own, once before." She says, not meeting my eyes.

She... when did...

"When did you...?" I begin, and she gets it because she nods.

"When you silenced me, in the hall. I wanted to see my father." I say, and I hope that'll be enough.

I did want to see father, not a lie.

I, forbye, wished to taste the freedom I had been scourged of for four whole years. She would understand this, I know as much. But she has been through so much today and does so every day. Who am I to add to her list by instilling a paranoia that I wish to be anywhere but here? When really, I only wish to be anywhere and everywhere with her- and now I can't even do that.

From the corner of my eye, I watch her as she moves to me, crouching by her bedside. A bed that she shares with me each night without question. I wish so badly to feel her in my arms- really feel her.

Soon, my darling.

She places a hand on my knee, the weight enough to get me to look up and meet her eyes.

"Thankyou," I say, and her eyes widen, "For today. For the adventure. For- for my mum. I don't," I clench my jaw-

I wish she wouldn't do that

-trying my best not to get emotional, "I don't know how I'll ever repay you."

I am unworthy.

I watch the thoughts flit through her head, unheeded, and I wait. I can't get mad at her for wanting to see her father after four years. I would be the same. I'd sent her away and she had used the time to try and see family, not that she seemed too fussed on it. The way she said '*father*' made me tense, like it was a harsh topic; a bitter taste.

Her mother though, she is someone I'd talk to again.

I can still feel the burns on my head. I don't know why she did it. Maybe to prove the barrier can be broken? *Maybe a warning?*

It felt like... I must be going crazy, but it felt like... a gift?

"Did you get to speak with her at least?" I ask, my shoulders sagging, "I know my mother's intrusion disrupted it, but I had hoped I'd bought you at least a little time?"

I nod, the feeling of my mum's arms around me still lingering. I haven't had her embrace in seven years, haven't seen her smile or felt her warmth or been the recipient of her love in the better part of a decade.

Until Aletheia gave her back to me, however brief it was- I

wouldn't change it for the world.

"You gave her back to me," I say, running my hands through strands of her hair, "For so long, I have been burdened with the last image of my mum being that of a corpse on a table... of her not being *her* anymore." I clench my jaw against the abrasive memory, washing it aside with the new one. "But now, now my last memory of mum is her holding me, of telling me she loves me. My mum is my mum again because of *you*, Aletheia."

Why, when she says such things, is my heart now only heavy with guilt.

Too many secrets.

My mother, my father, Leidha, Kuro, the Fates and even the entirety of how I feel about her. I'm not sure how much longer I can do this before I stop being me.

"I wish to rest, my darling." I say instead, and I feel the weight of my own making settling on my chest.

Too many secrets.

But she's not ready, and I must be patient. I shall double my efforts, triple them, in trying to break this barrier and forego the punishing hands of the Fates.

But for now? For now, I only wish to hold her.

I smile, the weariness in her eyes testament to the day we've had. I can't blame her. I wasn't even the one wielding the dimensions, and I feel like I could sleep for a week.

I've seen my mum again, and I have only Aletheia to thank for it.

"Okay," I say, and she nods, her head falling back on the bed and her body slinking its way to her allotted side, "I'll be right back."

I stand, stroking along her leg as I go.

It's only when I'm closing the door over quietly behind me that I see her curl in on herself; like the voices of the Gods are damning her.

I will fight them all for her.

The demon girl who showed me alternate realms.

The demi-god who teaches me how to live freely again.

The girl who gave me back my mum.

The woman who chooses to stay by my side when the rest of the universe awaits her.

She is the purest of souls, and I will work every day to earn her company.

But for now, we will rest.

CHAPTER 22
LIEDER LIEDHA

She rests beside me, her face still peacefully set in deep sleep. It happens occasionally, I leave my dream-beach before she does, and I wait for her to surface in her own time.

We've been this way for the days since realm hopping, driven closer by venturing further it would seem.

Her hair spills out over half the bed, and I woke today facing her; one of my arms tucked under her neck. Her lips are slightly parted, rustling the baby-hairs close to her face, bringing them towards her and away with every breath.

I've never had this.

Not with anyone.

I don't know what I'm doing, but I know that this is one of the most precious things in my life right now. She is. Whatever that means, a friendship, *more*...

I dare not think about more.

Yes, she calls me her darling. Yes, she stays here with me over everything else. Yes, she's the most incredible person I've ever met.

But I'm too messy.

My situation from work to home life is just too complicated to wrap her up in.

She deserves to be free.

I still wish I could feel her skin against my own though, know how it feels to really hold her instead of just the weight she maintains. It's as if she's slowly bleeding through. I didn't used to be able to smell her- but every now and again it's there, the hint of it.

Earth and sea and blue and green.

Her lashes stir, and I make a show of yawning and turning onto my back as she slowly rouses. I slip my arm from under her and grab my usual clothes from the chair.

"Another day of homework?" I grumble from the bed.

My body craves adventure, not moments into wakefulness and I'm already itching for something new.

My only remedy is my darling, standing across from me in her nightshirt and nothing else; the satin traipsing halfway down her thighs, the back rising higher-up, riding her curves.

Blessed be these mundane items in their effective simplicity.

She knows so much about me. From my emotions that were streamlined to her for four years, to my home life that she's been privy to for as long as she's been here. She's met Rylan, she's seen my other friends, and she knows my daily routine as easy as she knows how to breathe at this point.

And what do I know of her?

She's born of Relinque and a God of the stars, she drank when she was just a teenager in order to get through the days, and she has a kitsune as a familiar who currently holds residency on my skin.

But other than that?

I swing around to her, so quickly that she doesn't lift her eyes quick enough for me not to notice where they'd been resting.

I fight the urge to tug my shirt further down. Ridiculous,

having spent the night curled up beside her, to then become prudish in the light of day.

"Do you want to... get coffee with me?" I ask hurriedly, hoping the anxiousness isn't radiating off me in the way it feels like.

I shouldn't feel worried, I should feel calm.

But inside my stomach rages the war of the butterflies so drastic I fear they may fly free at any moment.

Aletheia raises an eyebrow, one arm lifting to rest behind her head on the bed as she scrutinises me.

"You wish to deviate from routine... again?" She asks, her tone sceptical, *"Why?"*

Why indeed.

I shrug as nonchalantly as possible, "I fancy it, Hydra is out on errands today, I haven't got lectures lined up or diner work- and I'd like to get out of the house."

She screws her eyes up at me, and I know she sees through the first layer of crap. It's not completely a lie, those factors do make the venture more possible. But they're not the only reason.

I sigh, looking away bashfully, "I would also, kinda, like to uhh, get to know you... *better*?"

My heartbeat sounds like a drum through my body.

She...

I smile, swinging my legs off and stepping up beside her so that I can get her to look at me. Let her see how happy she makes me without even trying.

"So- like a date?" I ask, and I watch as red floods her cheeks.

Don't let it show. Keep it down.

"Well, I wouldn't necessarily... I've never been on...."

"So your first date then." I finish for her, saving her.

I bow to her, "My darling, it would be my honour to partake in your first official date. I shall await your readiness downstairs." I smirk, swishing past her and pausing at the door, "Make haste!"

She whooshes out of my door before I can even make to correct her again, her words hanging in the air like weights above me.

I'm going on a date with a girl no one can see. As far as closeted dates go, I guess this is the easiest.

When I finally head downstairs, I come to an abrupt stop at the bottom step. Aletheia stands at the door, leaning to one side of it and swinging her leg.

She's pulled her hair back into a ponytail, her face and high-rising cheekbones now in full view and her elegant neck no longer shadowed by her waves. Even her pointed ears seem more prominent, with only a couple strands left forward to frame her face.

It's such a small change, insignificant.

Even so, I have to count myself down to take the last couple steps.

She raises her eyes to me, her wicked smile suggesting she knew exactly what she was doing as she gestures to the door.

"Shall we?"

I can only nod.

It takes us ten minutes of semi-comfortable silence before we make it into town, arriving at one of only two cafes in the whole of Siveyra. 'The quiet place', aptly named because it was rare for anyone other than the older folk to bother with it. The students preferred the more study-friendly café closer to the university.

But it will do for us.

"After you." I say, opening the door and then immediately cringing as the man behind me nods and barges past. Aletheia gives me a half-smile.

"The pitfalls of going on a date with an invisible girl- insanity is nearly always presumed."

I sigh, following her inside, "Perfect."

It's not the fanciest place, but it's a convenient one. A maroon room filled with hanging baskets coveting plants of various colour and species. The counter is covered with an assortment of cakes in spherical domes, attended to by two overly-chipper baristas; the rest of the space stolen by a host of coffee mugs.

Glaringly ordinary.

Which makes it all the more baffling that Aletheia is looking around like it's a realm she could never have fathomed.

She jumps up on the counter, which I have to try my damnedest to pretend I can't see, as she peers over the baristas shoulders, ogling as they froth milk and tamp down the coffee granules.

"What alchemy witchcraft is this?" Aletheia murmurs as she moves her hand out of the way so that the server can pour the latte art; her eyebrows raising.

"Artistic sorcery." She whispers, gripping onto a low hanging beam and swinging onto the coffee machine to inspect closer.

They're too busy to hear the machine's groans of protest.

"Can I help you?" A waiter asks, snapping me back to the room.

He's a tall, skinny-man, barely out of university, with a mop of honey-brown hair that matches his eyes.

"Oh- yes, table for... one." I reply.

I need to start getting better at pretending she doesn't exist. As it stands, I can't seem to take my eyes off her. She might break something, or cause a scene, or... disappear.

The waiter directs me over to a small booth in the corner, thankfully not by a window; the last thing I need is people passing by thinking I'm talking to myself.

Aletheia crawls over the booth tops, meandering around hats and heads alike until she plops herself in the seat opposite me, her face beaming.

"Segregated seats? In a public place? Oddities are truly infinite in the mortal realms." She says, already reaching for the menu; conveniently stacked behind a small potted plant.

I suppose it is odd, to go to a public place and expect to be seated privately.

"Do you... know what things *are*?" I ask, in what I hope isn't a patronising voice.

She didn't know what tea was, so I'm not holding out huge hope that she will be able to deduce what a skinny oat-macchiato is.

She frowns, skimming the page before flattening it on the table in annoyance.

"We uhhh, we can go somewhere else? If you don't like-"

"I can't read your dialect." She grumbles, not meeting my eyes as blue stains her cheeks. *"We aren't permitted to learn it- since your lot are considered a 'dying race'."*

I can see she's embarrassed. I don't take the dying race bit to heart. We did summon the oldest creatures in creation because of the mess we made, I can't blame the rest of the universe for damning us.

But the reading- that's nothing to be embarrassed about. Although I guess as a being of ultimate knowledge- not being able to make your choice of what to order in such a simple civilisation, must be kind of a downer.

"You can speak it, but not read it?" I ask, confused to say the least.

She grimaces.

"I've heard a mental stream of consciousness for the past four years, I know how to speak it... it didn't come through in written format."

The utter humiliation.

I wanted to enjoy new experiences here with my darling, and I can't even read her native language.

...Unless

"Think of your language." I say, reaching forward and grabbing the back of her neck to shove both our foreheads together.

I don't think I've ever seen her so red.

She moved so quickly, one moment she's sat back in a grump-

the next she's bashed our heads together.

"What- what do you-"

"Just trust me- think of your language."

Aletheia closes her eyes, her freckles beginning to glow and slithers of white and blue lines begin bleeding from her head across to mine.

It's like being struck by lightning.

One second I'm in the café, the next my mental being is wrapped in white and blue light and I'm paralysed.

"Breathe through it my darling," her voice says in my head, *"Think of your dialect- how it's written."*

It doesn't hurt per say, but it's not comfortable.

I can't feel my physical body, and I can only imagine what it looks like to everyone else in the cafe. I can only pray the waiter hasn't come back over to take an order.

I think back to English, back to school, back to college.

I try to picture the letter cards, the order of sentences on pages, the teacher who didn't care- but slogged through the work anyway. The homework, the books, the way they sound in my head.

Her hand on the back of my neck

Her hand in my hair

Her face so close to my face

Her eyes her lips

Her hands falling away from a child's- the girl's body bursting into flames as it falls-

"-Ma'am?" The waiter's voice sends me back to my body and I fall against the booth with a thud; my limbs slack.

He's looking at me with mild concern, and I beg there are no cameras that caught how that must've looked.

"Yes- yes sorry, my order, uhh-" I scan the menu, trying to bring my brain back.

"I'll have a cappuccino." Aletheia smirks from the other side of the booth.

I think I preferred it when she couldn't read.

"I'll have a c-cappuccino and a flat white- p-please?" I ask, flipping over the menu and smiling apologetically up at the man.

He raises his eyebrows at the mention of two caffeinated drinks, but doesn't question it as he takes the menus from me.

"Are you sure you're alright, miss?" He asks, looking me up and down in a way that suggests what he'd witnessed wasn't exactly *'normal'*.

"I- I haven't been sleeping okay, m-m-must be getting to me." I stammer, thumping my leg in annoyance.

He nods respectfully before taking away the menus and busying himself with the drinks.

"You did well, not many people can-"

"Who was she?" I interrupt, not meeting her eyes.

The image burns undeterred through my mind. The girl must've been younger than ten, Tabi's age. Purple eyes huge with terror and her brown hair flying out in front of her as she plummets- her body self-combusting into a thousand tiny embers in moments.

Aletheia killed a child.

She can read as much on my face, because hers hardens.

She doesn't say a word for so long. Long enough that the waiter comes along and silently delivers my drinks, offering nothing to lighten the mood.

Her hands curl around her cup, staring into the brown swirls with such self-loathing that it's a palpable thing.

So, it's real.

That image was a real memory.

She wasn't meant to find out this way. She'll hate me. reject me as father has and I'll be left alone again.

But she has to know now. I won't lie.

"Let me explain, then you can choose to damn me or not. If you decide once I've finished that you wish for me to leave- I'll go."

She doesn't move for a moment, her eyes still reliving my mental feed. She slowly reaches forward for her own drink, flicking her eyes up to mine and nodding.

This was not how today was supposed to go.

It was supposed to be easy, getting to know her and spending time with her.

I guess I'm learning more than I bargained for.

"I grew up in Empryrailla, as you know, for my childhood up until the age of eight." I say, taking a deep breath and blowing on my drink, "My father, the uninvolved and endlessly preoccupied God that he is, allowed me the freedom of the entirety of the diamond isles." She grimaces, "There, and wherever I could get to. Difficulty was- he didn't know I would be able to travel between dimensions. Neither did I- until Liedha and I did it without thinking."

Her hand tightens on her cup, my own tensing at the reaction.

"We were eight. Liedha was my best friend, a pure soul and a kindred spirit. She was timid but strong, with a desire to know the unknowable akin to my own. She was... being around her felt like being awake." I say, the words burning through me as I remember her.

I don't push the memories away like my darling does. I let them burn through me, scar their way through my being as part of me. It doesn't mean they don't hurt, but at least I know that I can face them.

"We weren't always on each-other's side though," I continue, my jaw tense, "And this one day, we tore through Empryrailla with voices that made the flowers shrivel, the suns turned from us and the waters ran dry. I wanted to go visit father during his meeting, I wanted to speak with him about being able to see mother. Liedha... she wasn't exactly my father's biggest fan. She had a few choice words to say about his fatherly efforts- words that as a child, I wouldn't hear." I shake my head, her wilful eyes still a strong memory that bore into me as I recall her.

"She berated me, relentlessly, and for the first time she wasn't too timid to express herself in front of others- she was a strong and ferocious girl with a heart of gold. I was so blinded by rage, so inescapably determined to

defend the man that never cared for me... that I clawed for her."

I raise my hand to my face, extending my nails until they're points. They would've hurt her for sure, but no one stays hurt on Empryrailla for long.

"I never even touched her. My nails dragged through a rift in the fabric of the realm, tearing it open- fuelled by my burning defiance and hurt. My deepest darkest thoughts directing our trajectory in the mindless heat of the moment. We fell through, one of my hands still in Empryrailla anchoring me... but Liedha... She had nothing to hold."

"She fell into the new realm, the world made of fire, the one that her child-body had never prepared to bear witness to- let alone be thrust into. I shan't detail how it looked- you know." I say, gritting my teeth and not looking up.

"I managed to pull free of the flames, crawling and howling back to my father. He wouldn't so much as hear me out. Others had already testified that I had been abusing Liedha throughout the day with my verbal assaults. They posed that I had done it on purpose without realising the severity and longevity of my actions. In part, I guess they were right- I had no idea what I was doing. Liedha's mother in particular desired my ruination, not that I could blame her- I'd essentially killed her daughter. Father... sentenced me to death, by will of the Fates."

My darling sucks in a breath through her teeth, but I don't take the pity that comes with it. I deserved the sentence, a life for a life.

"That's when mother swooped in on burning legs, an all-too-soon reminder of the death of my best friend in living format. She stole me away, from right under their noses- not that they could've stopped her. But that's how I ended up bound to Selheim for the better part of a decade."

She looks at me then, helpless.

"You see now? I killed my best friend. That, that is my darkest hour and my worst nightmare that you were just privy to. Do you feel like you know me now?"

She says it angrily, like a challenge.

Take my worst side and see if you can handle it.

Thing is- I can.

She didn't want it to happen. A tragedy and a traumatic experience, the loss of her only friend when she had only an absent father figure for family. She lost everything in the moment she lost her temper, as a child no less. And her whole world turned their backs on her.

I reach across and take her hand, her body jumping at the suddenness of my action.

"You were a *child*," I say, trying to bury the anger I hold towards her father and just console her, "You weren't taught how to control your ability, you weren't tended to, and you were trying to defend the groundless." Her eyes steal over.

"He was ruler of the diamond isles- he..."

But I can't. not anymore. I can't defend him for being as absent as hers is. Who am I trying to fool?

I shove down the desperate inner-child that begs me to fight for him. He has tried to have me killed nearly once a year for the past decade- at some point I have to count my losses.

"I am so sorry for your loss, and I'm sorry for the complete negligence of your father. But I'm not sorry that I found out, because yes, I do know you better now." I squeeze her hand, fighting her thoughts for her attention, "And I want to continue to do so... if you'll let me?"

There is so much I want to say to her.

I wish to tell her of Liedha, my darling is the first one this side of my childhood to even ask about her. I yearn to tell her the antics we used to get up to, about the hidden tunnels under Empryrailla, about the prophecy vault under the bath house.

There's so much she has yet to know.

We have time.

"I won't try and steal your mental feed without warning again," I mumble somewhat awkwardly, taking the cup towards my lips, "But yes, my darling, you can get to know me better. As much as you can until you're

sick of me."

Her shoulders curl in and she becomes smaller, but her lips curve into a small smile as she takes a sip.

Her eyes widen and she inhales the cup deeply, a borderline-euphoric expression crossing her face.

"Glad we came here then?" I joke, taking a sip from my own mug.

She nods, leaning forwards and smiling properly, *"What was it your college professor used to say?"* She says, taking another sip as she recalls my stolen memories, *"Oh, yes- 'swings and roundabouts'."*

We ended up talking for hours. At first it was a little difficult, but once she started on about her childhood and Liedha, she couldn't seem to stop. It was as if fifteen years of repressed emotions and memories came flooding forwards, unstoppable in their magnitude.

I was only too happy to listen.

She explained the games, the adventures to neighbouring stars in 'hunting season'- that demanded the children be able to take down a beast at least three times their size; when dropped in an unknown environment and left for as long as it took.

The underwater training where their bodies learnt to develop new breathing patterns in order to survive. Her body works in such peculiar, wonderful ways, completely adaptable and able to change in minute ways that enable her continuity.

I told her about earth schools, more on what she'd seen in my memory- explaining university and how it had changed in the past century. How we no longer solely focus on one thing but branch to three-to-five topics in order to be fully knowledgeable for a specific job role.

I told her about Mum's love of potions, about her collection of novels, detailing her research and projects- ones Aletheia has since demanded she sees as soon as we get home.

It's been easy, fluid, the conversation effortless and endlessly entertaining. I want to know about her and her life as desperately as she wants to know mine. Earth stories seem so mundane in comparison, but she loves it.

She's in the middle of telling me about one time she was at a tavern in Selheim- the first bar fight she ever witnessed, on her thirteenth birthday- when Amaya rears her head from round the side of the booth.

"Hey!" Amaya squeals, darting into the booth-side opposite me, Aletheia cursing and scooching back quick enough to dodge being squished, "I didn't know you'd be here! You get the day off from the training then?" She asks.

I cringe subtly at Aletheia, apologising as much as I can do with a look alone. Amaya is under the impression that I can't come out even when lectures are off, because of the 'jiu-jitzu training' I do. A solid enough excuse and a safety-net, in case wounds are still visible on different weekdays.

I don't make a habit of leaving the house, so I don't usually have to worry about getting caught. Other than today, currently sat *'on my own'* without even a book- and two empty coffee cups.

Doesn't look suspicious at all.

I shrug as casually as I can, "Coach gave us the week off."

I'm still not too sure on how to act around Amaya now. We've gotten back to semi-normal, but I'm not sure whether that would still be the case if she knew I was on an almost-date-like-situation with a girl.

It's not a date.

But it's not *not* a date.

"And you didn't think to tell me? Rude." She says sarcastically, unpacking slightly and making herself comfortable.

I push my leg further under the booth until it meets Aletheia's, her eyes glancing up at mine in a wickedly evil moment- before she dives under the table; scurrying up on my side and using my leg to anchor herself onto the seat.

She smirks at me, *"Well, hello there."*

I glare at her but place a hand down next to hers, our arms brushing. Well, as much as they can.

"I didn't think you'd be around, or else preoccupied with our absent third party." I say sarcastically.

She has the decency to look at least somewhat apologetic.

"Like I said, we were working on it." She says, "And anyways- you didn't tell me that you were head over heels in *luuurv* with Maddy, did you?"

She is not in love with her

I can feel Aletheia bristle at the comment.

"I'm not in '*luuurv*' with her," I say, my cheeks warming, "I have a... childhood crush... on her." I say, keeping my eyes on Amaya and trying not to notice Aletheia silently seething to my right. "And I think we both know why I didn't."

It's Amaya's turn to cringe, "Point taken."

Amaya leans in conspiratorially, gripping my hand on the table, "Do you have plans for the 'sleepover' though?" She says, a smirk spanning her face, "I mean, it seems pretty clear to me that the girl wants you."

"Wants your attention, there's a difference." I hiss, fighting the urge to smack her friend's hand away.

I smooth Amaya's hand before pulling away, her expression slightly hurt; gone in an instant.

"I don't know what she wants, but- the sleepover should be fun, anyway." I say, dodging the topic as quickly as possible.

I can see Aletheia growing more and more agitated and know we need to leave.

"I'm sorry 'Maya- we- I need to get home for supper, dad will have a field-day if I'm late." I say, sliding to the end of the booth with Aletheia's hand grasped tightly in mine.

"Oh- well, okay, yeah. Look, are we-" She fumbles, her eyebrows creasing in awkward apology.

"I promise you, we're okay." I say before she can finish the sentence, her small smile returning, "I don't want to lose my best friend, however manic she may be."

She tuts at me, swatting at my arm in mock-annoyance.

"This best friend is gunna get you a date, you hear?" She grins, and I really wish she hadn't.

I feel Aletheia tug me away and I wave Amaya off, "Say hi to Rylan for me!" I yell as I'm dragged away, Amaya blushing but... something else. I catch the hint of sadness in her features before the café door closes behind me.

Did he tell her?

Did she find out what he's going through?

...did he tell her about Hydra?

I shake off the worries as I pace it to match step with Aletheia, her arms swinging furiously.

This is going to be harder than I thought. I don't even know what Maddy wants- what Aletheia wants in the end.

I don't think I can ever have what I want.

CHAPTER 23

YOUR NEEDS, MY NEEDS

"I thought you said it was a *sleepover*??" Amaya says accusingly, the scepticism thick in her tone as we wait outside Maddy's front door; the hinges vibrating with the base that pulsates from inside.

Technicoloured lights blink on and off, bleeding through the blinds. Music thrums from the walls, accompanied by raised voices and the drunken yells of fellow students.

The place itself is more of a mansion, three floors high and two houses wide, the lawn spanning bigger than my entire house; and I'm pretty sure there's a back-garden hidden somewhere behind the estate.

Amaya clutches her pillow closer to her chest, having prepared for a small get-together, you could say we're all feeling a little out of our depths. Even Rylan looks ready to bolt- and he's usually up for a bit of chaos.

Chaos-incarnate at my side is no different, her nose turned up and arms folded as she leans against the side of the building with as much disdain as is physically possible to muster.

"Trust the basilisk to snake you guys into something entirely different from her promises." She sniffs, *"She won't even come open the door for you gu-"*

One of the giant oak doors swings open and Maddy appears on the other side of it, beaming from ear to ear.

"*Tenny*!" She squeals, grabbing clumsily for my hands and dragging me inside.

"This doesn't make her good." I hear Aletheia mutter from behind me, but I can barely hear anything over the hubbub of people.

Amaya and Rylan track behind me, shuffling as best they can through the bodies lingering in the hallway.

Balloons and streamers hang about haphazardly, as random and miscellaneous as the people who linger around them.

Upon entering, the house segments off. A giant curved stairwell opposite the front door, and doors to the left or right into equally massive living rooms.

Plural.

Something I hadn't realised from the many years I've been obsessing over Maddy- her parents are minted.

"I thought you said *sleepover*?" I yell, squeezing her hand to get her attention as we take a left into a kitchen area.

Dozens of red cups and cans litter the marble countertop, accompanied by cigarette butts and other such things that seemed more like Irene's territory than Maddy's.

Maddy merely shrugs, squeezing my hand back and swinging me round the counter so I bump into a couple bottles before releasing me.

"Plans change!" She slurs, pointing to Amaya and Rylan, "Dump that shtuff in the cupboards here so people won't see 'n steal it, alright?"

Rylan and Amaya exchange nervous looks, before slowly opening up various doors and placing their bags inside. Aletheia finally appears around the side of the kitchen archway, and I try my best to subtly wave her over.

"I've *missed* you!" Maddy swoons, grabbing me around the shoulders in a big hug that has her face in my collarbone.

I don't know what to do.

She smells of alcohol, people's sweat and sugary sweet perfume. I can't just stand here motionless, so I reach my hand round, patting her back in response; my eyes lingering on Aletheia as she takes a big breath through her nose.

Whilst the others are looking this way, or else snuggling into my side, I watch as Aletheia plucks a bottle of vodka from the table. My eyes widening as she promptly uncaps it and downs a third of the contents.

Never breaking eye contact with me.

I've led a hurricane into a household.

"You guys-" Maddy says, lifting off me momentarily to point at us, "-*need* to catch up!"

For a moment no one says anything, stuck in a state of total bewilderment.

Rylan is the first to break the awkwardness, clapping his hands together and rubbing them as he moves towards the drinks.

"Well, no time like the present I guess." He grins sheepishly.

But I can see the pained look in his eyes as he takes in the table of addiction. The fear circulating in his body as he probably recalls different bottles from different bad days at home.

"Rylan- you don't have to-" I begin, but he's already taken up a half-empty bottle of whiskey.

"This'll be a good start," He says with a flourish, offering it up to Amaya, "Mademoiselle?"

Amaya's cheeks darken and she smiles, taking two cups in hand before pausing and looking to me, hovering over a third.

I can feel Aletheia watching me, testing me.

"I don't know, it's not really my thing..." I say, switching between glancing at Aletheia and Amaya.

Amaya does a double take behind her to the empty space where Aletheia stands, Rylan's eyes growing wider as he realises what- and who- I'm looking at, quickly redirecting Amaya's attention with an arm around her waist that makes her giggle.

Maddy pouts, leaning in front of me so the black tank top she wears falls forward, and nearly everything spills out.

"*Puhleeeease* Tenny?" She whines, my eyes trying to look anywhere but the gap her shirt left, "For *me*?"

She bats her eyelashes and part of me melts. Oddly though, not as much as I would've expected. How can I- when I have an invisible demi-demon in my periphery giving me the evils.

I cave, "One drink?" I ask, more of a question to Aletheia than the rest.

Maddy shakes her head, placing the contents of one drink into the contents of another, "Two at least!" she grins, biting her bottom lip between her teeth as she hands me the polluted chalice.

I bring the cup tentatively to my lips.

"Ten," Rylan pipes up, as the smell of cheap gin leaks its way into my nostrils, "You don't have to if you don't want to."

What if hydra can smell it on me when I get back?

What if dad does?

What if...

Maddy lounges closer to me, and Aletheia literally hisses- like a wild cat- in her direction.

"...I think I'll need it tonight." I concede, taking a couple large swigs.

"Atta girl!" Rylan jeers, the liquid scolding poisoned pathways down my throat.

"Yesssss!" Maddy bounces ecstatically, already searching around for her own cup.

I turn when I feel Aletheia's hand on my elbow, her big eyes boring into mine pleadingly.

"I don't like this, darling." She murmurs, hand tightening on my arm, a plea to leave.

Before I can even calculate an escape route, Maddy has me by my other elbow and begins dragging us towards the main room; Aletheia's hand slipping from me.

"You lot have a couple options- Numero uno!" She exclaims as we enter the hallway, "Down the hall is the dance-floor- aka the living room. If you want to powder your nose and get into a bit of drama, there's your room." She turns and points to a room below the stairs, practically hidden from the rest of the house, "Then you have the closet of misfit toys- that's where Irene, Emmy and that lot like to spend most of their time." She points to a third and final door on the other side of the house, "And then there's le Pick-Me-Up, otherwise known as the drinking game corner. The obligatory 'never have I evers', truths and dares, and spin the bottle malarky that gets you prepped and geared up to enter the other rooms. SO-!"

She twirls herself around on my fingers and gestures around at the options theatrically, "What'll it be?"

We all exchange similar looks of fear and apprehension, before Rylan once again takes the lead and saunters towards 'le Pick Me Up'; swaggering with the confidence of ten men.

"This room sounds like catch-up central if you ask me," He turns, inclining his head towards the door, "Shall we, my dears?"

Aletheia closes in, Maddy does the same- and I can't look at either of them. It's never been my choice, I avoid making choices.

But even Maddy is looking at me like my word is law.

I pass an apologetic look to Aletheia, who looks mad enough to start throwing things now, and take hold of Amaya's arm.

I nod to Rylan, walking us forward and sealing our fates.

I can't find Rylan.

It's the first coherent thought I've managed in a while, so I figure it's an important one.

Above the drum and base that pounds through everybody in the vicinity, I can hear the alarm bells in my head going off. What if he's having a panic attack? What if he acts like his father does? No- that's *his* fear, I know Rylan won't be like that.

Not with Amaya.

The world is blue and red and purple, lights streaming and swimming through a sea of people.

How did I get to room number one? Numero Uno?

I can't recall.

The world tilts and I flail out my hands to try and balance it, unprepared for the weight of the room to need my assistance in righting itself.

Arms wrap around my middle. Strong, broad, male arms that are unfamiliar to me.

I twist and find the very handsome face of a guy from creature studies staring back at me; his irises the size of moons.

"You're so beautiful." He slurs, his blonde hair flopping in every direction, slick with sweat.

He leans in so that our bodies are flush front to front, one hand on my lower back keeping me standing and his face buried in my neck.

I feel his tongue snake against my skin as he begins to kiss a line upwards.

"N-no sorry no *thanky-*"

I'm hurled backwards and out of his arms with strength unparalleled in this realm. Aletheia's face is pure fury as she stares daggers at the guy, who now looks around confused; having no clue how I magically zipped halfway across the room.

He doesn't seem too deterred though, as he calls the next girl he sees 'gorgeous' and prepares the same routine all over again.

Aletheia's ribs seem to be glowing on one side. That's when I remember that she can draw a lethal weapon from her body. She is a walking arsenal of immense force, and I brought her to a party full of drunks and maniacs.

Maniacs who flirted with me. Maniacs that she watched touch me without consent.

I take her hand and drag it in the opposite direction.

I don't know where we're going but we have to move, get out, away- *find Rylan.*

That's what I'd been trying to do.

Yes, we need to find Rylan.

We make it to the main hallway somehow, stuck between the stairway and the front door.

"Darling, I want to go home."

The suddenness of her words has me stumped.

She looks so angry, furious.

But also- sad.

Listen to me, please my darling you- we- are not in our right minds.

I don't want to have to watch you with another girl or guy and pretend it doesn't hurt- just because you're not ready to recognise what we have.

I don't want to watch people grope you and do things to you because they don't care what you think, and you're so stuck in your own head to know you have a voice that can say no.

I don't...

I don't say any of this out loud.

She won't hear me.

She doesn't care yet.

I shake my head, trying to see one of Aletheia, instead of two angry demon faces. But she is part demon- so maybe there are two of her?

No, there's only one Aletheia.

My Aletheia

"I gotta... find Rylan- and Amaya-" I manage to say, looking around as if they're hidden behind a pillar. Maybe they are- maybe we were playing hide and seek? That would explain why I was in a room without them, they'd never have guessed I'd go in there.

Great hiding spot.

Go me.

She's smiling to herself, completely wasted.

I thought I could leave her be for an hour or two, have my fill and give her space and then we could leave.

Together.

Turns out- my darling is a complete and total lightweight.

"They are safe, my darling- you're drunk. We should just go-"

"*Pssst!*"

I whip around and have to squint to understand what I'm seeing.

A ginger head is poking out from a near-invisible half-door under the stairs, grinning manically.

"*Amaya*?? What're you-"

A hand darts out from the door next to Amaya's head, to a chorus of giggles and a plume of smoke.

"Come see, young child, the secrets of the universe await you." The hand says with a flourish, the door cracking open a little more so that technicoloured light swirls out onto the white ceramic.

There's another bout of giggles, followed by the hint of sage and something else...

"Hello '*Tenny*'!" Irene coos from behind the door.

"Hey! Only *I* can call her that!" Maddy's voice clammers, a light smack registering from inside.

A pink ball of life tumbles from the room, forward-rolling all the way across the floor till it unfurls at my feet.

Two legs, two arms and two giant pink bunny ears stare up at me, glitter covering the better half of her face.

"Come join us," Sayra cajoles elatedly, "It's wayyyy cosier in there than out here."

She shivers for dramatic effect, and I can't help but giggle at the absurdity.

"Out there is the big bad." Irene calls.

"So big and so bad." Sayra agrees, taking my hand in hers but remaining in a gremlin crouch, as she leads me towards the cubby.

"I concur." Amaya pipes up.

"My sentiments exactly!"

It's Rylan's voice that has me allowing Sayra to walk me to the room under the stairs.

That was what I'd been looking to do, right? Find Rylan?

I'm either drunk or insane or both- but it's a harsh mix. Their voices are hard to pin-point and I don't think I can feel my legs- or remember what they feel like normally.

"Darling...." It's my last attempt to salvage this, reaching for her just before she touches the door, my hand curling around her wrist protectively.

She doesn't know what she's doing.

She doesn't even realise I'm hurt, if she did- we wouldn't be here, right?

But she would run away if I loved her louder. Maybe... maybe she's just too afraid of others' eyes to accept my hands.

"Tenny come *on*."

The basilisk has a hold of her other wrist now and is tugging her towards the room of clouds.

I stand firm. I won't budge.

She can come with me if she chooses.

I won't let her be mindlessly dragged from one place to the next just because she bends to the desires of others with as much resistance as a magnet to iron will.

The snake may tug but I will simply stand.

I don't know what to do.

My friends are in there, and they're safe. I know Aletheia would get along with them, all of them- but Maddy...

I don't want to hurt anyone.

I turn to Aletheia, the one on the other side of seven. How can I explain to her that I'm wanting to stay because of my friends and not because of Maddy?

But maybe I can't, because maybe... maybe that would be lying.

I don't think I say these things out loud, but Aletheia's face drains of colour all the same.

One day I'll tell her that I can feel her emotions as strong as if they were sentences. One day I'll tell her and maybe she will feel bad about it. Or maybe that day will never come, and I just have to outwait this damned barrier and leave.

Maybe it's better this way.

One day I will not have to ask for her love, one day she will love me just because she wants to. But... that day is not today.

Aletheia's eyes harden.

"I'll make this easy for you then."

Aletheia drops my hand, my body catapulting forwards into the room.

I barely have time to watch her leave, glancing at her mid-freefall as she swipes up a bottle of something from the hallway

and brings it to her mouth.
  What have I done...

CHAPTER 24

BLINDED BY THE LIGHTS

"Yes!!" several voices cheer similar phrases of approval as I fall face-first into a pile of squish.

It's barely six metres in any direction, the walls indescribable-mainly because not an inch of them is on show. It's like an astrologist and a hippie interior-designer got together, ate some dodgy mushrooms, and puked up a room. Tapestries and fabric have been haphazardly stapled to every exposed bit of white, covering them in reds and blues and a multicoloured madness of mandala and geometric designs. The floor is no easier to interpret, pillows of all shapes and sizes crammed into every crevice.

I'm not fully certain there *is* a floor.

Rugs of different shades and texture are layered to the point where I'm not prepared for where steady ground is; unsure of the give and take of the very earth.

Little cubes of steadily changing colour are planted in several spots around the room, never displaying the same colour as the next; so that the lights battle for colour-dominance in the air around us.

Emmy and Corbin lie on one side, Maddy next to them. Sayra scrambles over to Amaya and Rylan on the other side, curling up by their feet and fiddling with a cube that seems to be infinite; unwinding and winding up again without ever breaking apart.

That's kind of what the universe does when you realm hop, I guess. Unwinding and unravelling to then re-knit itself in the place you want to travel to.

Maybe we are inside an infinity cube...

"You made it then." Irene muses, sat in the middle of the wall- opposite the door- a smile toying at her lips.

I'm on my front, propped up by my elbows, the world still righting itself. Irene's eyes widen slightly, as she reaches behind me, hastily pulling the door shut and my skirt back over me in the process.

"Bit of a clutsy drunk, aren't ya?" She says not unkindly, taking me by the hand and lifting me to sit next to her; her other hand clasped around a joint.

Amaya giggles, "She's *never* been drunk before."

I have to practically hold my jaw shut to stop my mouth from falling open.

Amaya lies languidly across Rylan's lap, her head lolling back to stare at the cacophony of colours and lights dancing across the ceiling. She's never laid down in public, other than to sleep I didn't think she *did* that. She never even slouches, let alone whatever she's doing right now. She's humming a tune that harmonises well enough with the dull tones and music that are coming from a mini speaker in the corner, Rylan's fingers running through her hair in smoothing motions. He's got headphones on that I can vaguely here base tones from, strong and rhythmic and loud enough that they should be vibrating him at that rate.

They look at peace.

This room is way better than room Numero Uno.

"Rylan, are you...?" I try to ask, not sure what to ask or how to ask it in a room full of people.

He lifts his head groggily as Amaya pokes him into consciousness, removing one side of the headphones. A smile splits his face in two and his hair flops over one eye as he squints at me through the haze.

"Dad's doing it all wrong, Ten." He drawls, as if everyone else isn't here to witness, "*This* is what it's made for."

He leans back again, replacing the headphone and returning his attention to Amaya's hair and the ceiling.

But they'll ask what he means- he'll have to explain what his dad's like, then one of them will call the police or get involved or tell him he should be doing something, *anything* to stop it...

No one bats an eye.

Everyone is in their own little world, even Maddy is hypnotised by Sayra's technical-movements with the infinity-cube, and the colours that wind their way through the room in and amongst the clouds of smoke.

"No one will notice if you leave it." Irene mutters from the left side of her mouth, eyeing me up as she takes another drag- the end glowing orange as the room turns red, "Concentration's a little sporadic at the moment, don't think too much on it."

Does she... how could she possibly know?

She pauses, looking me up and down. Sizing me up.

Before extending the joint to me, "In fact, don't think at all."

The long green cigarette burns in front of my face, a challenge-

"It's not a challenge," Irene says, as if reading my mind, "Just a suggestion. I find these things easier to enjoy with a little help." Her eyes meet mine and I watch as they soften with sincerity, as if the rest of the people truly aren't here, "I'll take care of you, walk you through it, if you want to. It's your choice."

But I don't want more choices

"I... I uhh..."

I glance around at them all. Emmy and Corbin winding their

hands together slowly like it's the most magical thing they've ever done. Maddy and Sayra seeing into the cube like it holds the secrets of the universe, and Amaya and Rylan- both at peace in their own worlds but still holding each other.

And then there is Irene.

She looks exactly how she normally does.

"Are you always...?" I half-ask.

She grins, Cheshire-cat-like and powerful.

"Eighty-twenty, but that's not a brag," She says, smoke tendrils snaking their way from mouth to nostrils, "We all have our vices- and their reasons for conception."

I nod, glancing at Rylan and seeing Irene smile in my periphery. Maybe I wasn't being as subtle as usual, or maybe she just understands me easier than most.

I take the thing between my fingers and drag the smoke into my lungs.

Huh, that wasn't so bad.

That was actually pretty *smoo-*

My lungs heave and it's like they're on fire, my coughs stirring everyone from their individual trances and drawing their attention to me and my first toke.

I'm dying- I'm pretty sure that's what this is. The uncontrollable coughing and eye-watering and the hellfire running down my oesophagus. But as Irene titters the others join in, restoring the balance with an emotion as easy as calming the water by holding the bucket still.

Irene is control personified.

She raises the joint to me again, taking my chin in her hand as the coughs dwindle and I go cross-eyed as she places the end of it to my lips.

My pulse jumps through my veins and she smiles.

"Higher heart rate will help it circulate," She smirks, watching me eagerly as I take in another drag, "As will the coughing, so don't panic." It burns a little less this time, "You've got this."

My heart continues to shove its way out of my chest with an unprecedented purpose, focused on the feeling of Irene's painted fingers on my jawline.

"That was rude." I rasp, Irene simply chuckling and my cheeks blushing at the intimacy of the action.

-And how I'd wished it was Aletheia, how her face went through my brain unhindered and how I'd yearned that I could really feel her fingers on my skin-

"Just you wait Tenny," Maddy says suddenly, throwing herself across the room and placing her head in my lap, "You'll *love* it."

The room is vibrating, or maybe it's my leg.

Up and down and up and down and-

I've been watching the colours drift and change over this specific mandala tapestry for over half an hour- or an hour- or maybe less or more I'm not sure.

Irene was talking about... no, Sayra was doing headstands, and Amaya was trying and failing- she fell and hit Maddy in the head with her arm.

Yes, that happened and then... then Emmy was saying about determinism I think- that we were always going to be here and do this, so prophecies could be real and exist somewhere if someone had the ability to predict the velocity and '*something else*' of every particle. Irene said I felt like I was destined or something.

"Tenaya?" Amaya is sat in front of me, her hands on either side of my face, Maddy still lain in my lap.

Irene is on my right.

Emmy and Corbin on my left.

Rylan in the corner.

This room is very small, but I think I like it being small. More homely, more corners more ground more soft and safe and things and people and-

"Tenaya? *Can you hear me*? Is she okay?" Amaya asks, I think she's distressed, and I want to tell her I'm good- but words are locked inside right now.

Can't say the thoughts- but I am having them. Because I can hear them. See? I can yell them in my head-

I AM FINE.

But they can't hear inside my head, I think Aletheia can though, it feels like Irene can too sometimes.

Irene pulls on my shoulder and my eyes meet hers, her irises large and searching my face for things I'm not sure of.

"Nod for good." She says, simple and straight to it.

I take a moment before my body reacts for me.

I nod.

She nods back, pushing me back to looking at Amaya.

"She's okay- first time. Give her an hour." Irene says. I'm so thankful there's someone here who can speak for me.

Amaya's hands stroke up and down my arms, which I'm okay with- maybe they feel weird, her hands certainly do. I'm not used to being touched, let alone stroked and lain on- other than Aletheia, and even then...

"What- hey are you-" Amaya moves away to the corner and Maddy's hand comes up to poke my cheek.

To get my attention.

I look down, the colour cubes are shading her face blue, and her lips are parted; the red under blue light making them dark and bold.

Aletheia's skin turns blue, maybe it's her? No, Maddy's hair is brown and eyes not-diamond and skin not actually blue. But for a moment she morphs, her lips growing lighter and kinder, her hair colouring fairer and she's Aletheia. But she's Maddy, and she's talking- so I should listen.

I must try to pay attention.

Get the gist at least- *come on Tenaya.*

"My parents won't be back till tomorrow, so you can stay as long as you like," She says, her eyes growing sadder, "They're never home for long anymore."

Distantly, I hear pillows moving and people shuffling, but Maddy is talking and looks very sad- so I should pay attention.

I nod, which seems to be the right thing to do. She doesn't seem to need more encouragement than that.

"Dad works abroad, and mum goes with him when she gets the chance. They don't really like each other anymore though." She closes her eyes, "Sometimes I don't think they like *me* much either."

Is she... I should be sympathetic- empathetic.

But that's... why is that difficult?

She has a house full of people, friends who adore her, money to go anywhere, a university that others would kill to be in, parents who give her everything and skin so primed it may never have been bruised...

That's why.

"Rylan- Rylan it's oka-*AH!*" Amaya's exclamation draws my attention away from Maddy as I watch her fall to the ground, Rylan looking pale as a ghost as he shoves himself up and out of the room.

He opened the door.

There's a world outside this room and he just went and walked out into it.

I feel sick.

I should be following him.

Amaya cradles her head for a second, pausing for only a moment before scrambling after him and out the door too.

I should *definitely* be following them.

"It's not like they don't *try*," Maddy continues, as if what just happened hadn't actually happened... did it happen?

"Mum takes me out on the weekends she's home, and Dad does his best on the evenings he's not busy. But I just thought I'd be more of a priority, you know? I'm their *daughter*, you'd think they would make more time for me before I leave." She sighs, "Sucks to be the least favourite only child."

Be empathetic. Be kind.

This is hard for her.

She's... she's *so* stuck in the victim personality and I am far too high to be able to give her the attention she's searching for. Especially when my friends might be in trouble.

I want to speak but I can't, and Irene is busy with Sayra because Sayra is upset the door is open when it shouldn't be.

To be fair- I'm upset about that too.

Emmy leans over, Corbin falling forwards with her, "Don't worry pet, Rylan was getting panicky and knocked her accidentally, I saw the whole thing." She gives my arm a soft stroke, "Try not to fret too much- or you'll be lookin' like..." She trails off, indicating to where Sayra is being rocked back and forth on the floor with Irene wrapped around her, fending off fervid whimpers as Irene reaches with one hand for the door.

I need to follow Rylan and Amaya out.

"S-sorry, Maddy I need to-" I say whilst already moving, Maddy rolling off me with an *'oomph'* as I make for the door.

The floor tilts and turns and the colours bleed together but still I push forwards until I reach the exit. Irene's hand lands on my wrist, halting me.

"I can't follow you right now," She says, gesturing to Sayra, "You sure you're gunna be okay?"

"I'll come with!" Maddy exclaims before I can reply, her hand reaching down and taking mine before dragging me out of the room.

The last thing I see before the colourful room is snatched from my view is Irene, her mouth bent into a frown and her eyebrows set low over her purple eyes.

Have I upset her?

"Nah, I'm sure she's *fine.*" Maddy says, *did I say that last bit out loud?*

The world is dark grey and cold, vibrations still pulsating through the floorboards on account of 'Room Numero Uno'. Raucous laughter and yells still emanate from behind 'Pick Me Up'.

I forgot such places even existed.

They were forever ago.

Maddy's hand in mine continues to drag me even though I don't move my legs, they are their own sentience and they only follow.

"Where- do you know?" I don't think that was a full sentence but it's the best I can do.

Maddy grins, pulling me up the spiral stairway. Spirals are a bad plan right now, as the drinks and the smoke start to blend and merge together inside of me and threaten to deplete over the side of the railing.

"Wait- *Why*?"

"You'll see." She sing-songs as we reach the second floor... third floor? This place is massive.

And she still complains- no. That's not fair, people can still be lonely in big places. People can struggle even in luxury.

But she does still get tended to by both parents- even if she can't see it.

We meander through a hallway that's straight but sways, or I do- I'm not sure. There's a darkness at the fringes of my vision that I'm not sure is really there.

We stop outside a door that's lilac with white rims, the hallway also white- but appearing grey in the dark.

Everything looks grey.

I want to go back to the room.

She presses a finger to her lips, as if I could speak or make noise right now if I wanted to, before beckoning me to put an ear to the door.

I do so, and immediately wish I hadn't.

A noise I've never heard Amaya make before pierces my eardrums, followed by the creaking and groaning from what I assume is a four-poster-bed.

I push away from the door and cover my ears with my hands, closing my eyes as if this will remove me from the moment.

Well, at least Rylan isn't panicked and Amaya is... well she's just fine.

With my senses removed I suddenly register the light-headedness for what it is, my eyes springing open just as I start to fall.

"Woah- hey- come on, let's get you back to the party huh?"

I don't- I think-

She leads me down some stairs, but I don't remember getting to the bottom.

I don't remember drinking more but I know I must have.

I don't remember going back into room Numero Uno but I know I did, because I remember Maddy's arm around my waist and her twirling me around and something silver silver silver

She was there, always there- but I don't...

I'm-

It's dark.

That I'm sure of.

It's dark and it's quiet but my ears are loud and thick with it; a high-pitched tone still ringing in them.

I'm lying on a sofa in a room I don't recognise. There's a chandelier, and wallpaper that looks textured and fancy, with a bookcase and a desk in my periphery. So, I'm probably still somewhere in Maddy's mansion.

But not in any of the three rooms.

There's no bed, so I'm not in the room with Rylan and

Amaya either.

From the ground comes a light tune, one that registers over the thrumming in my ears, and I manage to turn my head enough to see Maddy. She's lying on top of a blow-up-mattress, a blanket covering her and a single pillow under her head as she hums a melody I don't recognise.

Her eyes are open, and she stares at me a long while, her humming stopped as she just takes me in.

The silence is so thick that it's like a physical weight on my chest. My mouth is dry and my eyes can barely keep themselves open, they strain in their efforts.

This feels important.

Her red lips are full and open just the tiniest amount, her big green eyes- huge and glittering in the faint light of the moon. Her lashes cast fine shadows across her painted cheekbones.

"I like you, Tenny." She says into the darkness, so softly that I think she may not have said it at all.

But she did.

And I can say nothing back, I don't know how to speak right now. I just blink back at her with my heart catapulting inside of my chest and my brain working overtime to try and keep me conscious.

She smiles, "I like you, and I want to keep getting to know you... as more than a friend." She says, her bottom lip fitting briefly between her teeth.

This can't be real.

This can't... this is what I've wanted for years...

So why doesn't it feel okay?

"I'm not talking to Max anymore, he's gone- if that's your worry." She says, reaching a hand up to gently clasp mine in the darkness, "But... I want to take this slow. Do it right. I don't know how to be as open as you are, so... can we keep this as just our thing? For now?"

As... as *open* as *me*?

She has the wrong person.

She can't possibly think that I am open with anyone, that I am wholly honest about how I think or feel or what I go through on a daily basis. Do I truly do such a good job at hiding things that she's just taken what I display for the world at face value?

Does she think that what I've shown her is all that I am?

Maybe if she knew, she'd be less likely to complain about a slightly-absent parent relationship at the age of twenty.

But all I do is nod.

"I- I think I can do that." I say in a croak, because I don't know what else to say.

It seems to be enough though, as she smiles.

"Good." She says softly, as if all her jigsaw pieces just fell magically into place.

She closes her eyes and begins to hum again, rocking her head gently from side to side.

I roll back onto my back, one hand still clasped in hers, allowing the darkness to take me once again.

I've kept bigger secrets from the rest of the world, what's one more, I guess.

CHAPTER 25
FOREVER DRUNK

She's dancing.

She was in the tiny room for a while, not that I could just leave her. I can't. I tried and failed and here I am, watching her- protecting her.

Always protecting her.

I don't take issue with dancing in general, quite the opposite. I do, however, have a problem with the human-sized leach grabbing onto her when the lights are dim enough.

Does my darling not notice? Does she not see that the sadistic succubus only moves to touch her when all eyes are elsewhere. That she only comes close if she can get out again just as quickly? I slip from the edge of the room, moving to the front door where I lean on its edge, my previous drinks littered around this spot.

My spot.

The advantage of copious drinking perhaps- blissful ignorance to a painful reality.

Why it doesn't have that same effect on me is confounding.

The floor sways and the lights flicker and- I'm pretty sure the door used to be straight... I can't be sure.

There are people with six- wait, no- four? Maybe four or two arms, definitely not six.

But she's dancing dancing dancing

And I'm surrounded by the bottles I've downed, leant against a sinking door.

The door is sinking, yes, or- or no I may be falling.

This may hurt.

My knees give way and I expect the floor-

"Hey- woah there, careful gorgeous!" She smells of sage and green, her purple eyes locked in on my own.

And she held me up- is holding me up. I can't feel her, but she can... see me?

"Can you herr me?" I try, my words fumbled after not using my voice in so long, and the drinks; probably mostly the drinks.

She tilts her head at me, her brown and violet hair so pinpoint straight for someone perceived by everyone to be chaotic.

"Yeah, I can hear you- what of it?" She asks, shaking her head and offering me her hand, "I'm... Irene." She pauses, her eyes growing sad before she shakes her head. She gives me the up and down, her hand moving to the wall behind my head as I didn't immediately take it- taking to leaning. "Love the dress."

Her wrist is chained by a tiny sliver of silver, an engraving on a section of metal that reads; "She believed she could, so she did".

Curious.

Irene- the friend from the diner. This is the friend with the pink girlfriend.

And she's standing very close.

Maybe too close?

"Isn't the pink one your darling?" I ask as she presses in, her body coming into contact with mine and her eyes almost completely black, surrounded by the slimmest ring of purple.

If I thought I was far gone- this girl was a whole new story. I don't even think she can see what's right in front of her... yet, she can see me.

She touches my chin with her finger, lifting me to eye level, "We have what one might call an 'open agreement'," She muses, the metal ball on her tongue flicking against her teeth, "We're... polyamorous. But- I'm more curious than interested in that way, don't worry... I forgot about the diamonds in your eyes..."

She pours her gaze over me like cold water, dousing me with her stare as she deciphers me. This is not what I expected, but I guess maybe she's on something- or maybe I'm on something.

Maybe all of this is in my head, or maybe...

Has the barrier-

Regardless of her saying she wasn't interested, her face moves closer to mine, so close- too close. Her nose brushes mine and her eyes flutter closed as she presses the softest of kisses to my cheek.

Not my lips.

She pulls away, a sadness hovering over her again like a wraith; darkness folding over her features like nightfall.

What is happening- why did that feel...

"Ireeeene- what're you doing you're about to peak!" A pink puffball rolls from the door under the stairs, floating over to where we stand.

"Baby, I'm talking to... my new friend, yeah, she- she-" Irene's eyes seem to haze over for a second then come back, "She is kind of phasing in and out... am I tripping?"

The girl 'baby' sighs, grabbing her arm, her eyes not registering my existence as she drags Irene away and back to the hidden hole in the house.

"Come on, outside bad right now- inside good." Girl-baby says as she dips into the hovel.

Irene pauses at the entrance to the cave, her eyes landing on me again and a curious kind of smile spanning her face.

"I've found you before- around Tenaya." She says, and for a moment she's almost touching sobriety, "Stick around, and if you can- look after her. That girl needs an entire squadron to get through this year."

I nod, hypnotised with wonder that this girl has managed through a drug-induced haze, to pass through the visual barriers to see me.

She waves me off, "See you later, star-girl!"

The door to the tiny dimension in the house closes and the smell slowly fades from the hall.

Found me before... star girl...

I can travel the stars

I didn't think I summoned the crease but it's there, right in front of my face, coaxing me to do what I'm pretty sure I'm not allowed to do.

But my hand is already reaching for it and I can still see the snakes arm wrapped around her shoulders as she dances dances dances-

Mother will kill me, but I don't care.

I can't be here anymore.

The world rips away in a whirlwind of nothing and I'm freefalling in a state of ambiguous trust that the universe will take me where I need to go. Not back to her, I can't be next to her right now. She is young and naïve and so hellbent on making her own mistakes that I may as well be invisible.

I am invisible, I just thought I was less-so to her.

The world comes crashing back and I'm planted face first in onyx and silver rugs. The fuzzy texture smushes against my face, and I have to prepare myself to heave off of the thing; throwing myself upright- or as upright as the tilted world will allow. I don't remember my mother's bedroom being on an angle.

She watches me from her chaise longue, her body dulled to a less threatening temperature in the safety of her own house. She practically becomes her furniture- her usually burning and crimson flesh now a muted charcoal; the bedroom itself being mostly obsidian, with silver and the occasional red embroidery.

"Hello, mother dearest," I say, as snidely and coherently as possible, she needn't know I'm drunk- never noticed as a child anyway, "Fancy seeing you 'ere. 'Tis your bedroom though, so perhaps weirder that I'm 'ere."

I use an arm to casually lean against one of the beams of her four-poster-bed, the curtains roped to the beams during the day. Or is it the night?

I can't be sure.

Time differences across worlds is a weird one, you'd think time would be the one universal constant.

But no.

She folds over the book she was reading, the cover as black as the rest of the room; the crisp white pages a startling contrast.

"That was quite the entrance dear," She says, her tone clipped, "Not that it isn't a pleasure to see you- but I thought I'd told you to stay put?"

Stay put, don't leave, sit at home, remain in Selheim, don't realm hop, don't move, stay away from father, stay on earth, stay put-

Stay put

Stay put

"That's how it always is, isn't it?" I grit out, the words burning sulphur on my tongue, "Follow your orders, stay in one place, don't cause trouble. But- what if I want to leave? What if, I don't want to be under your thumb anymore?" I spit, watching her as she places the book to the side and moves to sit forward, eyes tracked on me.

"I'm sure I don't know what you-"

"You know." I interrupt, her eyes widening, "All my life, the moment you came into it- you put me in a box and prayed I'd stay there. You left me alone just as much as father did but went one step further. You took my freedom." The fury that's built for years is bubbling up and I don't think I'm able to push it down.

I don't think I want to anymore.

Darling does. All the time.

She pushes it down down down until there's nothing on the surface anymore. I've had to dig through so many layers just to scratch at the ones that actually matter. She doesn't let anything in.

Not even me.

"I killed my best friend and you said nothing." I hiss, aching at the memory, "You didn't even ask me if I wanted to talk about it. I was a chore to you. A pet to keep safe- but a house pet through and through. But I am so much more." I stand, trying to hold the ground still under my feet.

She doesn't say a word.

"You never wanted me."

It's the thought I've never let through. The one I know to be true but hurts too much to say.

I don't even notice I'm crying until mother stands, swaying over to me in the weirdly disjointed but elegant way she does, like a stop-motion video; and wipes my cheek.

I try to turn away, but she holds my cheek in a vice-like grip, twisting me back to her; her own eyes burning now.

"I never wanted a daughter," She says quietly, and it feels like a harpoon through my heart, "I wasn't allowed to have one. The Fates thought they saw to that."

Her words hit weirdly, taking their time in registering on my foggy brain.

"What do you- what?" I ask, my mouth dry.

"Your father took you from me the day of your birth," She says softly, "Wouldn't let me visit- and at the time I was weak, foolish, still aching for my own freedom." She shakes her head, "But the day I heard they were going to execute you- I burned holes in the fabric of the universe to get to you."

The heat radiates from her body and I can see amber hues glowing through the cracks.

"I don't know how to be a mother, I never have." She says, stroking my damp cheek with her thumb and causing them to steam away, "All I knew- all I know- is that I must keep you safe. I wouldn't let you leave as a child because I knew your father and the Fates were after you. I can't save you from halfway across the galaxy, my love. You have surpassed my expectations in so many ways, and I know I have failed you in just as many." She lowers her hand, and I feel my heart begging for her to return it, "I only wish for you to live."

I don't move for a moment, I'm too busy picking up the pieces of my shattered reality. I never thought my father was the good guy, but I definitely had my mother pinned as the bad one.

Wordlessly I rush forward and embrace her around her waist, clinging to her like that boy in the park had done to his own mother. I yearn for that connection so badly, perhaps this is the closest I will ever get.

Her arms wrap around my shoulders and hold me to her.

"I don't know how to be a daughter either." I mumble into her side.

I've always rejected her, never let her even try to be a mother. Always fighting to be loved by a father who never acted like one.

I still do.

"A daughter isn't a role to be played, or a duty. You are my daughter, no matter how you act. And I am your mother- if you will have me." She says, kneeling down so that my arms can go around her shoulders and hers around my middle.

Is this what having a home feels like?

Is it my fault I never had it? Because I didn't ask?

"Why are you choosing now, to say these things?" She asks.

The question is fair. Drunkenness may be the skin-level answer, but...

"I need my darling to be honest with those she loves." I say, knowing that's why I was driven here in the first place. "She lets people attach themselves who don't love her, she lets people abuse her and doesn't stop them, she... she won't set herself free."

Mother nods, pulling back to look me in the eyes.

"Are you sure she is right for you, my dear?"

It's not the first time I've thought it, but it's the first time it's been said out loud.

"My darling is a reticent soul, a giver," I say slowly, building the answer as I go, "She is shy, and meek, and never chooses to help herself. But under it all she is fierce and desperate for adventure. She is beautiful in body and soul." I smile at the memory, "The first time I saw her she was in the arms of my future self, fated to be so. I saw two of her that day, and that was the last thing I glimpsed before I was imprisoned. But for those few moments- time seemed to slow. She was the beginning and the end and for a second- I saw my life in her. I know she is meant to be mine, and I hers... she just needs time to see it."

Mother smiles, and I wobble a little- maybe more than a little, because she scoops me up in her arms; cradling me like the baby she never got to hold.

"Then that's exactly where you should be, my child." She says, drawing a blue line through the veil of the dimension and leaning through it.

One moment I'm in mother's bedroom, the next I'm being lowered onto the sleeping body of my darling.

"Stay safe, daughter." Mother says, before the veil seals behind her.

My darling is out cold. Usually such a movement would wake her, but many substances clearly forbid her brain from wakefulness. The full weight of my body is folded atop hers from where mother placed me, yet she doesn't stir. She breathes heavily, her mouth ajar and her hair plastered over her face in a deep drunken sleep; her steady snores the only thing to pierce the silence.

I move without thinking, my own eyelids drooping, as I slip the strands from her face and mouth. I curl into her, tucking myself under the throw. She doesn't rouse, but one arm comes up around me, wrapping me against her so my face is snug against her neck.

Tonight is the night I learnt I have two homes.

CHAPTER 26
TAG, YOU'RE IT

Light pounds into the side of my skull from the booth in the diner, the tiny streams of blinding cruelty searing into my corneas without mercy.

Hangovers- turns out- suck.

Irene sits opposite me, holding a bedraggled Sayra at her side. Beside them is Corbin, and Rylan by the window. Amaya opposite him with Emmy, Aletheia and I making up the opposite the side.

Maddy had other plans today. That's okay, there's not enough room in the booth anyway.

None of us look okay though.

They'd all tagged along to my morning shift, by the end of which I'm feeling like death incarnate and they're all barely conscious. Aletheia seemingly worst of all, and Irene appearing like the most put-together one; not that that's anything new.

I didn't know hell was featured in this realm, but currently my mind resides there. I've scoured many a mythical hellscape in my time, the Duat, Underworld, Dubnos and everything in between, yet I still feel the pain of substance abuse like knives through my cranium. If only my abilities could heal the aftereffects of alcohol, how merry my life would be.

My pain is at least shared by the table. The girl Irene keeps flicking glances at me, almost like she can see me- but not quite.

I'll work out how to test it when my brain stops crying.

I don't know how to feel about what happened between Maddy and I, I don't even know if I'm happy. Shouldn't I be happy that my childhood crush also likes me?

But then I woke curled up with another girl- not just another girl- Aletheia. The woman who has single-handedly turned my life on its axis; for better or for worse.

The woman I can't touch.

The goddess I am *beyond* unworthy of.

"So," Irene says too loudly, breaking the silence with a sledgehammer, "What're people's plans for Halloween?"

There's a collective soft groan from everyone, at the prospect of more alcohol. I think I may throw up.

It's for sure a possibility.

"Well, count me and Rylan out of the mainstream mania," Amaya says, reaching across to take his hand, "We've been planning a Halloween movie marathon- which you're all invited to if you feel like it."

Irene flicks Sayra's bunny-ears, Sayra's face is mostly obstructed by sunglasses, so big and impenetrable and completely reflective that there's barely any of her 'face' on show. She doesn't respond, her mouth remaining a thin line, but she raises a thumbs up and lowers it again robotically.

Irene chuckles, bouncing Sayra slightly so that she winces.

"If we are able to stand without the potential of passing out by that point," Corbin mumbles with his head in his arms on the table, "Then we're in."

Emmy grimaces but shrugs, her face similarly smushed in her hands, "Ordinarily I wouldn't be spoken on behalf of," She pauses to burp internally, "As of right now though, it's a necessity."

I try to tuck myself smaller as the table turns to me.

"We're down," Irene says, looking to me sceptically, "What about you?"

It's a loaded question, one that doesn't go amiss by anyone at the table. They're all aware that Maddy is throwing a Halloween party as well, and they all know I came from the same room as Maddy did this morning.

Moral conundrum 101, long-term crush or my best friends that I see on the daily. Friends that- from the looks they're giving me- will *definitely* hold my decision against me.

I sigh, holding my pounding head, "Can I think about it? It's not for another two weeks yet."

They all give each other sideways glances, and shrug. Since when did Rylan and Amaya get so buddy-buddy with Irene's lot?

"We could stay at home if you'd like?" I offer, placing a hand on her arm.

She stiffens slightly before relaxing and giving me a small look of appreciation, moving her hand to be next to my own.

She seems different. I'm not sure if it's the dwindling effects of substance abuse, or something passed between herself and the basilisk.

The misshapen group continues to sip at their coffees and share in their collective pain.

But it's Irene that catches my attention.

Memories of the night before slip into my brain and I feel her eyes on me, just like then, dousing me in a cold gaze.

I'm not sure if she can really see me, surely she would say something?

But she just sits there, cool as anything, keeping Sayra aloft and nursing her coffee with the other hand.

"I'm onto you." I hiss, not sure if I mean it as a threat or a curiosity.

She doesn't so much as bat an eye.

"Tenaya," Casimir's voice rings through the diner, and it takes me a moment to turn and stand- Aletheia squirming out the seat to allow me past, "Can I speak to you in here for a minute?"

To most people it seems like a polite request.

A request from my manager- why should I refuse?

I gulp back my distrust and nod, waving off the table as I go.

He moves back just enough that I can squeeze by, but not so much that his hand doesn't graze my ass on the way past. Barely a whisper, but it makes me recoil further into myself, praying this exchange is fast.

The kitchen door swings shut behind her and I'm left with her ragtag group of misfits. I'm not sure why I chose to remain here, instead of following my darling. Probably something to do with the defiant force on the table opposite me, staring daggers in the direction they left in.

She knows.

"I think I should-" Irene begins.

"If you swoop in every time he tries to talk to her, he'll just ban you from the Diner." Sayra grumbles, clearly annoyed that she had to use her voice.

"Swoop in? Why would there be swooping?" Rylan asks, looking to Irene in confusion.

Ah, so my darling keeps different things hidden from different people- not wise.

Choose your secrets and keep them- or don't, the moment you tell one; you complicate it.

"Every time you say 'swooping'- I nearly puke. Choose a new word." Amaya whines, slumping forward on the table but keeping her eyes up, "But yeah, what do you mean by... it?"

Irene flicks Sayra on her actual head this time, Sayra's hands flying up in defence.

"It's not my place to say, and I don't know anything really," Irene says, looking from them to the door and back, "All I know is that he isn't to be trusted."

Amaya looks hurt, her bottom lip jutting out indignantly.

"Why wouldn't she tell us? We're her best friends, we should know about this stuff."

Irene raises a judgmental eyebrow, "Didn't you nearly condemn her the other week- for reasons we shan't readdress?"

The table goes silent as the statement settles. Unspoken words heard by the transgender, pansexual and polyamorous people.

Amaya has gone a shade of red unrivalled by her hair, avoiding their eyes.

"I never condemned her." She grumbles, but doesn't argue further.

The table falls into an uncomfortable silence as time drags on.

Irene's eyes keep flicking to me, almost imperceptibly, but I can feel when she does.

The time draws out and my skin starts to itch, agitated.

"I don't appreciate you bad-mouthing me to your little friends." Casimir postures, having stood me in the corner by the fire exit.

His arms are folded atop his belly, looking down at me across his nose like someone might a naughty dog.

"I c-can assure you, I don't know-"

"Don't. Play. Dumb." He spits, his fist embedding itself in the countertop.

Only into the chopping-board though- he's making an effort to muffle his intimidations.

He can't hurt me- my friends are outside.

I need to believe this.

I need my body to understand this, so it stops trembling.

"That witch who painted the mural, she looks at me like I'm dirt under foot." He growls, stalking forwards until I'm backed up against the door, "Do I *look* like dirt under foot, to you?"

One of my hands rests on the bar that releases the doors, I have an escape- know it, body *know it.*

"N-n-n-no," I stutter, trying and failing to compose myself, "I haven't s-s-said an-n-n-nything."

I need this job

I need this money

For Tabi Tabi Tabi

He smiles then, arm extended to lean over me so that he's close enough that I can smell his putrid breath.

"Tell me, I'm curious, how does someone as prudish and *pathetic* as you, deal with sex?"

The question has my heart in my throat, a lump in my oesophagus.

What did he just ask me?

"I... I don't..." I can't think.

"I could help you, you clearly need it," He smirks, "I mean, have you ever even been *touched*?"

His lowered hand moves in the directions of my skirts and my own hand tenses on the escape latch.

Which he sees.

His hand lashes out and slams my wrist up and against the door, crushing it in his paws.

"You think you're so *clever*," He snarls, spittle flecking onto my cheek, "So self-assured. Well, your little friend is done with her *precious* painting." Ice spills down my back even with the pressure of his hand clamped around my wrist, "So behave, maybe I'll still offer to *help* you- if you're a good little girl."

He comes in closer then, his face so close I can see his pores and the dirt that resides there.

Submerge, go in, push down.

I feel Kuro raise his hackles on my skin, vibrating in a way that tells me he wants off. That he will protect me if I let him.

But he can't come off without my permission- or Aletheia's.

So he's staying put.

You're okay, just don't be here, heart can beat, body can buckle, but *tuck your brain away*.

Push it down down down

Safe.

"You breathe a word of this to anyone, and you'll be out of

a job so quick you won't have time to remove your apron," He grins, "Oh, and probably a home too- I've been hearing murmurs from your table of a certain orientation," *push it down*, "Let me see if I can swing you back the other way. For both our sakes."

He shoves into me and in doing so pushes my hips back into the door-levers.

He releases me in the same moment I fall backwards into the alley, my ankle twisting painfully as I collapse on the grimy concrete.

Casimir sneers, arms folded as he watches me scramble.

Screw this.

I stand up from the table at the same time Irene rises, our eyes suddenly meeting across the table when there's a crash from the kitchen.

Neither of us hesitates before leaping over people and tables alike towards the kitchen doors.

She turns for only a second as we go- motioning for Rylan to stay put, as he halts in his move to follow.

I let Irene go first, slamming through the opening and rushing to the open escape doors.

"What happened?" Irene demands as she pushes past the manager without so much as a glance to him, moving to help her up.

"My darling, what did he do to you?" I ask, covering her ankle with my hands and healing what I can as she tries to stand.

It's sprained, not broken.

She shakes her head, looking briefly up at her manager, then back to us.

"I-I t-t-tripped." She stammers.

I know her stuttering only happens when she's around the blonde demon- or intimidated.

I wheel on the man, stood in the kitchen with his arms crossed. I move lightning fast, rising in the air so I'm hovering in front of him- above him.

"You shall perish the moment I can feel the pulse in your neck between my fingers." I hiss, fury burning through me.

"C-Casimir was just t-t-telling me to watch my step with the door, b-b-because it's loose." *She finds her footing and I turn to her, confused.*

She's lying.

Why is she lying for him?

Irene clearly feels the same as me as she pushes her, "Tenaya, you don't have to-"

"Really, I'm fine." *She snaps, and I can see she's reached some sort of breaking point, because she moves Irene's hands aside,* "I just need to take more care next time."

The monster- Casimir, nods in agreement.

"Clever plan," He says, gesturing behind him, "Now both of you- out of my kitchen."

I move back to her side, touching lightly to her arm but she flinches, dragging her arms around herself and moving faster than me and Irene, out of the room.

I make to follow her, having nearly made it out of the kitchen, when I hear Irene's voice.

"Don't think you'll get away with this." She seethes, and I stop to watch as she sizes him up, strong and fearless even at a head shorter.

He frowns, looking down at her through his nose.

"You'd do best to keep walking." He grits, his anger barely concealed.

I take a step back towards her but stop as she moves closer to him- a threat.

"Through all your efforts and false bravado, you still fail to intimidate me," She growls with a smile, pointing a finger into his chest so he flinches, his lips twitching frantically and chin jutting like they're possessed, "That girl is under my protection. So, you'd do best, to back off."

Irene sanuters past me, defiant rage flaring in her eyes as she does so, and for the briefest of seconds they almost appear to be glowing.

I've never wanted someone to be my friend more in my life.

The door closes behind her and I pause.

Waiting.

His lips continue to spasm, like someone's taken a live wire to the underside of his face, his arms shaking. In one movement he slams his full weight through his hand and into the chopping boards.

The sound won't be heard from the other room.

But there's a crack going down the centre of the board, others splintering off from it.

He shakes his head, taking up the fragments and thrusting them unceremoniously into the bin; slamming over the lid, rising like nothing happened

I get it now.

I leave after he does, slipping through the door that he opens and squeezing back into the booth. The air is tense, and I can tell she's just spent the last minute or so convincing them all she's fine and nothing happened.

Eventually, they all begin to chat again. Covering the tension with amusements and slipping a veil over the occurrence to avoid tension.

Bring the tension

bring the fallout

just save her.

It's all I can think as I watch her pull the arm of her jumper lower, allowing the sleeve to conceal the bruising that peppers her skin like raindrops on snow.

My darling, please let us save you. Or better yet- save yourself.

I only move to her though, resting my head on her and linking my arms though hers.

Holding her.

Irene simmers in the corner, barely concealing her true feelings in the same way that I'm doing. She looks at my darling, her eyes growing softer as she recognises her for who she is. My darling is strong, intelligent, beautiful and kind.

So strong that she is willing to break for what she believes is right.

And I have to watch as she does so.

CHAPTER 27
PINKY PROMISES

"I think that one looks like a winged-beast," I say, pointing up to a particularly avian-shaped cloud, "Don't you agree?"

"Mmm." *She nods, unenthusiastically.*

She's receded over the last couple days. Getting through university with the most minimal effort required, responding to comments with half her usual spark.

I know she's counting down the days till she must go back. The Diner has shut for the next week or so, undergoing repairs. So, she has chosen to sit idly by and wait until her fate comes knocking.

I tried to talk to her about it, not that it got me anywhere but the silent treatment for most of the day. The bruising may be fading but I haven't forgotten.

It's a half-day of university, and we've been lying in the back garden since we got back, cloud busting- or at least that's what I've been doing- whilst Tabi plays with the grey feline. Her father and the blonde demon have gone hunting for supper- so we're in charge of the boy.

She's wearing a light pink jumper and joggers, the most concealing clothing I've ever seen her in. Even so, she's lying with her hands behind her head, her belly exposed and Kuro's head resting sleepily in the sun.

I move on impulse, smoothing across his head- and her stomach in the process.

She gasps, her eyes flying open. When she realises what I'm doing some of the tension goes, but not all of it.

Kuro's eyes blink open, watching me with an angry stare.

What do you want me to do, huh? I try and send with my eyes, his teeth baring as he reads me.

I know what he wants. He wants off- he wants to hunt down and maim the man who laid a hand on my darling. He wants to rip the blonde demon's hair out and tear her limb from limb. He wants all the things I want and more- but he doesn't hear what my darling wants. And I value her choices. This is her world, lest we forget- her reality. We can't go imposing our every will, even if we think we know best.

It's not ours.

But I'm also reaching breaking point.

He understands, tucking his head in the flurry of his tails and ducking out of the sun.

I miss having him on me sometimes, but it means that much more to me that he's bonding with darling. He will be ours now, and us- his

Tabi races over to us and I glimpse Kuro slip up underneath her jumper.

Tabi flops down between us, narrowly missing my arm in his excitement. The grey cat pauses in joining us, looking in my direction and hissing.

Tabi looks confused for a second before shaking his head at it, "There's no one there, silly."

...

Did the boy just...?

I don't think on it more because I'm too busy watching my darling crack a smile as she latches onto him; Tabi squeals as she hoists him into her arms.

"How're you doing Tabi-cat? How's school?" I ask, finding

my voice.

The joints in my shoulders scream in protest as I hug-onto Tabi. Hydra had recognised the hangover for what it was. Gods, I wish she hadn't been holding the kettle.

I don't know how to be myself right now. I don't even know if I can talk to Aletheia. Nowhere seems safe.

I think I'm slowly losing myself.

Even Irene sees it, though she won't say as much. I can tell they're all tiring of me and my seemingly endless drama.

But I'll put on a face- for Tabi.

He shrugs, "S'okay."

From the way he picks at the grass and his closed expression though, it's quite obviously not okay. Gods I hope he hasn't learnt this from me.

"You can tell me," I say, stroking Hyacinth's tail as she goes to Tabi's side, "Hyacinth's not the only one you can trust to keep a secret you know."

Hyacinth the feline companion- so the boy child is a young mage after all. Will curiosities never cease.

His face is scrunched up as he rips at the tiny blades of grass in his hands.

"They pick on me." He grumbles, not meeting my eyes.

I've never been the violent sort, never once raised a fist to anyone. But the moment the words have left his lips I feel my fury rise, wishing more than anything to crush anyone or anything that has caused him upset.

The feeling isn't helped by Kuro's sudden arousal, his own hackles rising, and it feels like a vibration on my skin as he growls; goosebumps erecting along my abdomen.

A smile plays at my lips.

So, my darling can feel defiant rage.
Good to know.

"What do you mean they pick on you?" I ask as calmly as possible, raising onto an elbow to look at him.

Tabi shrugs, flicking the slithers of green away and breathing out a heavy sigh.

"There was a fox on school grounds." He says, folding his arms, "I know you said not to tell anyone what I can do- I didn't." He says pointedly, "But I was just telling it to visit somewhere else, so it was safe, because school isn't kind to '*pests*'. Synthia had followed me out, and she ran back and told Marek and Henthol, and they told the bigger guys- and by that point most of the class was whispering about it." He reaches for Hyacinth, who obediently runs into his open palm, "Now most of class calls me '*pest control*'. And they... they put..." He frowns, fighting off getting upset by looking away and cinching his lips together.

He definitely got that from me.

"What did they do?" I ask gently, placing a hand on his arm.

He strokes Hyacinth, using the feel of her fur to calm him.

"The school dealt with the fox; I didn't see it happen. But the big kids in my class found out. They also found out my locker number, and a way to stuff its body in there." He winces at the memory, and I feel an unholy wrath come over me that I struggle to tamp down.

"There were flies on his muzzle, even the teacher couldn't look at it long." He frowns, "He was my friend. I don't think I want anyone who allowed them to put him in there as my friend."

I can feel my darling's rage like a physical presence, her hand closest to me bunched into a fist.

If I had it my way, we would go and find these bullies together. Make sure they knew never to mess with the boy-Tabi again.

But I know that's not her method.

I take in one steady breath after another.

"Your friends will find you when they find you- trust me," I say instead, "It took me till university to make anything close. You'll do better than me." I say, ruffling his hair affectionately.

"But," I say slowly, "Until you do, maybe you should be using what you can do to make things a little easier for yourself... or harder for others."

Tabi stops stroking Hyacinth long enough to look up at me, his brow furrowed.

"What do you mean?" He asks.

The breeze is cooling through my hair, and I lean back against the grass, my strands falling in between the blades effortlessly.

"Did you know I turned my entire class green when they bullied a girl?" I say, a smug smile tugging at the edges of my lips at the memory.

Tabi's eyes grow huge with admiration, sitting up on his knees to look at me, "No freaking way!"

I smirk, and I can see Aletheia watching me with fascination from his other side.

"Yes-sir," I smile, "I also swapped lotions for itching solutions for the girls that picked on others, put foul smelling incense in the lockers of boys who thought they were bigger and better than everyone else. I even added lavamian-drops- liquid fire- to my teachers' foods if they doled out punishment unfairly."

His eyes have gone from saucers to worlds as I proudly proclaim my not-so-innocent past antics; Aletheia's sly grin not going amiss.

"Now that's my darling." I purr, biting my lip and making her blush.
It's clear I'm not the only devil amongst us, my darling has a wicked streak.

"What I'm trying to say, Tabi-cat," I continue, trying and failing to ignore Aletheia for even a moment, "Is that just because people pick on you- doesn't mean you have to take it." I poke him in the ribs, causing him to keel over, "You're powerful, make birds poop on nasty girls, rats to leave droppings in boys' lockers, or even bigger animals to scare bad teachers." I grin as his eyes gleam, "No one picks on my baby brother."

His mouth twists into a begrudging smile and he shrugs, glancing up at the sky.

It's not that I want him to become a troublemaker, quite the opposite. But... he's still my brother, and he has the power I'd wished I could've had since I knew what magic was. He could be the most popular boy at school if he wanted, it just might take a little nudge from me, and transferring schools next year, to properly see it.

"Maybe I could see what the rats are like at school." He mumbles, Hyacinth meowing angrily at the prospect of him befriending her lunch.

"What're you looking at anyways?" He asks, searching the sky for something worth his time.

He's grown up in a world full of mindless entertainment, so extricated from nature.

Mum would be so upset. Maybe by me pushing him towards animals, dragging him out to the garden- to the woods and one day to the beach again, maybe I can bring a bit of the natural world back to his life.

"It's called 'cloud busting'," I say, drawing my finger around the white fluffy balls in the sky, "Just looking at the clouds, seeing what things you can see in them. Like that one-" I point, and he tracks it, "-Looks like a bit like a cat's head."

Hyacinth meows excitedly, also following my finger.

Tabi scrunches his nose to begin with. But then, as I let the silence drag on, he points.

"A fox?" He asks cautiously, outlining a particularly fox-like cloud with his tiny fingers.

I nod emphatically, and he takes this as encouragement; hurriedly listing off any and every shape of cloud in his eyeline.

He smiles at the sky, squinting up and fighting the sun for a glimpse.

"That one looks like an aeroplane!" He says, and I ruffle his hair as I look over at Aletheia, meeting her eyes properly for the first time in days.

Things have been tense- different. I know that's my fault. But if I let her in, into my messy life where I'm just trying to get through the year. If I let her in, then she has to see what I go through.

But that doesn't stop me from feeling the way I do, having my heart doing double-time in my ribs- at just a look.

I don't know how close I can have her, but I know I don't want her to leave.

"Actually... I think that one looks more like a bird." I say, Aletheia's brows raising before her hand reaches over Tabi's head to hold mine out of his eyeline.

Maybe she isn't quite as lost as I thought she was, maybe she can save herself from this- if she takes her own advice...

"Tabi dear!"

The moment is broken as her call rings out from the backdoor, the shrill tone sending tension ricocheting through my body.

It was nice while it lasted.

Tabi kicks up into a sit and I follow suit, up to my elbows. Hydra is in the doorway, bags of groceries in her arms and dad still shuffling a couple more in from the car. Dad wouldn't've called Tabi away, he would've come out and cloud-busted with us.

To Hydra's credit though- I prefer her taking Tabi inside than joining us.

"It's high time you finished your homework young man," She trills, her fake smile stretched thinner than ever, "Your father's in the living room for the big game, so you'll have to work in your bedroom today."

Tabi frowns, "Can't I go in the kitchen?"

I watch the smile she painted start to crumble, to fray, as the small challenge registers hard.

He's a kid, he doesn't realise that his words are sticks and she's a bear.

"I need the space to make dinner sweet-pea." She coos, somewhat strained, ushering him inside.

He sighs, scraping himself up off the grass before hoisting Hyacinth into his arms and trudging towards the door. He couldn't have more attitude if he tried.

Tabi can get away with it though, I've made sure of that.

"You know at any given moment you could call Kuro off and he would eliminate any threat to you." I say, her eyes turning to me and strands of loose hair blowing in the breeze.

"Why are you telling me this?" I ask, quiet and using my hair as cover in case Hydra is still looking, "In my realm, we go to prison for the needless killing of others- and our pets are put down."

I scoff, shaking my head at her, "My darling, it most certainly would not be needless," I say, reaching over to touch Kuro's snout that has since reappeared by her trouser-line at the mention of his name, "And Kuro is no pet."

I touch her hand with mine, holding it against my stomach where Kuro lies.

"I don't need anyone else to suffer," I say, my voice tightening,

"These are *my* choices, I will choose how to live with them."

Stubborn mortal, why must I love you?

"Tenaya," I snap my head back so fast it's a miracle it doesn't break, looking to the kitchen window where Hydra lurks, "Come help with the groceries."

She's used up all her niceties for the day.

I rise but hesitate.

She's not being nice.

She's had a bad day.

"Aletheia," I say as casually as I can, "Would you mind checking on-"

"No."

The suddenness startles me, and I look over to see her eyes like daggers.

I can't have her see this.

"Aletheia please, just see if Tabi-"

"I said no."

I won't let her hide this from me anymore. I'm not naïve. I know what the demon is capable of- I saw what my darling looked like that first morning and I know Kuro's been healing her before I can see any proper damage.

But she is being damaged, broken, bit by bit, and she's going to have to deal with me seeing.

Maybe then she will do something about it.

Maybe...

"Tenaya." My name sounds like a curse on her lips, "Now."

"C-c-coming, Hydra." I reply, already feeling my body tense

up as I move to follow her through the house, begging Aletheia with my eyes to leave and go upstairs.

Just for a couple of minutes.

Please go upstairs

The TV blares from the other room, even with the door closed. Dad never closes the door, which is another sign that I really need Aletheia to make herself scarce. Instead, she trails behind me, pausing at the stairs.

Please

Hydra places a couple of bags on the counter and begins busying herself with prepping food. Hyacinth scrambles from beneath the table and sits in the hallway-

Watching.

"The fruit bag first dear, then the pastries." She instructs, and I do my best not to flinch.

"Okay." I reply, as meekly as I can.

I duck my head down and grab for the first bag, moving past her as she picks up four plates and places them on the counter.

Plates aren't usually a concern.

I dip into the pantry and make light work of sorting the fruit into the allocated bowls, moving around some cereals and hastily retreating back into the kitchen.

Aletheia hasn't moved.

I grab for the second bag, my palms sweaty as I begin shifting the flours and sugars up into the cabinet above the worktop; my exposed ribs not a foot away from Hydra.

I watch as she works, sweat pouring off her as she hurries; exuding stress levels similar to that of a warrior coming up against a beast ten times their size.

I slowly lower myself to the cat's level, her ears going back in preparation to hiss at me.

I place a finger to her snout before she can, putting another finger to my own lips in the same movement.

The cat- Hyacinth – quirks her head at me.

"I wish to save my darling," I say quietly, darting glances to the kitchen and back, "Your human cares deeply about mine." I say, and I pray I'm not making a huge mistake.

"Summon him here."

The cat's eyes go wide and I can tell she understands, also knowing that what I'm asking is crossing a major boundary.

I don't care.

Maybe if I can get him to tell her, then she will finally understand.

Hyacinth races past me and up the stairs on paws so lithe that even my ears strain to track her movements.

An ally perhaps.

"How was university?"

The question comes out of nowhere, taking me aback. She never asks about me. I may as well not exist unless I move directly in her way, like a pawn in the path of the queen.

So why now?

"I-it was good, thanks," I say, uncertainly, "Mr Spelinski is t-teaching us how t-t-to man-nipulate dangerous weeds into non-t-t-toxic veg-ge-tation."

She rolls her shoulders, placing a couple of tins on the counter.

"Is that so?"

It sounds more like a challenge than a query.

I choose not to elaborate, she might snap because I talked too much. It wouldn't be the first time. I'm not sure if there's a version of reality where I leave this room unscathed, but I'm sure as heck going to try.

"Is-s that all I c-can-"

"Hold these for me a sec?" she interrupts abrasively, placing four plates in my hands before I can protest.

Not that I ever would.

I stand stoic.

Don't move- comply-

Don't rock the boat-

Don't breathe too loudly-

Sink into the background-

"I am not a *blasted weed*."

The crack registers first, right across my temple.

I should've noticed her pulling out the rolling pin.

My head flies back into the doorframe at the same time two of the plates fall and smash on the floor, pieces scattering every which way.

There's a ringing in my ears and a pounding in my temples, stars blinking in and out of my vision. I feel Kuro snapping and raging as he races up the back of my neck to my pounding head; already working to heal me.

It's then that I hear the whimpering, and my heart drops through my chest.

Through the floor.

Down down down

"Now look what you've done!" Hydra hisses angrily, as I raise my battered head to the hallway.

Tabi stands at the bottom of the stairs, his arms clutching Hyacinth tightly to his chest and his eyes shining.

...He saw everything.

And behind him, arms folded and face stormy, stands Aletheia.

I look between Hyacinth and Aletheia, the cat's eyes averted from my own in a way that they wouldn't usually, and Aletheia staring back at me; resolute.

...She did this?

"Go," Hydra spits, yanking the remaining plates from my hands, "Take your brother upstairs, you've done enough damage."

Hydra slams them down on the kitchen table, storming to the pantry for the dustpan and brush.

I peel myself off the doorframe, Kuro still growling in fury, a hostile and bloodthirsty presence on my own flesh; craving release.

"Ta- Tabi?" I sooth, trying to think rationally, shuffling over to where he quivers.

He looks nervously to the living room door and back again, uncertainty strewn across his face. He holds Hyacinth tighter as I approach, tears leaking from his eyes.

"Tabi- it's *okay.*" I murmur.

He shakes his head, a little at first and then violently, his chin wobbling.

"No- no it's *not* okay!" He practically yells, racing up the stairs before I can reach him; his sobs echoing down the stairs as he goes.

I make it to the bannister, to the bottom step, not looking at Aletheia, and following after him. I place my fingers lightly to my head, drawing them back with crimson staining their tips.

The living-room door opens suddenly, and I place my hand back to my head, turning in a direction that blocks the damage from view.

Dad looks baffled, his glasses hanging off his nose and his shirt ruffled. He takes in the scene, Hydra still a no-show in the pantry, the shattered plates in the kitchen and me at the base of the stairs.

"Is everything okay, poppet?" he asks, peering around the bannister as if his son would still be there, "Is Tabi quite alright?"

No

No dad, everything isn't okay.

Tabi is not alright.

And neither am I.

"Yes, s-sorry dad," I say instead, "Tabi knocked some plates off the table and got upset about it. I'm going to go check on him- H-Hydra's in the pantry."

I can feel Aletheia seething to the side of me but it's nothing-

Nothing

Compared to how angry I am.

I make to go up the stairs after Tabi, keeping one hand to my head in case it drips anywhere.

"You can call her mum, poppet." He says sombrely, not meeting my eyes, "It's been... long enough."

Neither of us moves for a second, the gravity of what he just said weighing on my shoulders; planting me where I stand.

He can't mean that.

He doesn't really think that I could ever...

But he's stood firm, awaiting a response.

"...Yes dad, of-course."

It feels like swallowing more than just my pride.

She's going to let it happen again, sweep it under the rug and pretend it never happened. Not again.

Please not again.

I reach for her arm, trying to get her to look at me.

"What're you doing? You could tell him-"

"I'm going to check on Tabi." I say harshly, cutting through her as if she'd never spoken.

Dad nods and continues into the kitchen as I ascend, and I take the last few steps at double the speed.

His door is shut, and I have the decency to knock lightly.

"Tabi-cat?" I murmur as I creak open the door, Aletheia still trailing behind me like an ethereal shadow.

Tabi sits curled in a ball by his bed, sobbing softly into Hyacinths' fur. He raises his head, and I can vaguely make out the redness around his eyes- and the hurt that resides there.

"You *pinky*-swore..."

The last of me cracks and breaks on his words, aching as I

realise how deeply I've let him down.

This is what I never wanted to happen.

This is what I work so hard every day to avoid.

I close over the door, temporarily enveloping us in darkness as I make my way over to the night lamp by his desk. I flick it on and he cowers away from it.

He doesn't want to see me like this.

"I'm going to show him," I say to Aletheia, even though Tabi can hear me talking to myself- I don't care, "I'm going to show him Kuro and that is going to have to be okay with you."

I stand in the corner, arms folded and not making a sound. She doesn't so much as turn to me as she makes decisions about my own familiar. Doesn't even look at me as she dictates what will be, with or without my consent.

Of-course she can show Tabi. She can show the world.

When will she understand that it's not me who seeks to hide?

"Who are you talking to?" Tabi whimpers, and I know I'm going to have to explain.

I never wanted him mixed up in all this.

I sigh, coming over to sit by his side, giving Hyacinth a tentative stroke; which she takes, her eyes blinking guiltily back at me.

I don't blame her.

When a goddess demands you do something- you do it.

"You know how you have stuff that you're not allowed to talk about, that you get into trouble at school about if kids suspect you?" I say, waiting until he nods for me to continue.

"Well," I breathe, "I have that too. Not the same as yours though. I-." I look in Aletheia's direction briefly.

I don't even know how to talk about her right now.

"I travelled through realms, Tabi-cat." I say, and he shoots up.

"You *what*?!"

I can't help but smile a bit, "I found people who had the means to, and I did. And I... I met someone, a girl." I say, taking a deep breath, "The girl followed me back- and I'm the only one who can see her."

Tabi's eyes dart around the room, squinting as if limiting his field of vision will somehow allow him to spot her from a different level of reality.

From my periphery I see Aletheia move forwards slightly, perhaps thinking she will make him aware of her like she did to Lily.

Things have changed.

"She's not here right now." I say coldly.

My arms drop to my sides in shock.

My darling... what're you doing?

"I'm right here." I say, as if perhaps she had forgotten, or not realised her mistake.

Because I am- she knows I am.

"My darling, why-"

"She's busy." I continue over her, refusing to pay her any attention.

Tabi needs me.

Tabi needs me because *she* made him need me.

"But she left me her familiar," I say, lifting my shirt slightly and Tabi gasps, his body lurching forward so he can inspect the sizeable tattoo on my abdomen, "This is Kuro, a kitsune."

He runs his fingers over the tattoo tentatively, his eyes lighting up and his fingers flinching as Kuro twitches his nose and flicks his tails at him.

"Kuro protects me," I say, and Tabi looks up at me, his glassy eyes still rimmed red, "He makes sure that even if I get hurt- it doesn't last. See?" I say, leaning forwards so he can see the perfectly smooth skin that's been reknit on my head.

His bottom lip juts out, curious and wanting to be excited- but the reminder of the incident hindering him.

"But... why did Hydra..." He whispers, almost scared to ask the question.

I shake my head, "That's between me and her, Tabi-cat. It was a misunderstanding. Hyacinth was good to come get you- but I'm okay." I say, trying to distract him with the cat even now.

It usually works.

This time though it looks like I'll be needing a bigger distraction. Good thing one is lying on my stomach.

"Would you like to meet him?" I ask quietly, pointing to Kuro with a small smile.

His eyes grow somehow wider and his mouth falls open. "You mean he can... he can be *real* real?" He squeals as quietly as he can.

I smirk, "Kuro- *off*."

The kitsune tattoo grins, teeth bared briefly before he stretches and bursts into a million glowing dots of amber and gold. The sparks flit up and around Tabi's head, spiralling through his hair and twirling around his arms and fingers; before settling in Kuro's shape. They solidify in moments, and suddenly the room is lit by the ethereal glow of a dog-sized kitsune, sat between me and my baby brother.

Which then begins to growl.

Because we just brought a mythical magic-bound fox into a room with a house-cat.

"Kuro- no," I say, grabbing his scruff and tugging backwards slightly, "Leave Hyacinth alone."

For the second time since meeting him he stills, and it's like the anger is ever-so-temporarily cast in my direction. His eyes pool a jet-black before swirling back gold and orange.

"Woah." Tabi exclaims, his eyes reflecting the hues emitted

by Kuro's fur.

Hyacinth hisses before moving to cower behind Tabi.

"How old are you?" He asks Kuro, and I smile- of course he believes Kuro will speak back.

Kuro's mouth lolls open and his tongue flicks, my smile dropping as Tabi nods.

"Can you- can you communicate with him?" I ask, shocked that I hadn't considered this a possibility before.

From the corner I see Aletheia shift, her body coming into my periphery.

She's nervous. Anxious, even-

Why doesn't she want Kuro talking to Tabi?

Tabi nods, "He says he's twenty-seven human years old, and that he won't eat the cat." He pauses, his eyebrows creasing, "What do you mean by '*this*-"

Kuro moves forward, pressing his head to Tabi's, quietening him. Kuro's canines appear briefly from under his curled lips. Tabi doesn't move, and I'm dying to know what Kuro's saying- what he sounds like. Tabi's arms go up and around Kuro's fur, brushing down his shoulders and then over his head; smoothing off the glowing specks that dot around before reattaching.

"Why can't I say?" Tabi asks Kuro timidly.

He'd better not be threatening Tabi.

If I wasn't currently trying to distract him and earn back his trust, I'd be pushier about knowing what it is that's so important. As for now- he can have his secrets.

"He heals me," I say, cutting into their silent discussion, "He keeps me safe, even if I get hurt- I'll be okay." I say, moving forwards and ruffling his hair.

Kuro yips at me and I smile, doing the same to him.

"You and me," I say to Tabi, "We'll be out of here within the year. I promise."

The frown returns to his face, and he folds his little arms,

"You pinky-swore last time."

I jump as the door to the bedroom door suddenly opens and slams shut, Aletheia nowhere to be seen.

Tabi jumps to his feet and Kuro bounds around him, excited for action even knowing that it was just his master; he can smell the courage on Tabi, I'm sure of it.

"That was just-"

"Aletheia, I know," Tabi says with more angst than necessary, "Kuro told me. Why have you guys fallen out? He won't say."

I turn to Kuro, his snout down as he steps over to me and bumps his head against my knee. He's a good boy. He wants to help, and I can tell having me and her at a disagreement is uncomfortable for him; especially now that he shares both our skin.

I shake my head.

I don't want him to be upset, but what she did...

"I just have some things to sort out." I say, hugging Tabi, his little arms wrapping around my waist.

"I've planned to get us out of here for years now, Tabi-cat," I say as he squeezes me tighter, "I know it's hard, but if we just hold out a little longer, it'll all be okay in the end."

I don't tell him that I won't get hurt, I don't promise him that he won't have to see it again- because that would be a lie. But I will get him out of here, however hard it may be.

I will save him.

CHAPTER 28

TAKE IT BACK, PAINT IT BLACK

With Kuro returned to my arm, I pause outside my room, fingertips brushing the handle.

I try to breathe but the air is thick, tense. Like someone's holding me just below the surface and I'm itching to unburden my lungs.

But the weights are those of my own devices. I think this time I'll let them pull me down.

I've never been this angry.

I shove into the room, closing the door firmly but quietly behind me before turning to face her.

And it's like she's punched me in the gut.

She looks broken, pearly tears streaming from her usually smiling face as she spins away from the window to face me; her silvery hair practically glowing in the moonlight.

I can't let this sway me- I can't.

She... she hurt Tabi.

“You had no right.” I say, steeling myself and pushing past the part of me that longs to comfort her, to heal her.

She hurt Tabi.

“My darling, she’s hurting you. He’s hurting you-”

She pleads, her hands twisting together.

“You. Had. No. Right.” I snap, and it’s like I’m letting go of whatever reins I had control of.

The part of me that’s used to pushing forwards, the part that takes over when she hits me and rises up to the surface when he gets too close.

The version of me that must not care in order to carry on and do what must be done.

She takes the reins.

I’m losing her, I know I am.

I know I pushed her, and I know that she’s hurting just as bad.

But I can’t do this anymore.

“You don’t have to love me,” I whisper, and she sucks in a breath hard through her teeth, “You don’t even have to like me. But please, my darling, for the sake of those who care for you- love yourself enough to save yourself.” I hug my arms around myself as the memory of her being beaten, of her lying in the alley, of her pulling down the sleeve and placing a hand to her temple to hide the damage, all replaying in my mind. Throwing the fact repeatedly in my face- that I am helpless to save her.

“I can’t keep standing by and watching you get hurt.”

She shudders, her tears pearlescent in the near darkness. I can’t be who she wants me to be. I have a plan. I have a timeframe. I have lived this life for nearly seven years, and I intend to do it for one more.

I can’t be her darling, I can only be there for Tabi.

And she hurt him.

"Then leave."

- She says, in a voice so monotone and hollow that at first, I don't believe it's her that speaks.

"You don't mean that-"

"I said leave." My voice comes out cold and unforgiving, but I push on- barely seeing her anymore,

"I choose this. This is *my* world- *my* life. And I'll live it how I see fit. I'll go to *my* work, and I'll live in *my* house, and I will protect *my* baby brother how *I* decide to."

My heart is beating hard, but I ignore it, numb to the thrumming of my own blood in my veins, "If that pains you too much, then go."

Don't say it don't say it don't say it-

"...I can't." I say, and it's like the string that holds the weight on my heart is cut free. The onerous pressure that came with keeping it from her lifting- leaving me hollow.

"Can't or *won't*?" I snap...

But something clicks.

Something I had refused to consider.

Something I thought couldn't be true.

The moment feels thicker than mud, blood, concrete-

"Can't."

I slump down to the floor, my arms folding over my legs, unable to look at her as I unburden myself with the truth.

"The Fates attack me if I go too far from you."

The world feels like it's condensing, the realisation flooding in-

"I can't leave your side... they'll take me back."

...I was never special to her. I was never worth sticking around for - at least not just for who I am.

I'm not her darling, I'm not worth anything to her.

I'm just a method of staying alive.

"You never wanted to stay."

My eyes fly up to her, and I can see her shutting down- out- away-

"That's not true-"

"You'd have hopped right from one dimension and into the next without a second thought if you could've." I say, speaking the realisations as they dawn on me, harsher and truer than I've had in a long time.

Everything making the clearest of sense in the most painful of ways.

"You've been bored since the moment you arrived. Biding your time till you could find a loophole out of here."

She's twisting it, forcing it, pushing a mentality that will allow her to separate from me.

"My darling that's not fair-"

"Don't you *dare* speak to me about *fair*." I borderline-yell, angry for the first-time, red-hot anger; rising like a tidal wave.

Hurt.

"You came into *my* life, proclaiming to be this '*saviour*', that cared *so much* for me- your '*darling*'," the word tastes bitter on my tongue and Aletheia flinches, "But I was just a means of survival for you. Nothing more."

Images of the beach, mum's beach, her sat atop the diner counter- across my lap- lying in bed, the different dimensions and the feeling of being infinite with someone I thought I might... I thought I was beginning to...

The memories are tainted now.

Water running through the canvases, marring the images. Spoiling what I thought was mine.

She was never mine to have.

I'm losing her...
"That's not-"

"Nothing. More."

She stares through me, unseeing. A girl I barely recognise with a will so determined and self-assured that I know there is no pushing through to her.

Not in this moment.

I take a breath, a steadying one. Unclenching my fists that I hadn't even realised were bunched.

"Stay as close as you need to, to survive," I open my door and point out of it, "No closer. I never want to see you again."

Please don't do this...

"...Tenaya..."

It's the first time she's used my name, and it burns a hole right through my chest.

I didn't know I could hurt more than I already did.

"Get out."

I know the words are final.

I know I can't get her to see reason right now.

Slowly, heavily, I nod and pick myself up off the floor. My hair slinks along behind me, trailing across her rug to the door.

I'm so close to her now, I could reach out and touch her- or at least, try to. I could hold her, and I could promise to never leave her side and that I love...

But the thought that she might push me away, that she might not hold me back, that she might step away from me; it keeps me from bridging the gap.

"Kuro," I say, not meeting her eyes as I see the faintest glimpse of shock pass over her features, "Come."

He slips from her skin, reforming on the floor by my feet, smaller than usual.

He doesn't jump to my skin in the way he usually would, and he won't meet my eyes.

He won't look at either of us.

Instead, he simply moves to my darling, lifting his snout and giving her hand a tentative lick. She doesn't pull away, but she turns her head; not willing to look at either of us.

"Goodbye, my darling." I say softly, taking the last couple steps out of her door.

And out of her life.

The door closes and the tsunami crashes down upon me.

I slip silently to the floor, falling beneath the waves of hurt and betrayal, huddling in on myself in a puddle of my own tears.

She really left.

CHAPTER 29

THE POT AND THE KETTLE

It's been three days. No sign of her.

We're under the stairs of university, Irene and the rest of the group; minus Amaya and Rylan this time. Emmy and Sayra have their makeup bags out, coloured palettes and lipsticks of every garish shade scattering the pavement. Sayra waggles the makeup-brush in front of Irene's nose, so close that specks of glittery eyeshadow fleck onto her skin like freckles.

like stardust

"I'm thinking we still dress-up for the Halloween movie marathon." Corbin says, deftly gripping the eyeliner as he places it to Emmy's eyelid, "What says us?"

Emmy places a taloned hand over his, "Right idea, wrong question my love- the *real* query, is what on earth are we going to dress up *as*?"

Corbin sticks his tongue out at her affectionately, threatening to stab her eye with the liner. An eyeliner battle ensues, Emmy near enough breaking Corbin's arm in order to escape unscathed. The smile I would usually wear doesn't reach my face.

"Something the matter, nerd?" Irene asks, her elbow connecting lightly with my arm.

I don't even know where to start.

Casimir, Aletheia, Hydra, Tabi, Kuro, Dad, Maddy-

"Nothing." I say stoically.

If they weren't so engaged in their dress-up ideas, they probably would've caught me on that.

I don't even know how to act like myself anymore.

"Well, that wasn't *entirely* convincing," Irene murmurs out the side of her mouth, trying not to draw the attention of the others, "I don't know, maybe it just seems like there's something missing?"

How...

Impossible, she can't know about her.

Irene scoops a hand into her bag, rifling around until she draws out a leather-bound notebook.

"This book is usually reserved for magic and potions, or anything out of this world," She says, flipping the book open to a page before placing it in my lap, "I figured she qualified."

Sketched out in blues and pencil etchings, drawn leant up against a doorframe, then poised by my shoulder, again lying on the stairwell, and atop the counter of the diner.

She's captured Aletheia, not once, but half a dozen times in an extraordinary likeness. From her hair to her eyes to her devilish expressions, even one of her younger; like she would've looked as a child.

"How did you... *when* did you..."

"I first proper spotted her at Maddy's party," Irene smirks, pointing to where a drunk-looking Aletheia leans, "I was on a whole load of crap, so I wasn't sure she was real. But then her outline or her hair or her shadow would appear ever-so-faintly whenever you were around." She points to the different poses, the one in the centre where she's sketched her and me- Aletheia wearing a massive grin with her arms around me whilst I share a secret smile with her.

"I figured she was yours."

I blink at the page, my fingers tracing the intricate waves of her hair, the delicate placement of her arms. Her smile.

I slam the book shut with a bit too much force, Sayra's head poking up from her palettes like a meerkat.

"She's not mine, she never was." I spit bitterly.

She only stayed to save herself.

Irene quirks an eyebrow, aware of the eavesdropping imp sat a couple paces away from us.

"Oh? Did something happen?" She asks.

Something happened that means I can never look at her the same. That broke the immediate trust I had in her- that reminded me that I am not worthy of that.

Of her.

Someone like her could never truly fall for someone like me. And I'd known it from the start, that it had been too good to be true. That a magical angel from the stars could never take a liking to a boring messed up mortal girl.

How pathetic was I, that I believed her for even a second.

"We just didn't agree on... things." I mumble, not meeting Irene's eyes.

Sayra glances at us, at the notebook still gripped firmly in my hands.

She dances over, reaching for it, "Watcha *readi-*"

I snatch the book against my chest without thinking, Sayra's fingers still extended in mid-air.

The movement was so sudden, I hadn't planned to do it.

"S-sorry." I say, still choosing to hand it to Irene rather than Sayra.

I don't know why I'm still trying to keep her hidden.

Sayra pouts, folding her arms, "There's no need to be like *that* about it."

"Sayra." Irene admonishes, reaching for her hand, "*Leave it.*"

I look between them, the shared understanding, the secrecy. I now know what it feels like to be on the other side of a paradigm.

Sayra frowns, stubborn.

"No- I won't. She's been quiet and moody, and now she's being rude. It's not fair." She says, stomping her foot.

Not fair...

Not. Fair.

Not fair

"Not *fair*? What are you- a *child*?" I snap.

The moment the words have left my lips I know I've lost it.

I can't go back from this.

I don't want to.

Irene frowns, "Hey, Tenaya, calm down-"

"We're only trying to help you, you're the one being moody and letting things happen to you." Sayra grumbles, looking down at me, "Not our fault you won't let us help."

Rage.

That's what this feeling is.

Pure and unadulterated rage.

I stand, my height dwarfing Sayra and I can see the uncertainty leaking into her features.

"And how *exactly* would *you* help, huh? Little miss 'I'm a toddler when I feel like it'?" I snarl, my hands clenched at my sides.

"Tenaya, there's no need-" Emmy comforts, my outburst pulling their attention away from their play-fight.

"No- there is." I hiss, whirling back on Sayra, "You think I'm moody and quiet and rude- who are *you* to cast any judgement on *me*?" I don't bother lowering my voice, my breathing suddenly difficult to control. "Maybe I'm '*quiet*' because if I wasn't- I'd never stop shouting- *screaming*. Maybe there're things going on in my life that your tiny pre-adolescent mind couldn't even *fathom*." I say, stepping forwards as Sayra takes a nervous step back.

Corbin and Emmy sit to the side, watching me with shocked expressions but not moving to Sayra's defence.

"At least *I* live in the real world-*function*, in the here and now, without the aid of a babysitter." I say coldly, pushing past Sayra harshly so that she stumbles; caught by Irene.

"Tenaya- *wait- TENAYA*!" Irene yells from behind me but I keep walking.

I don't need them. I can make it on my own.

I've lived this long without them. I can do another year.

Just one more year.

Without them.

Without her.

CHAPTER 30
GODS HELP HER

"Tenaya!" Irene yells after her, stopped only by a tantrum-bound Sayra.

Oh my darling, you're unravelling.

I've existed like this for three days. On the underside of walls, always minimum twenty steps behind, sleeping on the roof and squatting outside of lecture halls. Not even Kuro to keep me company. He turned tail and ran the moment I left her room; saying something about protecting the Syn's.

I can't be dealing with him right now anyway. Not when she keeps putting herself in danger.

I listened last night, as the blonde demon used her fathers' belt to punish her for sitting with them in the kitchen too long.

I listened as my darling didn't even shed a tear at the event, but how the child Tabi sobbed in the room next door; the buckle loud enough to alert him.

She isn't me, she can't hear his cries through walls and doors. If she could, maybe she would do things differently.

I... I don't know how to exist without her anymore. I was free before I met her, scouring galaxies and spiralling through realms carefree and wild.

Now? Now I only want to do that if she's there to watch me, to join me- to make the jump with me, over and over again for the rest of time as we know it.

"Let me go after her- Sayra I know she was cruel-"

"She was horrid!" Sayra whines pitifully to Irene, Emmy rubbing her back consolingly.

"Honey- sweets, we don't know what she's going through," Emmy soothes, "We only know her work life- and if that's anything to go by, what if her home life is worse?"

Irene nods, her face solemn.

My darling is foolish to cast these ones aside. They may be the only beings in this Gods-forsaken town worth the time of day.

"That doesn't mean she gets to take it out on me." Sayra grumbles, rubbing her red eyes with her sleeves.

Irene sighs, and I watch as she bends down to her darling, stroking her pink hair behind her elfin ears.

"I know baby, she was mean. And that's not okay." I step in closer, around the edge of the wall so I can get a proper look, "I'm not saying she's in the right. I'm saying it's not about right or wrong- she's in a bad place. And as her friends, it's our job to help her out of it."

My heart flutters as I watch the tender exchange between the two, Sayra's fingers looping briefly with Irene's.

"But..."

"You wanted us to be her friend, right?" Irene asks, to which Sayra gives a begrudging nod.

Irene smiles, flicking her metal incision against her canines, "Good, then I'm going to go and do something that might help her- as her friend. Okay?"

Irene's eyes meet mine across the expanse and I'm glued to the spot.

She winks at me.

"I'll be right back." She says to them, not breaking eye contact with me as she separates from them and struts over to me.

In another life, this woman was a god. The walk, the confidence- unparalleled.

"Walk with me." She says under her breath as she passes, her hands

routing around in her satchel.

I don't think twice before marching into step with her, my hands behind my back and my legs working double-time to keep up.

"Can you hear me, too?" I ask, my voice breaking and crackling after not being used in days.

She looks at me, her eyes roaming my features in a way that feels like an examination.

"A little." She replies, reaching out suddenly to take my arm in hers- unashamed to look like she's holding thin-air.

My darling would never.

Not that I don't understand, my darling is a recluse to say the least; her survival tactic being camouflage to the nth degree.

I can't feel Irene though, so the barrier remains in-tact.

"Home life or work life?" Irene muses as we walk through the semipermeable halls of the university, students hastily dodging her to allow us to part through the centre like a battleship through water.

A loaded question. But there'd be little sense in keeping the information to myself when I can't help her- when Irene might be able to.

"Both." I admit, squeezing in close as a freshman passes by.

Irene frowns, her purple lips thinning.

"I figured as much."

There's the sound of ripping paper and I look down to see her re-pocketing a notebook, a couple pages still in hand.

"And you tried to change one? Assumedly without her consent?" She asks, and I nod. "Figures."

I watch as she dismantles our arms in order to fold up the paper in a manner so that she can slot the first three quarters through the lip in my darling's locker- the last bit hanging through so that the pages will be on display when she opens it.

Irene tucks a couple strands behind her ear, shrugging at me.

"None of us have it easy," She says, looking left and right before leaning back against the lockers, "But when you have it as hard as I assume she does- it often feels easier to carry it alone." She pauses, "Safer."

"She is not safe." I say, my voice tight with emotion as I make my sentences concise in hopes I'm heard. "I cannot save her."

She looks at me, squinting as if doing so is particularly difficult.

"You did what you thought was right, star-girl," She says, eyebrows raised, "But it's her life that you tried to take the reins of. And from how she acts, it looks like she's never dropped them." She shakes her head, "You were never going to persuade her."

I twist, moving so that I'm leant beside her on the lockers, close enough that she chooses to lean down and rest her head on my shoulder.

I stiffen involuntarily.

"You know no one else can see me, right?" I ask sceptically, unused to such casual public displays of affection.

"It's as much for you as it is for me," She replies, "I give you what I'd hope is perceived as comfort- and I have the reassurance that you're real." She pokes my shoulder for effect, "You're weighty."

Weighty, definitely weighed down.

My heart aches as I see her walking down the hall. Amaya on one side and Rylan on the other, her last remaining safety nets.

"She thinks that I do not love her." I admit, her image blurring as my eyes cloud over again. "I kept a secret from her, a big one." I continue, "I am being hunted within an inch of my life, kept safe by the radius that surrounds my darling. She- she believes that because she is the reason I remain alive, that she isn't also my reason for living."

There's a pause where she lets me feel this. Allows me to admit these feelings.

"Then prove it." She says, swaying upright to look me in the eyes.

She moves in front of me and places one hand on the locker behind my head, shielding us from the rest of the hallway.

She has purple sparks in her eyes.

"Be around for the little moments, make an entrance on the big ones, and prove that you want to be around her for more than just the safety she provides." She leans in, taking me by the shoulders and bringing me into a hug, her face going into my shoulder.

I haven't been hugged in over three days.

"Show her that you love her."

She smells of sage and home, the weight she places on me like a blanket; a comfort. I yearn for the feel of my darling's arms, to a point that it creates a painful ache in my chest- which only intensifies in the arms of those who aren't her. I hold Irene tightly even so, squeezing as hard as the Fates will allow.

She pulls back all too soon, smiling as she waves me off, her own eyes appearing misty.

"She needs us right now." She says, and I nod, "See you soon, star-girl."

She turns to leave.

"My name is Aletheia." I say, slipping from the lockers and into the fray with her, knowing I must follow my darling further down the hall.

Irene smiles somewhat sadly, winking at me as she goes, "That's a cute name, but I'll stick with star-girl for now, if it's all the same to you?"

Distantly, I spot a pink puffball flying down the hall, too far for her human eyes to notice; accompanied by her bodyguards.

"I've never obtained a real sobriquet," I say, mulling it over, "I see no issue, so long as my darling approves."

Irene smiles, the gleam returned to her eyes.

"Go ask her then." She grins, before disappearing into the throng.

I begin the trek to the lecture hall, or right outside it at least, my heart in my mouth.

The basilisk's ball is two nights from now, and likelihood is- with all that just occurred with Sayra- my darling would rather attend a snake's-pit than a perceived-to-be-rickety safety-net.

I crack my knuckles, bringing my arms behind my back to release the tension there.

Time to kill the cobra.

CHAPTER 31

•••

I wake up, get dressed, leave.

University is long, lectures are short, my patience is thin.

The pages from Irene's notebook glare back at me, the depiction of Aletheia uncanny in its likeness. I fold them up and place them in my pocket.

Safe.

Amaya and Rylan want to talk about why we aren't hanging out with Irene's lot. I told them to go with them and find out.

I'm eating lunch from the vending machine alone in Spelinski's lecture hall.

It's quiet here.

I get home, I avoid everyone, I go to bed.

I wake up-

CHAPTER 32
DARLING

The room pulsates with warm bodies and heavy music, the thrum of which runs through my veins faster than the liquid courage I just downed.

For the second time in my life, I'm drunk in the middle of Maddy's living room, swaying to music I don't know with people I've never spoken with.

And she's here- Aletheia. I knew it as soon as I stepped foot in the front door I could feel it-

Her.

Her eyes on the back of my neck, her hair flowing past doorways.

No sign of Maddy though.

She didn't open the door this time, or invite me to the kitchen. I found my way of course, and six or so drinks later- here I am. Leaning into the throng of bodies that move and grind to noises louder than life. Their eyes don't see me here.

I may as well be invisible, their sights clouded in a drunken haze that will steal their memories of my face by morning.

As if I never existed.

I don't even know why I'm here.

Hydra will beat me for attending, dad will reprimand me for drinking, my friends are streets away and Maddy isn't even around.

I can sense her moving- Aletheia- a palpable presence even when she sticks to the shadows.

I'd be lying though if I said I wasn't glad she did. I don't want to never see her again, and a cruel part of me hopes the Fates hunt her forever.

I don't know what I'd do if...

It's only then that I realise what she's been doing. By sticking to the shadows, by circling this room. By keeping me away from where I want to be.

She's blocking me from Maddy.

I stand still in the rise and fall of limbs, glaring at Aletheia- who leans against the door to an office on the opposite side of the living room.

She glares right back.

I move without much thought, sifting through the maze of people till I reach the door.

She moves in front of me.

"My-" I begin, biting my lip at the last moment and looking away. She reeks of liquor, several layers of the stuff exuding from her pores in an attempt to extract the poison from her body.

I can't blame her.

"You don't want to do this."

She can't even look at me. Somehow, that hurts more.

I wish she would look at me.

"I'll decide what I want to do." I say, and she stiffens, before her shoulders sag in defeat.

"I only wish to help you." I murmur, knowing it will do me no good.

I don't need help.

Irene, Sayra, Emmy and now Aletheia. I don't need help, I just need to survive.

Just let me get through this year

I can't think straight, and I can barely stand upright, but Aletheia still moves to the side. Her arms are folded and eyes still not meeting mine as I make my way past her and into the concealed hallway that bridges between room Numero Uno and an office-room part of the party.

I can't think about Aletheia or the Fates or her lies. I just want to see Maddy's face and hear her say she's been waiting for me to arrive. Missing me?

I don't... I don't know what I want anymore.

The first wave is shock.

I take in the scene in excruciating detail, the layout of the office-library of her family home. The worn books with their frayed edges, the desk that houses the behinds' of second-and-third-year students, and their associated beverages. The yellow lighting that's been dimmed to an almost-painful degree, and the music that sounds from the antique record player. The 10-12 pairs of eyes that land on me as I enter, the leather armchair which she had been lounging on.

Her arms wrapped around him as she jumped into him.

His arms that coil around and hold her tight and spin her gleefully.

The seconds that turn into more than I'd like to express,

before they both look up.

The way his mouth twists into a smirk as she waves at me, his hand also raising- cajolingly, or innocently, depending on the eyes.

"How're you doing, Taya?" Max grins, the words irrefutably laced with spite.

I watch as his hands curl around her waist tighter, Madeline's face a mask of indifference as he so-obviously claims her.

The second wave is cold.

I take a breath.

I smile.

I pick up a lonely cup with a concoction of miscellaneous contents in its plastic depths, and bring it to my lips, tipping it at her. I turn around, leaving the hellhole I just intruded on.

How could I have been so foolish. *Naïve*. At what point had she ever shown me she was capable of establishing boundaries with him. With *anyone*.

When had she ever suggested that she would put any feelings I had above *his*? She was so comfortable being close with him and hiding me from the rest of the world. She doesn't even realise what she's doing... or maybe she does.

And maybe Aletheia has been right all along.

Perhaps this is no different than how I treated her.

"Hey!"

Maddy's voice churns up a sickness in my stomach that the mysterious drink hasn't aided. Still, I down the rest of it before I turn to her.

"Yes?" I ask as calmly and coherently as I can.

She moves in to hug me, like she had at the last party, only this time it's just one of her arms coming around my shoulders.

"No, no- I don't think-" I begin to protest.

"*What*?" She interrupts indignantly, scrunching her sculpted eyebrows drunkenly at me- and for the first time since knowing her, I see the hints of anger marring her faux-perfect features.

"What do you mean '*no*'?"

I sigh, trying to compose myself. I look over her shoulder from where she came from, but it seems this, at least, is a solo endeavour.

"What do you mean, '*what do I mean*'?" I say, gesturing in the direction of the backroom, "You were just-"

"I've done nothing wrong," She interrupts again, shaking her head drunkenly at me, "He's been all over me, trying to get close to me. And I've already started enough arguments tonight trying to stop it." She says, her eyes boring into mine in a way that suggests that this whole situation is somehow my fault.

That *I* am the reason she's having to set boundaries with her ex.

"I-" I start, but the look she gives me makes me falter, and I feel the lump rise in my throat, the tears gathering behind my eyes.

The third wave pulls me under.

"I'm sorry." I say.

Defeated.

She nods, her eyebrows lifting a little.

"I- I didn't realise." I go on.

"Yeah, you didn't." She snaps, but slightly less than before, "It's been really difficult. The night's not exactly gone smoothly already. I can't help it if he wants to be close to me, you know."

She has her arms folded, her body bristling from me challenging her. I wonder, does anyone ever question her authority? She said she would stay away from him and didn't... but that's *my* fault?

"Of course," I find myself saying robotically instead, "I'm sorry, I didn't know- I'm sorry."

The words taste foul on my tongue, but I don't stop her as she moves in and steals a kiss.

It's brief-

It leaves me empty.

"You must try to understand, darling." She says sombrely, without the smile I saw her give him so easily- as he wrapped himself around her like a python.

"That's My darling, you bitch."

Without warning, Aletheia sweeps past me and throws out her hands into Madeline's chest, her eyes a warpath and her hands glowing with a golden vengeance that hits its' mark.

Madeline flies backwards into the wall. Her spine bends and head cracks as her body slumps forwards in a haze of shock.

Aletheia stares at her hands in awe and confusion, at the same time people crowd into the hallway to look between me and Madeline with similar disbelief.

Madeline lifts her head, her hand going up to cradle her neck.

"Tenaya *what*- wait- who are *you*...?!"

I look between Aletheia and Madeline, her hands now shaking as we both come to terms with what this means.

That what Maddy just said can only mean one thing.

Without a word I grab her hand.

I grab her hand.

Her hand that radiates warmth and life and I can feel feel-

feel her.

I take hold of Aletheia's hand in mine, and we *run*.

CHAPTER 33

MINE

I don't stop at the front door.

She doesn't stop when we reach the street

I'm flying down the road, dead centre and sprinting with her in hand. My hand. Her warm- real- alive- here hand- in mine.

She won't let go of my hand

I don't think I'll ever let go again.
She's real real real

We're running out of air

We're almost there

We're together, she's bringing me with her

One more corner and it's there. In my eyeline is Amaya's house. Tall and lit up like a lighthouse in the dark.

She turns me around, twirls me through her fingers that feel smooth and soft. I swing her around and pull her in, pausing for barely a moment before cupping her cheeks with my palms and- -*She kisses me.*

It's like burning up and my heart aches and- -It feels like coming home and becoming whole and my heart aches.

And- *she's*- here- *with*- me.

My hands are in her hair and it's like running them through water, like *silk*, my fingertips brushing against her sloping neck and pulling her deeper.

Drowning us.

My hands wrap her waist and pull her closer, diving beneath the hem of her shirt and stealing touches across her back, sloping down with it and anchoring her to me.

I feel the tears running down my cheeks before I can stop them, Aletheia's eyes springing open in shock.

"My darling what's wrong? Is this too much?" I ask, beginning to pull away but she tugs me back.

"No- no, nothing like that." I whisper, her eyes and freckles lighting up the darkness, "I just- I- I'm not worthy- of you." I manage, closing my eyes and begging above all else for this to be real and mine.

Please let her be mine

I smile, her words tugging on my heartstrings more than I thought possible. "My darling- my love," I say, her eyes opening upon the word to gaze into my own, "It is I, who wishes to be worthy of you. Never doubt that."

I blink at her, dumbfounded.

My hands find purchase wherever they can, on her neck, on

her hands, on her arms, on her face. Wherever they can find skin on skin.

No more barriers.

"No more barriers," I say out loud, "No more secrets, no more hiding, no more *stupid* childhood crushes," I say the last part with bile still rising in my throat, "I am *yours*, Aletheia... if you still want me?"

I wait for her to reply, I wait, and hold my breath and pray to every god in existence. I pray to *her*.

Aletheia, Aletheia, ***Aletheia***

"And I," I whisper, my name in her mind a calling of the deepest nature, "Am yours."

Her forehead leans against mine and we just stand, breathing in each-others air and feeling the other between our fingers, being real in this moment- in the same plain of existence.

She is mine.

And I will die before I let another person lay a hand on her.

-But that's a conversation for another time.

I can still smell the waves of alcohol rolling off her, even though I can hear the truth in what she's been saying, I can also feel the weight of her against me; leaning for support.

"I think it may be time to get you home, my love."

She's real and here and really here-

-I think I might throw up.

The colour drains from her face so quickly and she looks like she may pass out.

"Or- or, where are your friends?" I ask, trying to get her eyes to hold mine. Distract her from the thought spiral I just accidentally sent her on.

There are two of her, two Aletheia's and two houses with the lights still on behind her. I'm going to try not to throw up.

Really *really* try.

I point as best as I can towards the house, "That one."

I look behind us to the mansion with the pristine garden, hosting a water feature of the most ostentatious nature.

Of course this is where Amaya lives.

"Okay- okay my love, we're going to get you there, okay?"

She looks at me like I'm her entire world, nodding and instantly regretting it as she pales again. I scoop her up against me so her arm is over my shoulder and mine around her waist; hobbling slowly up the drive to Amaya's house.

The world is very spinny. Maybe running after drinking isn't quite the way to go.

We were running together though.

I'm her darling, *was* her darling, now her love love *love*

"Yes, my love, you are." I smirk as she speaks her mind, perhaps without even realising it.

I press the button next to the door, waiting as the chimes summon a flurry of footsteps to the door. I count six sets of feet flying across ceramic before the door flies open.

"See! I knew she'd..." Amaya begins to say but stops dead when her eyes meet mine.

A zombie, a vampire, a cat, a witch, a ghost and an alien stand on the other side of the door. They all pause just inside, mouths open and eyes wide. All except for Irene, who looks me up and down with devilish approval.

"You proved it to her then?" Irene-the-witch smirks, the first to move forward and place her arm under darling's other side.

I sigh in relief.

"Something like that." I reply, somewhat meekly under the scrutiny of all my darling's friends.

I can understand their hesitancy. A girl with alien features arrives at the door holding the semi-conscious body of their closest friend.

I'd be wary too.

"She's nothing to worry about guys," Irene announces as we pile in through the front door, "She's just Tenaya's secret girlfriend."

Rylan-the-ghost and I share a look then, his eyes going wide as he points at me.

"The line in the dirt!" He exclaims, drunkenly.

Amaya-the-vampire turns on him then, her eyebrows angry, "You knew about her? And didn't tell me?!" She whines, swatting him on the arm.

Rylan only holds his hands up in surrender as we struggle up the stairs to Amaya's spare bedroom.

"Look, I didn't know she was some hot alien chick, okay? All I saw was a line in the ground." He says, blushing before amending, "And I mean hot in the objective sense, obviously you're the hottest person alive to me. I'm just stating the facts, you don't-"

"Rylan," Corbin-the-zombie pipes up, slapping him on the back, "Stop digging."

"Right, right." Rylan says, hanging his head a little.

Up the winding stairs that feel like they were made from a fairy-tale, we finally reach the landing and the adjacent room that they'd clearly been making into a hovel. Drinks of various colours and fills litter the floor and window-sill. Two double-beds in one gigantic room, plus two single-mattresses and a bunch of colourful pillows on the floor- is all that makes up the room.

"She's not a secret anymore." I say, the colours on the floor blending into one, making me dizzy.

The sentence goes around and around like a merry-go-round in my head- secret girlfriend. Is she my- yes, yes- girlfriend makes the most sense.

"What was that?" Amaya asks, coming close enough that I can see the blood smeared under her false fangs.

"*My* girlfriend." I mumble, hugging Aletheia to me and sending her toppling on top of me on the bed.

When did we get on the bed? When did they turn off the lights?

The room descends into giggles as I try and extricate myself from her, brushing her hair aside so she can see me. Her mouth breaks into a smile when she does.

"Mine." *She says, pointing a finger into my collarbone and giggling.*

I can't help but smile back, holding her pointed finger in my hand.

"Yes, my love, yours." I say, setting myself into a seated position and facing the group; now sitting and watching us expectantly.

I take her by the shoulders and lie her in my lap, her eyes closing almost as soon as her face meets my legs. I'm glad she's conked out- she doesn't get to see the abhorrent shade of blue my face goes at the closeness; her laboured breaths sending goosebumps along my inner-thighs.

"What's your name then?" Sayra-the-cat pipes up, arms folded.

The attitude earns her a shove from Irene, who stands and makes her way over to sit next to me on the bed; bumping her shoulder with mine. I'm not quite certain when exactly I won Irene's approval, but I'm not sure I would be able to sit here much longer without it.

Not with the eyes of all my love's closest friends on me.

I'm not even sure what they want from me.

"Just start by telling them your name, star-girl," Irene smiles, "And maybe how you got here?"

I look to each expectant face in turn, all of them eager- most of them wary.

I sigh, sitting up a little straighter and trying my best to focus.

"My name is Aletheia. I am demi-god of the diamond isles and demon kin of Relinque. I am the greatest threat to the Fates and as a consequence of such- have been running and hiding from them since my teenage years."

I pause, checking they're still with me.

I take their silence as understanding and my queue to continue.

"I was captured because I realm-hopped through time- the act that got you mortals put on the proverbial naughty step. When that happened though I met my love," I muse, stroking her hair back from her face, "She kept me company, for four years trapped in the realm of the Fates, and after learning my name- she summoned me. There's power in a demon's name you see, otherworldly power when it comes from someone who loves them- or has the potential to." I pause, remembering a final detail, "Oh, and you were all there when she found me in the Fates realm- don't go back there."

Silence falls on the room.

And then a cacophony of questions.

"You're a demon?!"

"You're a Goddess?!"

"How can you move through time?"

"Are the Fates still after you?"

"How long have you known each other?"

"Why don't we remember you if we saw you?"

My ears fold down at the rush of questions, and I try not to allow the agitation into my face. They are merely curious mortals, eager to learn- I cannot fault them for that.

I'm very glad I chose not to drink excessively like last time, my head may have imploded by now had I done.

I stretch, cracking my knuckles and waiting for the questions to dim to a dull hum.

This is going to be a long night.

I spent the next hour or so filling them in on all that had transgressed. I even explained that the Fates are still hunting me- thought it best to get that out in the open early this time.

Talking led to chatting led to drinking led to laughing.

Somewhere in the madness of the evening I allowed Irene to braid a single slip of my hair. It took her the best part of an hour to accomplish, but by the end she was happy at least.

I thumb the intricately woven strands.

"I wonder if I can infuse this to make it whip-like." I muse.

Irene's eyes gleam, "Do it."

Sayra looks between me and Irene with something akin to distrust, or at least discomfort.

"Hey," I catch Sayra's attention, "You're a little obsessed with the colour pink, right?"

She scrunches her face, but only momentarily before it lights up in wonder. I summon the starting points for realm hopping, zoning in and focusing my efforts on the vertical links- the pink ones; leaving out the horizontal blue ones. It's a wonder that my love was ever able to travel at all without even the fundamentals in inter-realm travel.

Sayra exists in a network of pink lines that glow and dance around her, the lights making her eyes burn a vivid fuchsia.

Emmy comes over to squat by me, "I hope you realise you're now going to have to do that every day- possibly for the rest of your life."

Irene can't take her eyes off of Sayra as she dances between the lines, Sayra herself simply lost in them.

I lean subtly towards Emmy, one hand extended towards her conspiratorially, "Once a week and you have an accord."

We shake on it.

"So, you don't know how to escape them?" Rylan slurs as we approach witching hour, slouching on the bed with an arm around a semi-conscious Corbin. "Have you tried, like, talking to them about it?" Amaya snorts, lying on her belly on the floor mattress next to Emmy, "I don't think the most powerful beings in all of creation are that open to debate." She says, flicking his foot.

"I... I'm not sure." I say.

We're on the bed closest the door, my love lies parallel to me, her arms around my middle and her face in the crook of my arm as I prop myself on an elbow to address her friends. She still hasn't roused, and I don't have it in me to wake her.

"I've never actually tried the conversational route," I muse, smirking at the thought even through the fear, "Next time they attempt to kill me I'll be sure to request a formal hearing."

The room titters for a moment before falling silent, all exchanging similar looks of concern.

They've barely known me a couple of hours, and they already fear for my safety. My love chooses her friends wisely, she is fortunate they chose her in return.

"Hey-" I push up a little more, "They haven't gotten to me yet."

Corbin rises from the dead to address me, deftly dodging under Rylan's arm and paling as he does so. Half the people in this room are on the verge of spewing.

"So, what happens now the barrier is gone?" He asks.

The question I've tried to push to the back of my mind since it broke.

Because I don't know.

I didn't understand the barrier when it was in place, and I'm even more bewildered at the logistics now that it isn't.

And I'm not willing to get run over by a vehicle to test it out this time.

I shrug, "That's for time to tell I'm afraid, I am no seer- I know not what the future holds." I say, stroking my love's hair behind her ear.

I only know that I want her in it.

Sayra shifts uncomfortably as I do so, her mouth twisting with the effort of keeping her thoughts to herself.

"You are still upset with her." I assess, squinting down at Sayra.

She does a double-take, unaware of being observed. She now tries to make herself smaller against Irene; who holds her loosely as she fights consciousness on the other floor-mattress.

"She... hurt me." Sayra mumbles, barely audible through her sleeve.

Irene tries to shush her, but the words are already out in the air, and everyone else looks elsewhere. My darling did her best to push them all away, and whilst they're still here- some of them clearly hold grudges better than others.

I take a deep breath before speaking, "She hurt me too," I say, Sayra's face lifting from her clothing shield, "She cast me out, told me things I didn't believe and wouldn't speak to me." I nod to Amaya and Rylan, "She pushed you two away when you asked too many questions," I return to Sayra, "And she insulted you- because she knew telling you to get lost wouldn't be enough. My love is brave and strong but she is also terribly scared and stubborn. Irene once told me that she would need an entire squadron to get through this year, and I now know her words to be true." I hold her tighter against me and sigh, "I know she hurt you, she shouldn't have. But I choose to love her every day, and will continue to do so even if she snaps or hurts me. You get to choose if doing the same is worth your time... it always will be for me."

Sayra considers my words, her eyebrows knitting together in a war between grudges and love.

Rylan is the first to speak.

"I'll always choose to." He mumbles, eyes shut but mouth smiling, "Any trouble she brings should be fun anyways. Usually is."

Amaya grins up at him, using the sheets to drag herself onto the bed until she's tucked against his side, "Same here, the girl needs us."

Emmy yawns loudly, "Count me in, even when she's mean, she's worth it." Corbin dismantles himself from Rylan and joins Emmy on the floor-mattress, "I second that." He concurs.

Irene smirks at me, clutching Sayra closer to her chest, "That girl couldn't get rid of me if she tried."

It's just the pink girl, Sayra, left. Her lips so pressed together that her mouth is but a line.

It takes her only a moment longer before she breathes out a heavy sigh, like a balloon deflating and her shoulders sag with the release of tension.

"I suppose she did give me a three-tiered-milkshake, I owe her one." She concedes.

"That's my girl." Irene appraises, squeezing her till Sayra giggles in protest.

I hold my own love tighter, her body tucked as close to me as the Fates will allow.

You see, my darling, my love. You have an entire squadron behind you, and whether you like it or not- we will help you.

I will save you.

My love you are home.

CHAPTER 34
ANSWERED PRAYERS

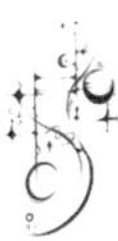

I don't know how I made it to the landing, all I know is there's a bannister here demanding to be slid down.

I let the blue and pink lines send me smoothly along the handrail, spiralling down until my feet touch upon carpeted floors.

My feet are still unsteady but that's okay, I can wobble if no one's here to see me. Mrs and Mr Amaya are probably long asleep, so I can traipse across their living-room semi-naked if I want to; a skirt had felt far too restrictive, my long-shirt and tights suffice.

The living-room is wide and dark, the sofa and two armchairs facing the wall, which I know opens up for the massive wall-television. They are judgement-fearing people, the Amaya's. They keep their more luxurious items hidden.

You can't hide a mansion though.

The moonlight streams in through ceiling-high window-doors, translucent lilac curtains billowing inwards from a door left ajar. White beams of starlight cascade across the room to my feet as I make my way to them.

It's not cold outside.

My bear-feet step onto the grass and leaves that crunch under-foot.

The breeze occasionally sweeps a circle of leaves up and through my hair, whizzing around my body and again there are the blues and pinks. Pretty lines that help the wind along- help *me.*

There's a small hut at the end of Amaya's garden, new and furbished on the outside; white paint and grey-lined doors, windows and ceilings. It's barely a room of a hut, but it has a hanging chair and blankets and pillows. It's a place of solitude and a brief reprieve from the expectations she faces at the house.

At least, that's how Amaya described it when she used to go on and on about the noise the builders made during construction.

I'd kill for a place like this- a place wholly my own.

The paint is dusty on the inside, my fingers drawing back white. There is a pile of books, magazines and a small collection of nail polishes and toe-separators by the hanging chair, that suggest Amaya's choice-use of the place. There's a bulb in the centre of the ceiling that I don't bother turning on and a red and purple swirling rug that I bury my feet in. Windows that face the front and glass-paned doors; that allow me to just about see the living-room I came from. I fall backwards into the network of pillows and blankets that adorn the basket-chair, my body sinking into fur and fabric, my joints singing as they relax.

Aletheia is... she's *real.*

She's real and here and really here, with me and *for* me; for Gods knows how long. And she said... she said she was mine.

And I'm hers.

If I'm honest, I have been for a long time. Since she came to me when I needed her, since she fell through the barrier and into Spelinski's lecture hall.

Since I heard her name calling to me in my dreams.

I let myself believe she didn't want me, that I wasn't worthy of someone like her- I'm still not. But... I want to be.

Maddy wasn't who I thought she was. She was never the idolised version that I dreamt up as a child. She's just her, with all the complications and intricacies that come with that. She doesn't know what she wants- or maybe she does. Either way, it's not me, and it's not my concern anymore. *She* isn't my concern anymore.

Aletheia is.

The room tilts as I push my foot on the floor and off again

Off and on

On and off

Making it spin- the chair can move in all directions, I can make it turn completely around-

Around and around again

I spin it until all I see are colours and moonlight and white and grey. This is how it felt to be in the vortex with Aletheia, to be at the centre of something going faster than you ever thought possible, held together by a singular person.

Aletheia Aletheia ***Aletheia***

The chair comes to an abrupt stop, facing what I imagine is the door, but there's silver in the way. Silver and porcelain and diamond eyes.

"I've told you before, my darling- my love," She murmurs, leaning over me and blocking the light, her leg slipping in-between mine, *"If you're going to pray my name, you should be on your knees."*

My world keeps spinning but my eyes are locked on hers and the way her mouth quirks up on one side as she leans down to kiss me.

Her cold fingers wrap around the back of my neck and draw me deeper, urging me closer as she moves one leg either side of mine and mounts me in the chair; rocking us precariously for a moment as she descends.

Her lips taste of cider and sugar, her tongue chasing the flavour into my mouth; delicately tracing the line of my bottom lip and making me gasp.

My hands roam under her dress, taking hold of her waist on either side and pulling her in. I can't get enough of how she feels, all lean muscle and smooth skin; with curves that flow gracefully into each other.

I knew I couldn't trust her to stay put, but the absence of her beach and the summoning from my sleep led me to her easy enough.

I don't think I've been more in love with her than when I saw her in this chair, legs open and eager for me, and her face one of total wonder. She craves me like I crave her, and it's palpable. I press myself closer, and I know wholeheartedly- I will never get enough of how this feels.

How she feels.

After the excruciating separation and physical barrier. This- this was worth the wait.

She was- is, always will be.

She's intoxicating. I'm drunk on her, falling into everything that she is with total abandonment and-

-and I'm terrified.

"W-wait." I say, my voice feeling harsh in the near-darkness of the hut.

She peers down at me, her starlight freckles casting a glow over our faces.

"*What is it?*" She asks, "*Is this too much-?*"

She moves backwards, off, away-

I don't think I've ever moved so quickly, one hand on her back rising her dress up so anyone in the house would be getting a full-view.

"N-no, nothing like that... it's just I... I've never..."

I've not done this before,

and-

I've never wanted something this badly.

She only smiles, knowingly, slowly lowering back down onto me.

"*It's okay, my love.*" She says, her voice like a song.

She moves, gently taking my hand in hers and intertwining our fingers momentarily. Her actions are effortless and purposeful, like she knows- like she's known what she wanted since the dawn of time.

I'm so lost and I always have been.

"Just do what you want to do," She breathes, lowering our joined hands to her stomach, *"What feels right,"* lower, *"What makes your heart race and what makes me..."* her hand comes free of mine as I take hold of her.

Her sentence finishes in a gasp so artful that I can't even think straight, as I grip her to me and continue to move my fingers against her.

Her diamond eyes close as she rocks into me, her bottom lip held between her teeth.

I move with her, around and against and- *in*.

I can't -won't hold it back.

Everything in me clenches around her and I'm arched, my heartbeat urging me to push harder and faster into her. I take her face in one hand, circling her bottom lip with my thumb, holding tighter and pulling her lips to mine as her movements increase in tempo.

Her lips are soft and eager and I lose myself in her, forget myself in her presence.

I have longed for this since I first set eyes on her.

She moans, a soft but aching vibration against my lips and I hold back from tearing at her stardust dress. I take her bottom lip between my teeth and nip, dragging her in before reclaiming her mouth with mine. Her spine arches and I can feel she's close, the tension in her building building *building*

My eyes stop seeing and I am nothing but euphoric sensation as I topple over the edge, riding wave after wave of her blissful pleasure.

Once her movements rest and the room slows its' spinning, I manage to draw my eyes to hers. She's looking at me like I'm the solitary star in the night's sky, like I'm a singular body in a sea of blue.

Like I'm the only thing in the universe that matters in this moment.

She's the only thing that matters. Right here, right now-there's no doubt in my mind.

I love her.

The thought runs through me, a message sent without intention, but received nevertheless.

I love her.

Wordlessly, I take her face in my hands, bestowing kisses first to her forehead. Then her cheeks, her nose, a chaste kiss upon her lips that leaves her yearning for more.

I slip downwards, her lap slick with me, my legs sliding down to the floor as I trail my kisses down her torso. I take my time, moving from her chest to her navel, to the very edge of her pant-line. I draw my tongue along it as I lower her tights, and she raises her hips on instinct to allow for me.

My mouth finds purchase on her inner-thigh and I bite down a little so that she gasps, her hands clenched on the outer-ropes of the chair.

"Now, my love," I say, slinking her damp thong down past her knees, revelling in the way her eyes widen as I press my lips to her, "Let me show you what I mean when I say 'pray'."

CHAPTER 35
THE CALM

The birds rouse me first, their light-chirping a distant siren to my subconscious.

Then the light, kept mildly at bay by the roof and the surrounding trees.

Then the memories.

My head pounds but I can almost ignore it through the bliss of what happened in the space of 24 hours. We didn't get to sleep till the first light of dawn stretched across the sky, all too consumed in exploring and re-learning each other over and over again. She is euphoria personified, a literal demon and a benevolent goddess; I intend to spend the better part of eternity worshipping her.

Aletheia is curled around me, asleep in the swinging basket, her soft snores drifting out of her slightly parted lips. Our bodies slink around each other with very little of us not-touching. The breeze has the chair rocking gently back and forth, steadily moving us like the morning tide.

The next thing that rouses us is less of a soft awakening and more of an abrupt intrusion.

"Found them!" Irene calls halfway between the house and the little hut, wrapping a dressing gown tighter around her in the crisp morning-air as she rushes in our direction.

I swiftly move and pull Aletheia's dress down to cover her as she stirs, but there's little to be done about my long-shirt-no-tights look.

Irene pokes her head though the door, her eyes darting around the small room, taking in my ripped and disregarded tights and the cascade of pillows that litter the floor.

She smirks at us, leaning on the doorframe with arms folded, "Well, haven't you two been busy."

Aletheia raises her head enough to glance in Irene's direction.

"That could indeed be inferred."

The cold barely registers on my skin, our little cocoon hiding us from the crisp morning air. Irene clearly feels it though, as she looks from the garden to us with deliberation.

She shrugs, "Ah sod it- it's cold."

Before either of us can protest, she's scurried the last couple steps and landed on top of us, cosying in the middle and stealing our warmth.

I'd be vaguely annoyed, had she not been the sole other friend in the mortal realm that could see me for the time my love and I were apart.

"Make yourself at home then." I mumble, scooching in closer to fend off the cold she brings.

"I always do." *She grins back, shuffling herself so she's the middle penguin in our mini-huddle.*

I stroke Aletheia's shoulder, the rest of my arm crushed and cradling a frozen Irene. I quirk an eyebrow at her, "Isn't that Mrs Amaya's dressing gown?"

She tugs the purple garment closer into her chest, "It matches my hair."

"You're such a tea-leaf." I say, shaking my head but smiling.

This, here and now, is the happiest I've been in a very long time.

Irene presses a frozen hand to both of our individual cheeks, sighing and pulling our heads together; clashing them against hers a little too harshly.

"Now, my dear flowers, we have some preparation and understandings to be had. So prick up your mortal and intergalactic ears- and hush up." She says, her eyes locked on the world outside in a comical pantomime.

"For one, we have about T-minus-two minutes before a powerful pink bloodhound comes a-sniffing- followed closely by her confidantes," Her rambling starts to bend a smile into her features, before she shakes her head and resumes her shenanigans, "In addition, we also have the matter at hand, that news has travelled around the grapevine- that an associate of Miss Tenaya Syn brutally assaulted the reigning ruler of Southlakes," She looks at Aletheia pointedly, "Congratulations by the way."

I grin, nuzzling closer at the memory, "'Twas nothing."

I glance past Irene's lashes to check for my love's reaction, but she appears unconcerned. Perhaps my intrusion had been more of a saving grace than a selfish vengeance after all.

"In any case, the final quandary if you will-"

"Are you mocking Aletheia?" I interrupt, watching as the dimples appear in Irene's cheeks.

"Me? Imitate a burlesque caricature of your dearest darling purely for my own amusement?" She pulls me in closer and presses a chaste peck to my cheek, "Wouldn't dream of it."

"Is that truly what I sound like?" I ask, having not realised there was anything comical or out of sorts in her phrasing.

Perhaps I am less attuned with earthling vernacular than I had first presumed.

She strokes my shoulder consolingly, which I take as a kindness. If she likes the way I speak, then that's all that matters.

"Furthermore," Irene says, slightly louder for effect; the

chorus of voices that emanate from the outside world serving as a human countdown, "What are you going to do about living situations, now our invisible star-girl is, well- visible?"

The warmth I'd managed to sustain turns to ice in my veins, the thought having not even occurred to me. Of-course she would live with me... right?

"Found them!" Sayra yells, scampering across the grass on all fours like a wild-cat possessed, grinning maniacally.

Irene grimaces before leaning up and out of the cot, "To be continued," She grabs both our hands, our faces both plastered in pale uncertainty, "Meaning the stress is to be continued too, we have to breakfast with the Amaya's, remember?"

She was right, we would need our mental fortitude. And so help Aletheia if she didn't sit up straight like the rest of us.

Breakfast passes by without much of a hitch, aside from a couple remarks from Mrs Amaya on the shortness of Aletheia's dress; not aided by Mr Amaya's sideways glances. They don't stay at the table long regardless, Mrs Amaya heading off to work and Mr Amaya making himself scarce to the office. He's a wiry little man, but he means well. He just, well, he has to tend to Mrs Amaya day in and day out- without messing up; a task and a half in and of itself.

Everyone else is pretty bleary-eyed and bed-headed, even Rylan has spent most of the morning with his head in his hands; the white ghost face-paint still lingering around his ears and temple.

I don't think I need to worry about his alcohol intake, he's well aware of his limits in that respect. Besides, the only bottle I see him reaching for this morning is the orange juice, taking a swig before grimacing and slowly lowering it to the table with a quiet menace.

"Which one- of you *monsters*- thought it was okay," He pauses looking at each of us in turn, "To buy *pulpy* orange juice- and not mention it to a man *before* he drinks?"

We all share mildly concerned glances before descending into a pile of giggles. Rylan's stern glare, never faltering, only making it that much funnier.

Amaya slowly raises her hand from beside him, shrugging apologetically, "Guilty."

He looks her up and down, shaking his head before lying his forehead back in the crook of his arms, "Despicable."

Aletheia hasn't let go of my hand under the table the entire time, keeping suspiciously quiet as the rest of the table talks amongst themselves. I wonder what went on last night, what they all talked about- how much they know.

It feels so good to be seen.
To be observed, recognised and accepted.
To be part of her world and her community.
This is the home I sought after for so long-
hers.

"So," Corbin says from the driver's seat, one hand on the gear stick attached to Emmy's hand, as they drive Aletheia and I back to mine, "What's the plan?"

My mind goes blank, looking from Corbin's eyes in the mirror to Emmy's in confusion.

"The... the plan?"

"Yeah," Emmy interjects, turning so she can see us better, her large hoop-earrings clinking, "Which is it going to be first? The 'coming out' talk? Or the 'interdimensional-girlfriend needing a place to crash' one?"

My breakfast threatens to become lunch on the floor of their car.

"Personally," Corbin continues, bringing his hand up theatrically, "I'd go for neither, sneak her up to your room and then attempt the coming out one."

"Oh yeah, because that worked out *so* well for us." Emmy quips, flicking him on the ear.

"How did you two manage?" I pipe up, Emmy's attention immediately on me, "Was there parental conflict when the two of you announced your love?"

They share a look then, a kind one, a beautifully human one.

"Well, my parents aren't exactly traditional." Corbin says slowly.

"And mine kinda knew I wasn't exactly happy as I had been, they were pretty accepting throughout the transition." Emmy says, pursing her painted-blue lips at the memory, "Dad... took a minute to fully get there, but he never used my dead name. We have a good relationship now." She says, smiling fondly, even though I can tell it wasn't quite as smooth sailing as she was suggesting.

Corbin shrugs, "My mum didn't get it for a while," he scruffs his hair as he makes a sharp turning, "One day I'd be ranting about girls, the next day guys, then trying to explain the rabbit hole that is gender ambiguity and non-binary folk. She was a little confused as to what she was meant to be accepting."

His eyes meet mine in the mirror, "It takes time, but eventually- the ones that love you, the real you, will love you regardless of the love you seek out for yourself."

I look to her then, my darling, her face pale but brow set.

I give her arm a squeeze, "We will do this at your pace my love," I say, her hand landing in mine, "I'll follow your lead."

The car pulls into the driveway, and I feel my heart ricocheting inside my chest.

I accept Aletheia, my love for her, I want her in my life and in my home and bed.

This time I'm not even most worried about Hydra- more *for* her than anything else. I'm scared that dad won't have it.

"I... I don't..."

"Duck!" Corbin yells, reaching through the back and shoving Aletheia's head down behind his seat as Hydra exits the house.

Not fast enough though.

She's wearing a formal pant-suit, white shirt and a fascinator that slicks down her straight blonde hair in a painful-looking manner.

She spots us, her sneer morphing into a fake-smile as she saunters over to the little red car, her nails tip-tapping on the window-side encouragingly.

Demandingly.

Like little red daggers, ready to slice through my cheek at the first opportunity.

I shift away from the window but press down the button that then begins rolling down the glass; until her plastered-on friendly face is on view to everyone.

Corbin and Emmy don't know, they suspect this is my mother. The thought bubbles angrily in my head until I can't help but say something.

"Well dear, who-"

"C-corbin, Emmy- this is Hydra," I say pointedly, Hydra's eyes narrowing, "M-my st-tep-mother."

Hydra's mouth pinches at the term, I knew I'd guessed it right. Dad hadn't wanted me to call her mum.

She had.

Emmy flicks her gaze between Hydra and me warily, her brow furrowed. Even without me saying to her the ins and outs of my family life, my stammer gives away the gist that something isn't right.

Gods damned fearful stutter.

"Delightful to meet you all. Tenaya honey," She continues, still bristling, "I'll be away for work meetings for the next couple of days, as will your father and brother- you best hurry on in so they can explain some small housekeeping rules."

Aletheia emerges from the stooped position she was in, her eyes murderous and demon-teeth bared.

"Blonde de-" My hand whips out over her mouth before she can finish the statement.

I try and beg her with my eyes to just stay silent, to be complacent just this once before I announce her to the rest of the family.

She closes her eyes, breathing through her nose before nodding slightly.

"And Tenaya, sweetness, you know the house isn't ready for guests yet." She says accusingly.

Ah yes, this was indeed the excuse she had been using for the past six years to forbid me from having friends over. Not that I wanted to bring anyone close to my haunted house of a family home; but her word made that decision final.

"I know, d-don't worry," I say hurriedly, "They were just dr-ropping me home."

Her thin smile relaxes some, but her eyes still roam the new faces in the vehicle with mild distrust.

"Hi," Corbin says, hurling himself through the gap in the middle and extending a manicured hand to Hydra, "I'm Corbin, pleasure to meet you."

She baulks at the gesture, sniffing before tentatively taking his hand. I had never bothered to work out her views on individuality, I suppose her reproach gives me my answer.

"Truly." She says, daintily placing Corbin's hand back inside the car.

She looks to Emmy, but Emmy remains forward-facing, her face unreadable.

Corbin cringes, motioning to Emmy, "And this is my girlfriend, Emmy."

Hydra nods, her smile faltering.

And then she clocks onto the girl beside me. The girl who's hand is now firmly planted on my knee. The girl in the slip of a dress, who's sitting far too close and whom she's never seen or heard of before.

She leans down to take a closer look, and I can feel Aletheia itching to rip into her; literally.

"And who might *this* be?" She coos, her manic smile returned.

Undoubtedly she thought this was something she could use against me, with dad. Gods I pray I get to him first.

Aletheia moves over me before I can stop her, her fingers pressing hard on the window button; Hydra stumbling backwards as it shuts abruptly.

"*Aletheia* what are you-"

"My choice too now." She utters, opening the car door and slamming it behind her.

I grip the handle, trying and failing to pry it open.

She locked us in.

She locked *me* in.

I slam my fists against the glass, practically growling at the audacity of being imprisoned in my own driveway by my new girlfriend.

"Hey- woah there, take it easy on Otamatone, would ya?" Corbin pleads from the front.

"I thought you said it's name was Meepbeep?" Emmy mutters and Corbin sighs.

"If you heard how many noises this thing makes on the daily- you'd understand the renaming."

I try to drone them out and focus in on what Aletheia is saying to Hydra, but the glass is thick and Aletheia's back blocks both their faces from view.

I'm powerless to stop this.

She stands a head taller than me, eyes wide and her hands raised slightly; as if someone moving of their own volition spooked her.

She hasn't been threatened in years. Ever?

The suit she wears makes her pointy. Sharp shoulders, sharp angles-

sharp tongue. I saw the way my darling squirmed and I won't negate how flippantly she disregarded her new friends.

My new friends.

I watch as she takes me in, from my dress to my eyes and ears, to my hair that moves a little too much to just be hovering on the wind.

She takes a sstep back, and I smile.

"My name is Aletheia," I say, stalking forwards so that she's mere inches away, till I can see the stressed red lines in her eyes, "And the mortal Tenaya- is now permanently and forever, under my protection."

She straightens to her full height, her arms coming to cross over her chest defiantly.

"I am certain I have no idea what you're talking about."

Oh, cruel captor, I shall truly relish breaking you.

"I am implying," I say slowly, "That your predilection for torturous games and consistent attempts to impute faults on my darling, shall henceforth be terminated." I step closer, "For your own safety."

Her red lips part in shock and her stick-like brows attack her eyelashes in outrage.

"Are you threatening me? On my own property?" She hisses, and I smirk.

I shouldn't do it.

I know I shouldn't do it.

I allow myself to float from the ground, only until my height matches hers; inches over it.

I revel as her face contorts in a mix of confusion and fear. I can smell the fear.

I let my eyes glow faintly, my hair zipping around me.

"Yes," I whisper, grinning so my canines are on full show, "Now run."

She pauses.

She pauses a moment too long, my hand jutting out and flicking her in the shoulder. The force I'd put into it sends her reeling back, barely catching herself on her stiletto style footwear.

"I. Said. Run." I say, returning to the ground and stalking towards her enough that she gets the picture.

She's lucky I don't unleash my third familiar.

She scuttles like the cockroach she is, one hand clasping her handbag and the other digging around for her car keys.

She's probably never left a driveway so fast in her life.

As the blonde demon speeds off the drive, I flick my fingers to open Corbin's car. She has yet to know the extent of my abilities, I just hope I haven't made her too angry with this particular display.

I'm angry for all of two seconds before I see her face. She won't look me in the eyes and her hands twist together awkwardly as she waits for me to berate her.

I did this.

With my secrets and my inability to defend myself, I caused the person I love to feel bad for trying to help me.

And I don't know how to stop.

"I... I only told her you were under my protection, to preclude you from further harm," She murmurs, her face downcast, *"...and for her to run. But that was more because she pissed me off."*

I won't laugh, I'm not allowed.

This is serious.... *But.*

I wrap my arms around her shoulders, squeezing until she returns it.

"I'm not mad," I say, swallowing the anger down along with my pride, "Just- in my house, in my driveway- please let me make the decisions? Or at the very least, don't stop me from making my own." I say, drawing her back to look her in the eyes, one hand raising to cup her cheek, "Kapeesh?"

I close my hand over hers and nod, "Understood."

Emmy winds down her window, frowning.

"Hey- so, we've kinda got the feeling there's a complicated situation going on here-" Emmy says.

"So figured it's probably best we skedaddle," Corbin finishes, looking between us expectantly, "You guys good for now?"

I go to answer but stop myself.

This is her driveway.

I turn to her, looking for her confirmation and she smiles; laughing and bumping my hip.

"Yeah, we're good."

They wave us off, the little red bucket wheeling out of the drive and zooming down the estate with as much grace as a drunk man at a tea party.

I take a deep breath, looking at the front door like it might rise up and eat me. It's just a house, it's just dad, it's just a conversation.

I've got this.

We've got this.

Before I can even make the first step towards it though, Aletheia has me round the waist again.

"My love, I must leave you but for a moment." I say, watching as the emotions of confusion and relief cross over her features, settling on uncertainty.

"Have I done something?" *She asks, her hand landing on my arm, sending goosebumps along my skin.*

Oh, how I long to lie with her tonight and not have a barrier between us- or a drunkenness that blurs precious memories.

"No my love, but if you've not realised- I am missing a familiar." I say, gesturing to her, "And as I ascertained last night, from blissfully thorough searching, he did not remain with you either."

Her blush is adorable.

The way she was with me, the bitter ecstasy she experienced and the elated sense of being that I bestowed upon her; perhaps for the first time in her life.

It was the greatest night of my existence.

Her hand tightens on me, as if she can sense the memory on my skin.

"Don't go too far." *She murmurs, her fingers tracing the distance between my freckles with the lightest of touches.*

I push the hair back from her face, kissing her forehead.

"I wouldn't dream of it." I say, pulling away, her hand dropping mine as I move out of reach, "I'll be back before you know it. He's not one to journey far without me."

I nod nervously, waving her off as she darts over the hedge that separates my house from the next. How I survived without her by my side for days, I have no idea; my pulse already double-timing it with the anxiety of her departure.

I sigh, grateful that Hydra has left for a couple days, but still fearful of the talk I know I have to have with dad, in order to keep Aletheia safe.

The handle feels weightier than usual as I step inside, closing the door as quietly as possible.

"Naya!" Tabi yells down to me from his room, his voice louder than life when Hydra isn't home.

I wish I had his ability to switch between modes, mine remaining stuck in the not-seen not-heard persona.

"She'll be up in a second Tabs!" Dad calls, saving me from raising my voice as he steps out of the kitchen; a backpack in his hands.

He's wearing football gear, a startling sight after not seeing him out of shirts and chinos in over six years.

"Tenaya- poppet, umm..." He starts, leaning against the bannister to the stairs and not meeting my eyes as he searches for the words.

"Yes, dad?" I ask hesitantly, stepping out of my shoes and walking closer till I'm just the other side of the railing.

He tracks my footsteps until he manages to meet my eyes, a nervousness there.

"Well, umm- Well, Hid-your mother, she's gone away for a couple of days on business, and uhh, well, Tabi wanted to go see the game this week in the city. Do you- will you be okay? On your own here, that is?"

My chest relaxes and I breathe a sigh out, nodding.

“That’s fine dad, I’m perfectly capable of not burning the house down for a weekend.”

He chuckles lightly, tersely, “Yes, yes I’m quite sure you are.”

I make to go upstairs, but he holds out a hand, tapping the bannister closer to me; but not quite touching me.

He hasn’t bridged that gap in years.

“Poppet, I uhh, I have to ask. Who...”

He saw.

He saw us outside. Not with Hydra or he would have come out and done something.

But he saw Aletheia and I in the driveway.

“The girl in the dress?” I ask, and he nods; sealing the fact that it is now or never.

I take a deep breath, “That uhh... well that’s Aletheia, my... my girlfriend.” I say, the terminology so weird for the level of intimacy we already have.

A childish label.

But a label nonetheless, and one I know dad has grown to be uncomfortable with; one that his religion dictates as inherently wrong.

His face says as much, as he battles with himself for a response.

He might send me away, he might not talk to me, he might-

“Are you happy?”

The question comes from nowhere and I’m shellshocked, rocked and unprepared for such a query. He’s never asked how I’m feeling really, and now, when I pose a conundrum that should have me bags-packed and life altered- *now* is when he wants to know?

I take in his pained expression and nod.

“Yes dad, I... I think I might be.”

He takes a moment, looking into the bag he holds as if it will herald him answers.

“You haven’t been happy in a very long time,” He says heavily, the words landing like stones on water- sending ripples of emotion outwards in every direction, "I'm glad that you've found something- someone, that brings you happiness."

I don't know how to respond, my mouth opening and closing like a fish out of water as I grasp for words.

He smiles sadly at my reaction, half-turning before patting my hand and squeezing it; reaching over the gap for the briefest of moments.

"Never let it go."

And with that, he heads back into the kitchen, already rifling around for something that must reside at the very bottom of the bag.

My feet take me up the stairs but my mind is elsewhere. I feel relief of course, happy that he will accept Aletheia and I for what we are, despite his religious beliefs.

But I'm also... *angry*.

Hurt. Furious that he's recognised my semi-constant state of dejection, and failed to lift a finger to alter it. He's my dad, he claims to care for me and Tabi above all else, yet when I am shown to be depressed or despondent under his own roof; he does *nothing*.

He knew I was hurting and did nothing.

So what if he didn't know the extent or the cause, he's my *dad*.

He's supposed to love me- to show it.

I know what love is now, I've seen its true form in the shape of a realm-hopping goddess. A ferocious spirit who will stop at nothing to protect those she cares for, and wreak holy hellfire down upon those who threaten it.

What he shows, it's not that.

I bite it back. It's not something I can change, and at the end of the day- I was after his acceptance, not his attentions.

I only need the one.

I swing open Tabi's door without knocking and am immediately swept off my feet by giant orange paws. I land on my butt just outside his room. Kuro, the size of a small donkey, having bawled me over before I could even say hello.

"Did you know he can grow to whatever size he wants?!" Tabi squeals, not pausing before leaping on top of Kuro's back and squirming his way up until his face pokes over Kuro's shoulder.

"Kuro?!" I ask dumbly, my head still reeling from the fall.

"He's been with me for a couple of days," Tabi says, wriggling down Kuro's side and coming to crouch where my head is, my body still pinned beneath fur, "He explained a little."

Tabi's face looks frustrated, and I turn my glare on Kuro; my anger reignited.

"That was *not* his information to share." I grit out, shoving onto my elbows but failing to budge him from me.

His eyes narrow, his teeth baring and lip curling as he lets out a warning growl; his head coming down to bump mine.

I get the message- *don't test me.*

I sigh, lifting my hand to scratch him behind the ear, "Sorry, Kuro, I know these days must have been difficult for you too." I press my face into the fur of his forehead, "It's not you I'm angry at. Or her."

It's me.

He nuzzles back before pushing off of me, stalking into the room and returning to me with Hyacinth perched on his head.

"You- *huh*?!" I say, pointing to them in confusion.

Tabi only giggles, "He wants to show you that he didn't eat her."

Kuro sniffs, wagging his many tails and shrinking down slowly, magically, until he's the same proportions as Hyacinth. They roll and burst out into a chase, Hyacinth zipping away, running for her life with Kuro in hot-pursuit.

"...for the most part, they're good." Tabi shrugs, giving me a hand up as I dust myself off.

I smile, ruffling his hair as he starts telling me about the game this weekend. About how his favourite player will be there, and that he's bringing countless objects for her to sign.

I pay as much attention as I can, even with my mind on where Aletheia will go looking for Kuro if he's right here. I'm sure she'll realise soon enough and head back.

My phone buzzes from my pocket, a notif, and I take a glance at it whilst Tabi packs, the animals rough-housing around me:

Diner's fixed- be in for 5pm tomorrow.
Won't be in for morning - I'll be in for lock-up at 10pm.
Don't be late.
- Casimir

Just as one demon leaves, another must return. I try to push down the fear and focus on Tabi, on anything but the notif and the prospect of going into work alone tomorrow.

Gods I hope she gets back soon.

My body strains and my heart burns with the effort of trying to pry my limbs out.

Their purple and black tendrils wrap around every inch of me. I can only watch through tear-filled eyes as her house has a blue line split down the middle of it; cracking and marring her world before tearing from view.

There is black, and there is white, and there is grey.

There are the Fates and there is me, stuck at the centre of their void like a prize-catch framed and mounted.

There is nothing else.

I scream and cry and thrash but I know, from years of experience I know; there is no hope.

There is the black, and there is the white, and I am eternally stuck in the in-between.

I never even got to say goodbye.

CHAPTER 36
THE STORM

The diner is open when I get there, presumably Casimir had one of the other employees open-up for him. Barely anyone comes in, save a couple regulars who complement me- telling me I look refreshed after the time away.

I feel anything but refreshed.

Aletheia didn't come home last night, nor did she arrive this morning. Not even attempting to summon her had brought her to me. I mentioned it to Kuro, and Tabi translated that he said not to worry and that she was a free spirit.

Don't I know it.

But he didn't need to translate the concerned look that bled into the features of the kitsune when he thought my back was turned.

Dad and Tabi left early this morning, saying they'd be back in a couple days, but weren't sure if it'd be Sunday evening or start of next week. I don't mind, having the house alone is a blessing I must have had maybe a handful of times in my life. I just wish I could have it alone with *her*.

It's coming towards closing-up, customers having left over an hour ago, and I'm just about finished with the last chores of the day. It feels weird to not have Irene here to keep me company, or Sayra bouncing off the walls for us to hurry up and leave.

I still haven't apologised to Sayra for how I acted. She didn't seem to hold a grudge, but perhaps that's why Irene hasn't come back to visit today.

It's dark, and I have barely anything left to do before lock-up, save mopping. Casimir is still a no-show.

There's a rustling from the back room, a slamming and a clinking that has me frozen to the spot.

"Hello?" I call stupidly, cursing myself for the cliché reaction to a foreign noise. I stop myself from asking *'who's there'*. I push through the kitchen door, holding it in case I have to run back.

The place is too dark, too quiet.

Quiet enough that I can hear the lock of the front door click into place behind me.

Without a sound, I run through the kitchen, heading straight for the fire exit.

I was warned.

Everyone said if he was willing to do one thing- he would do the next, given the chance.

Irene left, he got his opportunity.

I stop dead by the fire exit, my body going cold as I register the thick metal chains lashed around the handle; a hefty black-padlock securing them in place; visible through the gap to the outside.

Blocking me in.

And now I'm in a corner. Trapped. With nowhere to hide.

"Aletheia," I whisper into the silence, "I don't know where you are, but I need you. I really *really* need you. Aletheia-"

For a large man, he moves so quietly.

His hand comes around my neck from behind. Sausage fingers cutting off my airways as the other arm slams me into the fire-exit; the metal clanging loudly.

"You didn't want to be my friend," He snarls, spittle hitting the back of my neck with every lisped word as he swings me around like I'm nothing, shoving me against the countertop; the edges digging angrily into my hipbones, "Fine, I guess I'll have to be *extra* friendly to compensate."

I can't move, my hands can't find purchase on the slippery, clean work-surface and tears blur my vision.

He's too big to fight. I've always known that. But I didn't think he would ever catch me so off-guard, or try anything like this- not when he has so much to lose if he's found out.

Maybe that's what his perverted mind gets off to, the thrill of the almost-getting-caught, the rule-break where he never usually does.

He's sick.

And there's no reasoning with that.

"ALETHEIA! HELP! ALTH-" my words are cut off as his hand closes down further on my windpipe.

"Be a good girl and shut the fuck up." His rancid breath is the only thing that manages to pass into my lungs; I gag on it.

She's summoning me.

My heart burns with a vengeful hellfire and my chest pulls forwards against the restraints on my wrists.

I can't move, they won't let me move.

But she needs me. She needs me more than she's ever needed me before.

"LET ME OUT! LET ME SAVE HER!" I scream at them as her summoning grows harsher, more desperate.

Ink black and purple swirls come forth from the depths of all directions. They morph and blend until they stand before me, three bodies in one with their backs sewn together and their hooded heads folded in three directions. The only thing to pierce the darkness is their three sets of glowing white eyes that stare back at me, mercilessly.

Aletheia Aletheia Aletheia

She's pouring her prayers out into the universe, praying them, choking on them.

And I'm burning up on them.

My fingers touch on the wrack of knives ahead of me and I don't think twice. I grab the closest and drive it backwards into his stomach.

He howls, releasing me for a moment.

The moment is all I need to duck under his arm and sprint for the doors. Through the swinging ones, hurdling over the bar counter and slamming into-

Locked doors.

I heard him lock them- why did I forget? Why didn't I *think*. Why did I think, if I got away from one corner, he wouldn't be able to follow me to the next-

Sharp and off-key whistling sounds from the kitchen passageway, and from it steps Casimir, swinging the keys around his fingers in a lazy circle. He takes his time placing the bloodied knife down on the bar, delicately even; so that I barely register the clink of it over my own racing heartbeat.

He sniffs, allowing the keys to fall on the extension cord to his side.

"Now?" He snarls, dragging his trousers up a little and snapping the waistband, "Not so friendly." He grins at me through laboured breaths.

I sprint left around the booths- but not fast enough, his grubby hands twisting harshly in my hair and thrusting me backwards onto the floor so I see bright flashes.

"**ALETHEIA**! Aletheia please help me- please *PLEASE!* Help *AGH-*" I choke on the words as he pulls me up by my hair again, dangling me like a fish on a line.

"Didn't I tell you to be *quiet*?" He spits, throwing my head down onto a booth table on the last word and blackness digs into my periphery, threatening my consciousness.

She's going to break, separate- I can feel her snapping.

If she goes under I don't know if I'll be able to get her back. Finding her- the real her- in the first place had been hard enough.

But now...

Every time she screams my name- another harpoon of fire strikes me through the chest and pulls me towards her by my heartstrings. Lightning through my soul. Fire in my lungs. Screaming in my head. Screaming fighting crying-

"LET ME OUT LET ME OUT LET ME OUT!"

But they won't.

I hear the buckle clink just before he kicks my legs out from under me so that I'm bent over the table. My legs are shaking and he's too strong for me to stop him from pushing my legs further aside as he unzips his trousers; the noise thunderous in the dead silence of the diner.

"Al... Aletheia..." I sob in barely a whisper, my face damp from the tears that now smear across the table.

"You'll like it. Yeah, you'll take it and you won't say a word like a good little girl. That's right."

He's insane.

He's actually lost it.

Talking to himself like we're conversing and convincing himself that what he's about to do is justified. That what's about to happen to me is okay.

Normal.

Fine.

Fair.

"Please... *no*..." I try one last time, perhaps to reason with him, perhaps just to show I tried.

He snorts, phlegm catching in the back of his throat as

he catapults me harder against the edge of the table, his face contorted in manic rage.

"Don't pretend you don't *want* this."

His tongue between his teeth, he takes my skirt zipper in hand, winding it down till it falls to the floor and I whimper pathetically.

He's going to rape me.

"LET ME SAVE HER!"

He has me and there's no way out. No one's coming to save me, I can't save myself, and he will never get caught because who believes a respectable diner owner over an emotionally unstable young girl.

If I just go into my head, if I just lie here, it will be over soon.

"DARLING HOLD ON! PLEASE! I'M TRYING - LET ME SAVE HER!"

His grimy fingers snag my tights, pulling them around and down.

It'll be over soon.

"No... My darling, no...." I can feel her giving up.

I feel it graze me, flesh on flesh.

It'll be over soon.

"...."

The clang of metal against bone is the first thing I register as his weight falls free of me and crashes to the floor.

I don't move. I don't breathe. I don't even think I blink.

My eyes move though, as I track backwards to where Irene stands, brandishing a fire extinguisher over her head. Her hair is wild and her eyes are frantic as she looks between Casimir's unconscious form, his lower half exposed- and my bent-over body.

"*Tenaya...*"

It's all I need to hear to break.

I take in a breath that sounds like a wail, from depths I didn't know I possessed, and slip to the floor where my skirt already lies.

It didn't happen.

She didn't let it happen.

I'm okay.

He didn't...

My darling you're okay, I will find you again.

I swear it.

I try to rock these things into my brain as I grip my arms around my body and try to piece myself back together. I scramble further from him across the floor, putting as much space as I can between us before curling into a ball.

"Hold on there, honey. I'll be right back." Irene says, one hand gently stroking my back before she darts into the kitchen area.

I hear a clanging and a scraping before she emerges not a minute later, dragging the heavy chains with her. She smiles slyly at my gobsmacked expression.

"Rule number one of catching the dodgy ones- always make a copy of their keys." She lifts a bundle so full there's almost no room for them to jangle, "And I mean *every* key."

She wastes no time in slumping him onto his front and lashing his arms together, pulling them so tight that his shoulder-blades protrude through the fat.

She secures the chains in place. As an afterthought, she runs to the counter, pushing up on it and grabbing a paper bag from the other side, shoving it forcefully over his head.

She makes a show of slapping her hands together.

"Good luck explaining yourself out of this one." She spits.

I feel like I'm watching everything in slow motion, through a pane of glass. Like I'm sat in a movie theatre and I'm watching the scene play out on a screen.

Irene comes over to me then, her eyes soft as she crouches by me, breaking the fourth wall. She doesn't say anything. I just watch as she picks up my skirt, cautiously getting me to stand; placing me like a mannequin so that she can redress me. She shimmies the skirt up my legs, pulling up my tights as she goes, careful not to linger on my skin. She takes off her camo-jacket, placing it over my shoulders- before walking me out of the Diner.

We don't talk as she guides me by the hand, with each step away from the place I feel a little bit of me come back. The pavement under my feet, the breeze on my cheeks, the stars in the sky, Irene's hand in mine taking me away

away

away from there-

him.

I got away from him.

My steps falter as we reach the park, my feet dragging me away from the path and onto the grass as my knees buckle beneath me and I shatter.

Irene's arms are around me and I collapse into a bundle of emotions, raw and painful, in her arms. I don't know if it's relief, the fear coming in for a second wave, the fact that I nearly lost myself or that she saved me when I thought no one would.

I just *break.*

I don't care that my cries are probably disturbing half the neighbourhood.

I don't care that I look like a baby curled in Irene's arms.

I don't care about what Hydra will think or that I need a new job or that my friends had been right all along.

I only care that my friend is here, and she is holding me so tightly that the rest of the world doesn't matter right now. The entire universe is taking pause so I can piece myself back together.

"It's okay, it's okay- you're safe. I've got you." Irene repeats, over and over again in a tone barely above a whisper.

"I didn't think- I didn't- no one was coming and I thought-" I sob, my voicc hoarse and broken as I grip onto her like a life-ring.

"I know, I know," She hums, "And I know you said you'd be fine. But that's what friends are for- we turn up uninvited sometimes."

I squeeze my eyes shut, tears leaking out unhindered as I curl into her shoulder in shame.

"I was-, to S-sayra I never even ap-pologised, I d-d-didn't-." I stammer.

Irene only scoffs, shaking her head at me.

"You really are a silly sausage, you know that?" She smirks, and a little bit of it passes onto me as my sob cracks into a half-smile. "Just because you told us once to go screw ourselves doesn't mean we're suddenly going to abandon you." She tuts, flicking me lightly on the forehead, "Not on your life."

I've never had this.

For most of my life I've been hiding at least three things at a time from everyone. Always having them at arms-length to protect myself, or my family, or my environment from change. Never have I had people around me who know me, who want to keep knowing me even when everything is on show.

"I-I don't..." I say, shaking my head against another bout of tears, "*Thankyou.*"

She holds me until the early hours of the morning. Our joints aching and my eyes sore. She holds me up on the walk back to mine and she holds the door open to my house. She holds me up as we take the stairs and she holds my hand as I curl into bed, unwilling to undress just yet. And she doesn't leave.

To feel known is to feel held, yes. Funnily enough, in some cases, to be held is also to feel known- if held by the right arms.

CHAPTER 37
ROUGH WATERS

Saturday comes and goes, the morning hours bleeding into the afternoon without so much as a lunch break. Irene stays with me the whole day.

Even when I get the notif from dad saying they won't be back till Monday.

She stayed.

When I got a call from the police, and had to explain the exact time and placement of events. When they announced that a small girl in bunny ears dropped off a tape that showed diner-CCTV footage of events. When they told me they wouldn't be asking me too many questions, that that would come later under court terms.

She stayed.

And even though she stayed, even though I don't know how I would have gotten through the day without her; all I can think is of *her*.

Aletheia.

She left me.

She didn't come, she ran. Ran away.

When she got the chance to leave... she left.

No my love, I would never have left you. I had no choice...

"Come get coffee with me?" Irene asks out of nowhere.

We've been sitting in silence in the living room, watching whatever comes on from the default setting. I haven't touched my tea, *Leaf juice*, that Irene made me, and my stomach curdles at the concept of food.

She stands, stretching,

her stardust dress itching skywards-

before extending a hand to me, "We've gotta get you out before your body tells you that home is the only safe place."

I snort without meaning to, shaking my head as I take her hand and rise, "Trust me, that is *never* going to happen."

She gives me a begrudging smile as we grab our coats and leave; umbrella's up and heads down to fend off the rain.

Can you fly us

It takes us twenty minutes of casual conversation and dodging puddles before we make it to the café. I've never gone outside in sweatpants before, Hydra would never have allowed it. The baggy jumper serves to shield my body from the world as much as possible. ***His hands on my body on my waist tearing my hair ripping my clothes down down down***

"Irene..." I breathe, the memory temporarily blinding me and I clasp her arm as we huddle just outside the café, under the canopy.

Not here. I don't want to be like this, I don't want this happening here-

His breath in my ear his hips crushing mine flesh on flesh on flesh on

"I... I can't..." I can't breathe is what I want to say, but all I can see is the ***table-top of the diner as he-***

"Okay, it's okay- breathe with me- my breaths, see?" She places a hand to each of my cheeks and tries to get my eyes to meet hers; her bracelet catching in my periphery-*"She believed she could, so she did"*-

she left me

she left me and he got me and she didn't stop him

"Tenaya- it's okay, come with me." She commands, drawing me backwards until my back is against the outer-wall of the café, my body sliding down to crouch; head between my legs.

And I'm *heaving.*

Great lung-fulls of air which end in sobs that I can't dampen. I'm so tired of crying, but I can't seem to stop.

She's gone

He got me

"I don't w-w-want this," I manage, my fists clenched in the fabric of my trousers, "I don't... I *don't...*"

"I know you don't sweet-pea," She murmurs, stroking my hair back and squatting out the way of people coming in and out of the café, "It wasn't your fault. You didn't ask for this- none of it."

I lift my head then, my heart slowing but the ache dwelling.

I don't think it will ever go away.

"No- I mean yes, but that's not..." I grit my teeth, jaw tensing as I fight off another bout of hyperventilating.

She waits patiently as I wrestle my body for control.

I can't stay this way, I have to stay strong for Tabi, even if I'm breaking or broken- he can't see me this way.

But...

"I... I don't want to live in a world without- *her.*" I say, my voice breaking on the last word.

I can't even say her name right now.

She said I was under her protection

That I was her darling, her love, that she'd never leave me...

"Honey..." She starts, but then her eyes track on something approaching, she frowns, rubbing my knee and whispering, "To be continued."

She stands, and I watch as she rushes up to Amaya and Rylan on the opposite side of the street.

The rain drowns out their words, Irene's body huddled under their umbrella obscuring Amaya's face from view. But I can just about see through the rainfall, the expression on Rylan's face-

hardening.

Turning to something rage-fuelled and powerful. The enmity he exudes, strong enough to be felt from across the road.

It's then that he sees me, crumpled and tear-stained at the base of the café doorway, as I raise one hand slowly in greeting.

He doesn't say a word, just touches Amaya's shoulder as he passes her the umbrella. He takes each step in a measured way. The rain may as well have been sunbeams for all it did to deter him, as he stalks across the road.

He stands over me, tall, rain-soaked and looking for all intents and purposes like a man ready to wage war; his hair slicked to his face.

Wordlessly, he crouches, scooping me up and into his arms, and standing with me still hanging onto him. He clutches me to him like it's the last time he's ever going to see me, or the first time in decades. He holds me like I may fall apart or disappear at any moment. He grips me to him in a way that, without the need of words, tells me that he will never let it happen again. That it should never have happened, and that if he ever sees him- he's a dead man.

He doesn't say any of this, but I feel it.

I feel it in the way that his knuckles blanch white with their grip on me and his eyes stay fixed on something behind me; like if he sees the aftermath then all hell will break loose. In the way that he lowers me to the ground and still keeps an arm around my shoulder.

My arms go around his waist and I blink away the last couple tears, "Thankyou."

Rylan is my best friend, the funny one, the charismatic other-half that I couldn't live without. But when someone he cares about gets put in harm's way- he would tear apart the world to save them.

He grunts, squeezing me against his side and muttering out the side of his mouth, "Wipe them away before she gets here or you'll have *her* waterworks to compete with."

I laugh despite myself, turning my face towards his body to wipe them off as discretely as possible.

I feel him suck in a breath, "Ah, nah, too late. Worth a shot."

I turn in time to see Amaya's blubbering face huddled under the umbrella Irene has since taken control of, Irene's expression one of total un-amusement as Amaya's face breaks in the most unattractive way, and she launches herself at me.

"I'm so sorry we weren't there- it's all my fault I'm so sorry-" The rest of her cries are muffled in my shoulder as I now stand, held up by Rylan- whilst also now holding up Amaya against me.

Rylan presses his lips together, "Yeah, see- she wouldn't be like this, but I did kinda drop a bit of a bombshell on her last night as well- no innuendo intended."

Her sobs intensify and her little body shakes with the effort, I tiptoe to look at him over the mass of orange hair.

"You..." I begin, not sure how to ask it in company, Irene's ears pricking up even as she tries to look inconspicuous.

He nods with a grimace, "Shall we go inside?"

Once we're all in the process of drying off and Amaya's sobs have turned to sniffles, the coffee ordered and arrived, I feel my bones start to relax. Sat in the corner next to Irene and opposite my two best friends in the world.

But still without her

"So," Rylan says, cutting through the silence and dragging the attention to himself; as per usual. And as per usual, I'm more than happy to give it to him.

"Since making this little madam my girlfriend," He says, hugging a rather dishevelled looking Amaya to his side, "It felt only right to trauma dump on the poor girl."

Amaya scoffs, elbowing him lightly before brushing his side, "That's putting it lightly."

He nods, he averts his gaze from me before saying, "Which uhh, kind of meant explaining a little into your umm... similar predicament."

Amaya crosses her arms, and he budges her, "Which, she *promised* she wouldn't throw a hissy about, and knows doing so right now would be especially and *wholly* inappropriate," He says pointedly, "Right?"

Amaya mumbles something about being left out of the loop before he nudges her again, and she sighs.

"Yeah, so- I'm not going to say anything," She mutters, looking down, "But Rylan is moving out with his baby sister." She says, side-eyeing me, "And we think you should too."

Usually, I'd have the energy to be annoyed that Rylan had told the best kept secret of my life without my permission. But right now, all I can seem to do is blink in response.

Rylan... moved out?

"Why... how did your mum let you...?" I ask, not working out how to form a full sentence; he got the gist.

He shrugs, leaning back with both arms over the booth, "She didn't have much of a choice about it," He says, his smile strained as he recalls it, "It was either I take Lily and she can see her- or I called social services and she never sees her again." He grimaces, "Authorities would be in the house all of two seconds before they'd have taken Lily away."

Amaya shuffles, and I can tell she's past the sympathy and onto the internal annoyance stage. A stage only born from wanting to help those you care about, but with her fire and temper, it's not always easy to see that.

I lean forward on the table, clutching my mug in my hands, "You did what you thought was right for Lily at the time," I say, talking to Rylan but hinting at Amaya, "It's not easy telling your mother that you're taking away both of her children because of her husband."

Amaya's cheeks burn before she nods, leaning into Rylan.

"That doesn't mean you shouldn't do it though," Amaya murmurs, struggling to look me in the eyes, "I don't want to push you, but... just because getting you and Tabi out would be difficult, doesn't mean you shouldn't do it." She looks between Rylan and me with apprehensive eyes, "Your dad might even let you take him, if it's the right thing?"

She doesn't know what she's saying.

The key difference between Rylan's situation and mine- his dad doesn't care. Mine at least says he does, even if he doesn't act like it all the time. Rylan's mum would happily see Lily and Rylan in a better place, whereas Hydra would rather I stayed firmly planted under her thumb.

"It's not quite that easy, Amaya." I say as kindly as I can, "I appreciate it- and I'm working on it, but it's not as simple as a conversation with a rational parent." I grimace, "I don't really have one of those."

Just the idea of asking dad to allow me to take Tabi and live on my own without him. The outrage from Hydra, the despair from dad, and Tabi stuck in the middle of it- fully conscious that the people who love him most in the world are fighting over him.

No.

I've chosen this course of action because it ends the easiest for Tabi. It has always been for him, and I'm not changing that now just for the sake of my friends' sanctity of mind.

I watch as Amaya flicks Rylan on the cheek, his hand having been hovering over her cup in false-menace.

Her legs across my lap in the diner, flicking me on the forehead, her hair up and around us

I try to squeeze the memories out of my mind, screwing my eyes shut against the flood of pain.

"What if the Fates took her?"

Irene's words pierce the silence and I turn to her, almost in slow motion.

Did she... how did she know I was thinking about...

"I'm kind of psychic," She says with a wink, "And you're easy to read. *And,* you're missing the biggest most obvious conclusion and it's driving me insane- just because you don't believe yourself to be enough to stick around for." She shakes her head, mouthing silently into her mug the word '*Women*'.

"I'll cheers to-" Rylan begins.

"No, you won't." Amaya lowers his mug back to the table with her palm over the top.

What if... but then wouldn't Kuro... I can't wait until Monday to know if she ran or was taken.

"How can I find out?" I ask, as if they'd know the answers.

Irene just smirks, leaning into the corner and draping one leg after the other across my lap.

Like Aletheia did.

"Well, *one* of us little tea-leafs, still has a portal stashed away somewhere." She muses.

"You *what*?!" Amaya practically shrieks at Irene.

My blood goes cold.

"And it *isn't* me." She hisses at Amaya, sending her the finger before inclining her head in my direction.

She knows.

She's always known.

Or maybe she found it when she was at the house earlier. Either way- she knows I stole from her.

"I... I wasn't going to-"

"Ah, lighten up would ya?" She says, bumping me on the shoulder, "I'm just playing with you, I know you only took it to get back to your girlfriend." She smiles, "And that's exactly what you're going to do."

She can't be saying what she's saying.

"I am," She says, and I'd be lying if I said I'm not spooked, "Go home, get the Veturcaela, go find your girlfriend, and get yourself a happy ending." She looks up at the sky, smirking.

"Gods knows she needs one." Irene winks, looking at you.

CHAPTER 38

RUN

Get out get out GET OUT

RUN

My darling

Please no

You need to leave

she's coming for you…

CHAPTER 39

WHO SAVES THE SAVIOUR

The house is empty when I get home.

Amaya doesn't truly understand the situation, even Rylan could see that- which was why we hadn't told her in the first place. But that's a whole can of worms for another time.

Could Aletheia really have been taken by the Fates? More importantly, can I find her?

I turn the key in the lock, pushing the door open with a feint click and creak.

My shadow extends into the hallway, no lights are on- but the streetlamps illuminate enough that I can feel my way into the hall; closing the door and locking it behind me.

It's been so long since I've been completely alone. Not just without Aletheia, but anyone. The house has never felt so... cold.

My eyes slowly adjust to the dark, the ink black of night dusting the grey walls. Hydra painted them grey when she moved in. Sucked the life out of them and then us, one after the other.

I make it a couple paces towards the steps before I stop short.

The hairs on the back of my neck rise, almost imperceptibly.

The air feels cold but thick, solid.

There's a creak from behind me, from feet that have never had to learn where the silent spots are; but who's wholly responsible for why I do.

I dart forwards, but not fast enough to evade the swing of the mallet that connects brutally with the side of my skull.

The world goes dark, my legs lose feeling and I fall in a crumpled heap on the floor. My body won't move fast enough, and I watch as my blood seeps from my head across the wood; her dainty black daps stepping into it.

There's a sting in my neck, and moments later I watch an empty hypodermic needle and syringe fall to the floor with a clink.

She got me.

Her face appears at my shoulder as she rolls me onto my back. Her face is manic, eyes wide and teeth bared.

"You silly little *bitch*." She spits, flecks frothing at the sides of her mouth like a rabid dog.

"Look what you've done. Making a mess. I'm going to have to clean all this up by myself later." She tuts, as if it's my fault that the floorboards will be stained crimson.

There's a physical barrier between me and the rest of the world, I can feel nothing. And for a moment, I think- this is how Aletheia felt.

I can't even feel the blood that seeps from my temple.

There is no pain.

I watch as she takes up the mallet again, her eyes roaming my body.

"Well, if I have to clean it anyway- best to take precautions."

The mallet collides with my right ankle, and I hear the break that I can't feel. Then my left.

C-r-a-c-k

She takes one of my mutilated legs in hand and begins to drag me upstairs.

I see the ceiling above the steps as my head bangs harshly against each step. Lolling then dragging, lolling and dragging. Until we reach the landing.

It's almost funny, but it feels like this was how it was always meant to go. She wasn't meant to get caught, go to prison. I wasn't meant to have a happy ending with the girl I love. I wasn't meant to escape my rapist. I wasn't meant to make it this far at all.

I guess I have Aletheia to thank for that.

I hope she will save Tabi for me. If anyone could- she can.

I can't my darling, you need to fight- I can't get to you...

She will get her. Even if it takes her an eternity, there's no way Hydra gets off scot-free, so I guess there's a comfort in that.

She drags me down past my bedroom, past hers and to the bathroom where she leaves me momentarily.

I should've known she would go this far. I should've known that Casimir would too.

I'm sorry mum, I should've done better- but I will be with you soon.

So soon.

I hear the tap on the bath go and everything in me freezes.

She's... she's going to *drown* me?

My eyes track to where she's crouched by it, not checking the water but checking it's plugged properly. She turns to me, her crooked smile only ramming home what I'd thought inconceivable.

"Y-y-you- iwed- huh." I choke, my tongue a lifeless slug in my mouth and my vocal chords barely responsive. All that's coming out is wheezing- but I know she understands-

-As she smiles wider.

"She struggled harder than you," She says, "I'll give her that."

No.

No mum drowned in the sea-

She died a natural death and was found after drowning...

I can't look away from Hydra, squatted next to the water.

"...ai?"

"Why- you ask?" She says, her eyebrows creasing in confusion. "Well, because your dad is obsessed with me, of course!" She squeals, as if it's the most blindingly obvious thing in the world.

She's insane.

This insane lady killed my mum.

She's going to kill *me*.

"Your father," She carries on, unhindered and frantic, like some sick old-timey movie villain, "Has always had a crush on me, you see. But there was always something or some*one* in the way. In school it was a girl called Patrice. She hooked herself round him and never let go," She sighs, reminiscing, "Even at eleven I could see he was desperate for me. And she was in the way, that is- until her tragic accident in the pool house." She shakes her head at the memory, taking up my arms and hauling me towards the tub in jerky movements.

"Then there was Celeste, harsh and *needy* Celeste in college, she always wanted his attention- and your father's *far* too giving in nature to say no. Fortunately for him, she went cliff-diving in the summer and never came back."

She shoves one of my arms over the side of the tub, followed by my shoulders.

"And then there was your mother, your *precious mother*. Tara, hag that she was, had him on some sort of potion for years. She was my best friend for ages you see, knew I was infatuated with him, and him me- but still she insisted they had a connection I couldn't see. That's how I knew it was a potion. She practically *admitted* guilt. She was a lot harder to get rid of, took a lot longer to plan."

It's not true. She's insane.

She's killed three people and I'm next.

My lower half is hauled inside the tub and I'm just staring down at my legs. Bent at awkward angles and knees jutting out. My ankles...

My ankles are shattered and pooling blood, like ink into the water. Painting it *red-*

"And then there's you, my dear," She titters, grabbing my face with her nails, digging in till I see blood oozing down my cheeks from her touch. She pulls my flesh till I'm facing her, and I can see the blood red lines that map her eyes.

"You were the final obstacle. He will truly *need* me when his precious little first born suddenly kills herself in his bathtub when everyone's out of the house- his dutiful wife out of town on business. Oh- can't have this then."

She says, noticing the marks she's made on my face for the first time. She grabs at my hands, placing hers over mine and using my own nails to rake down my face.

Blood seeps from the gashes into the water.

"And this of course." She mumbles to herself, placing the mallet in one of my lifeless hands and back into the water.

She would have everyone believe I went insane, bashed in my own ankles, mutilated my face then offed myself.

She's crazy.

And I... I've allowed her to live in this house, with my younger brother and father, for *years*. The woman who murdered my mother and brutalised me on a near-daily basis.

But... others might believe her story.

Rylan and Amaya would know, and Tabi would suspect, but what proof would they have?

"He will finally be all mine." She sing-songs, taking a seat by the tub and pushing my face back to neutral as I slide down the tub so that my knees poke above the water and my chin hits it.

I watch as the faucet thrusts water into the tub, specks freckling my face from the opposite end.

So this is it then.

My fate.

To watch my death slowly approach as the bath fills with water and then go out in the same way mum did. By the same hands no less.

I hear the crinkle of a seal being broken, watching from my periphery as she undoes the nail polish and begins to meticulously attack her stubs.

Aletheia Aletheia Aletheia

If I call her she will come

Aletheia Aletheia Aletheia

Please. ***Aletheia.***

Aletheia please save me.

I feel every time she calls me. I know what she's experiencing, I can sense the thud of her heart and the way the poison coasts her bloodstream.

The Fates hover before me, their three sets of eyes trained on my face.

Never blinking.

"She will die." I say, defeated.

I've cried and wailed and thrashed so much. My wrists are drenched in my own blood, my eyes have no more tears to give and my throat is raw.

They don't so much as shift their tendrils in response.

My wings are broken, my scythe unreachable, Kuro in another dimension, and Circé can't travel alone.

"My darling, an innocent mortal woman- she will die by the hands of the criminally insane, if you do not let me save her- please." I beg again, even though I know it's pointless.

She has so much left to live for, she hasn't even begun.

I should never have lied to her, hidden the Fates from her.

We had so much left to see.

I feel the tug of fear and I know it's nearly over. She's going to die, and I can't save her.

I let my head fall forwards, watching the last of my tears fall into the depths and disappear.

"Please. I will give my life. I will die here and now if she can live. Just let me save my darling."

There's only silence. Thick and tense.

Then-

"You would give us your life?"

Their voice comes out ragged, three in one, crackling like electricity and omnipotence personified.

I raise my eyes to theirs, my heart beating double time, triple time, as they hear me.

By Gods, Rylan was right- the conversational route can work.

They're finally hearing me.

"Yes- YES!" I say hurriedly, straining desperately with newfound determination against the restraints, "Anything and everything that I am, is yours- if she can live."

I look between their heads, and for the first time, I watch as the two on the sides turn to the one in the middle.

They're in disagreement.

The two on the sides want to take me, want to agree to my offer, dispel of me and save her.

But the third-

"We will not kill you." The middle one says, moving them forwards slightly and standing a little taller than the others.

I feel my hope splintering, and alongside that is the feeling of her slipping under.

She's dying.

"But she... she'll..." I can't say it again, not when the end is so close.

"If she saves herself," The middle one declares, reaching to hold the hands of the other two in synchronicity, "We shall spare you both. If she lives- she will set you free."

The other two reach around and place their other hands on the thirds' chest, nodding, then turning to me; and for the first time the middle one looks confused. Then angry.

Then resigned as it nods to them-

Allows them to tell me-

"Call to her," they command in unison, "Let her hear you. Help her find a way out."

Find a way...

She has one.

The genius thief of a woman has a Veturcaela, and she didn't think to tell me.

I smile even through my terror.

I take a deep breath and don't think twice as I nod to them each in turn.

I scream her name loud enough so that the entire universe might bear witness. So that it may carry it to her.

Tenaya, my darling- hear me.

I can't get to her right now, that's understood. But I can send help.

With my left hand I tear a rift- through it I can see her, eyes staring blankly upwards and slowly sinking as the blonde demon remodels her digits. I do it so quick and purposeful the Fates don't know what to do. I don't think they even know what they're allowed to do right now; for once in a state of indecision.

I don't think they've ever been in disagreement before.

I can't talk to her through it- and the Fates won't let her see me- but I can do something.

With my right hand I rip another, this time appearing in front of Tabi's face in the car.

The boy's eyes go wide, and I can see her father too, mouthing something about 'what the devil is that'. Another time I might've found that amusing.

'Tabi', I mouth to the magic boy-child whose eyes light up in understanding, 'your sister is in danger - Hydra is murdering her'. Get home.

I see him yelling, his face terrified but strong. Her father pales, and for a moment- I think he won't believe him. That's when I throw both rifts together so they are an open window for just a few seconds. My fingers strain and bend, I can't hold them both open much longer- but he needs to see.

Fury beyond that of the Fates contorts his face and I watch as Tabi is flung back against his seat and his father slams on the pedals as he watches his daughter drown.

He can do this, I think to myself as the rifts squeeze closed again and the energy from opening two rifts suddenly registers on my body.

I slump, but I heave in lung-fulls of air, preparing to scream to her again and again and as long as it takes.

We can all save her.

Together.

There are no bubbles.

I think if I were to really commit, then I would at least make the last bath I were to ever take, have bubbles. Maybe even a bath bomb.

As it stands, all that I have is the constant swaying motion of the filling tub. The water has reached my mouth, my lips thankfully closed, and is steadily approaching my nose.

"It'll be over soon dear," Hydra coos from the side of the tub, in what must be the kindest voice she's ever used with me, "Of all the people who have gone out like you have, you're probably the luckiest- you won't even feel pain."

She's onto her toes, painting away as she talks, paying me no real mind as my body slides slightly on the ceramic. My heart thuds faster but is nowhere near close to pushing the poison from my veins; no matter how many beats per minute it travels. I've tried hyperventilating to speed it up, but it's had no effect.

"Of course, you have your mother to thank for that." She continues mindlessly, "She had books on books of stupid potions and spells- yes, spells. Your mother was attempting to perform and practise illegal acts under the same roof as her children. Can you *believe* some people?"

I wonder what dimension Hydra lives in.

Clearly not this one.

"But yes, your mother devised the serum for the physical paralysis you're experiencing. It's not permanent and well- oh, you don't need to know about side effects anyways." She titters to herself.

My mind goes blank, and I close my eyes.

I-

I don't-

I don't want to die.

My heart aches both from the physical strain, and the painful desire to change my fate. I want to scour the galaxies, speak Aletheia's name across the cosmos and travel interdimensionally for the rest of my days.

I want to know that Tabi is safe.

I want to see dad how he used to be.

I want to watch Rylan flourish on his own and move in with Amaya, and one day nanny their kids.

I want to be a part of Irene's group and feel wanted.

I want to learn, and teach, and live live *live*

Gods I wish I could have lived.

TENAYA

The voice comes from inside my own head, like the shattering of a barricade. Strong and forceful and like the final battle-cry of a thousand warriors.

Aletheia...

DARLING FIGHT, TENAYA YOU MUST SAVE YOURSELF

Does she know what's happening?

But I can feel her now, her consciousness and the way it's... trapped. Irene was right all along- she's been taken by the Fates.

She's trapped.

That's why she didn't rescue me from the diner, it's why she can't save me now.

Aletheia...

I can't move a muscle, I can't even feel my own body in the water but...

I'll try.

I roll my eyes back so I can only see the blackness of my eyelids. My mind wanders down past the bottom of the tub. Past the tubing and the panels and through the floorboards to where I left it-

hid it-

saved it.

The Veturcaela.

I throw out my mind around it, feeling for its energy- for a pulse to suggest it feels me too- even though I can't physically reach it.

Blue and pink lines swirl into my mind right as I know the water is hitting my nose and I sink further.

I am submerged.

I am drowning.

I have moments.

I stand in my mind, my body working here, and I throw my arms out to the energy, pulling and pushing; weaving it around me and conjuring where I need to go.

Lend me your power

I think, sending a message to the heart of the Veturcaela, *For a moment, let my arm lift, let me get there.*

I'm screaming so loud in my own head that it mixes with Aletheia's and I can't think straight because I'm *dying*.

The colours burst and reknit and swirl around me and my heart judders. My lungs burn and my body heaves without my conscious doing, as the water pours into me; muscles spasming and spine bending out of my control in search of air.

I roll my eyes back so they're looking up at the sky from underwater, the colours still swimming around me even in the physical world. In and under the water, pooling and circling my arm.

Raising it

Bringing it up and out of the water to the crease.

Hydra hasn't noticed- I know she hasn't- and I have barely seconds of consciousness left.

My mind bleeds and I feel my head shattering.

From the burn marks Relinque made so long ago I feel things burst and rise from my skull. Things that give me the strength to take the crease between my fingers. I hold it as tight as I can, and *rip* it- shoving my hand through it in the same motion.

My darling is grabbing onto the cloaks of the Fates.

"SHE SAVED HERSELF LET ME-"

Before I can even finish the sentence the bonds that hold me release, and I'm hurtling across the space. My ragged wings drag my aching limbs faster than ever before.

She did it she saved herself she saved me

Her hand is in mine and I'm ripping away the dimension to get to her.

Damn it all damn it all DAMN IT ALL

There's space enough to get through and I dive. I will thank them later, for now she needs me.

I plunge into the icy water on top of her, her eyes closed and the lights gone. I tear her from the water, pressing her face into my shoulder and holding her in the air.

"My darling- my love- I am here." I say over and over again, for her and for me as I register her heart ever so ever so faintly beating.

She made it.

Two short stumps, barely three inches high, extend from her head. It takes me a moment to realise it but when it hits me, I can't believe I didn't realise sooner.

Mother has gifted my darling her blessing.

She gifted her dimension travel by bestowing her with the potential for her horns- antlers it looks more like- should she manage to unlock it.

And she did.

I hear a rustle to my left. The blonde demon cowers on the floor, her face whiter than the ceramic tub.

I've never wanted vengeance this badly before. It tastes hot and wild and inevitable.

And I can smell the fear plastered on her skin.

That- that will taste good.

The bathroom door crashes open and in comes her father, eyes wild and hair ragged as he takes in the scene. His eyes locking with the unconscious form of his daughter, then me squatted protectively over her, then the demon.

Before he can even take a step- I stand, lifting my darling into my arms, the water adding to her weight, but I barely register it.

"Take her to the hospital." I command, holding her out to him like an offering.

"What- what's happening- who-"

"Father of Tenaya and Tabi, husband of Tara, there is no time," I say and his mouth falls open, "We have saved your daughter thus far, but she requires urgent medical attention. You must leave, and I-" I say, pointedly looking at the dishevelled excuse of a mortal on the floor, "-I must stay a while longer."

The blonde demon hisses and scampers back, clawing towards him on the floor.

"No- no dearest you must believe me I would never- she took her I was trying to save- dearest please-"

His boot collides with her temple hard enough to send her back into the bathroom cabinets; her body crumpling, wails escaping her now-crooked mouth.

"Nononono NO! I didn't you mustn't- I'm yours you were meant to be all mineminemine-" she wheezes into the floor, her matted hair covering her face and spilling into her mouth as she continues to mindlessly babble.

She finally broke.

"Do what you must."

He says to me, his eyes unseeing and the realisation not quite setting in, but nodding as he holds his daughter aloft.

I manage a small smile. It would be nice, I suppose, to have her family accept me.

Tabi's voice whimpers from down the hall and I scurry past her father and Tenaya's body, down the hall- scampering on all fours until I reach him; finding him sat on the penultimate step from the top.

His little arms are wrapped around Kuro's neck.

Kuro blinks at me, his nine tails shining and his body still in the process of shrinking down; his back rising and falling in heavy pants. He'd clearly been part-and-part of how they got here so fast.

I extend a hand to Tabi slowly, not wanting to startle him any more than he likely is.

"You've been keeping him safe for me, huh?" I ask softly, gesturing to Kuro as I stroke down the boy Tabi's hair.

The boy Tabi nods emphatically, hesitating a moment, before bypassing my hand and jumping into my arms.

It takes me a second to balance, before I wrap my arms around him.

"Thank you," He whines into my shoulder, his body trembling, "Thank you for saving my sister."

I didn't know my heart was capable of breaking so many times in 48 hours.

"She saved herself, boy Tabi-cat," I say into his hair, breathing in what smells so much like her- but different in the most amazing of ways, "She is the best thing in all of creation- and I shall spend the rest of my days making sure she is safe."

He leans back, examining me for my words and nodding.

"Now, I have something to take care of." I say, rising to my full height and touching his head as I do so.

Behind me come her fathers' footfalls, heavier with her added weight. Tabi rushes to his side and grabs for her hand.

"You will meet us there?" Her father asks me, more of a command than a question; but I respect it, nonetheless.

I nod, and that seems to be enough for him.

They both descend the stairs, and I watch as her hair leaves a trail of water from end to end of the house. Water that nearly took her out in the same way as her mother. Water that pooled into her lungs and starved her of breath and nearly stole her from me forever.

Water that she put there.

But my love will live.

Kuro pauses at the front door, awaiting my command. I can tell where he wants to be though, he's seen me do this a handful of times- even gotten involved with a couple.

He needn't see this one though. This one will be different in the most sadistically brutal of ways.

For my love.

"Go with them." I say, and he hears the coldness in my tone, darting quickly out of the house with a yip.

The last thing I see is Tabi's little hands pulling the front door closed behind them.

I wait to hear the car start and the crunch of gravel as they pull off the drive.

My scythe slowly extends from my ribs.

I take my time, footfall after footfall on the wooden floor, the cool metal dragging noisily behind me with every step.

The floorboards feel cold and the air smells damp and the world feels feels feels

So much.

The door crashes open off its hinges, as I flick it with a solitary finger, my eyes burning as I take in my prey.

She cowers, helpless and insane against the cabinets, eating her hair with every ragged breath.

That may be the place to start.

I ascend into the air, hovering there and gripping up her locks in one hand, raising her to eye level as I float. Her face is basked in golden white light that transcends from my flesh- and I know I must be raging but I barely feel it. All I feel is a calm certainty in what I must do next.

What I've ached to do for so long now.

She hollers, clawing at my hand but leaving no mark as she manically kicks and twists, suspended in the air by her hair.

My scythe cuts through it, slashing diagonally and tearing through part of her scalp in the process. She screams as she drops, deadweight to the ground; I let the strands feather around her from my palms.

"You hurt my darling," I say, bringing the scythe up to my shoulder casually, "You were going to kill my darling."

I let it fall straight through her thigh.

Her guttural scream barely registers, and I slam my hand against her mouth as she cries- so hard her head collides with the tiling behind her and the tip of her tongue falls freely to the floor- severed by her own teeth.

"But I shall show you mercy, eventually- because death, my dearest demon, would be too much of a kindness for the likes of you."

She whimpers, and I stand, cracking my knuckles and twisting my spine in preparation.

She will need to make it to the hospital before prison, that's for sure.

But for now-

I fall atop her and dig my thumbs in, slowly and purposefully, straight through her eyes; blood curdling and spurting from her mouth and sockets.

I grin, as I begin her demise.

CHAPTER 40
TO FEEL KNOWN

I feel my body come back to me piece by broken piece, cell by damaged cell. Each part that gains sentience eliciting new bouts of pain as consciousness digs at my eyelids.

I don't open them.

I don't want to see Tabi's tear-stained face as he takes in the broken body of his sister who failed to protect him.

I don't want to see dad's tired eyes and defeated shoulders, as he realises what he's subjected me to since the day of mum's death.

And I don't want to live in a world where I don't open my eyes to see her face.

Aletheia's.

But then again, it's never really been about what *I* want.

The last thing I saw was Aletheia, chained in the Fate's dimension, my fingers brushing the cloaked-edges of the most omnipotent beings in all reality.

The stiff white sheets beneath my broken body only further confirm my suspicions that I'm in hospital. I can't move my feet due to heavy restraints, that feel like cement blocks around my ankles.

I know there's someone to my left.

I don't know how long I've been unconscious, I don't know who has come and gone.

But I know it's not her.

She'd be lying across me, on me, holding my hand or stroking my face just to be close to me; just to be sure she still could.

This person barely has a foot on the bed as they rock themselves on the hind-legs of their chair.

Whether I want it or not, this is the reality I have to wake up to.

"Is she here?" I croak, my vocal chords strained, "Is she in this realm?"

There's silence.

The chair legs stop rocking and the air feels tense, like they hadn't expected me to wake up.

"Answer me!" I say, louder this time and my voice breaks on impact.

There's a soft chuckle and a flick on my forehead that demands my eyes fling open.

"You're a feisty lil fawn aren't ya." Irene muses, as the bright white lights etch coloured blotches into my cornea's.

I'm in a small hospital-room, four cream walls, green curtains draping over windows that overlook the woods behind the building. There's a solitary vase of flowers placed on the table next to a clipboard. A heart monitor, a fluid-drip- Gods knows I don't need more water.

I shake my head to clear it.

"Irene- seriously, is she... did you just say *fawn*?!" I begin but get side-tracked, her words stirring a whisper of a memory from beneath the water.

I reach one hand up, noting my nails have been scrubbed clean of dead skin and blood, tentatively touching the crown of my head.

Just past my hairline, protruding from my skull, are two dual-pronged horns.

Antlers.

I have baby antlers sticking out of my head.

Irene grins, her piercing between her teeth as she watches my face change from shock, to awe, to horror and back again.

"I debated between fawn and Cernunnos, but figured you weren't big into your ancient Celtic deities." She remarks.

I can tell the flippancy is for my benefit, that she's avoiding the seriousness of the situation, trying her best to be jovial in a moment where panic is likely.

"Irene," I say slowly, my fingers tracing the bark-like lines of the horns, "Why do I have antlers?"

There's a flurry of sheets and suddenly, from under the bed, a giant ball of orange and gold whips up onto my lap.

"Kuro- where did you-?" I exclaim, as he licks excitedly at my cheeks.

"He's not really allowed in hospitals," Irene explains, giving his back a stroke, "But he's quick, and by the Gods he can shrink to stupid sizes." She says, placing her thumb and finger barely centimetres apart to demonstrate.

His ears fall flat and he growls a little, his face pressed down into my chest as he licks my chin; his eyes angry but appeased somehow.

I know it's his way of saying I worried him, that he missed me.

"How long was I out?" I ask as I stroke him reassuringly, Irene snorts.

"You mean, dead?" She says, and from the bugging of my eyes, she must know that was *not* what I meant. "Ah, well yeah. Okay so you died a little on the way to the hospital," She cringes, holding her hands up placatingly as she watches the line on my heart monitor spike, "BUT- but but but, you're here, you're alive. Tabi is okay, your dad is okay, Hydra is in prison and, uhhh, maimed to the point of no repair-"

"What do you mean *maimed*?" I ask, my heart still double timing it from learning that I died.

I was dead.

Gone.

Irene smirks suddenly, stretching before planting all legs of the chair down and sauntering over to the door to my room.

"This'll be my queue to leave for a bit," She smiles, gesturing at the closed door and bringing both hands out as if they're holding things, "but it will also answer your first question at least."

My heart thunders at her words as the door flies open.

Aletheia

Aletheia Aletheia ***Alethiea***

She stands dishevelled in the doorway, two steaming cups in her hands- cups which Irene briskly takes from her.

"The ONE time I'm told I have to shower, and you go and wake up?!" She practically yells, sprinting towards me and leaping, landing on both me and Kuro with little-to-no grace and holding me tighter than I thought possible.

From the doorway I hear Irene laughing before the door swings shut behind her.

The tears well up before I can move to stop them because she smells of sea and blue and earth and green and feels like home home *home*

She's awake and she's here and I can feel the magic in her veins that she hasn't even registered yet.

We will be unstoppable.

We can scour the universe and tiptoe from galaxy to galaxy without anyone to stop us. And it's all thanks to her.

I notice the tears then, the scent of despair and aching and I raise my head from her neck as the drops fall from her cheeks.

"None of this is your fault." Aletheia says, one hand moving up to brush the first couple tears from under my eyes.

But it is.

Who else is to blame for this disaster but me?

"It is- I let it happen," I blubber, my tears uncontrollable and my lower lip quivering as I struggle for breath, "I let *her* stay- I let *him* stay- *I* stayed- that's why..."

"You didn't ask for any of this." She interrupts abruptly, sitting up on me and shoving Kuro to the end of the bed in the process, straddling me, *"You didn't want any of this. You did what you thought you could to stop this. None of this is your fault- or your doing."*

Staring up at her now, I think I finally understand why people worship statues of deities.

If they look like this, let me pray.

I shake my head even so, "This isn't your problem to fix, you didn't make any of this happen."

She pauses, eyes only on me as she carefully chooses her words. She takes the back of my neck in her hand, raising me up gently so that I'm sat up with her legs either side of my lap; one of my hands supporting me on the bed and the other going to her waist.

"Being here with you is the greatest privilege of my life." I say, stroking my fingers through the hair at the back of her neck, forever thankful that I can finally feel her, "You are the purpose for my existence, and the sole reason that I stay. Your problems, my darling- my love, are my honour to help fix, regardless of their cause."

I...

I don't think I've ever felt so loved.

Not in nearly a decade, and not like this.

This is... this is what it feels like to be whole.

"But..."

"If you won't let me help you- at least let me hold you." She says, pressing my face to her chest and cradling me, *"My love, I can't bear to see you like this."*

My lower lip trembles and my shoulders shake.

Every time I see her, she heals something inside of me that

she was never responsible for breaking.

"Hush, my love, I'm not leaving- I'm real and here and really here- with you." She says, smiling into my hair.

I could have lost all of this. Her. She could have been taken from me.

And it all comes back to me.

The Fates, the diner, the house, the things Hydra admitted to me as she drowned me-

"She murdered my mum."

I feel Aletheia stiffen.

She brings my face back to look at her, her brows low on her face and her mouth set in a line.

"I have taken vengeance upon the blonde demon," I say, my blood re-boiling at the memory, "I know nothing I do, can right the wrongs she did. But she will never know happiness." My voice becomes clipped as I recall what I put her through.

Not enough.

It would never have been enough.

"She will never see the eyes of someone who loves her," I say, meeting her own as I do so, "Never step through the door to a place she calls home. She will never hold offspring or own the title 'Mother'. She will live out the rest of her days in semi-permanent agony, without ever being able to touch on true joy or elation, ever again." I hold her hand in mine, "I swear it."

Her words should scare me, terrify me even- but they don't.

I don't know what she's done, and I don't think I ever want to. But knowing that she can't get to Tabi ever again is the only solace I ever needed to feel *that* much better.

The door to the room swings open unannounced and, as if on queue, in steps dad and Tabi.

Dad gasps and then immediately cringes, averting his eyes and pressing his lips together, "I said you had my blessing, that doesn't mean I wish to see every inch of the repercussions." He grumbles, my cheeks going scarlet as Aletheia slowly extricates her body from mine; taking the seat next to the bed but never letting go of my hand.

Tabi's eyes light up, his smile growing wider as he notes Kuro lounging at the edge of the bed.

"You're awake!" He squeals, rushing over and shoving his arms around my neck, Kuro nuzzling up to him.

I'm alive, I think but don't say. Maybe he doesn't know I died, it's probably better that way.

"How're you feeling, poppet?" Dad says from the doorway, his hands in his pockets as he makes his way over to stand by the heart monitor.

He looks... drained. I can't say I blame him, he did just find out the woman he's been attached to for six years was abusing his first born. Not to mention if he knows that she killed mum.

I look up at him, my heart in my mouth.

I don't know what I can say that won't break him.

"I'm fine." I say.

I can feel Aletheia's eyes on me narrowing, even Tabi draws back, his brow furrowed as he looks me up and down; from the marks that likely still mar my face to the casts on my feet.

"Don't." Dad says suddenly, his jaw tense, "Don't play down your feelings to me. Ever." He shakes his head, his blue-grey eyes meeting mine, and I can see the years in them; the pain, "I know that's what you've been doing. For me, and for Tabi. You're your mother's daughter through and through. But stop it." He steps closer, his hand reaching down to mine, "I am your dad, I will shoulder what comes. You don't need to save me from life Tenaya. Life happens, and you keep going."

He takes a shuddering breath, squeezing his eyes shut before blinking them open again; a glassy film covering them.

"So, I'll ask you again- how're you feeling, poppet?"

There's a lump in my throat, and an ache in my chest that has nothing to do with why I'm hospitalised.

"Like shit." I say, monotone and honestly.

Aletheia snorts and Tabi gasps and Dad actually manages to chuckle; even Kuro lets out a low rumble.

He gives my hand a squeeze, Tabi holds my middle and Aletheia has my other hand, Kuro capturing my feet. I am held down and together by the people who love me most in this world, and I wouldn't have it any other way.

It took dying for me to get here, but the outcome? I wouldn't change it for the world.

"So..." Tabi mumbles, raising up and tapping at my antlers hesitantly, "Do we need to file these off, or...?"

CHAPTER 41
SURPRISE

From outside the hospital door, I can hear them laughing together, the sound music to my ears.

Finally, am I right?

I know I can't stay long, Sayra will be in need of updating and I have meetings with several authorities on the Diner-incident still to attend to. Not to mention hunting down Melinoë, now that the prophecy has been recognised.

But I can spare a few more minutes.

I really thought she would never get here- or die trying. Turns out she did, so maybe I was right all along. The hospital hallways are pretty deserted, her dad having paid out half a fortune to get Tenaya her own private room; it was the least he could do, given the circumstances.

I twirl the coloured strands of my hair between my fingers, smiling as I produce purple sparks that fray and fizzle around me.

So, what happens now? Now that I'm talking to you, just you, and you know all that you think you know?

I flick the metal ball against my teeth, coming to the end of the hall and booting open the hospital doors with more effort than is needed, my magic getting the better of me.

Well, I suppose that's up to you.

You, and whatever happens next. Remember that Tabi knows something we don't- or at least you don't.

Yet.

CHAPTER 42

LOOSE ENDS, EXTRA THREAD

"I am not a childminder- I do not need to go and check that Tabi has 'packed his lunch properly'." Aletheia whines, mimicking me with little-to-no grace.

It's been a rather stressful couple of weeks to say the least.

We are in the process of moving house. It was one of the things I'd asked for, the big thing, and dad was only too willing to oblige. Any remnants of mum in the house had been tainted by Hydra long ago. Now it's just a living reminder of six years of torment, and the day I died.

He couldn't really fight me on it.

My room looks barren, boxes and bags littering the walls and bedframe. Aletheia stands in the doorway with her arms folded.

"Look, the sooner you check- the sooner we can take him." I say, watching as the glint returns to her eyes.

We had discussed with dad the possibility of realm hopping with Tabi. It'd taken a week of asking, begging and bartering-

but finally, after many *many* ground rules had been set and standardised, he conceded.

We are going to take Tabi into another realm, only briefly, but still. He was all too excited and ready to go- I don't trust him to know his lefts from his rights, let alone trust him enough to pack himself edible food.

She sighs, lazing her way out of the door,

"You know, you've become way more entitled since you got those antlers. Don't think I'm beyond magicking them off."

She mockingly places two fingers above her head and saunters from the room, grumbling something like 'dear oh dear'.

She'd already told me how happy- and not at all jealous- she was about me getting her mother's blessing. She isn't the best at hiding her emotions, she hasn't had to practise it nearly as much. I can clearly see the yearning looks she gives the horns on my head whenever I mention them.

So I try my best not to, for the most part.

I've been back to university of course, now wearing a ridiculous hat 24/7 so they don't take me in for magic use- the hospital was paid off on that account. I'm not dropping out of university just because I got sexually assaulted, mortally wounded and died.

That's just not me.

Spelinski was his usual self, happy to have his favourite student back in the hall.

I can't say the same for Madeline.

She remains the queen regent of Southlakes, but I can tell her pride has been wounded. Not that she tried to talk to me, and there are already countless boys and girls queueing up to take my place. Aletheia shot her devil-eyes every time she turned to me, having not left my side since I woke from hospital, and university was no exception. She was all too ready to fight anyone or anything that put a foot towards me- especially if that person was Madeline.

But she never did.

Amaya and Rylan have had Aletheia and I around their new flat several times already, Rylan taking no pause in absolutely rinsing my new headpiece. Corbin and Emmy were marginally more tactful, but when Sayra burst into the room and immediately jumped on me- grabbing my antlers to ride me around the room- any and all sense of decorum was lost.

The Diner is being taken care of, not that I'll ever go back whilst it stands as it does. Not for the foreseeable future. Irene is handling it for the most part, the videotape will have him locked away for the time being; but with us moving towns now, it doesn't matter to me much. So long as he can't go near me or anyone else at risk again, that will do.

And then there's Hydra.

Blind, hairless, scalped, beaten, stabbed, diseased and mentally disturbed Hydra. She's locked up in some sort of institution for the dangerous and deranged. I'm sure they have a nicer name for it there, but to be honest- I don't want to know. I want to forget her face, I want to accept what's happened and move on. I don't want to think of her; suffering or otherwise.

To me, I find peace thinking that she just doesn't exist anymore. It's Aletheia that delights in remembering the ways in which she brutalised and tormented her within an inch of her life. It was nice the first time, vengeful even. But I would just like to be free of it now.

I'm setting myself free, navigating the cosmos with the woman I love.

There's a flash of colour in my periphery, and I turn to what I thought was Aletheia.

A man stands in my doorway.

He's tall enough that he has to duck under the doorframe, with auburn hair tied back in a ponytail. He wears a cream top with corset-like string at the collar, baggy brown trousers splay out around his bare feet. His eyes are a deep red, with looks that place him in his late-twenties; he's the most beautiful man I've ever seen.

But he's still a random man in my bedroom, who somehow managed to get past my dad, Tabi, Kuro and most pertinently- Aletheia.

"Who- what're you doing in my-?" I try to ask, but the words won't form the right sentence.

I... I'm starstruck.

"Hello, darling." He purrs in a deep voice, one hand coming to rest on the top half of the doorframe, "Fail to recognise me?"

His eyes roam me, adventurous and untamed.

"I don't- who-?" I try again, but no better.

He moves faster than humanly possible, his body suddenly behind mine.

"How about now?" He asks, his throat rumbling against my ear.

He has my back firmly against his chest, one hand to my collarbone and the other snagging my waist. He leans down and presses his face to my neck; the heat rolling off him in a way that has become familiar to me.

There's no way...

Aletheia would have said something. Surely he's not...

"*K-kuro*?!" I exclaim, my heart beating out of my chest as I try and wrap my head around this.

But it makes so much sense.

Aletheia called him pervy.

Said I was always protected when he was around.

Why she wouldn't let me take him to the shower with me.

Why, when I took hold of him, he looked like a man about to fight someone, a man who doesn't like being told what to do- or manhandled.

Why Tabi asked why he couldn't tell me something... Tabi knew who he was all along.

"In the *alternate* flesh." He murmurs against my neck, and I shiver, chills running unhindered down my spine.

This is too weird; this can't be happening.

"She's been keeping you all to herself, our little Aletheia." He muses, snaking a lock of hair between his fingers and twirling it in front of my face, "It's high time I got a chance to play."

He grins, turning my face to his with the same hand, "Seems only fair, no?"

"Kuro."

Aletheia's voice sounds from the doorway, and I turn to see her- hands clenched and hair spiralling around her in all directions.

"Time to go." He growls, and I watch the colour drain from her face as Kuro slashes a crease into existence behind us.

The realm rips from view and I'm tumbling through the voids, held captive by a human Kitsune.

The last thing I see is Aletheia's shocked face, her hands outstretched but not quite reaching me. The blue and pink swirls encase us, stealing me away in a spiral of orange and *gold*.

ACKNOWLEDGEMENTS

First of all- thank you, the reader, for picking up my book and getting to this point. I've been working on *The In-Between* for the better part of two years, and every moment has led to this.

Thank you so much to Arkbound, who took a chance on *The In-Between*, and gave me the opportunity to make my dream of publishing a reality. A massive thanks to Bridget, without whom my book would still be in the shambles of its first draft. Bridget has been the biggest help in both the editing stage and promotional plans. She's been dependable, supportive and all around incredible, and I couldn't have asked for a better person to aid in my publishing journey.

Thank you to my parents, for their unending support and belief in me and my writing. I am so very lucky to have the kind of parents that believe that I can do whatever I put my mind to. Since my very first attempt at writing a book back in school, to here and now with my first publication, their support and love has been unwavering.

Thank you to Nicole, my best friend and flatmate. The unbelievably talented artist, who produced the front cover and inside art for this book- and never stopped believing in me. She's been here for the first ideas, for help in plot twists and for all the nonsensical ideas I have for both this book and potential sequels... Thank the Gods she's patient. She is one of the most impressive, funniest, and incredible people I have ever met- there will never be enough thanks for her.

Thank you to all my friends who have offered their support, from proofreads to insight on cover designs, I am so grateful. As well as all of those who donated and supported my Crowdbound campaign- without which The *In-Between* would still be a pipe dream. Relatives, friends and those who just came across my advertisements and saw it as something worth investing in, you've done more for me than you know.

It's always been my biggest ambition to publish my own book, to walk into a random book shop and see it on the shelves. For people to pick up my writing and enjoy what I've created, for them to see the characters I've worked so long on. Ever since I first got into reading- all the way back to age 9, when I found a copy of *The Girl Who Could Fly* under a chair in the waiting room at school... It's mine now I'm keeping it. Nevertheless, without that first book- I don't know whether I would be sitting here writing an acknowledgments section of my own.

And finally, again, thank you to you- the reader. I can only hope this book gave you the same joy to read as it was for me to write... minus the stresses of editing, rewrites and trying to get published... I digress. This book has been a journey and a half, and I'm so happy you can be a part of it. Thank you for picking up this book, and giving *The In-Between* a chance- hopefully it lived up to your expectations. And, if you did enjoy it, I hope you join me for the sequel- *The World Beyond.*

MEET THE AUTHOR

Molly O'Dowd, a Bristol-based author, has always been drawn to storytelling, inspired by the books that shaped her childhood—starting with *The Girl Who Could Fly* and *The Trylle Trilogy*, and later in life books such as *Faebound, Wolfsong,* and *The Shepherd King* series. A longtime lover of fantasy, she explores LGBTQ+ romances in her own fantastical worlds, aiming to fill the gap in representation within the genre. Influenced by anime and series like *Re:Zero* and *Arcane*, as well as authors like TJ Klune, she blends magic, romance, and complex interpersonal dynamics in her writing. When she's not working on her next book, Molly enjoys painting, drawing, and unwinding with her favourite TV series. She hopes readers walk away from her stories with a love for her characters—and maybe a bit of impatience for the sequel she's already writing.

Writing · Publishing · Diversity · Inclusion

Our unyielding mission is to open up the world of literature, journalism and publishing to everyone through delivering mentoring, workshops, events and sponsorship. We believe that empowering people through writing is a way towards building a stronger, fairer and more enlightened society.

Building Futures. Bridging Divides.